SKY CHASE

Joe Kenyon saw that the F-16s were creating a north-south line over central Scotland, forming a barrier to the east. They were going to try and fence him off and then herd him out into the Atlantic until he no longer had enough fuel to make it to the Soviet Union. In this way, they hoped he would finally be forced to land somewhere back in British territory— or bail out over the ocean. They would, of course, prefer anything to letting him take the SR80 through their net to Russia. And that meant they ultimately would not hesitate in blowing him out of the sky.

Joe Kenyon didn't want to go to the Soviet Union. He *had* to. Perhaps they even knew that. But it didn't matter. As he climbed ever higher, ever faster, it was Joe Kenyon and the SR80 against the entire combined air forces of the free world. And there was a part of Joe Kenyon that was hoping they were good enough to shoot him down.

BLOOD RED SKY

By Anton Emmerton

General
— PAPERBACKS —

A Division of General Publishing Co. Limited
Toronto, Canada

A General Paperback Edition
Published under license from Panda Books, Inc.
475 Park Avenue South
New York, NY 10016

ISBN 0-7737-8379-2

First printing: May 1985

Printed in the United States of America

CHAPTER ONE

Everybody was cocked with at least three drinks. The room was full of smoke and the loud babble of conversation, with the laughs of elegantly dressed women tinkling above the lower multinational accents of the diplomats.

A quick glance past the florid face of the Bulgarian attaché revealed that Joe's wife Suzie had been cornered by Dimitri Olenko, the Soviet air attaché, Joe's opposite number in London. It looked as though Dimitri was telling Suzie a joke, Joe thought, by the way she suddenly leaned back on her heels and laughed delightedly. Kenyon thought that Olenko was a nice guy. It was a pity they couldn't get to know each other better. . . .

"—which I am hearink," the big Bulgarian was saying, "is so important in America now, *da?*"

"I'm sorry, Yevgeny?" Joe turned his attention unwillingly to Galakhov again. "I missed that."

At every diplomatic function the Bulgarian attaché did his best to corner Joe and breathe fetid garlic breath into his face while he asked the same old boring questions in the same old theatrical Eastern European accent. It was a tactic of most of the

Warsaw Pact diplomats to lead with obvious ques
tions, then get together subsequently to compare
notes and reactions, endlessly playing back the party
from tiny tape recorders secreted in the depths of their
heavy suits.

"Uvvercroft!" General Galakhov said, and
belched. He rumbled a triumphant chuckle up from
his huge stomach. "I em hearink iss important in
America now, yess?"

"Uvvercroft?" Joe looked puzzled. What was the
idiot on about now? Joe thought fleetingly of the
cottage he and Suzie had rented down in the depths of
the Wiltshire countryside, their escape at weekends.
Besides the work days at the embassy, which were
long enough, they both wearied of the endless rounds
of cocktail parties and socializing—dinners with the
French and Germans, massive seven-course meals
with the tireless, talkative Italians, and the ponderous
Warsaw Pact boys; the Aussies and Kiwis, Danes and
Norwegians—it could make you feel like a wilted
blimp by the end of the week. He forced his attention
back to the Bulgarian, who was now waving his arms.

"Da!" he growled. "Uvvercroft, yess? For going on
de vater and de landt?" Galakhov pursed his lips and
made a farting noise in explanation. "You onder-
stendt?"

"Ah!" Joe nodded, forcing a smile. "Hovercraft!"

Galakhov reached forward and smacked Joe's
shoulder. "Da, uvvercroft!" he cried, his thick lips
grinning widely. He excitedly, unknowingly, tilted is
drink onto the carpet.

Joe ignored this and adopted a frown of serious-
ness. "Oh yes," he said. He leaned toward the Bulgarian conspiratorially and looked quickly around as if to
be sure that no one would overhear him. Then he
dropped his voice. "Thousands of them," he mur-

6

mured. He brought his glass to his lips and peered from left to right again from beneath lowered brows, then said no more.

After a few moments the Bulgarian couldn't stand it. He leaned forward, his face thrust close to Joe's, eyebrows raised.

"Vy?" the Bulgarian whispered.

Kenyon looked up. "Why?" he repeated.

The Bulgarian nodded quickly. *"Da—vy?"*

"Well," Kenyon said, keeping his voice low. "Remember what happened to Napoleon?"

Galakhov frowned, puzzled, "Napoleon?"

Kenyon nodded.

"Vot 'as uvvercroft got to do vid Napoleon?" Galakhov held his breath.

Joe said, "When Napoleon tried to take Moscow on foot he got bogged down in the mud, right?"

"Zo?"

"Well," Joe whispered. "We're not gonna make that mistake! We're gonna use hovercraft, see?"

Galakhov stiffened. "You are making a yoke!"

"Keep it to yourself, General," Kenyon said, with a straight face.

He left the Bulgarian leaning back on his heels with his stomach thrust out, looking puzzled, small eyes narrowed in thought. Joe grinned to himself. They'll talk that one over for days, he thought. Last time he'd told Galakhov that the U.S. was close to production of a self-destructing nuclear tank capable of Kamikazi attacks in excess of a hundred miles an hour. The subject of tanks had popped up all over London at various cocktail parties for quite a while afterwards.

Dimitri Olenko, he saw, was now talking with someone Joe had not yet met. Kenyon noticed the lank, black hair slicked down on the head with some sort of retaining grease, a fairly thin face, and small,

7

dark eyes. As Kenyon moved toward the couple, Dimitri broke off the conversation, turned his back on the man, and smiled across at Joe. Who the hell is he? Joe thought. Suzie had noticed Joe break loose from the Bulgarian, and in turn eased herself away from the Italian attaché and his wife. The Italian was making airplane maneuvers with his cigar, while his blond wife smiled patronizingly. She had the best pair of boobs in the whole group, Joe thought.

"How're we doing?" Suzie asked as they met in the center of the crowded room.

Joe put an arm around her bare shoulders. He was about five ten and Suzie stood no more than five two. He kissed her on the forehead.

"Great. They're all telling crazy lies, as usual." He told her about the "uvvercroft" and she laughed delightedly. "What was Dimitri talking about?" he asked her.

"About home," she said. "He seemed real interested."

"Oh? Anything specific?"

"Not really. Ordinary things—Like cars, how much they cost, and houses. Schools, shops." She looked puzzled for a moment. "He seemed real interested, though. He kept me talking for quite a while. Not the normal aircraft stuff tonight."

Joe looked thoughtful. "Well, tell me more afterwards. I'd better move around. Need another drink?"

She looked at her glass.

"Screwdriver?" Kenyon prompted. He smiled down at her. "The doc said it wouldn't hurt, didn't he? It's not kicking, is it?" he whispered, grinning.

She glanced quickly down, then back up to him, smiling. It was a secret they intended to keep. "At two months!" she whispered, laughing. "Go on—get me that drink."

8

"You take care," Kenyon told her. "Poet's day, tomorrow," he said as he left her.

Piss on everything, tomorrow's Saturday. Joe's friend in British Intelligence, David Pentland, usually called and announced this on a Friday. Tomorrow night they'd all be down in Wiltshire. Joe couldn't wait.

Olenko was getting very friendly these days, Joe thought as he went to mix the drinks. The Russian had arrived in London just after they had. Both of them were air force, and both test pilots. It would be great if they could have the freedom to sit down and compare notes over a few beers. He sensed that Olenko felt the same way. Olenko had a wife and two kids back in the Soviet Union. He said Suzie reminded him of Natalia. Perhaps the reason he was grilling Suzie on those domestic things was because he was homesick. Joe knew that Dimitri really liked Suzie. He called her "Zuzie."

Joe wormed his way through the crush of bodies back to his wife, who he located talking to the French couple, Jean and Samanthe Linet. Olenko was in a group nearby, standing with the East German and a Pole. The Russian caught Joe's eye and crooked his head for Joe to join them. Joe nodded, signalled "two minutes" with his free hand, and gave the drink to Suzie, at the same time greeting the French couple.

"Jean—Samanthe," he smiled. "Having a good time?"

Jean Linet dragged his eyes away from the Sophia Loren figure of the Italian attaché's wife. Captain Linet was somewhat of a roué, Joe thought. However, what man in the room didn't admire a pair of boobs like that, sheathed in plunging silk? But Samanthe was no slouch, either.

Samanthe smiled up at Joe. "Of course!" she said.

9

"And you—you are enjoying your own party?"

"Of course 'e is, is that not so, Joe?" Jean Linet said. The Frenchman turned to the girls. " 'E gets to talk with all the pretty girls while 'e gives them their drinks, yes?" He grinned wickedly at Kenyon. "I 'ave seen you looking down their dresses, Joe."

"I don't think I have ever seen you *not* looking down their dresses, mon ami," Joe retorted.

Samanthe feigned horror. "Does 'e do *that*?" she asked.

"He's doing it to you right now," Joe said. They all laughed, then Joe excused himself and went over to Dimitri Olenko. Dimitri saw the American coming and detached himself from his own small group.

"Good to see you, Dimitri," Joe said.

"Joe, always I enjoy your parties. Is possible because Zuzie is so beautiful, yes?"

"Well, I know it's not *my* good looks. But I tell you, Dimitri, I don't think it has anything to do with Suzie. You know what I think? I think it's that all Russians are boozers, that's what I think. How you guys ever become fliers beats me. But then the stuff you fly is pretty simple, right? How 'bout some fresh air?"

The September night was balmy and windless, and Suzie had opened the French windows to the small patio behind the tall old Queen Anne house in Brompton Square. High brick walls covered with roses and honeysuckle kept the traffic in close-by Knightsbridge to a low murmur. The small, stone-flagged patio was more like a secluded little country garden than the backyard of a diplomatic residence in the heart of London.

When they were outside, Joe offered the Russian a cigarette. While he was lighting both cigarettes, Joe told Dimitri about Yevgeny Galakhov's inane questions and how he had answered them, which made the Russian pilot laugh.

"Of course, he is only doing his work," Olenko said, smiling. Joe nodded and for a moment both men were silent, enjoying the relative peace outside.

Light spilled from the party out onto the patio, but there were deep shadows below the high walls. The man Joe had seen earlier moved into the square of light in the window, looked out into the darkness, then stepped quickly back into the party. From the side of his eye Joe caught Olenko's frown.

"Who is that guy?" he asked Olenko when the man had gone. "I don't know him, and if I don't know him, he wasn't invited. Friend of yours?"

He noticed the Russian had become tense, and there was rarely any tension between the two men. They were both professionals steeped in the disciplines of their respective services, and, aware of the parameters of any discussions between them, always stopped short of talking about things that might compromise them later.

Olenko shrugged and drew on his cigarette. "KGB," he murmured.

"What!" Joe exclaimed. "Then what the hell is he doing inside!" The security men from both sides usually stayed outside on the occasion of a diplomatic get-together.

"I'm sorry, Joe. He is an assistant attaché, newly arrived. I was ordered to familiarize him with the local scene. I thought you would not mind. He will not bother you. He is just new and takes his job seriously. I would have introduced you, but you were very busy, yes? Anyway, I myself am not enthusiastic about socializing with this kind of people, you understand?"

Joe nodded. "Okay." He paused for a moment and

11

sipped his drink. "Anyway, how're things?"

"Things, Joe?" Dimitri repeated. He smiled tightly. "As you know, things are quite cold, for the moment. Because of the breakdown in the talking at Geneva, and your missiles."

There was nothing new in that, Joe thought. Everyone knew the Russians were furious about the Pershings and the MX. "So?" he prodded quietly.

Olenko glanced around him. Both of them knew that by now there would be bugs throughout the entire house. The whole Eastern contingent came armed with them and planted them where they could—under toilet seats, in plant pots, below furniture, under tabletops—a sort of saturation exercise conducted, presumably, Joe thought with amusement, in the hope that perhaps one of them would escape detection, and then the hosts' private conversations would be monitored. However, both men also knew that after the guests left, the sweepers would arrive, and it would take them only an hour or so to locate all of the devices. It was an exercise in futility, a hangover from the old days of primitive bug detection.

Olenko decided to change the subject. "Is time we took some more exercise, Joe. Shall we play some more tennis next week?"

Kenyon remembered getting dressed for tonight's party and seeing the weight assembling around his waist from the excess of good food and drink, and the beginnings of age-sag below his eyes. He thought that being a diplomat was more like the job of a sophisticated barman. It was a far cry from the hands-on precision and the clean, empty skies of flight. As far as he was concerned, the years spent testing the SR80 had been the high point of his career.

"That's a good idea, Dimitri. How about Wednesday?"

12

"Yes," the Russian nodded. "I think Wednesday is good. Six o'clock—the usual place?"

"I'll be there," Joe said. "Your turn to bring the balls, right? Let's go in and get another drink."

Inside, people were beginning to leave, since it was close to eleven, and for the next hour Joe and Suzie Kenyon were busy with platitudes and good-byes.

After the front door had shut for the last time, they went to the sitting room and collapsed together into the depths of a sofa while the temporary staff cleaned up the glasses and hors d'oeuvres plates and went around cleaning and polishing the ashtrays. Twenty minutes after that the sweepers arrived and started to move through the house, while Joe and Suzie talked about the evening over a bedtime drink of vintage port, which they had both learned to enjoy since coming to England.

"So—how did I do?" Suzie asked, looking tired.

"Great. Just great. It was a good party." Joe undid his tie.

"I saw you talking to Dimitri outside," Suzie said.

"Yeah. He seemed to be a little on edge tonight. He was asked to bring some KGB guy along. I think he was embarrassed. Goddamn it," Joe said. "He *should* be. I was pissed, and he knew it."

"Do you think there might have been some ulterior motive?" Suzie asked.

"Maybe. I don't know. I'll talk to Allan Briggs, anyway. Maybe Allan has some background on the guy. Do you know the one I mean?"

She nodded. "Uh-huh. His name was Salin Renko. His English was bad." She shuddered for a moment and Joe raised an eyebrow. "He had awful eyes," Suzie said.

"How do you mean?"

"Cold—you know?"

13

Joe was silent for a few moments. They sat and drank the port. Then Joe said, "What about Dimitri asking you all that stuff about home?"

"Yes. I don't know what to make of that, Joe." She looked thoughtful.

One of the sweepers came into the room. "All finished, sir," he announced.

"How many tonight?" Joe asked.

The sweeper, who was a big, round-faced American—contrary to Joe's preconceived notion of a small, ferretlike person—grinned down at the attaché.

"Seven, sir. One in the reefer."

"In the refrigerator!" Suzie laughed. "What do they think we do? Stick our heads in there and discuss secrets over the dip?"

"There was one under the bed as well," the man said.

"Which bed?"

"Your bed, ma'am."

"But none of them should have been up there!"

"How about the patio?" Joe asked.

"Clean, sir." The sweeper looked at his watch. "Better be moving on, sir. Good night."

" 'Night," Joe murmured. "See you next time."

Joe got up to lock the front entrance, and sighed as he thought of the heavy schedule tomorrow. He came back into the room and looked down at his wife. "I think the three of us should get some shut-eye. Gonna be a long day tomorrow."

"Perhaps Dimitri wants to tell you something," Suzie said.

Joe raised an eyebrow. He had respect for his wife's intuition. "Now what made you say that?" he asked her.

"I don't know," she said. "But there's something different about his attitude."

14

"Yeah," Joe said thoughtfully, "yeah, maybe you're right."

"Anyway," Suzie said, rising from the sofa, it's Poet's day tomorrow."

The next day was hectic.

Two senators arrived at Heathrow for a so-called fact-finding tour of NATO, with London the kickoff point as a concession to the wives who salivated for the treasures of Harrods and the fashionable Chelsea shops. Evenings would be spent at the theatre and Anabel's and the Savoy. Not a great deal more would be known by the senators about NATO after similar tours of Paris, Brussels, and Bonn, but a good time would be had by all. However, the U.S. attachés in those places would attend like bellboys to point the party in the right directions throughout Europe, and next week Joe and Suzie Kenyon would start the ball rolling with a reception at Brompton Square.

After the senators and their wives had been met as VIPs at Heathrow and transported in a diplomatic limousine to the Savoy, Kenyon hurried back to the embassy at Grosvenor Square to catch up with the day's paperwork, and to return the phone calls of various aerospace concerns in Britain who were keen to sell the Americans the latest in electronic goods and armaments. Then there was the Friday afternoon report and meeting with the ambassador, and finally the closeout meeting with the CIA man. By this time it was after five-thirty and the traffic out of London would already have developed its normal hideous Friday afternoon panic of frustrated motorists half-choking in exhaust fumes as they bunched at the Chiswick roundabout at the beginning of the M4 Motorway to the west.

Joe sat down in a chair close to the lanky CIA man's desk. Allan Briggs was, like his name, not very notable. He was slightly taller and thinner than average. He was also slightly untidier in his dress than average. Even during these hot September days, Joe noticed, he wore a wooly, V-neck sweater below the jacket of his lightweight tweed suit, notably inappropriate dress for both the weather and the embassy. Joe Kenyon somehow always thought of Allan Briggs as a tired gunfighter. Perhaps there was a touch of Gary Cooper about him, Joe thought, a touch of the quiet whimsy. However, Allan Briggs was a top CIA man, evidenced by his posting as the chief security man in the London embassy. Kenyon knew that extraordinary efficiency and keenness lay behind the tired, whimsical eyes of the unnotable Briggs.

"I always try to get clear by three-thirty," Kenyon said tiredly. "Never made it yet, though." He grinned at Allan Briggs. "There's always some bugger like you to talk to first."

"You're lucky you've got a place to get away to, Joe," Briggs said ruefully.

"I suppose so. I'd go mad if we didn't have the cottage." Joe leaned forward and looked at his watch. "Anyway, only one thing of note, Allan. We threw a party last night for the whole attaché bunch, as you know. It was our turn. As usual, that Galakhov pumped me like a recruiting sergeant. I told him we were into hovercraft, preparatory to doing a Napoleon on Moscow. Funny thing is, sometimes I think the idiot believes me." Kenyon shook his head and Briggs smiled. He knew Galakhov well. "However," Kenyon went on, "Galakhov had a new boy with him. A tall guy; athletic looking, slicked-back black hair, long sallow face. Didn't say much; just followed Galakhov around the party and listened in. Later, Olenko confirmed he was KGB." Kenyon leaned back in his chair and took out a cigarette. "Why would the Bulgarian attaché bring a KGB boy into my party? They usually leave 'em outside."

"Can you remember the name he went by?" Briggs asked. He had taken a note of Joe's description of the KGB man.

"Yeah. It was something Renko. Might have been Salin Renko. Suzie'll remember. I'll confirm that on Monday."

"Okay. Anything else?"

"Well, Olenko was acting a bit strange. Perhaps I should say slightly out of character. Suzie thought so too. He asked her a lot about the States. What kind of schools, the kind of shops, how much things were, what American women did in their spare time—the kind of things a family man likes to ask if he's on a trip and his wife has asked him to get the information. With me?"

"Yeah. Go on."

"Later I got him out onto the patio. He seemed uneasy. When I asked him how he was doing, he said things were a bit cold on his home front. We all know this anyway, but he's never made a point of it before. He muttered on a bit about the Pershing and cruise missile decisions. When I pressed him, he changed the subject, cheered up, and asked me for a game of tennis next week. We're playing on Wednesday evening at six. The public courts in Hyde Park."

"Okay, Joe. Thanks. Maybe you can get a bit closer to Olenko on Wednesday and find out what's bugging him."

Kenyon frowned in recollection. "Yeah. He's a nice guy, Allan."

"Sure," Briggs smiled. "But don't forget he's a Soviet diplomat. And they don't send yoyos to London. You better measure every word Olenko says. He may be drawing you close for something, so stay ahead of him."

Joe felt a little surprised. "Sure, Allan." He got up to leave. "Have a nice weekend."

"And you, Joe. Bring me back a couple of trout."

In his third-floor office of the Whitehall Building, which housed all of the departments of MI5 and MI6, David Pentland was just about to put a call through to his girlfriend, a tall, dark-haired, Foreign Office secretary called Gail, when the phone rang, and the operator said it was Colonel Kenyon on the line.

Pentland looked at his watch and saw that it was after six. He and Joe Kenyon had met because they both got away at weekends to the same, small, Wiltshire village. Mutual friends in Wiltshire had introduced them and they had since formed a strong friendship. They had flying in common. David Pentland was a lieutenant commander in the Fleet Air Arm who had flown Harriers before volunteering for the SAS, after which he had been invited to join the Intelligence Service. So, in addition to getting to know each other socially in Wiltshire, they would often bump into each other on their rounds in London—when Pentland was not abroad, involved in covert operations for MI6.

Pentland lit a cigarette and picked up the phone.

"You're a bit late getting away, Joe," he said.

"You can say that again, David. I was wondering if you're going down?"

"Yes, I am. I was just about to ring Gail when you called."

"Great. Will you make it to the pub in time?"

Friday nights at the Queen's Head were when Joe and Suzie and David and Gail usually met up with friends from the surrounding area: farmers, doctors, and company owners who lived throughout the rolling Wiltshire countryside. A party or dinner at one of the homes was usually arranged for the Saturday night, and the men would discuss shooting, fishing, and flying, while the women chattered about London fashions and the latest gossip. The warm, convivial atmosphere was a nice closeout to the busy week.

"I'm going to do my damndest," Pentland said. "We should make it by nine or so, if Gail can get away. I'm pretty much clear."

"Okay, great. See you there," Joe said cheerfully, and hung up. Pentland replaced the receiver and called Gail.

"How does it look?" he said when he heard her familiar, soft, round voice. "The Kenyons are going down. The weather looks good; it should be a nice weekend. Can you get away soon, Gail?"

Gail Rayson worked in the Foreign Office as a personal assistant. Her weekends out of London depended on what kind of heat was burning in Britain's foreign affairs, but much to Pentland's relief, she said all was quiet at the moment, and she was about to leave for her flat.

"Could you pick me up at seven?" she asked.

"Seven it is. Pack tennis stuff and swimming things, and bring your fly rod."

It was always a surprise to the other women that Gail was an accomplished fly fisherman. She was a tall, slim girl, otherwise quite unathletic, who loved to cast a dry fly for the quick, little, brown trout living in the chalk streams of Wiltshire. She hated tennis.

"I'm not playing that bloody silly game, David," she said, referring to Pentland's suggestion that she

19

bring her tennis things.

"Just bring them and wear them so that I can get an eyeful of your legs. You look great in that tiny skirt with your knickers showing."

"You should learn to keep your eye on the ball, you dirty old man," Gail said. "See you at seven."

Pentland smiled and hung up, then went down to the underground car-park where he'd left the Aston.

Gail Rayson decided to take a taxi back to her flat. She normally caught a bus, but with the whole of London intent on getting out of town for what looked like a glorious summer weekend, the traffic was horrible. The streets were jammed with impatient drivers and the exhaust fumes gathered in the hot streets. Taxi drivers and motorists swore at each other as horns peeped and blared impatiently. Gail closed the windows in spite of the heat and sat back to suffer the ten minutes or so to her small mews flat in Chelsea. She was also looking forward to the weekend, and she thought of David Pentland.

She had grown to love him over the nine months or so since they had met, but she had been very careful not to let him know the extent of her feelings. He was very reticent about parts of his life, and was always disappearing abroad for weeks at a time, saying he was involved with the lower spectrum of an armed forces liaison with NATO for the Defense Ministry. So far there had been nothing stable about their relationship, but they got together as much as they could. Pentland was ten years older than she was, in his midthirties, and she knew he had been married before. She had never gotten him to talk about the marriage, and he had built up very definite walls when it came to discussing that kind of thing. What she liked about him were his quick sense of humor, his tall, slim, good looks and his ability to mix easily in any society. He loved flying and fishing, as she did, and he also loved birds, which opened up opportunities for them to get away to the wild spots of the British Isles, the mountains of Wales and Scotland, and the moors of the West country and Yorkshire. They invariably stayed at pubs in small villages, which they both preferred. They walked and climbed miles together in an easy relationship, enjoying the wind and the sky and the moors beneath their booted feet. Lately, she had fallen easily into the pleasant routine of summer weekends with his friends in Wiltshire. They all seemed to like her. And she was particularly looking forward to this weekend after an extremely hot week in London. She knew it would go by all too quickly.

When the taxi dropped her in the mews she rushed into her flat and threw her things into a soft bag, did the breakfast washing-up, fed her cat—who David had named Speedy Gonzales for its habit of sneaking into bed with them—took a quick shower, dressed in jeans and a revealing, short-sleeved cotton blouse, sorted out her fly rod, and sat down with a small gin and tonic to wait for the rumble of the Aston's big engine in the mews.

CHAPTER TWO

"Suzie thinks Olenko wants to tell me something," Joe said.

Pentland was lying on his stomach in the grass on the bank of the shallow trout stream that ran through the meadows half a mile to the south of the Kenyons' cottage. On the far side of the stream, beyond drooping willows and thigh-high seeding grass, a steep escarpment of the Wiltshire downs hazed up into the morning sunshine. A pair of mallards quacked quietly somewhere, hidden in the reeds. Joe cast his fly diagonally across the fast-running water and a fish made a lazy rise, blew water over the fly, which refused to sink, and sank back down in disgust. Gail had plodded off up the river, her feet scrunching on the shillets, and she was now out of sight, hidden by willows beyond a curve. Pentland was testing out the old theory of trout tickling, without any success.

Both men had mild hangovers.

It had been an especially good Friday evening, which had ended up with all of them, including the women, spoofing for a bottle of port. Joe Kenyon had lost and bought the port, inviting them all back to his cottage to drink it. Suzie had cooked sausage and eggs and they had sat around until the early hours talking and listening to music. It had been two-thirty before David and Gail had driven off to their own place and the others had left for their homes across the misty Wiltshire hills. David and Joe had impulsively decided to get an early start fishing, which they had regretted when they stumbled out of their beds a few hours later, at six-thirty. Nothing could keep Gail from fly fishing, and the three of them had met at the river when the early white mist was rising off the water like steam, and the sun had only just come peeking up over the downs.

Pentland rolled onto his side and picked a long grass stem which he stuck in the corner of his mouth. "Oh? Any ideas?"

"No. It's just a feeling. He wants to play tennis on Wednesday."

At that moment there was a sound of splashing up the river, and the mallards took off with wings whirring, quacking their alarms. A wood pigeon clattered out of a willow above their heads, noisily beating its wings.

"Sounds like Gail's got one," Pentland said with a grin. "Wait for it!"

"David! Bring the net! I've got one," they heard her call.

"See? Bloody good thing she came, Joe," Pentland said as he got to his feet. "Wouldn't be much breakfast without her, would there?"

Both men walked quickly along the bank upstream and found Gail up to her thighs in a place where the river slowed in a wide pool. Her rod was bent in a graceful curve, the line taut and snaking about at the far end of the pool. The trees were thick on the banks and the sun lit up small areas of the clear water in dappled patches. Gail's line ran out with the reel sizzling as the fish took off upstream. She moved after it, keeping the line taut, until she suddenly disappeared completely below the surface as she stepped into a deep hole. She came up spluttering, still keeping the rod-head high.

Joe and David stood on the bank and laughed delightedly.

"Bring the net, you silly buggers," Gail called.

However, it was difficult for them to concentrate because the water had made her blouse cling to her figure—which made a beautiful showing since she wasn't wearing a bra. Joe was quite sure that her knockers would beat those of the Italian attaché's wife, and David was grinning appreciatively as he waded into the river with the net.

By now the fish was tiring; Gail got it to within about ten feet of her, and David slipped the landing net beneath it. It was a good fish, enough for a tasty breakfast with the mushrooms they would find on the way back to the cottage.

As he waded ashore, David Pentland realized again how beautiful Gail Rayson was. She crouched over the fish, insisting on doing her own dirty work to remove the hook. Her long, wet hair clung to her face and neck and her cheeks glowed after her dip in the chilly stream.

"You'd better go on up to the cottage, Gail," Joe said. "Suzie should be up by now. Get some dry clothes and tell her to put the coffee on. We'll find some mushrooms and be back in about twenty minutes."

When she left them they watched her for a few moments, her hips swinging above the waders as she took long strides through the high grass of the meadow toward the cottage.

"That girl's a real dish," Kenyon said.

Pentland smiled and lit a cigarette. "She doesn't know it yet, Joe, but she's going to marry me before too long. When I get out of intelligence, and back into the navy—"

"I wouldn't blame you at all," Joe said. "Let's get the mushrooms."

"What time have you arranged for tennis with Olenko?" Pentland asked.

"Six. On Wednesday."

"See if you can get closer to him, Joe. Have a few extra beers afterward. Get him talking."

"It's not easy with your boys and the CIA and the KGB watching us play tennis and cluttering up the pub afterward," Joe grunted.

"I know, but you're used to that stuff."

Whenever two diplomats of the status of Kenyon and Olenko got together socially, they were covered by snoops of all three countries, and none of the snoops bothered to conceal their presence from the others. It was standard operating procedure, and served to remind the diplomats to be careful about what they said to each other. The KGB, particularly, kept a very careful watch on their people.

"What we ought to do," Pentland said as they crouched about the meadow looking for mushrooms, "is devise a way to bring him closer to you. Make him somehow feel dependent on you."

"I don't see how we could do that," Joe said.

"What do you do after tennis?"

"We don't usually change. We pull on some warm-ups and make tracks for the nearest pub. The Lion, usually. You know, the one close to the Grosvenor House?"

"Yes?"

"Then we have a couple of beers and talk generalities and go home."

25

"Do you ever get him to stay out for dinner?"

"I've never asked him."

"Try asking him this time." Pentland pulled a six-inch-diameter horse mushroom out of the long grass. "Wow, look at this beauty!"

"Okay, I'll give it a try."

They collected a dozen fresh mushrooms and now hungry in anticipation of breakfast, decided to get back to the cottage for a mouth-watering mixture of trout, mushrooms, eggs and bacon, toast, and coffee.

At the pub the previous night, David had passed the word that he and Gail would put on a barbecue party at David's cottage up on Cranborne Chase on Saturday evening; after the delicious breakfast with the Kenyons they decided to drive into Salisbury, eleven miles away from the village, to pick up supplies for the evening.

The clear, early-morning weather had ripened into a hot summer day, and before they left they put the top down on the Aston Martin. Gail's hair flew in the breeze as the big volante engine warbled throatily between the hedgerows of the narrow lanes on the way to the old city. The farmers had finished with harvest, and fields of sun-browned stubble curved on the backs of the rolling downs. Cows chewed their cuds lazily in the long, seeding grass of the water meadows by the road. The sky was cornflower blue and cloudless, and they felt the heat of the sun on their faces beneath the warm air swirling past the windshield.

David wore shorts, a T-shirt, and canvas shoes without socks. Gail, after her involuntary swim in the trout stream, had borrowed a light-blue cotton skirt from Suzie that, because Suzie was much shorter than Gail, resulted in a lot of exposed leg. She was also wearing one of Suzie's tennis tops and a pair of slip-ons. David found it difficult to keep his eyes off the expanse of sun-browned thighs beside him as he drove. She had lovely, long legs, he thought. What a weekend!

First the great evening at the pub last night, the trout fishing and mushrooms this morning, tennis with the Hollisters at their farm this afternoon, and then drinks and hamburgers at his place this evening. And no doubt something would be arranged for Sunday, but if not, he decided they would get up late and go for a long walk over the downs. Definitely get up late, he thought, glancing across at her again. This time she caught his glance and smiled back at him, lovely, fully lips spreading above her long chin.

"You've got that look in your eyes!" she said.

He threw back his head and laughed.

"You just concentrate on the driving, mister!"

He hadn't felt so happy for a long time, he thought.

Salisbury was filled with summer tourists and the streets were busy, but they found a parking place in the Cathedral Close, paid their fifty pence and walked out into the High Street through the North Gate, a marvelous stone archway which opened out into the Tudor street. Black and white timber-framed buildings leaned at impossible angles above the busy traffic.

Weekends like this were becoming small, bright periods to treasure, since he had become part of the sometimes life-threatening insecurity of MI6. The department was apt to send him on missions to the Eastern-bloc countries and on occasions he wondered if he would see England again. Those moments made him appreciate things he might have previously taken for granted, like the summer bustle in the medieval street before him, the exquisite symmetry of Salisbury Cathedral and its great, needle spire reaching up into the deep blue of the cloudless sky, and, particularly, the easy grace of the long-legged woman striding out beside him, her thick hair blowing across her face in the breeze. He glanced at her and saw the sparkle of her dark eyes as she returned his look, her full, red lips smiling back from white teeth.

"What thinkest thou, my lord?" she said.

"That thou maketh the fairest of pictures, my pretty maiden, and that they breasts appear as alluring creatures beneath thy seductive shirt—"

"David, for God's sake," she said, reddening.

Pentland put his arm around her shoulders as they walked. "What would Oi do wi'out 'em?" he said in a Wiltshire accent.

"You'll find out if you don't shut up," Gail replied. "Now. We need booze, bangers, buns, and things. Quite a lot of things. So you go off and get the booze, and I'll do the rest."

"Don't you want me to help?"

"Yes, but you won't. You'll embarrass me, get in the way and drop everything, so bugger off and I'll meet you back at the car in an hour." She swung off into Sainsbury's.

Pentland went back to Beech's bookshop near the Close gate and found a book on peregrine falcons, bought the booze a few minutes later, went back into the Close and lay down on the grass in the shade of a huge cypress tree where he opened the book and fell asleep. Her shadow woke him just as her foot prodded into his stomach and he toppled her with an ankle lock, bringing her down on top of him with a yell.

During the drive back to the village David was thinking about Dimitri Olenko and Joe Kenyon. It seemed to him from what Joe had told him that Olenko had made a subtle approach, and if he had something to say, whatever it was, it would be important. Joe said Olenko had vocalized again about Mother Russia's dissatisfaction concerning the breakdown of the SALT talks and the decision the Americans had made to install Pershing Twos and cruise missiles in Europe. However, concern for that had long swept up past attaché level, and even ambassadorial level. The heads of state were shouting at each other about that now, and there was no reason for Olenko to bring the matter up at Joe's party. Other than the pure banalities of cocktail parties, what was said at such a party was carefully edited, each attaché knowing that he was on the front lines of diplomacy, and his words would be considered carefully afterwards. It was odd, David thought. And the questions to Suzie. Did Olenko want perhaps to come over? Christ, that would put the cat among the pigeons.

Or was Olenko trying to set Joe up for something?

Joe wouldn't agree with that line of thought because he had made the mistake of growing to like Olenko. Joe wasn't objective any more, and that could turn out to be a problem, Pentland thought.

But there was one thing for sure, and that was that Olenko wasn't snuggling up to Joe for kicks. He wanted something from Joe, or he wanted to give Joe something. On Monday he would look into things a bit, he thought. Examine a few trends; shove a few things into the computer and see what emerged. And meanwhile have a bloody good weekend.

It was very hot during the afternoon.

Jan Hollister brought tea out onto the lawn in front of the house by the tennis court, and the six of them sprawled around the white cloth spread out on the grass loaded with homemade cakes and biscuits, and cold lemonade, and tea. Hugh Hollister, who was keen to play, had a difficult time whipping up a foursome for the court. Pentland was lying back on the grass, watching the swifts screaming around the trees and the eaves of the farmhouse, fascinated with the speed and maneuverability of their flight, while Joe Kenyon, who wanted everyone to think he was just closing his eyes to keep the sun out, not wishing to appear antisocial, betrayed the whole thing with a colossal snore. The loud laughter woke him up.

When Hugh finally managed to get David, Jan, and Suzie onto the court with him, they were all soon delirious with laughter as Hugh pranced his portly figure across the net, David saying that he looked like a pregnant fairy. But in spite of his unorthodox net play, he was very effective in killing a short ball.

After the set they returned to the lawn more fatigued with laughter than exercise, and lay back to let the sun dry the sweat.

Joe Kenyon had fallen asleep again.

As David lay back with Gail's head resting on his stomach, he remembered some of the things Joe had told him about the test flying at Edwards Air Force Base in the Mojave Desert, over in California. Joe's last assignment before posting to London had been the flight testing of the SR80—Lockheed's very weird-looking successor to the SR71, better known as the Blackbird. The details were classified, but David remembered that Joe had touched on how far the design had gone to integrate the biochemistry of the pilot with the electronics and flight systems of the aircraft. A vein in the right arm of the pilot was computer-fed with appropriate drugs to match his metabolism to the mission profile: benzedrine when things became busy, and valium when they became routine, David imagined. Operational flying was becoming more and more like science fiction when it started plugging in your bloodstream—and, therefore, your brain—to on-board computers and fly-by-wire systems to deal with a mission. He looked across at Joe, sleeping on the grass, with a sense of wonder at the achievements of the stocky, middle-aged colonel. They say a good man needs a good woman behind him, he thought, and he found himself looking at Gail, who had gotten up to chat with Jan Hollister as she pruned some leaves at a nearby flower bed.

He thought he might become quite an achiever with a woman like Gail at his side.

They had rounded up eight couples for the barbecue, who were beginning to trickle from the pub up to the cottage in merry moods, just as the sun was setting behind the hills.

David had bought the old stone-and-thatched cottage two years ago as a weekend retreat, and as a place to catch up with himself between some of the more extended operations that the Department sent him out on. The cottage sat high up in the hills of Cranborne Chase, just under a belt of rough woodland called Haddon Wood. A long, dirt track led up to it from the nearest road.

He had added a bathroom off the tiny kitchen, and installed a Swedish wood-burning stove, and repaired the thatch. Cooking was done on a wood-burning Aga stove, which doubled as a water heater. There was no telephone or television, but there were a lot of books. The cottage was one room up and one down, plus the built-in bathroom, and the stairs from the lower room up to the single bedroom were more like a ladder.

31

Once up, it was impossible to stand upright because of the steeply sloping ceiling. There was only standing room in the middle, but that was where the bed had to go, so if you wanted to stand upright you had to stand on the bed.

But the walls were two-feet thick, and the cottage was cool in the summer and warm in the winter.

Most of the half-acre outside was a jumble of fruit trees and bushes gone wild—a haven for small birds—which was the way Pentland liked it, but he had carved a small lawn out of the jungle, which ran down to the woods. He had cut the grass short with a push-mower, after they had gotten back from tennis, while Gail had bathed and washed her hair for the evening.

David and Gail now sat on the small lawn in deck chairs, holding glasses of iced gin-and-tonics, watching the red orb of the sun ease down behind the hills, which turned purple as the shadows crept up from the valleys, floating on a white summer mist. The air was still and smelled of the sweetness of freshly mown grass. A bonfire smoldered below the moist grass cuttings and added a nostaligic pungency. Magpies chattered unseen in the wood and a blackbird poured its remarkable liquid notes into the evening.

As the sun went down and the woods at the end of the lawn deepened into a broad band of blackness, David got up and lit the barbecue, which was when they heard the first of the cars grumbling up the track bringing their friends from the pub.

Light spilled from the open cottage door and windows onto the small lawn, and a tape played a quiet background of old stuff and new stuff and some David Brubeck jazz as everyone bit into juicy hamburgers, drank wine, and told jokes. Owls hooted, and a fox barked in the wood once, and after the sun had well-and-truly gone down, the stars came out and

32

the moon climbed up over the hills in the south, and bathed the rolling country in silver. It was good company, and a beautiful night, Pentland thought, and a fitting end to a marvelous weekend day. He found Gail near him and put his arms around her and danced slowly with her on the lawn to a song by Rod Stewart called "You're in My Heart, You're in My Soul," and after a few moments Joe and Suzie started dancing. One by one the other couples put their arms around each other and danced on the lawn.

"Look what you started," Gail murmured.

"They won't see how I finish," David said in her hair.

He held Gail close, their bodies touching as they swayed on the lawn. He smelled her scent, and her breasts felt warm and soft against him. She had put her arms over his shoulders and he felt one of her hands on his neck. He thought it was very sensuous, with the music, and the soft pools of light on the lawn, and the moon lighting up the hills, and not much talking as the eight couples danced. But when the Rod Stewart number finished, Michael Jackson came screaming on with "Thriller" which broke the mood, and the conversation started up again. More drinks were poured, and there was loud laughter when Joe said, "Just look at that!" and they saw Hugh Hollister's back as he stood with his legs apart in the darkness at the foot of the lawn relieving himself, thinking that no one could see him. He came back smiling at them and said, "It's good for the nettles. That's how they get their sting, don'cher know?"

Olenko had never been far from David's mind all day, because it was part of his job to think about that sort of thing, and Olenko had behaved oddly. David saw Joe alone for a moment, pouring a glass of wine, and Gail was chatting with Suzie, so he sauntered across and joined the air force colonel.

"This Olenko thing, Joe."

"Yeah," Joe said, looking up. "What's up?"

"I was thinking. Was there anything else about your party that stuck out?"

"How do you mean?"

"Well, what about the other boys from the Eastern block? Any of them acting strange? Out of character?"

"No. No, I don't think so. Pretty much the usual bunch." Joe took a pull at his wine and then frowned. "There was an uninvited guest, though. Some guy called Salin Renko. He came with that Bulgarian monster I told you about—Galakhov. Dimitri told me that Renko was KGB, and I thought that was a bit odd. Those boys usually stay outside."

"What did this Renko look like?"

"Tall guy, about six one, six two. Pale face, dark eyes, slicked-back hair. He was an ugly looking sod on the whole," Joe said with a smile. "He was wearing a white shirt and a white tie with a black suit, which made him look like a young Frankenstein." Joe laughed. "Creepy looking son of a bitch, come to think of it," he said.

"What was he doing at the party?"

"I don't know really. But he kept his eye on me and Dimitri. I remember he watched us go out onto the patio and then he came across and stood just inside the doors, but he didn't follow us outside. He left just after Olenko did."

"And you'd never seen this guy before?"

"Nope. Never."

"And Allan didn't seem to know him." Pentland drew on his cigarette. "How about I come to the pub on Wednesday? We'll see if this Renko turns up."

"Sure. Why not? We'll have a couple," Joe grinned, and then Jan came over to them.

"Talking shop?" she asked.

"No," Joe smiled. "We just decided to get together for a drink midweek."

"Sometimes I think that's all you men can think about," Jan said. "Boozing!"

Joe put his arm around her waist and told her that there *was* one other thing he thought about, which made her laugh.

Joe Kenyon and Jan Hollister were laughing together as they stood in front of the brightly lit open doorway to the cottage. Jan was a very pretty woman, David thought. She had a slim figure; strong legs; dark brown, almost black, hair; and big brown eyes. She dressed well, talked fast in a husky, sexy voice, and was a magnificent cook. David thought with a smile that Joe Kenyon had a soft spot for Jan Hollister. But they were all very good friends, this bunch. Most of them had known each other since they were teenagers.

David turned to look at his other friends on the lawn. Their figures were dark silhouettes with their faces lit occasionally in the glow of the bonfire. Some sat on the grass and others in deck chairs, talking. The party was winding down. It was close to one o'clock and they'd be drifting off home soon, he thought. Gail was chuckling over something Nat Adamson was saying. Nat's tall, heavy figure made her look small beside him. They were standing well down the lawn with the woodland dark behind them and it was then that David's eyes were drawn to something that briefly reflected in the trees beyond them. He studied the area carefully for a few seconds, but saw nothing more. He was about to turn away when he saw it again.

The bonfire had slowly dried the grass cuttings as it smoldered during the evening, and now tongues of small flames were breaking through the crust with hissing and crackling sounds. As the fire flared, the extra light at the side of the lawn reflected off something down in the woods. Both reflections seemed to have come from the same place. There was a clump of trees on the moonlit skyline of the downs beyond the woods, and when he had first seen the glimmer his eyes had fixed the position by the clump of trees.

At first he concluded that a deer stood there on the edge of the wood watching the antics of the bipeds on the lawn. But animal's eyes normally appeared green with a light on them at night, and both eyes would show, because when an animal stared at something, it did so with unwavering concentration.

There had been only one reflection—both times.

And the glimmer appeared to Pentland to be positioned too high for an animal's eyes.

He saw it again then, and the hairs on the back of his neck prickled. Someone was watching them.

He walked quietly to the side of the lawn into the darkness, and then ran silently down through the fruit trees to the edge of the wood. He glanced back before he stepped deep into the trees and saw that no one had noticed him leave; they were all in the same places and the murmur of conversation stayed at the same pitch. He stepped into the trees and penetrated to a depth of fifteen feet or so, then began to move as quietly as he could along the perimeter of the wood toward the place he had seen the reflection. The leaves were very dry underfoot and he placed his feet carefully, moving forward in slow-motion. It was pitch-black in the trees and he kept both hands extended in front of him to ward off trunks and underbrush, carefully easing the smaller branches aside and detouring around thick clumps of young birch and oak. He estimated that he would cover about four yards in five paces, and that whoever was there in the wood watching them was about forty yards from where he had entered the trees. He paused at every fifth pace and listened.

The fifth time he stopped he heard someone cough quietly ahead of him—the low rumble as a man cleared phlegm routinely.

Pentland looked to his right toward the cottage. Through the trees it was just possible to piece the scene together from where he stood. He could see the brightly lit windows and the vertical oblong of the open door on the far side of the lawn.

Joe Kenyon was still framed in the doorway talking to Jan, and as David watched he saw Joe throw his head back the way he always did when he laughed. The sound of his laughter drifted down into the trees.

Framed in the doorway.

The man ahead of him had just cleared his throat. When does a man instinctively clear his throat? Before you address yourself to some delicate little task, he thought. Clearing the throat is a part of the human body language that says "I'm about to say something," or "I'm about to *do* something."

Do *what*?

What had reflected? Spectacles? Field glasses? Neither, he thought, because they would have looked like eyes back up there on the lawn. What about a small telescope?

Or what about a telescopic rifle?

The thought hit Pentland's mind as he paused with his right foot reaching forward to make the next step, his left hand touching the rough bark of an invisible tree, his eyes staring into the blackness in front of him.

He leapt forward, crashing through the branches, his feet pounding down through the undergrowth. His arms smashed the small growth aside, but he missed some of the branches and they whipped into his face,

37

thorns tearing at his skin. Above his own noise he heard someone crashing away ahead of him, moving across to his left, and he swerved to intercept.

He found himself cannoning off tree trunks, running blind. He tripped over deadwood and heard the noise of the other man running ahead of him. A pheasant whirred off, *kek-kekking* through the trees in alarm, and wood pigeons clattered out of the upper branches.

Haddon Wood was crisscrossed by foresters' paths and rides. The section of wild woodland was a favorite place for horse riders and shooting men. The rides were ten feet wide or so, covered in long grass in the summer, and pockmarked with the dents of horses' hooves. Pentland burst out of the trees into a ride. It stretched away to either side of him, bathed in moonlight. To his right a black figure was running silently away fifty yards further up the turf. As he started off after the man he saw that whoever it was was tall and ran like an athlete. He appeared to be clutching something tubular in his right hand but it was impossible to see what it was. The man's head was tucked down as he put everything into his run, and he ran like the wind.

The ride led straight across the breadth of Haddon Wood and terminated in a four-foot deer fence of oak posts and chicken wire, which the man leapt in his stride, taking him out into the open pasture. The pasture swept uphill toward the skyline of the downs. The figure turned left at the edge of the wood and sprinted up to the deer fence, disappearing from Pentland's view. He arrived at the fence twenty seconds later, jumping over it, and ran fast along the edge of the woods in pursuit. He had only taken a few steps before he realized that there was now no one ahead of him. The field was deserted in the pale moonlight. He stopped, and heard his heart thudding, his breath coming in short gasps.

Son of a bitch, he thought.

Then something hit him on the nape of his neck, and his knees turned to jelly. He felt himself folding down to the turf, waves of blackness washing in from all sides to extinguish a pulsing, white-hot spot of pain-light in his brain. His vision faded as the turf rose slowly up into his face and he felt grass in his mouth; and the last thing he was aware of was the strange sensation of his own body bouncing slightly, strangely light, as it settled into the clumps of turf in the field in an untidy sprawl, by which time the blackness was complete.

CHAPTER THREE

He knew that the unconsciousness had been brief, just a moment of blackout, because the blow had been a short-term disabling strike, which paralyzed movement effectively for a short period. It had the effect of knocking the nervous system silly. A blow like that could kill if it was delivered hard enough. However, he knew he was alive because a flashlight shone into his eyes from a position above him, the light adding to the pain in his head.

He was quite unable to move for the moment, and he waited for the other's next move. Would it be a shot, or a kick, he wondered? Christ knows. But if the light moved, it might presage action by the man who held it, as he adjusted his position, and Pentland resolved to throw himself to one side if he could.

But the light didn't move.

He heard the man breathing deeply through his nose. Very controlled. He wasn't even out of breath. Very fit, Pentland thought.

Then the light went out, and he heard and felt the man's feet thump away through the grass.

He tried to get up but still couldn't move, and he realized that perhaps only fifteen seconds had passed since he had been knocked down. He was unable to stand for another thirty seconds and by the time his eyes had readjusted, the moonlit field was empty and silent.

Whoever that was now knows my face, Pentland thought.

Fifteen minutes later when he emerged from the trees onto the lawn, Gail was the first to see him, and came running toward him. The music had been turned off and the others were standing in a group by the cottage door, talking quietly.

Gail paused as she came up to him. Pentland stopped and opened his arms; she came into them, then pressed herself away from him with a mixture of a smile and a frown. He could see her face by the glow of the bonfire, which was still burning happily.

"Where on *earth* have you been?" she asked.

David kissed her, kept an arm around her shoulder, and started them both walking up to the cottage.

It had been a very professional blow, he thought.

"Just a short walk," he said.

"Then why are you so hot? You're all sweaty!"

"I jogged up a ride through the wood. Too much smoking and drinking. I felt like some exercise." He smiled at her sideways. "I like it in the woods at night. I'm weird!"

"David, your face is all scratched. Are you *sure* you're all right—"

"I got a bit lost. I had to scramble through the brambles, that's all."

She looked at him oddly for a moment, but something in his tone stopped further questions as they walked up to the others.

"We wondered where you'd buggered off to," Nat said.

"I'm sorry," David laughed. "Didn't realize how

41

much you'd all miss me! How's it going?"

"We're just off," Suzie said. "It was a lovely evening, David." She turned to Gail. "Thanks for everything, Gail."

Then everyone said their good-byes and went to the cars. Engines started, lights came on, and the cars slowly tangled and untangled as they turned around on the small parking spot David had carved out of the undergrowth.

"Queens Head at Twelve?" Hollister said from his car window.

"Queens Head at twelve," David nodded. "Good night."

They rumbled off, lights moving down the trees on each side of the track. Then the silence of the night closed in, and they turned and went back into the cottage, and went to bed.

They made long, lingering love on the double mattress beneath the low, sloping ceilings of the cottage bedroom, while mice rustled in the thatch above, and as a tawny owl hooted down in Haddon Wood.

David lay awake afterwards for a while with Gail's hair all over his chest, one arm around her bare shoulders and the other behind his head. He had a vivid picture in his mind of a dark running figure, black trees crowding close to the sides of the moonlit ride, and a section of the distant skyline of the downs bathed in silver.

David Pentland didn't wake up on Sunday morning until eight o'clock, and the first thing he saw when he opened his eyes was Gail. She was propped up on one elbow beside him, looking down into his face with her expression serious: lips set, and a frown. But he didn't notice her expression at first because the morning sun was slanting in through the window beyond the foot of the low bed, hitting the right-hand wall in a dazzling oblong and bouncing over to the two of them in the bed, leaving her face in shadow, while lighting the velvety golden texture of her skin. Her hair was mussed and clustered softly around her face like a thick, dark halo, and the light formed shadows between her breasts. The air was warm because of the sunlight and the bed sheet was down over her hips. Sparrows were chattering in the thatch, and rooks were cawing in the fields.

Sunday morning, he thought, and smiled as he reached for her, then winced at the pain in his neck and shoulder. It made him sink back onto the pillow with a groan.

She said, "I saw the back of your neck just now, before you turned over."

"Oh?" he said with his eyes shut.

"Yes."

"What's it look like?"

"You must have got that," she said, "during your little jaunt through the woods last night."

Pentland opened his eyes and grinned. "Kiss me."

"Which means you didn't tell me the truth."

"Didn't tell you the truth? Would I ever lie to—"

"You lied to me last night, didn't you?"

"Gail—" He reached for her, and she swatted his hand away impatiently.

"Your face is badly scratched, and you have a ghastly yellow bruise on the back of your neck, and you tell me that you went for a jog through Haddon Wood. It was after midnight, and we had guests, so that would have been silly enough by itself. Now, how did you get that bruise?"

"All right. I'll tell you if you give me a kiss and then

43

go and get some coffee."

Her lips softened into a grin and she leaned over him. A breast touched his shoulder and her hair settled over his face. As she kissed him, he tried to pull her down but she pulled away strongly.

"Oh, no!" she said primly.

"Bloody spoilsport," he grumbled.

She climbed out of bed and went across to the window. She stood looking out for a moment, the light silhouetting her figure. She had a long back and lovely hips.

"It's a beautiful morning. We've been so lucky with the weather this weekend, haven't we?" she said with her back to him. Then she turned and pulled on her bathrobe.

"All right. I'll make some coffee. You're so *lazy*."

While Gail was down in the small kitchen heating the coffee, Pentland thought about the watcher in the wood. In the clear light of morning, he thought that whatever the man had been carrying hadn't looked like a weapon. He pictured the scene again in the moonlit ride, the figure running about fifty yards ahead, holding what had looked like a thick tube in his right hand. There would have been plenty of opportunities for him to use the weapon while he stood in the edge of the wood, and it occurred to Pentland that the thick tubelike object could have been a camera with a long lens. Photographs in the dark? He could have been using infrared. But why photographs, anyway?

And the camera appeared to have been focused on Joe Kenyon, if that was what it was. It could have been the lens reflecting when he'd been talking to Joe Kenyon, both times.

He couldn't think why someone would want to take photographs of Joe Kenyon from the woods at night.

He heard Gail's feet on the stairs, and then she pushed the door open with her shoulder and came into the bedroom with a tray of coffee and sweet biscuits. She climbed back into the bed and passed him a cup of coffee. He reached for a cigarette and lit it.

"There was someone down in the wood watching us," he told her. "I didn't want to tell you last night. I thought it might ruin your evening."

"Watching us! How odd! Did you see who it was?"

"No. He ran when he heard me. I chased him through the wood. That's how I got the scratches." He sipped the hot coffee. "Ah!" he breathed. "He went through the woods and out onto the downs on the other side. I lost him in the darkness, but he was waiting for me. That's when he hit me."

"My God, David! Have you any idea who it could have been?"

"No. None. I never saw him properly. It was pitch-dark in the trees. Some Peeping Tom, I suppose."

"Well, you ought to tell the police."

"Perhaps. But old Constable Wick's only got a bike. Anyway, I think perhaps I scared the bloke off. I don't suppose it'll happen again."

"It's spooky though, isn't it?"

"Every village has its Peeping Tom, Gail. Forget it. I think it's better the others don't know about it; it'll only scare the girls. Okay?"

"I suppose so," she nodded. "All right, I won't say anything." She looked briefly at the lean planes of Pentland's chest, and his arms, which were long and well-muscled. He looked very fit. "He must have been an athletic sort of Peeping Tom," she said.

"Ar, bugger," Pentland said in a Wiltshire accent, "they do breed 'em strong in Wiltshire, look. And Oi baint so young as I used t'be."

45

They went for a long walk across the downs and wound their way along sheep tracks and farm roads down to the village and the Queens Head. They walked through the door of the old, shaded bar at twelve-thirty, hot and ready for a beer. At an appropriate moment, Pentland took Joe aside and told him what had happened the night before.

"I can't imagine why anyone would want to, but someone's taking photos of you and going to a lot of trouble do it. So keep your eyes open, Joe, and watch your mirror. Someone's keeping tabs on you."

"Yeah," Joe said thoughtfully. "It's funny, isn't it?"

By four-thirty on Wednesday afternoon, the high-pressure area which had produced the stable, sunny weather of the previous weekend had eased away to the east and was now bringing a heat wave to the fields of northern Europe and Scandinavia. As the normal series of low fronts came sweeping back over England from the southwest, the radio and TV meteorologists cheerfully announced that "winds would be light-to-moderate with sunny periods and scattered showers."

That was in the morning. By ten A.M. a ferocious storm had leapt upon the west country, producing sixty-mile-an-hour winds, driving rain, and hail, and causing no end of problems to hordes of holiday-makers on the highways and byways of Devon and Cornwall. But no one was really surprised.

London had so far remained dry, although cloudy.

David Pentland looked out of his office window and thought that if he had arranged a game of tennis for the evening he would have seriously considered cancelling it. But he hoped that Joe Kenyon and Dimitri

Olenko wouldn't be thinking the same way. He decided to call Joe at the embassy. The embassy told him that Joe had left for the day, so he called Brompton Square and spoke to Suzie.

"Hello, David," Suzie said. "Wasn't that a terrific weekend? We had such a *great* time."

Pentland smiled at Suzie's unfailing enthusiasm. "Marvelous," he said. "Is Joe there by any chance?"

"Yes, he just walked in. He's upstairs changing for tennis with Dimitri. Do you want me to get him?"

"No, that's fine. I was wondering if they're still going to play. The weather looks a bit threatening."

"Well, I guess they must be. It's not raining at the moment, is it? Joe's really keen to play to get the exercise. You guys are going to meet afterward for a drink, aren't you?"

"Yes. I thought I'd amble over to the park and watch them."

"Great. How's Gail?"

"She's fine. I called her last night. Just tell Joe that I'll see him at the pub."

"Will do. Bye, David."

"See you soon, Suzie."

So it was on, he thought. He decided not to go back to the flat to change. He caught a cab and was in the park by six. He bought a paper and strolled across the grass toward the tennis courts near the centrally located café. In spite of the dull afternoon, people were rowing lazily about the Serpentine in the lapstrake varnished rowing boats. Kids fed ducks, and seagulls beseiged the kids for a share with ringing cries. They reminded David of the sea. Pigeons strutted underfoot, nodding and pecking at crumbs.

Pentland looked no different than any other businessman taking the air after a stuffy day in the office. He held a raincoat over his left arm, and a briefcase in his right hand, which contained nothing but a pair of binoculars.

He saw that Joe's Citroen was in the car park, and as he spotted it, Dimitri Olenko's Mercedes turned in and parked. Joe got out of his car and the two attachés, wearing white tennis clothes, walked onto the courts swinging their racquets about and talking cheerfully.

Beyond the courts, Hyde Park stretched away, dotted with trees heavy with summer foliage. The browning grass was crisscrossed with the rides and footpaths that formed a network used by early-morning joggers and horse riders. On a sunny afternoon, the grass would have been littered with people soaking up the sun and couples happily necking, oblivious to others. Today, there were few joggers and no couples. Pentland walked to a green-painted seat, and after checking the location—back in the trees, sixty yards or so from the courts—sat down. He raised the newspaper and crossed his legs, settling down to watch. Joe and Dimitri had warmed up and were at the side of the court pulling sweaters over their heads.

A Ford Granada was parked at the side of the road that ran up to the cafe. Its driver wore a hat and his face was in shadow. He was also watching the courts. That would be Allan's man, Pentland thought.

He picked out Dimitri's man sitting at a table on the café patio, wearing his raincoat and pretending to read a book. Pentland shook his head and grinned. No one else was wearing a coat. It was too warm. For the same reason, very few people were wearing hats. The KGB man might just as well have hung a sign around his neck. Still, he thought, the Russian was just a bodyguard for the tennis game, and was probably bored stiff.

They were about to start the first game. Joe had

won the toss and was at the baseline, ready to serve. He was leaning over the ball, bouncing it very professionally, like McEnroe. He tossed the ball into the air and threw himself into a stylish serve like Jimmy Connors—and smashed the ball clean out of the court like Joe Kenyon.

Olenko laughed delightedly and a kid threw the ball back over the fence.

Joe went through the same procedure with the second serve, but finished by tapping it so lightly that Dimitri Olenko had to sprint like a hare to reach it before it bounced twice. By the time he got there the angle was impossible, and Dimitri was forced to hit a lob. Joe had foreseen a short return and was running at the net like a bull, so the ball sailed over his head. He skidded to a halt and went back after it, flailing wildly. It died before he got near it. Pentland heard Joe cry "shit!" and saw Dimitri laugh again. Joe was laughing too.

Good old Joe, Pentland thought. He should have practiced on Saturday at the Hollister's. This was an international match, after all.

Cars came in and out of the café car park; nannies walked by with prams and strollers; and pigeons went *who-whoooo* in the trees. The diplomats' faces grew steadily redder as they chased the ball around the court, doing their best to give each other fuzz sandwiches.

A brown Fiat had pulled onto the side of the road. Someone at the wheel was using a camera. Although the interior of the Fiat was in shadow, it looked as though he was photographing the tennis game. The CIA man hadn't noticed the Fiat. The American looked as though he was dozing.

Pentland folded his paper and got to his feet. He strolled away from the courts with his raincoat over his

49

shoulder and made his way gradually toward the left, crossing the road a hundred yards behind the Fiat. He was about to approach the car from the rear when the man in it opened the door and got out. He was quite tall, but he had his back to Pentland and he was too far away to distinguish details. He wore a trilby-style straw hat and a light-colored checked jacket. He looked like an American tourist in summer clothes.

Pentland went back across the road and moved through the trees to his original position as fast as he could without becoming noticeable. The man was making his way closer to the courts. Pentland was so intent on watching him that he narrowly avoided bumping into an old man who had risen from a park bench.

"Excuse me," Pentland murmured.

"Hey, guv!" the old man called as Pentland walked on. "Wait! C'n you spare a bob fer a veteran of two bloody wars, what's down on 'is uppers?"

"Look—" Pentland began.

"My old lady's bedridden. She carn't do nuffink fer 'erself, guv. I need a bob or two fer 'er medicine, don' I? Be a sport, guvner!"

Pentland noticed that the immediate air had become pungent with the smell of stale beer and tobacco smoke. He was sure the bedridden wife was pure imagination.

"I'll make it a quid if you'll do something for it," Pentland said.

A peculiar mixture of avarice and anxiety flitted across the old boy's eyes. "A quid, eh? Wot's the catch?"

"No catch." He passed over fifty pence. "You get the other half afterward."

"After wot?"

"See that bloke over there wearing a straw hat and a

50

checked jacket? All I want you to do is get him to take his hat off and turn this way so I can see his face. I'll be on that seat there. That's all."

"I'll do it fer a quid more."

"You old bugger."

"That's me, mate." He cackled and spat. "Only a quid, guv?" he whined.

"All right." Pentland looked up and saw Joe serve an ace. The man with the hat was standing on the grass with the camera up to his face.

The old man walked off and Pentland sat down to watch the action. He took out the binoculars. It took the old boy two minutes to edge up to the tall man with the camera. When he got close enough, the old bugger simply walked up and knocked the hat off with a quick flip of his mittened hand. It looked so funny that Pentland had difficulty controlling his laughter. The old man was backing toward Pentland with his arms spread out in supplication.

"Cor, sorry, guv!" Pentland could faintly hear him pleading. "I fort it was a friend, 'onest I did, I meant no 'arm—"

Pentland saw that the photographer had slicked-back dark hair, a long pale face and dark pits of eyes.

You must be Salin Renko, he thought.

For a moment it looked as though Renko was going to hit the old boy, but the cockney had dived for the hat and was offering it up like an olive branch, still keeping up a steady stream of apology. Renko snatched the hat and waved him away.

Pentland got off the seat and walked back into the trees, leaving a pound-note on the seat weighed down with a small stone. He stayed until he saw that the old boy, who had hurried back with a worried look when he saw that Pentland was no longer there, found the money.

51

It was probably Renko in Haddon Wood, Pentland thought.

So, Renko at Joe's party, Renko photographing Joe in the depths of Wiltshire, and now Renko photographing Joe playing tennis . . .

It was coming up to nine when Dimitri Olenko stood up, drained the remaining beer from his glass, shook hands with Joe, and left the pub. Two minutes later, the KGB man who had installed himself at the far end of the bar picked up his hat and coat, paid for his drink, and followed the Soviet attaché out the door.

Salin Renko had parked across the street and had moved himself into the left-hand seat of the Fiat so that he would be only a vague figure to anyone leaving the pub. Earlier, when Pentland's cab had pulled up outside, Pentland had kept his back turned to the Fiat, and had stooped his shoulders and limped a little as he went in through the doorway. There had been quite a few pedestrians on the pavement and he didn't think that the Russian would have spotted him.

Pentland had ordered up a piece of veal-and-ham pie and a pint of draft beer, sitting at the far ends of the room from the attachés. When Olenko left, Joe had caught his eye but Pentland had made a slight shake of the head, then gestured toward the toilets. After a few moments Joe had risen and walked to the toilet, and thirty seconds later Pentland followed him in. The CIA man was watching carefully, but he knew Pentland's face and stayed at his table.

"You're being followed everywhere you go, Joe," Pentland said. "You're being photographed by Salin Renko. We can't be seen together tonight or they'll suspect I might have noticed, because Renko had a good look at me in the woods last weekend—"

"You mean it was Renko in the wood?"

"Yes. Try and think why the hell they want pictures of you. I'll call you at the house later."

"Okay."

Joe left the pub five minutes later, and when Pentland left afterward, the Fiat was gone. Pentland took a cab back to his flat at the Brompton Road-end of Queen's Gate. When he got inside he poured himself a scotch and dialed Joe. When Joe answered, the scrambler made their voices sound hollow.

"Who won?" David asked.

"He did," Joe said, and laughed.

"You should have played on Saturday."

"Yeah. I suppose so. So it was the same guy who was in the wood Saturday night, eh?"

"I'm pretty sure it was."

"Renko's got some balls. Those guys aren't allowed more than twenty miles out of London."

"And we're not allowed outside Moscow's Central District, right?"

"Rules—" Joe said.

"Are made for the guidance of wise men and the obedience of fools."

"Who said that?"

"Beats me, Joe. But look—why do you think the Soviets are taking photos of you? There's got to be a reason."

"They've probably got the equivalent of *Playgirl* over there and they want—"

"Joe," Pentland interrupted, "listen. The Russians aren't doing this for fun. Renko was taking a risk stamping around down in Wiltshire. And your buddy, Olenko, must have told him about the tennis this evening. They've got something cooking. Could you tell Allan Briggs I'd like to talk to him tomorrow? Tell him to come to number twelve, Esaw Road, Battersea. It's one of our flats. Ask him if he could get there at nine and tell him to make bloody sure he's not followed for any reason."

"Okay."

"How did Dimitri come across tonight, Joe?"

"He was on good form. He's invited me and Suzie to dinner tomorrow night at his flat in Holland Park."

"Have you been to his place before?"

"Yeah. A couple times, for cocktails. Not for dinner."

"He could get a lot of photos tomorrow night with the right equipment."

"I suppose he could."

"I'll get Allan to hide a mike on you. I'd like to hear everything Olenko says."

"Okay."

"Also, Joe, ask Allan to bring a list of your major appointments for the next month, could you?"

"Sure."

"Don't let anyone else at the embassy know. It would be better if you made the list straight from your diary yourself and gave it to him personally before he leaves. Can do?"

"Yes. Sure."

"Okay, Joe. Think hard. I'll be in touch."

Pentland replaced the receiver, switched off the scrambler, and dialed Gail. While he waited for her to answer, he looked across the room at a framed photograph of her on his desk. It wasn't the usual portrait. She was standing on the cliffs down in Cornwall at Bedruthan Steps in a strong wind that blew her hair across her face. Her eyes narrowed against the wind.

She answered at the fourth ring. "Hallo?" she said.

Pentland breathed heavily into the mouthpiece.

"Oh, it's you. How's your neck?"

"How did you know it was me?"

"I didn't," she said. "I just hoped it was."

"Well, I'm damned," David laughed.

"You got me out of the bath."

"That means you're all wet."

"Very funny. David, do you know what time it is?"

"Yes," Pentland said, "it's time I popped around for a drink."

"I'm awfully tired."

"Just a drink," he said with a grin.

"All right."

Pentland rarely used the Aston in London. Most of the time during his periods in town he left the car parked securely in the Department's underground park, and took cabs. Gail's flat was only ten minutes away by cab and all he had to do was walk to the top of Queens Gate and pick one up on the Brompton Road.

She was wrapped up in her dressing gown. Her hair was freshly washed and fluffy. He sat down on the sofa with his arm around her. Speedy Gonzales was up the chimney. "He's taken to doing that," Gail said, laughing. She turned to him. "Last weekend was lovely. They're such a nice lot down there."

Pentland said, "Company 'A' tells one of its employees to take hundreds of photos of Mr. X, without Mr. X knowing."

"How interesting," Gail yawned.

"Why would a company do that?"

Gail sighed. "I give up."

"No. Listen. Why *would* a company do that? It isn't a joke."

"Look, I don't want to play silly games tonight, David. I was about—"

"It isn't a game. I want to hear your ideas," Pentland said quietly.

Gail looked up and saw he was serious. She reached forward, got a cigarette and thought while she lit it. Speedy Gonzales scrambled out of the chimney and leapt across the room onto Pentland's lap. David pushed him off and the cat slunk into the kitchen.

"To compromise him," Gail said.

"No. Not that type of photo."

"He's not a celebrity?"

"No, not really. Not to justify that particular company taking the trouble, anyway."

"How about to make a model of him? Like Madame Tussauds?"

Why would the bloody Russians want a model of Joe Kenyon? "No, I don't think so."

"Well," Gail said, leaning back and yawning, "the Japanese take photos of everything they want to copy. Perhaps this company wants someone else to look like him."

CHAPTER FOUR

The next morning Pentland left for the safe-house in Battersea at seven-thirty.

It was pouring with rain and the sky hung around the tops of the taller buildings like grey moss. Pedestrians were hunched against a strong wind and pigeons blew across the streets like dirty paper. It was a miserable morning to go through the standard operating procedure for access to a safe-house, all that ridiculous dashing about.

Pentland walked up to Brompton Road and caught a cab back to the South Kensington tube station, where he traveled west to the Earl's Court station. At Earl's Court he walked quickly through the tunnel below Earl's Court Road, taking the side branch into the bowels of the huge exhibition hall, eventually running up the stairs to the main lobby above. He took a look around him, then slipped out of the main entrance and flagged down a cab that took him east along Kensington High Street to the Royal Garden Hotel, near Kensington Palace Gardens. He crossed the lobby to the elevator, went up to the third floor, got out, ran up the stairs one more floor, and caught the elevator back down to the car park in the basement.

He ran across the parking garage, through the cars, and up the fire-steps back out into Kensington High Street on the east side of the Royal Garden. After jay walking across the busy morning street to the far side, he caught a bus. His feet and legs were soaked. Bloody stupid game, he thought.

He got off the bus at Harrods, and then, as it moved off he ran after it and jumped back on, then got off again at Hyde Park corner. Then he caught a cab to Waterloo Station.

Once in the station he made a beeline for the toilets and ran down the steps into the morguelike, white-tiled interior. He fed a tenpenny piece into a cubicle door, went inside, reversed his raincoat, and put on a flat hat from one of the pockets. The raincoat was now a sleazy brown color. He left it hanging open and took off his tie, stuck a cigarette in the corner of his mouth, hunched his shoulders, drew in his chin to give him a half-baked, sloppy look, and went back up the steps into the station, slouched and hollow-chested.

The morning rush-hour crowd was streaming off the platforms and he had to stand in line for a cab. As far as he could see, he was the subject of no one's interest.

He took the cab across the Thames to Battersea. The river looked like a stream of sewage in the grey light, black mud glistening along its edges at half-tide. He left the cab and walked the last half-mile to Esaw Road.

There were dingy lace curtains in the window of number twelve, just like all the others in the rundown terraced row on both sides of the street. Over-the-hill cars lined the narrow road and the rain poured down. He let himself into number twelve just before nine o'clock.

Allan Briggs shambled past the window just before

nine-thirty. He was wearing workingman's overalls, a flat hat, and heavy black boots. A green cape covered his shoulders like a poncho. David let him in.

He led Allan into the small sitting room crowded with cheap, loose-covered chairs and a sofa, and across to a bookcase built into the wall alongside the fireplace. The bookcase swung back, revealing a door through the wall. They went through into an identical sitting room in the next house, number thirteen. A fat little woman in a flower-patterned apron was ironing clothes in front of a coal fire.

"Morning, Amy," Pentland said.

"Morning, gents," Amy said cheerfully. "You're out on a filthy morning, all right. I don't know!"

Amy's fireplace had a similar bookcase, which revealed a door opening into number fourteen.

"I'll be goddamned!" Briggs breathed.

"Drives you nuts, doesn't it?" Pentland said.

"Who was that?" Briggs asked, pointing at the wall.

"That," Pentland said, "is Amy Harrison, retired document shredder. Lovely old girl. She reminds me of my grandma. Let's make some coffee and go over things."

"They're taking a lot of photos of him, Allan," Pentland said. He told Briggs about Renko in Haddon Wood last Saturday night, and then about the tennis game and pub yesterday evening. "They seem to be in a hurry."

Briggs said, "Last Friday, before Joe left for the weekend, he told me that he thought Olenko was behaving oddly. And also that this KGB boy, Salin Renko, came to his party uninvited. The Bulgarian had brought him along. We're keeping the usual tabs on Joe, but so far there's been nothing to grip."

Briggs looked through the dingy curtains on the window at the dingier street. Pentland was sitting in one of the cheap Victorian armchairs with floral-patterned covers, his feet up on a small, square coffee table.

"So what do you think they're up to, David?" Briggs came back from the window and sat down heavily in the other chair. He leaned forward with his forearms on his knees and lit a cigarette.

"We might find out a bit more after tonight. Olenko's invited the Kenyons for dinner. Could you fit him out with a tape recorder? They won't search him, and he'll get by the metal detector in the hall with that, no problem. Joe'll keep his eyes open for camera lenses at Olenko's place. I've got a feeling that Olenko might drop something, and I'd like to go over everything he says afterward."

"No problem. Good idea. I can fix that."

"Good. Let's have a look at Joe's schedule for the month."

There were senators to meet, and diplomatic cocktail parties and dinners; Ministry of Defense conferences concerning air force compatibility roles in NATO; a public relations visit to the Rolls-Royce engine division, followed by a visiting Marine Corps team of generals from the States ironing out the details of the licensed production in the U.S.A. of the new super VTOL Harrier. This was followed by flight evaluations for two days at Boscombe Down. Then there was a garden party at Buckingham Palace for ranking diplomats and two days at the Farnborough Air Show. Before the Air Show, Joe would spend three days in Geneva with technical negotiators, in preparation for the upcoming round of SALT talks with the Soviets, where he would monitor approaches concerning the sensitivity to the cruise-missile emplacement.

These were the main items. Reading between the lines, both agents could visualize the extent of the preparation work Joe faced: the names and backgrounds of visiting VIP's, technical revues and State Department directives, intelligence and trends in the Warsaw Pact and the Middle East; besides this, he still had to consider time-management factors of scheduling and social obligations that involved both he and Suzie.

"Do you see anything in this lot they might be focusing on?" Pentland asked, looking up at Briggs from the list. Briggs was still studying the list, sipping noisily at his coffee. He looked up a couple of seconds later when he'd finished.

"Nothing that stands out, as far as I can judge. Except perhaps the Geneva bit. But he's small-fry there. More of an observer, and these aren't crisis talks, just preparatory stuff before the big guys come on. His schedule looks pretty routine to me."

"That's how it strikes me," Pentland said. He stood up, lit a cigarette, and sat on the edge of a yellowing, oak dining table with badly carved lions' feet. Rain pattered down the chimney into the fire grate and the occasional cars swished past along Esaw Road. "Back to the photography, Allan. What's your theory on that?"

Briggs drained his coffee and poured another cup, then leaned back in his chair, holding the cup and saucer in his lap. Americans never got used to saucers, Pentland thought.

"Okay," Briggs started. "I don't think they can be after a compromise deal, because Joe's not the type to give them an opening. And they weren't trying to trip Olenko on the charge of consorting with the enemy, because it's Olenko who pushed for the tennis, and he's not stupid. And it doesn't seem that Olenko has

61

tried to get Joe to be indiscreet at all. He probably knows Joe too well for that. So, at the moment they just want photos of him. Joe with friends, Joe walking down the street, Joe playing tennis, coming out of the pub, going into his house. Joe laughing, wearing suits, casuals, tennis gear. All about old Joe." Briggs held his hand palm upward. "What do you think?"

"I have a wild idea," Pentland said, "that they might want to make someone look like him."

Briggs looked down into his cup for a moment, then back up at Pentland. "That would fit," he said thoughtfully. "Yeah, that'd fit, all right." He nodded. "Okay. Why?"

"Well, now." Pentland started to walk around the room looking down at his feet with his hands behind his back. "Let's say this *is* what they're up to. They'll have a good opportunity to record his voice tonight when he's having dinner with Olenko. I gather they're the only guests. Pretty soon they'll have a look-alike and sound-alike. So, the question is—what will they do with this clone? There must be something Joe's involved with that is really important to them. It feels as if they're on a time schedule by the way they're going after it." He stopped and swiveled round to face Briggs. "So we have to assume that at some pertinent time they slide the clone into Joe's position, have him do or say whatever it is they want, and achieve their objective, right?"

"Sure," Briggs said. "Go on."

"That's as far as I've got."

"Shit, I thought you were about to do a big revealing act," Briggs said with a laugh. "You sounded like you'd got the thing all worked out!"

"Unfortunately not," Pentland said with a smile. "But this is the perspective from which I think we should look at this camera stuff."

"I agree."

"Okay, how about we sit down and make a list of anything that comes to mind that they could use Joe Kenyon for. We've got to start somewhere."

Half an hour later the room was filled with cigarette smoke. Pentland threw his pen down onto the table and leaned back and stretched. "Finished?"

"Yeah. I can't think of anything else," Briggs said.

"Let's put them together." He added the items that Briggs had written down onto his own list, and started reading aloud.

"Disinformation, embassy access, VIP contact, assassination, blackmail, defection, bugging, SR80—," he looked up. "What do you mean, SR80?"

"Joe was flight-testing it back at Edwards. I thought you knew that."

"So?"

"So, he knows all about it, doesn't he?"

"Yes, but the look-alike doesn't."

"Sure, but supposing they switch and leave the look-alike in Joe's place? They could get Joe to tell them all about it, couldn't they?"

Pentland thought for a moment. "I don't think so, Allan. Why would they need a look-alike for that? If they wanted to snatch Joe they'd just do it. That is," he smiled, "if you chaps were caught napping. If they *did* leave a look-alike in Joe's place he'd be tumbled as soon as he got home to Suzie."

"You may be right. However, I'm going to keep close tabs on Kenyon when he's away from home."

Pentland read the rest of the list to himself and tossed it onto the table when he finished.

"Most of these ideas are just different ways of saying the same thing. What they boil down to are— firstly, disinformation. Secondly, embassy access and all other privileged access, with a whole bunch of classified and secret information that could spring from that. Thirdly, VIP contact, which covers assassination, blackmail, bugging, trends and attitudes, and God knows what else. Then defection; and lastly, the SR80, in connection with a snatch. I think we should concentrate on access and VIP contact—"

"Don't rule out the snatch," Briggs said.

"I don't think we should rule out anything. But I don't think a snatch is likely. Politically, it would be utter stupidity for the Soviets to snatch an American diplomat in London."

"They always do things that I don't think are likely. There's no knowing with those bastards," Briggs said. "And who says they're not stupid?"

"All right. Let's keep building that list as ideas occur to us. When I get back to Whitehall I'll get checks going on both Olenko and Renko. Could you ask your boys to do the same, so that we can compare notes? Then I'm going to see Byrnes. I think we've got a counteroperation opening up here."

"I think you're right."

"Also, we'd better have a think-tank with Joe as soon as we can. We'll have to go over every detail of this schedule of his, and milk him for his ideas on what they could use his body for."

"When do you want to meet?"

"Find out from Joe when he can get away. Tonight after the dinner would be best. I'd like to meet here again because we know it's clean and safe. But it'll be tough getting Joe across town if they're tagging him." Pentland thought for a moment. "Tell you what, I'll do a travel schedule right now. Give it to Joe, and tell him to follow it accurately, Cabs, buses, whatever. You follow in his tracks and I'll bring up the rear. They might be expecting to see *you* people, but not me. If there's anyone on his tail I'll wipe him off."

As they cleaned up the papers, Pentland said, "I'm getting pretty worried about Joe."

Joe Kenyon wore black-tie and Suzie wore a silver off-the-shoulder evening dress with vertical blue lines. It was low-cut and showed off her figure. Her shoulders were wrapped in mink. Joe thought she looked like a million dollars. Her sapphire earrings flashed their blue depths as the cab made its way up Park Lane through the lights of the evening traffic. It was still raining and blowing a gale outside.

"You look like a million bucks," Joe said, taking her hand.

Suzie turned her head and smiled. Her hair was ash blond, cut fairly short and turned under, sweeping forward below her cheeks. It was a young style, somehow reminiscent of the abandon of the twenties, and went with her easy smile and blue eyes.

"Oh, sir!" she said in a southern accent, flashing her eyes at Joe, "you're just sweet talkin' me!"

"That's what Dimitri's going to be doing when he sees that dress," Joe said with a grin.

"Well, I hope he does!" Suzie laughed. "I'd be worried if he didn't!"

Joe's hand wandered up to the middle button of his waistcoat. A tiny wire was attached to the back of the button, sewn into the waistcoat lining. The wire led to a remarkable little tape recorder no bigger than a book of matches, attached also to the waistcoat lining just to the left of the small of Joe's back. He wouldn't feel the recorder sitting normally, only if he sat with a bias toward the left. He didn't feel it in the seat of the cab. The recorder was already on, and would be for the rest of the evening; it had a capacity of five hours. Suzie had no idea it was there, and Joe had said nothing to her concerning his new-found stardom with the London Soviet contingent.

The cab swung into Holland Park Road, a quiet precinct of tall Edwardian buildings, most of which housed foreign diplomats in London. The cab double-parked outside the building in which Dimitri Olenko lived on the fifth floor. Joe paid the driver, opened the door for Suzie, and sheltered her up the scrubbed stone steps to the porch of the building with his umbrella. Shiny-black iron railings guarded the drop to the basement on each side of the porch. Joe rang the bell and Olenko's voice said, "Who is it, please?"

Joe said, "Kenyon," as he shook out his umbrella.

The door opened automatically as Olenko's voice said, "Please come up, Joe."

There was a nice old elevator with square, brass accordion-grids for doors, and deep-pile carpeting. It hoisted them sedately up to the fifth floor. Olenko was waiting for them on the landing outside his apartment.

"Joe—Zuzie! Is so nice to see you!" He kissed Suzie's hand and shook Joe's warmly, and ushered them into his sitting room. He took Joe's topcoat and Suzie's mink, both of which were sprinkled with rain.

"I give you trink," he said, disappearing into a room with the coats. "Sit down. Make yourself comfortable," he shouted, then came back into the room, his eyes crinkled in a smile.

I wonder what you're up to, Dimitri, my friend, Joe thought.

Olenko was wearing a dinner jacket, beautifully cut, which was certainly not made in Moscow. More likely Saville Row.

"Now, please, tell me what you like for to trink?" He laced his hands in front of his chest and leaned toward Suzie. "You look *beautiful*, Zuzie," he said.

66

"So beautiful."

Suzie glanced delightedly at Joe, then looked back at Dimitri. "Well, thank you, Dimitri. How about a screwdriver? On the rocks?"

Joe laughed out loud at Olenko's expression. "Translated," he said, "that means vodka and orange juice with ice, Dimitri."

Okenko shook his head and smiled. "You Americans, with your trinks. Is amazing, Joe. In Russia we trink vodka most of the time, champagne when we can get it, and beer as little as possible."

"I think those are all you need," Joe said.

Olenko smiled. "Perhaps we should change places, Joe." He turned to look at Suzie with a twinkle in his eyes. "What you think of that, Zuzie?"

"I think I shall die of thirst if you don't get me that drink, Dimitri," Suzie laughed.

"Take her, Joe. Sit her down." He waved his hand at two sofas in front of a fireplace filled with flowers. "I get the trinks." He went out of the room.

Joe looked slowly around the room. Bookshelves lined the walls on each side of the fireplace. A TV and stereo system had been built into the right-hand shelves, and Chopin was playing quietly. On the left wall was a long, ebony sideboard. Above it hung a framed photo of Lenin, the severity of which was reduced by a large Monet print to its right. The door through which Dimitri had gone for the drinks was to the left of the sideboard. Joe remembered that the door led to the dining room. To the left of the door from the landing was a roll-top desk with two telephones, and to the right were a glass-fronted display cabinet with odds and ends of china and glassware, and a few ivory pieces from the Far East. A Soviet flying helmet rested on the top alongside a broken wood propeller from an early aircraft. There was also a photograph of a pretty round-faced woman with big dark eyes and short straight hair like Eva Bartok. That must be Natalia, Joe thought. The other wall set off a chess table and two rosewood chairs.

Joe couldn't spot any camera lenses.

He knew there would be one or two, plus sound-recording equipment. He felt the need to pick out one of them at least, so that he could be sure in his own mind that Olenko was involved directly in whatever operation the Soviets were mounting. Sometimes, he thought, the imaginations of MI6 and the CIA tended to be a bit paranoid.

Dimitri came back into the room with a silver tray holding drinks in cut-glass tumblers. He set the tray down on a glass-topped table between the opposing sofas set in front of the fireplace.

He passes Suzie her drink. "Your screwdriver, Zuzie," he said with a chuckle.

"Thank you, Dimitri."

"I did not ask you what you liked to trink, Joe, because I know what you like. Scotch and soda, I am right, yes?"

"Perfect." Joe took the drink. Dimitri sat down by Suzie, facing Joe.

Joe nodded at the flying helmet on the glass case. "Is there a story behind that?"

Olenko followed his eyes. "*Da*. Yes, is quite a story, Joe." He got to his feet, placed his glass of vodka on the table, and fetched the helmet. As he came back to the table, Joe could see that the helmet was heavily crazed and scratched. Olenko put it on the table in front of them, and sat down again.

"I was flying new type of airplane. Testing, yes? Like you, Joe, I was test pilot before coming here. This was test for spinning and this plane went into flat spin and stayed there. It became necessary for me to leave, but the ejector seat did not operate. When I climbed from the cockpit the air pushed me into the tail fin. My head hit this. I was lucky to land in a marsh because I was unconscious all the way down on the parachute. So I keep the helmet."

"What were you flying?"

Olenko paused and smiled. "Was strategic reconnaissance plane. You know, spy-plane like your new SR80."

"You mean our SR71, the Blackbird, don't you?"

"No, Joe, I do not mean that," Olenko said quietly. "But! We must not talk of airplanes. Zuzie will become bored." He leaned toward Suzie and took her hand.

"I'm used to airplane stories, Dimitri," Suzie said. "I like them. If I didn't, I'd have died of boredom long ago, having a pilot for a husband."

"This is what Natalia says," Olenko said. "You would like her."

"Why isn't she with you?" Suzie asked.

"This is not the way for diplomats of the Soviet. We are not sent with our families. Natalia is happy at home in Berezniky. I will go back to see her soon."

"Berezniky. That's close to the Ural Mountains, right?" Joe said.

Olenko nodded and sipped his vodka. "Yes. On the west side of the mountains. It is very beautiful there. Hunting and fishing, much forest and good walking. Good country to see from the airplane."

"Have you lived there long?" Suzie asked.

"For five years. But a lot of the time we stay in Moscow, of course."

Joe had heard someone moving about beyond the dining-room door; just then it opened and an elderly, severe-looking woman, dressed in black with a white turned-down collar, came into the room. She said something in Russian to Dimitri, and then withdrew.

"Dinner is ready," Dimitri announced. "Shall we go and eat?" He put his glass down and held out his hand to Suzie.

During the dinner Joe noticed that some of the bubble seemed to have gone out of Olenko's conversation. There was less crinkle around his eyes when he smiled. He asked endless questions about America, concentrating on where Joe and Suzie lived now, and where they had lived previously during Joe's air force career, their likes and dislikes, the kind of friends they had made, their hobbies, and where they went for vacations, and about school and children.

At one point, Joe, keeping his face straight, asked Olenko if he was considering moving to the United States. Joe said that the United States would be glad to have Olenko. Olenko reddened slightly and then made light of it by telling them that Natalia had asked him to tell her all about his new American friends. He said he hoped they didn't think him rude, with all the questions. However, Joe had noticed that most of the questions had been directed at him, which was unusual, because Olenko normally turned his charm on Suzie, often leaving Joe an amused bystander, content to watch his wife sparkle.

Olenko decided to swing the conversation back to flying.

"You are of course attending the Farnborough Air Show, Joe?"

"Wouldn't miss it for anything," Joe said. "And you?"

"Of course. I enjoy very much the Farnborough Show." He looked at the calendar dial on his watch. "Now is only ten days away. Sometimes I am glad

70

when it is finished because there is always so much work to be done for this show."

"Yeah. It really gets into my schedule." Joe had a lot of responsibility with things at Farnborough, particularly from a public relations standpoint. The place was always crammed full of VIPs from home, in addition to the national business prospects from representatives of attending nations, and their entertainment.

"I understand your country will be flying the B-1 bomber to this show. And possibly your new reconnaissance plane, Joe?"

"Do you?" Joe laughed. "They don't tell me anything, Dimitri. If you hear anything more, you must let me know. I could do with the advance information!"

Olenko laughed. "Of course! Which days are you there? We should arrange to meet."

"Well, I have to be in Geneva for the opening of the new SALT talks at the beginning of the week—through Wednesday—so I hope to get to the show Thursday through Saturday."

"In that case we should meet in Geneva! I shall also be there the same time as you, Joe, and therefore at Farnborough with you. Is a happy coincidence."

"That will be great, Dimitri. Bring your tennis things and perhaps we shall have the chance to get in a game or two over there. Do you know where you'll be staying?"

"Yes. I am registered at the 'Four Seasons.' And you?"

"I believe they'll book me at the 'Beau Rivage.' I'll let you know for sure."

"I am looking forward to it now that you say you will be there."

"You might not," Joe said. "We'll be on opposite

71

sides."

"But," Dimitri said with a smile, "we both want the same thing, is that not true?"

"Yes it is, Dimitri. We just cannot agree about how to set about it, can we?" Joe looked down at his watch. It was just before ten.

CHAPTER FIVE

At ten o'clock on a Thursday night the Brompton Road Air Terminal traffic was light. Most of the buses for the remaining flights of the evening had left for Heathrow. Downstairs, Arrivals was a lot busier. Pentland watched a couple of Indian cleaning people walking back and forth across the tiles pushing wide mops, one of them with a cigarette hanging out of his mouth, below disillusioned, heavy-lidded eyes. A few people were at the check-in counters and one or two more were making inquiries about vacation tickets at the ticket counter. The white-tiled floor was wet and dirty from peoples' feet, with the rain still deluging down outside.

Pentland expected Joe to come in through the automatic doors a little after ten. He would walk across to the ticket desk, ask for a timetable, go into the toilets, and then leave. If there were anyone on his tail, they would be forced to come into the hall because they would not be able to be sure that Joe wasn't heading for a plane. Then, they could lose the tail through Departures and never pick him up again on any of a dozen buses leaving continually for the airport.

It was ten after ten. Joe would have left Olenko's

place by now. First he'd drop Suzie off at Brompton Square and then it would only be a five-minute cab ride to the terminal. Pentland turned the page of his newspaper and kept an eye on the entrance. He realized that it was possible that Renko would not have Joe tagged routinely at all, because the Soviets would run the risk of revealing their interest in him. However, if they should decide to tag him tonight, the attache would lead them to a valuable safe-house, and Byrnes would be most upset if the Battersea house was blown. It was a lot of trouble and expense to set up a safe-house.

After the meeting with Allan, Pentland had gone straight back to Whitehall and met with the boss.

At first Colonel Byrnes had been somewhat irritated. When Pentland had been bringing him up to date, Byrnes had stood by the window looking down at the traffic swishing through the rain below, with his hands behind his back. There were four or five red-barred files on the circular rosewood table Byrnes used for a desk, and it was obvious that the MI6 chief was busy.

Byrnes was tall and thin, in his sixties, with silver hair curling slightly up above his collar. He smoked cigarettes through an ivory holder, and wore suits cut in a hacking style, giving his tall figure a look of elegance and panache.

"It's really their affair, you know, David," Byrnes murmured when Pentland finished. "It sounds like a job for the Cousins. Nothing to do with us, really." Byrnes swung round from the window on one heel to face Pentland who was sitting at the table. Byrnes drew on the cigarette and puffed smoke at the ceiling, then fixed his blue eyes on Pentland.

Every time he met with the boss, Pentland was impressed by his elegance. But it wasn't only the elegance, it was the man's lineage: Eton, Cambridge, the Royal Marines—then the SAS, and finally MI6. The colonel had apparently been a crackerjack behind-the-lines man during the last war, and had distinguished himself in espionage and penetration during the Cold War. There wasn't much Brynes didn't know about intelligence and penetration operations.

"Purely from the viewpoint that Colonel Kenyon is an American, I agree, sir," Pentland said. "But from a NATO standpoint we could have some responsibility to pursue things. With the CIA, of course," he added quickly, "until we develop a clearer idea of what the Soviets might be up to."

"Hmm," Brynes said. He ambled over to the table and sat down, then began patting the pockets of his suit for his lighter. Pentland leaned across and lit the cigarette for him.

"Thank you," Byrnes drawled. "Very kind." He drew on the new cigarette. "If I recall, David, you and this Colonel Kenyon are good friends, aren't you? Met him in Wiltshire, I believe you mentioned."

"Yes, sir."

"You don't think you might want to dive into this thing because of friendship, I hope?"

"My friendship with Kenyon is a major factor, Colonel. If it hadn't been for that, I doubt anyone would be aware that the Soviets were photographing him."

"No, of course," Brynes murmured. "Good point."

"The other point is that other than Kenyon's wife, and possibly Allan Briggs, I think I'm the only one who knows Kenyon well enough to spot a well-prepared stand-in."

"All right, David, what is it that you have in mind?"

"I think the Russians are in a hurry, to the extent that they could be judged to be operating incautiously. Olenko's concentration on Joe has increased substantially since Kenyon's diplomatic party last Thursday, and Renko took somewhat of a risk that night in Wiltshire, and again at Hyde Park. I'd like to stick with this for a week to see where it leads. Our own security could be involved, because Kenyon's work consists of a lot of evaluation, on behalf of the U.S. Air Force, of our own weapons and aircraft manufacture. He's on our side with the Harrier sale, for instance, and quite a lot of the electronics for the new SR80 are from Ferranti. Joe was the test pilot for that aircraft."

"That's their new spy-plane, isn't it, the SR80?"

"Yes. It uses electrobiochemical integration of the pilot and onboard systems."

"Ah, really? And what, pray, does that mean in English?"

"They plug the pilot's bloodstream into a computer on the aircraft. The computer supplies him with appropriate drugs in accordance with the mission profile. Effectively, the pilot becomes part of the aircraft, one of its systems. His own adrenaline rate increases the sensitivity of the aircraft's flight controls and weapons or reconnaissance systems. So, effectively, there's a direct link between the pilot's brain and the aircraft, and vice versa. When you combine that with helmet and eyeline gun and camera control, and pressure-sensitive flight controls and throttles, the reaction speed and response are phenomenal—"

"You like flying, don't you, David?" Byrnes said.

"I do, sir."

"You miss it, eh?"

"Yes. I'd like to get back to a Harrier squadron one of these days."

"I'd have thought you might have had enough of it after the Falklands."

"I suppose it's in my blood, sir."

"All right. Stick at this for a week. Give me a report daily."

"Thank you, sir." Pentland rose to leave. Byrnes leaned back in his chair.

"What do the Yanks call this new flight technology? Do they have a mnemonic for it yet? They have them for everything else."

"Yes, Colonel. They call it 'Flesh Touch.' "

"How obscene," Byrnes said.

Joe Kenyon came into the terminal at twenty past ten.

Pentland watched him walk to the ticket counter and wait behind a garrulous woman for a minute before he could pick up a timetable. Then he headed past Pentland and went into the toilets. He was wearing a black raincoat over the dinner jacket, with the collar up against the rain. As the toilet door swung shut behind him, a short, balding man wearing a brown raincoat walked into the terminal. He went across to stand below the main Departures board. Pentland laid the paper down, stood up, and walked casually past the man's back toward the exit doors. Joe came out of the toilet, passed Pentland, and went out to the line of waiting cabs. As Joe left the terminal, Pentland reeled up to the man in the brown raincoat.

" 'S'bloody *awful* weather, ain' it mate," Pentland announced loudly, wavering drunkenly with a stupid grin on his face. As he got close he tripped, shouted "whoops!" and fell forward, grabbing for the man's lapels with both hands. He was laughing drunkenly as he pulled the other to the floor. "Chrisht, sorry mate," he puffed, as he crawled across the struggling figure. "Ish these bloody floors—all shlippery. Here! Lemme help yer!"

"Get out of the fucking way, you drunken bastard," the man hissed as he struggled to his feet.

"No need ter be *nashty*," Pentland called as the bald man ran for the doors.

A few people gave Pentland disgusted looks as he followed the bald man outside a minute later. The man in the brown raincoat was climbing into a cab.

There was no sign of Joe Kenyon.

Pentland signaled a taxi and climbed in.

"Waterloo Station," he told the driver, and sat back and lit a cigarette.

Briggs would clear Joe at Piccadilly.

An hour later, after they had toured across London, with David and Allan Briggs pincering back and forth across Joe's wake, the two agents walked down Esaw Road, toward each other from opposite directions. The street was clean, and Joe was at the door of number thirteen. Amy Harrison opened it after he had rung the bell. David had forgotten to tell Joe about Amy.

"Hallo, dear," Amy greeted Joe at the door.

"Oh." Joe was confused. "I'm sorry. I must have got the wrong house." He turned to go.

"Well, never mind, dear," Amy said. "It's a terrible night, isn't it?" She could see Pentland approaching beyond Joe. "I think you'd better come in and get dry. I'll make you a nice cup of tea."

Joe heard Pentland's voice behind him say quietly, "Go on in, Joe."

Pentland walked past and went into number four-

78

teen next door. Joe followed Amy inside number thirteen.

"That's right, dear," Amy said comfortingly as she closed the door behind Joe.

Joe turned round to find the little stocky woman pointing an automatic at his belly. "We'll just wait until Mr. Pentland gets here, sir," she said. "I don't know you from Adam, do I?"

At that moment Pentland came smiling into the hallway. "It's okay, Amy, thank you. Sorry Joe, I forgot to tell you."

"You really ought to 'ave told the gentleman the right procedure, Mr. Pentland," Amy said, stuffing the gun below her pinafore. "Really, dear," she admonished.

Sheepishly, Pentland led Joe into number fourteen, with Kenyon laughing nervously behind. "I'll never understand you guys," he said.

"Token stuff. Routine," Pentland announced as the three of them settled in the living room of number fourteen. "What about back at Brompton Square, Allan?"

"Only one guy, the one with the brown raincoat. They'll assume Joe's in bed now."

"I wish I was," Joe said. He looked around him at the room. "You guys don't go in for luxury, do you?"

"We're the impoverished British Secret Service," Pentland said. "This isn't the CIA, you know. Why do you think I'm so poor?"

"Poor my ass," Allan Briggs scoffed. "You don't run an Aston Martin on peanuts!"

"My old auntie left me an inheritance, bless her heart," Pentland grinned. "Make some coffee, Allan, and I'll get the tape fixed up." He turned to Joe Kenyon. "It could be a long night, so make yourself comfortable, Joe."

Kenyon looked at odds with the dingy room, sitting in the cheap, old, flowered armchair in his dinner jacket, surrounded by walls decorated in a livid green wallpaper patterned with interlocking vines.

They drank coffee while they listened to the tape play back the conversation at Dimitri Olenko's flat.

At two-thirty in the morning Pentland and Briggs were practically interrogating Joe Kenyon.

Joe sat slumped in the armchair looking tired. The drinks with Olenko had worn off and he felt slightly hung over. He had ripped the bow tie off and opened the collar of his shirt, and his hair was roughed up. An ashtray by the chair was full to the brim and Joe was on his fifth cup of strong coffee.

Pentland sat at the dining table and Briggs was sitting on the floor leaning against the bookcase with his shoulder close to the tape recorder. The rain had stopped, but the wind still gusted strongly. The air in the small room was stale, full of cigarette smoke.

"Come on, Joe," Pentland urged. "You must have some idea of what it could be they want from you?"

Kenyon waved an exasperated hand. "Look, boys, I'm new at the diplomatic game, and old at being a pilot. What the hell do I know? I'm just an air force officer with a clean record."

"Could they have got wind of some new policy stuff on the cruise missiles? Something you guys might be planning to throw into the ring at Geneva? Maybe something you could hold them over a barrel for?"

"Nope," Joe shook his head. "There *isn't* anything new. Our position is to defend the deployment of the Pershings and cruise missiles and to stop them escalating their own deployment in the Pact countries."

"What about the SR80?" Briggs asked.

"Well, what about it?" Joe said, turning his head toward the CIA man.

Pentland looked across at Briggs. "You still think they might want to snatch Joe because of that plane?"

"Olenko mentioned the plane twice during the evening, right? Once in connection with his own test-flying experience, and again in connection with Farnborough."

"Yeah," Joe said. "But everyone knows we're flying it over to Farnborough. They can take all the pictures they want of it then."

"It wouldn't be pictures they want," Allan said. "They'll be after the systems."

"They sure as hell'd like to get their hands on that stuff," Joe said. He nodded. "They're way behind us on that."

"How many other pilots have flown that plane?" Briggs asked. He leaned forward.

"That's classified information, Allan."

"For Christ's sake, Joe!" Briggs said in exasperation.

"Would you like me to leave the room?" Pentland asked.

Joe smiled and shook his head. "There's only one other to date."

"One!" Pentland said. "You mean only one other guy besides you knows how to fly that thing?"

Briggs looked over at Pentland. "See what I mean?" He lit a cigarette. "Fifty percent of the accumulated knowledge of the SR80's flight envelope and systems is sitting in that beat-up old armchair. When he isn't doing that, the Soviets are following him around London photographing him." He looked back at Pentland. "Now will you take me seriously?"

"I still can't believe they're planning a snatch," Pentland said.

"A snatch?" Joe sat up. It was the first he'd heard of that theory. "Christ, they wouldn't do that. It would practically start a war."

"It depends on how they handled it," Pentland said thoughtfully. "I had no idea that you had only two pilots to operate the SR80."

"By now there'll be others coming through the simulator pipeline."

"Who's the other pilot?" Briggs asked.

"Chuck Lindley. He'll be flying it over for Farnborough."

"Maybe we're on the right track. Maybe we're not," Pentland said to Briggs. "However, I agree with you—a snatch moves to the top of the list. Let's collect our thoughts for a few minutes. I'll make some more coffee."

While Pentland was in the kitchen, Joe said, "Look, Allan, it's getting goddamn late. I've got a heavy day tomorrow. I need some sleep."

Pentland smiled as he heard Briggs say, "It's your body, Colonel. You'll have a heavier day if they snatch you. Call in sick, and cancel your appointments. This whole setup is beginning to stink badly. We're going to need to account for every minute of your time and exactly where you're going to be from now on."

Pentland walked back into the room with more coffee and set the pot down.

"The trouble is," he said, "we won't know when they're going to do whatever it is they're planning. Somehow we've got to dream up a way to get a step ahead of them. Let's get back to it." He turned to Kenyon.

"Why is the American government risking the SR80 at Farnborough, Joe? You kept the wraps on the SR71 for long enough."

"I guess it's a question of sales resulting from a

demonstration of advanced technology." Joe smiled. "We fly the highest, and we fly the fastest, and here is the aircraft to prove it. So buy your fighters from Uncle Sam. That kind of bullshit."

"So if they were to get their hands on you, they would be able to extract the secrets of the SR80's advanced systems, I suppose." Pentland frowned. "But would you know the details of that stuff, Joe? Or is your knowledge limited to how to operate the systems rather than their design?"

Joe leaned back in the chair and stretched his neck, rolling his head from side to side. "I guess they could get the basics out of me, yeah. But remember—they did that with Gary Powers and it didn't result in a surge of Soviet technological progress back then. Like him, I don't think I could tell them enough to make that kind of difference. I think you guys are on the wrong track, thinking about a snatch. It's too wild."

Allan, stifling a yawn, said, "They'd be better off snatching the goddamn plane. Then they'd have it all. Forget about Joe." He looked over at Pentland. "Right, David?"

"They wouldn't even get the thing rolling," Joe laughed.

"What do you mean, Joe? Couldn't any experienced fighter jock, given the opportunity, climb in and crank the SR80 up? Some Soviet Chuck Yeager type?"

"Nope," Joe said.

"How come?" Allan asked.

Joe raised his arms and dropped them resignedly back onto the arms of the chair. "Look, top-secret is just that. *Top-secret!* Just take my word for it. Right now, nobody but Chuck Lindley and myself can fly the aircraft. Without either of us in the cockpit, it's just a big aluminum tube stuffed with electronics, and

83

as useless as a eunuch at an orgy. It won't go!"

"You say 'at the moment.' You mean until your vacancy is filled?"

"Yeah. That should be any time now. The testing's complete. They'll start hands-on flight training after Farnborough. Operational pilots are in the process of finishing simulator training right now. I worked most on the flight parameters. Chuck's been working on the electronics applications."

"But they're not after Chuck," Allan said. "They're photographing you. We've got to stay on the theory that they might be planning to snatch you, or possibly the plane—"

"No, no, *no*," Joe said, shaking his head in exasperation. "The Soviets don't snatch people like me. I'm not a goddamn scientist. And I've told you, there's no possibility of them snatching the plane. There has to be another reason for these photos. We're going up the wrong path."

"I hope you're right," Pentland said. "But I'd like to know just why another pilot couldn't take the aircraft. We both have the highest security clearances anyone can have. I think it's very important we know. There may be an angle you're not considering, Joe."

Joe leaned forward in the chair and stared down at the faded brown carpeting for a moment. "Think of it this way, guys. The SR80 is like Dracula." He looked up and smiled across at the two agents. "But it will only drink my blood or Chuck's. It wouldn't touch yours. Or anyone else's."

"How obscene," Pentland said, echoing Colonel Byrnes.

Pentland told the cab driver to drop him off on the Brompton Road at the top of Queensgate. By the time

84

he got out of the cab it was four in the morning. He felt tired and stale after the intense night in the small smoky room.

Allan had taken a cab with Joe, and Pentland had caught the next one along. Now, as the cab slid to a halt only an occasional vehicle passed, and the road stretched dark, wet, and empty, with the tall old buildings looming to each side of the pavement. The wind still whistled in gusts down the street and around the buildings; otherwise, London was at its quietest at this ungodly hour.

Pentland flexed his shoulders and breathed the cool air into his lungs as he walked down Queensgate to his flat. He thought of Gail sleeping, ten minutes away, and had a strong urge to tell the cabby to drive on to Chelsea and drop him off at her place—but she would be definitely miffed if he sought her company at this time of the morning. The thought of her made him smile. She would be curled up with her head on one pillow in a mass of dark hair, with Speedy Gonzales on the other. Bloody cat . . .

He reached in his pocket for his keys and took the dozen or so steps up to the entrance porch two at a time. It was one of those porches with a small alcove to each side with ridiculous narrow stone seats built in, which he had always thought was a stupid piece of design. Who would want to sit huddled in a porch on Queensgate? The milkman used one of the seats for the bottles, and stray cats used the other. The area immediately in front of the entrance door to the building was therefore very dark. There should have been an overhead light, but the bulb had been out for more than a year and the landlord, in his usual desultory manner, had not yet gotten around to replacing it.

It could have been perhaps some minute reflection

from the blade, or possibly some denser quality than usual in the shadows of the porch, but there was no time to think about that, only time to sweep his right arm across his exposed body in a stiff-arm parry; better the knife in the arm than in the guts . . . fall back in sympathy with the lunge, to bring him out—hopefully off balance—while the adrenalin pumped into the bloodstream and the heart picked up instantaneously into a palpitating rhythm of survival.

He lunged himself forward to get inside as the knife glinted back in, this time from the side, and slammed the heel of his hand stiff-armed up at a pale, face-high oval as the red-heat of the blade cut through the clothes and skin on his back. As he felt the blade, the heel of his hand smashed upward into the shadow's lower jaw. A closed-mouth grunt of pain then, and breath forced out of a nose, and no time to lose. Four fingers of the right hand stiff into the plexus to stop him breathing while the ax-edge of the left hand chopped into his kidneys.

Thump—thump.

And a chop to the neck as he folded so that he stayed folded, and a lot of anger in that chop because of the feel of blood running down his skin and pooling into the buttocks, and the pain coming.

Then, for a moment, only his own harsh breathing in the porch and the blood pounding in his ears, the heart already beginning to slow, and the shock bringing in trembling reaction.

A car's engine roared into life on the far side of the road, very loud in the pre-dawn silence. A brown Fiat swung out of a row of parked cars, its tires screaming as the driver kept his foot down through the gears.

Salin Renko.

Who would this be at his feet?

In the tiny light of the pencil flashlight there was

blood in the mouth, blue eyes open wide above, short air hair, and a sandy mustache. He wore a dark sweater and grey pants, with rubber-soled boots. Pentland reached down and felt the man's neck, and also the sting in his own back as the skin stretched.

A sting in his own back, but Blue-eyes was dead.

He hadn't meant to kill. He would have liked to have asked him questions. But there'd been no time to measure a blow. At that moment it had been Blue-eyes or him. Tough luck, Blue-eyes.

Pentland heaved the lump of the body aside with his foot, unlocked the door, and went inside. He climbed slowly up the stairs to his apartment, poured a large scotch and phoned the D.O. He drank a large mouthful of the scotch as the call went through.

"Peter here," Pentland said tiredly. "I've got someone at my place who needs a lift badly, and could whoever comes bring along some aspirins?"

"Where will he be?"

"Waiting in the porch. Don't be too long."

"Is the pain bad?"

"I shan't die."

"Good. They're on their way—"

Fifteen minutes later, standing by the window overlooking the road, Pentland saw the white top of an ambulance, with the red cross looking black in the infrequent yellow street lights, slide quietly up to the curbside below. Three foreshortened figures, two of them in peaked hats and the third carrying a case, strode into the porch and disappeared from view. Thirty seconds later the two peaked hats came back into view carrying a stretcher which they loaded into the back of the vehicle, and then there was a quiet knock at the door. Pentland turned from the window and let the doctor in.

"Get your shirt off, lad," the doctor said. "Good,

87

now sit down there and lean forward. Ah. Hum you're lucky. Yes. Cut you nice and clean, as a matte of fact. If someone's going to cut you, pray for a sharp knife, and a clean one, eh? Where's the bloody needle—?''

When the doctor had gone, Pentland lay stiffly down on the bed and smoked a cigarette. Sleep wa now a lost cause, the mind too brittle.

First blood . . . he thought.

They must be very anxious to have tried that. They were in a hurry, and they wanted him out of the way.

Salin Renko wanted a clean run.

CHAPTER SIX

The Soviets took Joe Kenyon during the last minutes of his stay in Geneva.

All day, the Alps east of the city had been obscured by the grey bases of heavy cumulus clouds piled high into the sky like the gigantic peaks of the mountain range they obscured. Yellow rays of the sun slanted down through the gaps in the clouds to highlight rocky crags and dark valleys of the lower slopes in a stormy Renaissance scene.

While Joe was secure in the talks inside the Palace of the United Nations, David Pentland sat in a sailing dinghy half a mile out from the shore of Lac Leman, better known as Lake Geneva. The lake's surface was like a sheet of pewter in the lackluster, thundery air, scarred only now and then by wakes of ferries and small motorboats, quickly settling back into its original implacability. Like his own, other sailboats sat lifeless in the hot, still air, appearing distantly as unmoving sculptured islands, their sails hanging in folds: sagging triangles mirrored in the dull water.

The city of Geneva murmured with traffic to each side of this southern extremity of Lac Leman, heaving above itself a brown pall of exhaust-laden air which hung in a band over the grey buildings.

Pentland looked at his watch, which said quarter to four. Joe would emerge from the Palace of the United Nations at five, and he wanted to be close to the steps by then. He spat over the side of the dinghy and watched the patch diffuse, remaining next to the boat. He squinted up at the sails hanging in yellow folds from the mast, and cursed the lack of wind. There was a rumble of thunder in the distance. It went on and on like the irritable mutterings of some miserable giant, echoing back and forth in the mountains. Sweat ran down Pentland's face and he groaned at the thought of having to row the boat back. Then, the sweat would be pouring off him in buckets. He peered at the imposing Palace, beyond the Parc Mon Repos where he had hired the boat. People were scattered across the browning grass like tawdry-colored litter from this distance, tourists sunbathing, kids running around like blowing candy-wrappers.

Each morning he had driven Joe from the Hotel Beau Rivage, on the Quai Du Mont Blanc overlooking the lake, to the Palace of the United Nations; through the city's rush-hour traffic up the Quai W. Wilson, into the Avenue de France and around the Place des Nations, and up to the Palace; then watched the attaché carefully as he walked through the security checks into the safety of the cool gloom within. The process was reversed at five and they would fight the rush hour back to the hotel.

The first morning after he had seen Joe safely into the conference building, Pentland had met with his old friend and colleague, Maurice Fennel, the MI6 man in Geneva; the meeting arranged the previous night when he and Joe had checked in. As usual, Maurice gave directions to one of his haunts in the back streets, where the big Swiss preferred to conduct most of his business over endless glasses of Pernod.

When Pentland walked into the bar through its grimy door with opaque glass and grubby curtains, it took a few moments for his eyes to adjust to the gloom; he had to navigate mostly by the sound of the stentorian voice that greeted him with enthusiastic insults from the back of the room.

"Pentland! Over 'ere!" Fennel's voice boomed. "Are you blind? Claude!" he bellowed at the proprietor. "Pernod—*Mon Dieu*! This is an occasion! Where've you been, David? It 'as been so long! Or will you 'ave scotch, you depraved limey—!"

Pentland picked Fennel's bulk out of the gloom and smiled as he approached the table. The Swiss grinned back from thick lips, below heavy eyebrows and a nose like DeGaulle's. His voice was gravelly like Chevalier's, the accent pronounced over his American English.

"Maurice!" Pentland greeted his friend as he sat down. "How the hell are you, you old reprobate? My God, you're putting on weight."

"It 'as been earned, David. I am forced to build the reserves because of all the work London requires me to do for them, *hein*? Pernod?"

Fennel poured some white liquid from a fresh bottle on the plastic tablecloth and added water, then stirred the mixture into a white, milky cloud.

"So what are you doing in Geneva, *hein*? Tell me the news! 'Ow is Gail?" Fennel made a growling noise of appreciation in his throat. Pentland had brought Gail to Geneva for a long weekend during the last winter and had introduced Maurice Fennel as a business acquaintance. Fennel had wrapped a huge arm around her shoulders and shown her a great time, telling her wicked stories and keeping her laughing nonstop for the three days they were there. Gail loved the big charismatic Swiss agent.

"If she had known I was going to see you she would have sent a big kiss."

"Ah! Silence, while I imagine this!" Fennel sighed.

Pentland told Maurice about the Soviet interest in Joe Kenyon.

"So, you are guarding 'is body, *hein*? This is different for you—"

"He's an important man, and he's a good friend. I don't want to trust this to a surveillance unit, Maurice, until I know more about what the Soviets are after." Pentland sipped at the Pernod. "There's a *mokre dela* man called Salin Renko who appears to be the executive in the field. Here's the info on him." He handed Fennel a brown envelope. "Could you keep an eye out for him in Geneva? If you could find some way to nail him, unofficially of course, it would be a load off my mind. The bastard's already had one go at me, and I'd feel a lot more comfortable if he was out of the way."

"But, of course. I shall look. And if I find 'im, I will arrange something."

"In the meantime, how about joining Joe and myself for dinner tonight, at the Beau Rivage? Kenyon would enjoy meeting you. But no drinking competitions, Maurice."

Maurice Fennel enjoyed testing the mettle of a new acquaintance by arranging, usually late at night after a good dinner out, a drinking session to see who could outlast the other. When Pentland first met him, Fennel had taken him out for an excellent dinner, after which he had driven his Rover to a back-street bar. Fennel had marched in, kissed the proprietor on the cheek, hugged him, taken a bottle of scotch from the shelves behind the bar and sat down with two glasses. Fennel's sole companion was an Alaskan malamute called Sugarbush, who was used to waiting patiently for his master out in the Rover. The two men filled the glasses and talked, getting to know each other as the level of the amber liquor in the bottle dropped steadily lower. A couple of hours later, with barely an inch of whiskey left in the bottle, Pentland realized that if he moved he would probably fall over, and be unable to get up. He desperately needed to relieve himself. The toilets were down a flight of stone stairs leading off one corner of the room. The bar, by then, was deserted except for the proprietor yawning tiredly on his stool.

Fortunately Fennel felt a similar urge, and with a grunt heaved himself up from the table and walked ponderously toward the stairs, disappearing down into the darkness leaving Pentland at the table wondering how he could follow. The minutes went by, and eventually, through a haze of whiskey, Pentland began to wonder where Fennel was. Making an enormous effort, he managed to get up from the chair, and under the bored eyes of the proprietor, using the walls with drunken cunning, he lowered himself down the streep steps to the toilet.

There was no sign of Maurice, only a loud snore from one of the stalls. Pentland found the Swiss sitting on a toilet seat, his head back, mouth open, fast asleep.

Later, clutching each other, they managed to mount the steps. Fennel kissed the proprietor, and they staggered out into the street at three in the morning.

Sugarbush sat behind the wheel of the Rover with his tongue lolling out from between his huge teeth. Fennel got into the passenger side and Pentland into the back. Fennel reached across Sugarbush, started the Rover, and shifted into drive. The Rover moved off with Sugarbush at the wheel, Fennel steering with his left hand, and his left foot on the throttle.

"Take us 'ome, Sugarbush!" Maurice cried.

"Jesush Chrisht!" Pentland muttered drunkenly and closed his eyes.

The next thing that Pentland knew, the car was stopped and Sugarbush was panting at a policeman who was peering in through the driver's window with a worried look. Pentland followed the ensuing conversation in French.

"Why is this dog," the policeman said, "sitting in the seat of the driver?"

Sugarbush continued to pant and drool at the policeman's face.

"He is taking us home," Maurice replied, pronouncing the words carefully. "Because we are drunk, and he is not!"

"Mon Dieu!"

"He is just a dog," Maurice pointed out. Pentland giggled in the rear.

"This man who laughs in the rear," the policeman said, "he is also drunk?"

"That is my son of whom you speak," Maurice said. "He is just happy. When he is happy, he laughs. This is abnormal?"

Sugarbush barked deeply and excitedly as Pentland lost control, sinking back into the seat howling with laughter.

"He is very happy," Maurice observed.

There were now two policemen at the window.

The new arrival said: "It is Fennel!" in a knowing voice.

"Ah—*ca va*, Henri!" Maurice called.

"It is better you leave this automobile here, Maurice, my old friend," Henri said.

"Perhaps you are right," Maurice agreed.

Pentland then found himself sitting in the rear of a police Citroen, while Maurice, by his side, explained to Henri that in reality Sugarbush was a reliable chauffeur, as the two policemen drove them home to Maurice's apartment.

Sugarbush sat erect between the two policemen in front, taking a keen interest in the route.

It was occasions like this that prompted Pentland to forbid any drinking competitions after dinner with Joe Kenyon . . .

Maurice had been unsuccessful in locating Renko. The Swiss agent had been sure that the Russian was not in Geneva, which was a relief. As he began to row back to the park, Pentland thought about the trip back to London tonight. It would be good to get back. He hoped it would be cooler in London. And he looked forward to seeing Gail.

By all accounts Joe had been bored stiff with the talk preparations. Three days of dreary dialogue between the NATO and Soviet bloc people through interpreters' monologues, while behind the scenes the experts of both sides had responded to the summonses of the front-liners to produce sheets of backup material: explanations and charts, minutes of previous points of agreement and disagreement, technical summaries and extrapolations. Joe was there as an adviser to the team, an expert on strategic air weapons, and he had looked forward to being called, keen to make a point that perhaps would have a faint chance of making a difference; something that might conceivably light a spark in someone's eyes to create a perceived edge, so that a new pawn could be moved a square forward to progress the proceedings and set the talks on a path towards agreement.

But Joe had not been called. The voices below the high gothic ceilings rumbled on like Thor in the mountains, with not a sliver of electricity to spark the charge and release the tension.

As he rowed, Pentland could see the flags of nations hanging outside the Palace far away across the leaden water. They hung limply above sweating pedestrian sightseers, who perhaps read the morning papers with hope that East and West would issue a communique of progress.

What a bloody silly world it really was, Pentland thought as he sweated at the oars.

At breakfast this morning, Joe's mood had reflected his disillusionment with the progress, but then the attaché cheered up, which Pentland had put down to the fact that it was the last day, and they would both be returning to London that evening. Joe had leaned across the white tablecloth and looked swiftly to right and left, as though not wishing to be overheard, with a secretive gleam in his eye.

"David," he said, "I wasn't going to tell anyone for a while, but I just got to tell someone—"

Pentland looked up with a mouthful of toast.

"Suzie's pregnant!" Joe announced.

Pentland's eyes widened and he nearly choked on the toast. He knew that Joe and Suzie had wanted a child since they were married, but so far had been unsuccessful. He also knew that Suzie Kenyon had gone through two previous miscarriages, and thought that by now there was no hope, which accounted for his surprise.

"Joe, that's marvelous!"

"Yeah," Joe leaned back delightedly. "Suzie's wanted a kid for so long. Well, we both have. After this tour we want to put down some roots. Get a permanent place of our own, maybe in California, some place warm. Suzie's missed that all these years in the air force, following me around. After a while, somewhere permanent gets to be an obsession."

"I bet she's over the moon."

Joe nodded and smiled. "She's up there," he said. Then a hint of anxiety crept into his expression. "She can't afford to miscarry again," he said. "It could be real bad if that happened again. Real bad. The doctors say if that happened her chances of having a kid would be nil. So it's kind of nerve-wracking."

"How long have you known?"

"Two months. So far so good." Joe looked at his watch. "I'll be glad to get back. You seeing Gail before the weekend?"

"Tonight," Pentland grinned.

"Bring her down to the country. We'll have a party to celebrate."

"You're on, Joe."

"Great!" Joe finished his coffee. "What's the schedule for tonight?"

"I made reservations on the seven o'clock flight, and two others. One at eight-thirty and the last out at ten."

"That sounds good. I might be a bit late getting away tonight. There are bound to be loose ends. But I'll do my best."

"When we get back here, pack and get down to the lobby as fast as you can. I'll get the accounts ready. We'll get straight out to the airport and check the car in. We'll do any waiting there, rather than the hotel."

"You still worried about this guy Renko?" Joe asked.

"He hasn't shown up so far. But we can't relax until we're in the air, Joe. What news of Comrade Olenko?"

"He's as cheerful as ever. I'd say he's perked up a bit," Joe added. "A week ago, as I told you, he seemed preoccupied, but now he's back to his old self. We meet today at the talks. Anyway, no photographers in Geneva that I've noticed. I'm sure you guys were on the wrong track. Maybe they were just building their files."

"I doubt it, Joe," Pentland had said. "I doubt it—"

Pentland paused and rested the oars. He lit a cigarette, and after a few puffs, threw the butt over the side. He wiped sweat from his face and watched a big ripple spread as a fish came up to check out the possible food.

It was all a bit quiet, he thought.

After another minute, he picked up the oars and rowed the rest of the way back to the boat-rental place at the Parc Mon Repos.

Everything went fine.

Joe came out of the talks only ten minutes late and they got back to the Beau Rivage at five-thirty, which left plenty of time to pack, check out, and drive to Cointrin Airport in good time for the seven o'clock flight.

The hotel was very busy. Tourists were checking in and delegates checking out and the lobby was full of people. The two men parted at the elevator on the third floor and arranged to meet in the lobby as soon as they could. Pentland had already packed and all he had to do was collect his bag, take a quick look around the room to check for stray items, and go back down in the elevator to the lobby.

The elevator doors opened onto a busy scene. A large group stood waiting and Pentland pushed through them. Much to his surprise, he caught sight of Joe Kenyon on the far side of the lobby near the entrance, and wondered how in hell Joe could have possibly gotten back down from his room so quickly. The attaché caught Pentland's eye and waved. He had even found time to change, Pentland noticed. Joe now wore a sports jacket. Pentland made slow progress through the crush toward the cash desk.

Halfway across the lobby someone tripped him and he sprawled down into a forest of legs and baggage trolleys. On his way to the floor he thumped into a short fat Frenchwoman who shrieked as she fell over. As Pentland got to his feet, he saw Joe being hustled towards the porter's exit between two men. The Frenchwoman was remonstrating.

"Are you an 'ippy from the *Etats Unis*?" she cried. " 'Ave you no manners!"

She was being helped to her feet by her outraged husband, a little man in a loud checked jacket, who began to join in the general noise, to avoid any subsequent abuse should he not demonstrate his concern.

Pentland began to run through the crush, shoving people aside.

Someone yelled, *"Attendez!"* in an official voice, and another yelled, "Thief!"

This brought on cries of "Police!" as others in the crowd assumed he was a purse snatcher; people grabbed at him and a porter leapt in front of him, only to receive a thump in the stomach.

"Cochon!" the porter gasped, staggering back.

Someone blew a whistle, and uproar followed Pentland through the porter's doorway to the carpark.

He was in time to see a Mercedes roar from a parking slot and swerve for the exit with a squeal of tires. Joe's face was half-turned to peer from the rear window, white and anxious, sitting between two men with only the backs of their heads visible.

Pentland ran for the Peugeot, one hand groping for his keys.

"Bastards, bastards, *bastards!*" he cursed as he rammed the ignition key into the slot. The Peugeot's engine roared into life. Pentland drove out of the slot with the rear wheels skidding, and narrowly avoided the front of a Citroen limousine, which dipped its hood in an indignant hiss of air suspension as it braked. Pentland shot out into the rush-hour traffic, forcing his way into the stream in a cacophony of air horns.

The Mercedes was at least a quarter of a mile ahead.

You clever sonofabitch, Pentland thought, as he cut from lane to lane in an effort to close the gap. You clever bastard, Renko. You stay out of sight for three days—even avoid the attention of one of the best men in the service, Maurice Fennel—knowing that as each day passed, our defenses, our alertness, might slip a shade lower, and at the last—the best moment—when we're finished and going home, you slide in like a switchblade. And if I can't keep you in sight and think of some way to stop you, you'll have Joe Kenyon over the border in a matter of hours.

Pentland cut savagely across two lanes into a closing gap in front of the high cab of a transcontinental truck, getting an earful of twin airhorns and a blast of full-beam headlight in the rear-view mirror. He cut into the right-turn lane as the traffic slowed for a red light, and burst across the slowing traffic into the temporarily clear intersection, squeezing into the far lanes between a surge of cross-traffic from each side. Brakes screeched and horns blew as he drove flat out

fter the receding traffic ahead. The Mercedes, just
limpsed, looked as though it had increased the gap
etween them to nearly half a mile. The driver knew
vhat he was doing, Pentland thought.

He sweated in the enclosed car. There were no gaps
n the action to wind a window down, or hit the air-
onditioner lever, and the interior was as hot as an
ven. When both hands were not on the wheel, one
vas whipping the gearshift into the next slot as he cut
ind thrust to keep the Mercedes in sight. He noted
hat the gas tank was half-full.

So the move had been made, and he was on his
own.

No way to contact Fennel or Briggs; no time to
stop. There was every chance, he thought, that the
Soviets would get Joe clear, and if no one had
recognized Joe leaving the hotel escorted by two men,
there would be no proof that he had been snatched by
the KGB. Some terrorist group might take credit for
his disappearance, and the authorities would sigh and
do little while they waited for the ransom demand. It
was all too regular an occurrence these days.

Meanwhile, back in the Soviet Union, somewhere
deep in the Taiga, probably, Joe would be stripped of
his mind. Perhaps one day, if he survived—or if they
allowed him to survive, he corrected himself—they
might offer him in trade, if they would ever admit they
had him in the first place. And then he would return
to the United States as a zombie. Yes, Pentland
thought with dread, they would cut him soft, and cut
him hard, with the drugs that changed a man's inner
beliefs, until he wouldn't be Joe Kenyon any more,
and there would come a moment when Joe's own logic
saw no objection to sharing everything with them,
because he would no longer regard them as the enemy.
They would be his dear friends, his trusted colleagues.

And, dear Christ, what of poor, pregnant, Suzie

The crowded road ran into the Avenue Pictat Rochemont, which connected with the Rue de Chen to France and the Alps. A good proportion of th commuter traffic swung left onto the Route Fron tenex, which ran along the southern shore of L Leman and out into the residential areas closest to th city. By the time Pentland got the Peugeot screamin into the fast lane of the less-cluttered auto-route Chene, the Mercedes was barely discernible in th distance.

It appeared that the Soviets were headed for th Alps. Pentland could see the slopes more clearly no about fifteen miles ahead to the south, the lowerin sun lighting up the foothills below the thundercloud He knew the first snows would be settling on th highest peaks and the birch would be turning to gol So where the hell were they taking Joe? Throug Mont Blanc into Italy? The route led to the tunne How could he stop and warn Allan Briggs? Someho he would have to find a way, so that the CIA ma could get the ball rolling with Maurice, and cut the out with border blocks. Choppers could achieve th rest in minutes. But if he lost sight of the car, tha would be that.

They began to climb through the foothills of th Alps, the road twisting tortuously toward the bases heavy grey clouds which hung grumbling below th peaks. Pentland managed to catch glimpses of the ca ahead before it disappeared around each bend in th road, while he kept his foot flat to the floor and sen the Peugeot bucking and leaning through the bends They could turn off any time, he knew, and they wer bound to know that they were being followed. H recognized that the Mercedes was a faster car and tha the driver knew how to extract the best performanc from it. He would have to outdrive the other man conclusively if he was to keep them in sight.

Half a mile apart, with almost no other traffic on the road, the two cars roared toward the cloud bases, the air becoming gloomy and cooler. Tendrils of vapor clung to crags jutting into deep valleys that were already plunging into early gloom as the steep mountain slopes shut out the late sun. Deciduous trees gave way to pine forests and the road soon gave the appearance of having been carved out of solid granite.

Pentland wondered how much of the technical secrets of the SR80 Joe would have learned during the test flying. He would know how to use all the systems, of course, but would he be able to describe the principles and mechanics of their construction? He thought of the SR80's still-operational predecessor, the SR71 Blackbird, the greatest spy-plane ever produced, still able to hold the Soviets at bay cruising above a hundred and fifty thousand feet at mach three plus. If the Blackbird could do that, what could the new plane do, he wondered? How much more advanced were its systems, that it needed a computer complex to couple the brain of a man directly to the heart of its systems to operate at maximum capacity? And, in turn, tune the man with drugs so that he could achieve sufficiently fast reactions and comprehension to use the aircraft's potential. How *fast* could the SR80 fly if the Blackbird could leave an F-104 flat-out on afterburners as though it were standing still—and climb to its cruising altitude at three times the speed of sound?

As he thrashed the Peugeot in pursuit, Pentland remembered when the Russians had pulled out the stops and allocated a considerable portion of the Soviet defense budget to producing an aircraft to take the world speed and altitude records from the Americans. The result had been the MIG-25 Foxbat. The aircraft had briefly won those records—until the Blackbird had taken them back at over two thousand miles an hour, while apparently flying within normal operational limits. It was also clear that any of the Blackbird fleet could have achieved the speeds and altitudes required.

Then, the Russians had used the Foxbat to prevent SR71 overflights, and had found that not only was the Foxbat unable to approach the Blackbird's altitude, but that the American aircraft would suddenly accelerate to phenomenal speed—almost suborbital—and that the heat-seeking missiles fired hopelessly in the Foxbat's final zoom-up, before it fell away out of fuel, would explode in contact with an ECM ghost launched by the Blackbird's pilot. Pentland doubted whether any pilot of the Soviet air force had ever in fact sighted an SR71 on an overflight mission.

No wonder the Soviets had snatched Joe. They must be desperate. The Americans were making them look like fools, even to the extent of reporting changed locations of scientific and defense structures the day they occurred, and the structure and composition of every nuclear test carried out, with an analysis of its firing mechanisms and radioactive content before most of the Russian scientists themselves knew. It was small wonder that third world nations, which were strong customers for MIGs and Ilyushins, now bought F-20s from Northrop and F-16s from General Dynamics. The Russians were furious.

Pentland brought the Peugeot howling out of a left-hand bend in time to see the Mercedes disappear into a side road leading off to the right. A second later and he would have missed the change of direction, and he thanked God that they had left the denser cloud cover behind them. The great walls of the Alps had acted like a dam to keep the vapor from penetrating into the heart of the mountains. A few seconds later, leaving his braking until the last moment to obtain every possible advantage to close with the Mercedes, Pentland changed down through the gears and sent the Peugeot lurching into the side road.

The small road ran precipitously up into the heart of wild, rocky crags, its surface eroded by the effects of extreme winter cold and melting snows of spring. The sun was dropping fast in the western sky and the road ran along the side of a vertical drop to the right, with a cliff of rock to the left, the sun catching the peaks above in rosy evening light. He could not see the Mercedes at all for minutes, but there was nowhere for it to go—there were no turnoffs. Just cliff and precipice, and a low, stone, bordering wall just high enough to catch the axles of a sliding car and send it hurtling over into the cloud-filled depths below. The byroads of the Alps were notorious for their insecurity and their ancient narrowness, which would force one of two cars, should they meet, to back up for miles to be able to pass each other. Fast driving needed full concentration, and Pentland sweated as he worked the wheel and the gears, braking on the short straights and accelerating out of the bends.

A part of his mind wondered where in hell these people were headed for. Some lonely alpine farmhouse, perhaps.

Or a high rendezvous with a helicopter, which was more likely.

The valley to the side of him was becoming shallower, climbing up faster than the road, and flattening out below into a series of rocky canyons, steep-sided and bleak with a lack of trees, which were unable to find a purchase for their roots in the thin soil over a bedrock of granite. The old engineers had built the road wider here, with a few turnouts to provide passing places, or perhaps to contemplate the view. They were running up to the heights of the central Swiss plateau where the peaks were less precipitous and the valleys less sheer, and another few miles, he knew, would bring them to the high meadows and pine forests which were the centers of attraction for hikers and alpine botanists and ornithologists, who went to the highlands to watch the eagles and peregrines.

Pentland came screaming around a hairpin bend with the car hitting the rpm limit in second gear. He was in the process of changing up to third when the vehicle bucked, lurched into a skid, and swung broadside toward the retaining wall.

His first thought was that one of the front tires had blown out. His second was that someone had shot them out, and the third was that whatever he did with wheel and brakes, the car was going to slam into the low wall, and if it did, that it would flip over into the valley below.

The Peugeot hit the wall with the right rear wheel first, which brought the front wheel skidding into the wall with the body tilted outward. Then, in seeming slow-motion, the right lower bodywork caved in, and the Peugeot leapt into the air and spun sickeningly in space, down toward the rock below.

At the same moment that Pentland's Peugeot was skidding toward the parapet of the mountain road high up in the Swiss Alps, the telephone rang in Allan Briggs's office at the United States Embassy in Grosvenor Square, London. Allan reached for the phone.

"Yes?"

"Sir," the special CIA operator said. "There's

someone called Joe calling on a clear line from Switzerland."

Briggs leaned forward and said, "All right. Put him through, tape it, and trace it."

The operator said, "You're through to Mr. Briggs, sir."

Joe Kenyon's voice said, "Allan?"

"Joe," Allan Briggs said. "You're in the clear, you realize that?"

"Yeah. I'm sorry. I thought I should call you. David's disappeared."

Allan Briggs looked at his watch, which said six-fifty. Joe Kenyon and David Pentland should by now, he thought, be in the Departure Lounge for the British Airways flight to London, which left at seven o'clock. What the hell was going on? "Where are you, Joe?"

"Still at the hotel. We were supposed to meet in the lobby. He wasn't there. His car's gone. I don't know where he is."

"He didn't leave any message at the desk?"

"What do you take me for, Allan?"

"Sorry, Joe." Briggs paused for a moment. "Is there a back way out of the hotel?" he asked.

"Well, I guess so. There usually is."

"Well, find it. Leave your bags. Don't check out or pay the bill. Just leave. Get a cab to the airport and get through to Departures as soon as you can. Get me?"

"I don't feel like just leaving David, Allan—"

"Get your ass moving, Joe, you hear? I'll take care of things from this end. What time was the next flight?"

"Eight-thirty."

"Phone me from Departures just before you board, so that I know you'll be on it. Okay?"

107

"Okay."

"I'll meet you at Heathrow."

"Allan, I'll need to get to Farnborough direct from Heathrow. I won't have time to go home. Call Suzie, will you?"

"Sure, Joe. See you at Heathrow. Take care, you hear?"

Briggs replaced the receiver and reached for a cigarette. What the hell had happened to Pentland? Whatever had happened must have been some sort of emergency to leave Joe unsupervised, even for a few minutes, in a busy Swiss hotel. And the car was gone. Odd. Allan Briggs reached for another telephone, which rang automatically at MI6 HQ in Whitehall. The duty officer answered.

"Yes?" drawled an Oxford voice.

"Our friend Peter's gone missing since about five-thirty from the hotel Beau Rivage in Geneva."

"Oh? What were the circumstances?"

"He was meeting with Kenyon to come home. He didn't show and the Peugeot he hired is gone. Kenyon has no idea about it. Can you get someone on it?"

"Immediately."

"At the same time perhaps one of your chaps could cover Kenyon. He'll be taking a cab out to Cointrin. You might cover the road and make sure that when he gets to the airport someone sees him through to Departures. I don't like this turn of events."

"I'll do the best I can, old boy."

Allan put the phone down, feeling very uneasy. It was now seven and the eight-thirty flight from Geneva would not get to London until just after ten, and then he would have to get Joe to Farnborough. It looked like it was becoming a long evening. What the hell are you playing at, David? he thought.

Pentland had seen no sign of Renko in Geneva.

Could the Soviets have gone after Pentland to clear the way to get at Joe? Were they now waiting until the attaché left the building?

The embassy was quiet. A lot of the staff had gone home. Allan got up from his chair and started to pace around the office. He could relax a bit, he thought, once he heard that Joe was on the plane. But what about David? Shit! he thought. He felt helpless. He decided to call Suzie Kenyon. She would be disappointed if Joe didn't make it home tonight. He went over to his desk and buzzed the intercom.

"Yes, Mr. Briggs?" one of the night girls answered.

"Bring me some coffee, would you?"

"Certainly," the English girl said. He wondered which one it was this evening. They all sounded the same. He called the operator and asked her to call Joe Kenyon's home number.

The mournful English ringing tone went on repeating itself. There was no one in. Briggs replaced the receiver and picked up a radio handset. He pressed the transmit button.

"Zero-One, to One-Five," he said. The static hissed against a background of silence.

"Zero-One, to One-Five, come in," he repeated.

For Christ's sake, he thought. This was the round-the-clock watch to keep tabs on Suzie in case the Russkies decided to use her for collateral, and the goddamn watcher wasn't at his post. Sonofabitch!

"Zero-One to One-Five, Zero-One to One-Five, come in, over . . ."

Nothing.

Jesus!

The girl came in with the coffee and put it on the desk. Allan was at the window rubbing his face.

"Your coffee," she said.

"What?—Oh, thanks—"

The girl shrugged and left the office.

"Wait!" Briggs called, and she came back in.

"Who's on duty watch?"

"Jerry Anderson, sir."

"Send him in, would you?"

"Yes, Mr. Briggs."

Allan sipped the coffee absentmindedly. No watcher, and no Suzie Kenyon. And no David Pentland. His guts told him that things were not at all as they should be. Anderson came in.

"Jerry, take over from me here. There's no response from One-Five and I can't raise Joe Kenyon's wife. I'm going down there. Use the radio if anything comes in from MI6 or David Pentland."

"Will do, Allan."

"I should be back in an hour," Briggs said, heading for the door.

"I'll be here," Anderson said, smiling.

CHAPTER SEVEN

The seat belt kept Pentland from flying off the seat. As the car hit the retaining wall, he pulled his legs up and went into a tuck with his arms wrapped around his knees and his head down. The Peugeot hit the wall with a rending crash and toppled over into the valley. There was a brief moment of silence with gyroscopic forces, which felt like an aircraft in a flat spin, and then a violent impact as the rear of the car crashed down onto the slope below the road. The driving seat tore loose from its mountings, and Pentland was thrown back and pinned against the rear-seat cushions.

As the crumpled Peugeot, now considerably shorter than the manufacturer's specifications, rolled down the rocky slope, the rear right door was wrenched off and Pentland was ejected. The first part of him to hit the shale was his shoulder, closely followed by his face; the impact cut his cheek and knocked one of his teeth loose. He slid down the shale with arms and legs whirling and came to a stop twenty feet above the smashed car and against a granite rock, disoriented and barely conscious. The car below him was upside down with its wheels spinning.

Blood pooled on the shale below his mouth. He groaned and spat out the loose tooth and began to cough, waves of nausea sweeping over him, until he became violently sick. When the retching was over, his head felt clear and he found he could move his limbs. He sat upright, and saw that his pants were ripped the length of his left leg, which was badly grazed, blood seeping from the torn skin. He spat more blood out of his mouth.

There was a violent concussion in the shale beside him and rock chips flew into the air synchronous with the echoing crack of a rifle. Pentland threw himself sideways down the slope, half-rolling and half-scuttling on all fours into the cover of the upturned car. As he put the bodywork between himself and the road, a bullet smashed into the wreck with a loud clang, and another scattered the shale close-by.

He raised himself carefully, hugging the upturned grill of the Peugeot, its broken radiator hissing and steaming, and peered up at the road between the slowly turning, splayed front wheels. The road was seventy feet above the car at the top of a forty-five-degree slope. He picked out the ragged gap made by the Peugeot in the parapet; then he saw something else which made his genitals cringe and his heart thump heavily in his body.

Somebody was climbing down with a rifle slung diagonally across his back. He was making careful progress and was already thirty feet or so below the level of the road.

Pentland sank back down to the shale.

He had no weapon, and for a moment wondered what the hell he could do. He felt like a rabbit in the center of a highway at night with the big lights roaring down, paralyzed and unable to move.

The man climbing down wore dark clothes and

moved athletically; Pentland was sure it was Renko. He felt in no shape to run, but it was the only thing he could do for the moment.

He spat blood from his mouth and moved as fast as he could down the slope away from the car. He thought he would have about five minutes before Renko would get down to the car.

Two shots cracked past him as he ran, and he crouched lower. The slope was strewn with large rocks, and at times he was forced to leap from one to the other. On the patches of shale, he slid for the most part downward on his behind, breaking his momentum with the palms of his hands. The blood in his mouth clogged his throat and tasted metallic, and he realized that the taste was partly fear. He could not swallow the thick mess, forcing him to spit instead, the drying blood making him retch again.

At one point he glanced back up to the car, but Renko had not reached it yet. Pentland shifted to his left to keep the car between himself and the Russian as much as he could.

Then he realized with a sense of horror that the slope fell off into a cliff. The ground dropped away to nothing a few yards in front of him, and when he came to the edge he looked down onto a fast-running river with brownish greenery on its banks. It looked like a drop of a hundred feet and, with Renko behind, he felt a wild urge to leap over the edge like a hunted animal.

The mountains rose steeply to each side. If he tried to climb to either side, Renko would pick him off with ease. He was in a cul-de-sac, the end of which was a chasm. He looked back and saw that Renko had passed the car and was now bobbing down through the rocks toward him.

Pentland crouched low and peered over the edge of

the cliff, looking for hand and footholds. The rock was uneven, and not absolutely vertical the whole way down, although he saw that in places some part seemed to tuck back out of sight. There was no alternative, nowhere else to run. He went over the edge of the cliff, feeling with his feet for ledges and peering down between his arms for the next handhold, trying all the time to keep one foot and two hands, or two hands and one foot, gripping. Sweat began to run into his eyes and he could spare neither hand to wipe it away. It blurred his vision as he peered down for the next hold, but part of him was grateful that he could not clearly see the chasm which yawned below. He lost all perception of time, and the image of Renko coming down through the rocks submerged in his mind below the immediate fear of losing his grip on the face of the cliff, and falling to a certain death.

His limbs trembled with tension. The animal part of him sobbed out frantic breaths while the sweat poured into his eyes and smarted in the wound in his cheek. Part of him knew that he was only able to stomach the empty air below because of his greater fear of the bullets above.

Reach down with free foot, kick about and locate a ledge by feel, test it, transfer the weight from the upper foot, and do the same with the hands. Lower the body carefully, and crawl down the cliff like a chameleon in reverse. Spit blood and retch.

Where was Renko? He *must* be close to the top of the cliff by now. And if he was, he would find Pentland spread-eagled on the face halfway down. But there was nothing else to do, he thought, panic bubbling in his chest as he scrabbled down as fast as he could.

Then something caught his eye above.

Something darker against the thinning clouds.

Something hunched at the top of the cliff, which now seemed a long way up. Something rounded, and moving, and shifting position. He couldn't see clearly with the sweat in his eyes, but he knew it was Renko.

Pentland clung close to the cliff-face trying to make himself part of the rock. He would be just head and shoulders to the Russian. And then he thought with terror that if the Russian shot him, it would be in the head. Renko would shoot his life out of his head as he clung to the cliff-face . . .

But Renko did not shoot him in the head, or the shoulders. The Russian missed both, and shot two fingers off his left hand in a spray of blood and bone. The impact of the bullet blew Pentland's left arm off the rock and slammed it down against his body, dislodging him, and he fell into space.

After seconds of terror Pentland hit water so hard that his body felt birched, and only the agony in his hand prevented him from passing out completely. There was also an element of surprise. The river had looked fast and shallow from the top of the cliff, and as he fell he was convinced he would die; his mind had been full of the images of a shattered body and a crushed skull.

Instead, his lungs filled with water and he was rolled end over end, legs and arms flailing, bumping rocks, with the river roaring in his ears. Then, suddenly, there was no sound, no light, no movement, no weight. His only awareness was that his lungs hurt as though they were on fire.

He glimpsed a blurred flash of rippled silver and bright light beyond his eyelids for a second, and then it was as before . . . nothing. He kicked and flailed with the instincts of survival, and came to the surface spewing water from his mouth and nose, choking; he managed to stay in the light and focus his eyes.

Glimpsing rocks and branches close to him, he reached and kicked his legs, gripped and pulled found rock beneath him, and wedged his chin on a dry part and retched his guts up, convulsion after convulsion, hardly aware of anything except the need to rid his lungs of water and breathe again. He knew in the nucleus of his brain that his body was doing its best to take care of things, and he clutched a branch and the rock and let it get on with it until it had cleared the system. After a while he found himself lapping the water at his chin like a sick dog. The tooth-hole screamed in agony. He groaned and pulled himself clear of the water, into the deep shade of a thicket of young birch with sun-browned leaves.

He remembered a handkerchief in his pocket, and with his lips drawn back over his teeth in a rictus of pain he bound the wet cloth over the pieces of white bone and bloody skin that protruded from the stump of his left hand, where the fourth and fifth fingers would never be again. He felt a leaden weakness from shock and the loss of blood. His hand throbbed, like the rest of his body, but the adrenalin of fear coursed around his veins, and pain was not a major consideration. His muscles vibrated with tension like harp-strings, and the need to survive was fueled by the strength of a wild joy that he was in fact still alive.

Pentland turned his attention to the river. It looked as though the river had tumbled him sixty yards or so along the base of the cliff and swept him into the quiet water of a pool, which gurgled quietly in front of him, its banks thick with young mountain ash and high grass, and pieces of driftwood from the previous spring's melting snows. He was on the bank of the river nearest the cliff and shrubbery prevented him from being able to see the cliff-face. He presumed he was therefore hidden from Renko. He was developing

116

strong hope that Renko would leave it at that. The man would assume he was dead, and leave.

Pentland wondered how much time had gone by since he'd been shot from the cliff. When you think you're living out your last moments, he thought, things tend to become detailed, frame by frame, and time stands still. Perhaps no more than four or five minutes had passed.

He crawled through the grass and bushes in the upstream direction, peering through the foliage to catch sight of the cliff-face.

Renko was a third of the way down with the gun slung across his back. Pentland stared up at the Russian through the leaves, unable to comprehend, a real dread like a cold stone in his stomach.

Why did Renko want him so badly? They'd taken Joe Kenyon. They had plenty of time to do what they liked with him. Why this relentless animal pursuit?

Renko was coming down smoothly and deliberately, without a wasted movement. Careful, knowledgeable searches with feet and hands for the right places, traversing slightly toward Pentland for the moment, assessing the vertical topography like an expert. He was about seventy yards away, and still sixty feet or so up on the face. At the rate he was descending he would be down in not more than fifteen minutes.

Pentland crouched in the bushes looking up at the dark pursuer on the cliff. Mixed rage, pain and helplessness fought for predominance in his mind. He cradled his left wrist across his right forearm, conscious of the throbbing pain that synchronized with his heartbeat, the pain now so harsh in its intensity that it seemed to occupy his whole body. He looked around him desperately. The river ran at his back with the cliff paralleling its course in front of him. Beyond the river, the land rose steeply upward in unrelieved slopes of rock and a few clinging pines. There were two ways to go; upstream or downstream, along the course of the river. He looked back up at Renko, who was making steady progress. Did the Russian assume he was still alive? Or was he coming down because he had to be sure Pentland was dead? Why so much trouble, why so important for Renko to get rid of him?

Renko would be vulnerable on the last few feet of the cliff, when he would virtually be within reach from below, but still unable to use the weapon. That would be the time to take him. He watched Renko again for a few seconds, and saw the strength with which the man maneuvered himself on the cliff, and knew Renko would jump the last ten feet. Then it would be hand to hand. Pentland looked down briefly at the bloody stump of his fist. Two hands and a rifle to one hand, he thought; one fit Russian against an Englishman whose every limb ached from the battering in the car and his fall off the cliff, with God-knows-how-much blood missing, and a shattered hand. The odds, for the time being, were very much in the Russian's favor. He had to be out of range by the time Renko reached the river.

Pentland set off downstream, as fast as he could.

He ran through tumbled rocks, pines, and bushes close to the river. The cliff to the left often forced him into the cold water of the fast-running river, and then it was slow progress over slippery rocks hidden below the surface. At times, he plunged to his waist in deep holes and pools as the river became steadily deeper, gasping with the shock of the cold water. It was seven-thirty now, and the east-facing rock to the left was darkening in shadow as the September evening crept toward sunset. The peaks to the right were still bright

118

between clouds of thick, grey vapor dissipating as the air grew colder at the end of the day. At another time, in different circumstances, the river in its deep gorge, with the peaks of the Alps rearing up to more than ten thousand feet, would have been inspiringly beautiful. But now, the same cliffs and landscape were a prison of rock to either side, with unknown terrain ahead and a Soviet killer not more than ten minutes to the rear.

As he stumbled along the bank, Pentland tried to gather sufficient wits to analyze what had happened since he and Joe had gone separately to their rooms in the Beau Rivage Hotel. How had Joe gotten down to the lobby before him? Why had they merely tripped him when he had tried to cross the lobby? Why not any number of means of incapacitating him completely? A knife, a quick jab with a suitably tipped needle—even a heavily silenced weapon? Did they think Pentland knew too much, and that if he got back to London Olenko would be seized? That was reasonable. He had *seen* them take Joe. Perhaps they had counted on getting Joe away from the hotel before he could make it back down to the lobby, in which case there would be no evidence that Joe had been kidnapped by agents of the Soviet Union, and Olenko would be secure. Yes, he thought, that would have to be the reason. Renko would have been ordered to get rid of Pentland at all costs, because otherwise MI6 and the CIA would have Olenko's balls back in London when they got the word.

Now it looked distinctly as though there would be no word.

Pentland paused and looked back up the river. He knew that Renko would be down by now.

He ran on, and tried to consider his options. He could just try to plain outrun Renko until he reached civilization—some house or chalet, or mountain farmer—although he had no idea at all of the lay of the land. Or he could hide somewhere, and hope that Renko would give up and go away. Or he could somehow dream up a way of turning the tables on the Russian. Not very good options, he thought, with the breath rasping in his throat and the cooler air searing into the hole where the tooth had been. Not very good options. He looked quickly back over his shoulder again, and this time he thought he saw the Russian far back through the rocks and trees.

The gorge narrowed ahead and the land across the river became sheer—a mirror image of the cliff close to his left shoulder. The river was running faster and deeper between the rock walls and he was forced after a few more minutes to plunge in and swim. There was no alternative. He would have to let the river take him where it would.

He kept his jacket and shoes on, because he knew that when it became dark, if he survived that long, it would be bitterly cold in the mountains. He wanted to feel the cold, he thought, and see the stars. He wanted very much to survive until then, because the odds in the darkness would be more favorable.

The cold water knocked the breath out of his body, but numbed the pain in his hand which he held close to his body as he sidestroked with the current.

He couldn't have taken more than a dozen strokes when a bullet hit the water close to his face. He felt the compressive thud of it in the water around him just before he heard the familiar heavy crack of Renko's rifle echoing between the rock walls. He took a deep breath and rolled below the surface. The river was running even faster now and he felt himself tugged and spun by the current; the water was as cold as ice. When he came up for air he heard the weapon again, but felt nothing, and only stayed on the surface long enough to gulp air before plunging under again.

When he came up for the third time, he risked a glance around him and saw that the river was flowing into a left turn. The cliffs were now higher and dark, and shut out the light. The current was very strong and foamed past large rocks thrusting menacingly above the surface. He kept himself in the main stream and the river swept him past them. He sank below again, having heard no more gunfire, and when he surfaced he was well into the turn. Now, the only way Renko could maintain the pursuit, he thought with some satisfaction, would be for the Soviet bastard to jump in himself, and the river would equalize their individual progress to the point where, for the time being, the Russian would be unable to gain.

He tried to relax and allow the current to take him. He felt desperately cold, his limbs numb and his body cooled to the point where his teeth chattered together in uncontrollable shivering. This water was snow runoff, green and mean. Perhaps, he thought, the whole thing might come down to who in the end had the best circulation . . .

He had known when the cliffs closed in and the current speeded up what this river trip might develop into. Now he was sure. He could hear something above the familiar slap and hiss of the water around him. Things were really speeding up. The surface seemed to have settled somehow, hunched itself for action, green and smooth and serious. Back upstream where he had first entered it, the river had been more playful, but now it had matured, and its stream song had changed into a solid roar. There were falls ahead. *Now* would be the time to fool Renko, he thought. Get to the side and crawl out on the rocks, and hide if possible, and let Renko go past, and over the falls.

He'd never get back.

Pentland struck out across the stream for the rock wall to his left. The current beat sideways at him. It broke over him, submerging his face, and he found himself fighting it furiously. He put his head down and went into a crawl stroke, ignoring the pain in the hand, but the river rolled him over. It sucked at his legs and tumbled his body like a log. The only way he could stay on the surface was to go with the current. He tried breaststroking: the spread arms and legs were more stabilizing, but most of the time he was still half-drowning. The rocks were closer now, jumbled black heaps which surged in and out of his vision as he was swept sideways past them. Close to the rocks the water became rougher and noisier, and the background roar louder every second. He tried to grab the rocks with one hand, but every time he gripped the wet, cold stone the river dragged him loose and swept him away. Then he was slammed backwards into one of the rocks, and his head cracked against it. The water piled up over his face and the current dragged him under.

Once again he found himself rolling over, disoriented, fighting with waning strength and mounting hopelessness to get back to the surface.

He came up in the fast part of the current, gulping and retching, starved for oxygen. Through blurred eyes he saw that there was now a white mist between the rock walls, and a pounding, all-pervading roar filled the gorge. The water around him seemed to have developed a demonic, thrumming life of its own. The surface lagged behind the green power beneath, which grabbed at his legs and pulled him under again, twisting and shoving at his tangled limbs as the currents fought each other.

Everything seemed to curve suddenly downwards

and he fell with the river like a sodden piece of driftwood into a white storm.

The yellow streetlights were flicking on along Brompton Road as Allan Briggs drove into Knightsbridge. The September evenings were getting shorter, and the heat of the afternoon sun dissipated quickly. Briggs pulled off the still-busy West End road and parked the car one block to the west of Brompton Square. He clipped his transceiver to his belt below his jacket and walked through the evening pedestrian traffic.

One-Five would have parked his Ford Escort on the west side of the square, where he would be able to look across the miniature, central park through the trees to the entrance to the Kenyons' house on the far side. Cars were parked on both sides of the road and there were no empty slots. A car door slammed somewhere ahead and someone walked across the pavement and entered one of the tall, narrow, terraced houses. A dog roamed along the black-painted railings of the park, peeing every five yards, and two children, no more than ten years old, played at the end of the square with a ball beneath the light of one of the ornate, converted gas lamps. Otherwise, the square was quiet, and busy Knightsbridge was a mutter in the background.

Allan Briggs walked quietly past the parked cars, keeping to the left side of the pavement, checking each car for occupants and looking out for the dark blue Ford which One-Five was using. As he passed the houses to his left, he heard an assortment of comfortable noises: classical music from one, as someone practiced on a piano, sounds of laughter and the clink of cutlery from another, as the distinguished and

123

wealthy occupants of the fashionable little square got on with their evening. The cars were mostly Mercedes and Rovers, with a sprinkling of Rolls Royces, and a Ferrari or two. A jet, low on its final approach to Heathrow, lighted passenger windows glowing, roared across the clear black sky above the yellow lamps, its brief noise quickly silenced by the high houses.

Briggs picked out the agency's Ford Escort. He approached from behind, looked quickly around, then bent to peer through its rear window. Nothing. What the hell? Briggs thought. He slipped around the car to the front passenger door beside the curb and once again bent to look into the car's interior. Empty. One-Five's transceiver lay on the passenger seat below Briggs's eyes. It was switched to receive. He noted that the key was in the ignition and the driver's window was open.

Where the *hell* was One-Five?

Briggs looked across the car's roof at the Kenyons' house, and then made a careful perusal of the small park. Maybe One-Five had had a reason to get closer to the house—had had to leave the car for a few moments. Maybe he had gone for a leak in the bushes? Briggs grinned for a brief moment, expecting the agent's figure to appear momentarily from the bushes. But the man hadn't answered before. Why was the transceiver in the car? It didn't make sense. One-Five, like the rest of them in London, was good. Where the hell was he?

Briggs slipped into the Ford on the passenger side and looked around carefully, noting the nearly full ashtray, remembering that One-Five smoked. They were all Marlboro butts. The glove locker was empty—which meant that wherever the man was, he was armed. But there was nothing in the car to indicate conflict of any kind. He shook his head and

124

picked up One-Five's transceiver.

"Zero-One to Base, over."

"Base—go ahead."

"One-Five's missing. At present, I have no idea why. Log it. Check his last known contact report. I'm gonna check around. Advise me immediately if he should check in from someplace else, okay?"

"Roger."

"Out," Briggs finished.

He eased quietly out of the Ford, and once again keeping to the side of the pavement where the shadows were deeper, he walked quickly toward the playing children. He slowed his pace as he approached them, and put both hands in his pockets to give the impression he was out for a stroll.

"Hi," he called out. They were two boys, both English judging by their voices, as they threw a tennis ball back and forth. "Practicing?"

"Not really," the taller lad, who was closest to Briggs, called.

"We would be if we had a cricket ball," the other piped.

"That's hard, like a baseball, right?" Allan asked. He'd stopped walking.

"Yes," the taller lad said. "But we're not allowed to throw cricket balls out in the street—"

"He bust a window last week," the smaller one interrupted with a grin. "So that was that!"

"Only because you missed, idiot. It was an easy catch, butterfingers!"

Allan Briggs laughed agreeably.

"You're American, aren't you?" the older boy asked.

"Yeah. We play baseball there. No cricket."

"You're lucky. Cricket's boring a lot of the time."

"I've heard that," Briggs said.

"Not if you're good at it, it isn't," the younger one piped provocatively.

Allan forestalled the inevitable argument. "Colonel and Mrs. Kenyon live around here somewhere," he said, swiveling around on his heels, looking up and down the row of houses. "Don't they?"

The older boy nodded. "Yes," he said. "They live at number fifteen." He bounced the ball and suddenly threw it to his younger brother who caught it with a triumphant cry. Briggs grinned and looked around him, hoping to spot One-Five. The Ford sat quiet and empty back along the street. There was no one else around. His eyes took in the Kenyons' house, number fifteen, and then he focused back on the boys.

"Do you know them, then?" the young boy piped.

Briggs nodded. He swiveled his body with his hands in his trouser pockets. "Yep," he said. "Met 'em a while back," he told the boys. "Matter of fact," he added, "I was supposed to meet a guy here, and then we were gonna drop by to see the Kenyons." He flicked his head back toward the Ford. "His car's there, but he's not around—maybe he went for a walk or somethin' while he was waiting, I guess."

"Oh, yes," the older boy said. "He *was* there, in the car—just sitting. You must be very late. I bet he was bored!"

"Did you see him leave, then?" Briggs asked.

They were throwing the ball back and forth across the few paces that separated them, trying to make each other miss.

"I don't know where he went, after he spoke to that ambulance man—do you?" the older boy asked his brother.

"Ambulance man?" Briggs murmured. "Was he sick?"

The ball was missed by the younger boy and

126

bounced toward Briggs. Briggs caught it and tossed it up and down one-handed, looking down at the two boys. Ambulance? he thought. Ambulance? The young one grinned up at him.

"No—he wasn't *sick*!" he laughed. "Least," his face clouded uncertainly for a moment, "I don't *think* he was, because he was just talking, leaning out of the window—then he got out and stood for a little while—then he went with them—but he walked, so he must have been all right, mustn't he?" the boy added cheerfully.

"You mean," Briggs said, "he got *into* the ambulance?"

"Well, we had to go in then," the older boy said, almost apologetically. "So we didn't see him get *in* it." He glanced at the house behind him. "Mum called us, you see. It was suppertime. He looked at his younger brother. "He wasn't around when we came out, was he?"

"No." The small boy shook his head. He looked up at Briggs with big round eyes. "I hope your friend *wasn't* sick," he said.

Briggs tossed the ball back to the older boy. "So do I," he paused. "Can you remember when it was that the ambulance was here?"

"Just before it got dark," the older boy told him.

Briggs tried to make sense of it. An ambulance in Brompton Square just before dark. Someone from the ambulance talking to One-Five. One-Five gets out of the car and goes with the ambulance man to the ambulance. What the hell happened after that? He silently cursed the boys' mother. And nobody had been keeping an eye on Mrs. Kenyon, therefore, since dark. Christ! He glanced quickly at the Kenyons' house. One-Five had been spirited away by an ambulance. Who was sick? Was Mrs. Kenyon sick. . . ?

"Ah, well," Briggs said to the two boys with a sigh. "So long—nice talking to you." He moved off along the pavement toward the Kenyons' house.

"Good-bye," they called after him in unison.

Briggs waved a hand.

Jesus Christ! he thought. Could this fuckin' ambulance have something to do with Susie *Kenyon*?

A sodden carcass of a tree spun in the water, which was half-covered in yellow foam just beyond the maelstrom where the river fell into the pool.

Pentland's hand had grabbed this waterlogged raft after his head had collided with it on one of his increasingly rare excursions to the surface. The fingers of his right hand gripped it with a power of their own. For several minutes he and the log spun together, oscillating half-in and half-out of the maelstrom until he managed to summon the strength to hook his right arm over it. He was then able to keep his head more or less above the surface. In this way, most of the time barely conscious, he clung on and gradually replaced the water in his throat with air. He noticed that the shadows had deepened to the point where it was now nearly dark. The sky above, clear of clouds, was a deepening canopy of violets and magentas, nearly night.

He kicked his numbed legs feebly at the dark swirling water. In his exhaustion he felt the need to let go and slide off the half-submerged slime of the log. He no longer felt the cold, just a relaxing numbness, his whole mind and body in the lethargy of approaching death. Enough was enough, a soundless voice urged. He and the tree went round and round in the darkening water while he kicked feebly, the roar of the falls joining the roaring in his ears.

He realized some time later that he had stopped turning. The direction of the falls was steady, and instead of pounding at his head from every direction, he was aware that the sound of the water was focused to his side. He found he was at the edge of the pool, where the air was less laden with moisture, and the tree was now pinning him lightly but firmly against solid rock. He reached out with his right hand and gripped the rock. He turned himself away from the bobbing security of his raft, and using the last of his strength, he pulled his torso clear of the pool and lay draped across the rocks, part of his mind realizing that he should pull his legs from the water, but his muscles unable for the moment to respond.

When more of his awareness seeped back, it was dark. This knowledge kept a dull spark in him alive, because, although for the moment he had forgotten its significance, he knew darkness was hope. His thinking process churned sluggishly and he finally found the energy to drag his legs from the water. After this seemingly enormous effort he once more slumped back face-down on the rocks, and shivering, thought about Renko.

Renko had not followed him into the river, unless the Russian had followed him into the falls and drowned. If Renko was alive Pentland felt sure he would have made his presence felt by now. If he hadn't been carried down by the river he had probably climbed the cliff and followed the river's course from above. It would have taken him a good while to get to the top of the cliff. His own voyage had been swift, although he wondered how long he had drifted in the pool, but it couldn't have been that long or he knew he would have died from the cold. So at this moment the Russian could be looking for a way down to the pool. Pentland realized that he was wasting time and would have to move. At least he had darkness on his side, he thought in an exhausted haze.

Using the rocks around him as props, he managed to get himself upright. His teeth chattered uncontrollably with the cold, and for a few minutes, waves of dizziness swept over him. It took great effort to get his jacket and shirt off with the one good hand, and then to grip the ends of the garments between his knees to wring the water from them with his good hand. He did the same with his trousers, socks, and underpants while shivering naked in the darkness. He put the clothes back on and zipped the windcheater up tight to his neck. He had never felt so cold in his life, and knew that the only way to get warm would be to move, and force his body to produce heat to warm up the moisture trapped in the damp clothes next to his skin.

With no feeling in his feet he hobbled and shuffled up the rocks away from the pool like a crippled old man. With no idea of where Renko might be, he climbed with exaggerated caution, testing every painful foot and handhold up the sloping contours for any loose rocks which might tumble and give his presence away.

It was not so much a climb as an awkward upward negotiation of really rough ground covered with the same proportions of rocks as the slope where the Peugeot lay, and it was necessary to spend a great deal of time shifting back and forth in the darkness to find a way up the next few feet. After half an hour or so of this, the feeling began to return to his limbs; pins and needles, followed by excruciating pain as the blood forced its way back into the millions of shrunken blood vessels. The resurrection of feeling in his limbs brought back the throbbing agony to his left hand, and he could not imagine more pain than if someone

130

had been beating the fingers with a ball-peen hammer.

But movement and pain, he thought, were something to kick against. However unwelcome, they were a characteristic of life. He was alive, and it was dark, and, he thought with some comfort, you can't aim guns in the dark.

But mountains and desert are never completely dark. Away from the cities, there is always some light from the clear skies—enough to discern skylines, to make out the deeper blackness of solid rock against the softer darkness of a horizon. He knew that starlight, and later perhaps the moon, would turn the landscape into shades of silver-greys and blacks, so that only the colors of day would be absent. It was probably darker now than it would be at any other time during the night.

When he judged he was well up the rocky slope above the pool, he found himself a low shelter below a jutting rock, no more than a body-sized niche. He was now out of sight, in complete darkness a few feet below the skyline. He could hear the river below and the distant roar of the falls bursting from the gorge into the pool. He thought he was a hundred feet or so up, and some hundred and fifty yards back from the river. He saw that the land to his right climbed fairly steeply up to a flat skyline, which he concluded would be the top of the plateau above the river gorge.

Renko, if he had climbed the cliff, would not have crossed the river before doing so. Therefore, the Russian would be on the same side of the river as himself. By now Pentland was sure that Renko would have arrived at the lip of the plateau above the pool. This would put him not more than two hundred yards away. Now with time to reflect, while the cold air seeped back beneath his steaming clothes and chilled

131

him again, anger reared above the base instincts of survival which had driven him to this animal cave in the Alps, and with the anger came needed adrenalin that made his blood pump hot in his head even as his body shivered. Anger that this dark, ugly peasant-of-a-Soviet was hunting him to shoot the life from him. Anger that the man had already deprived him, irrevocably, of two of his fingers. Anger that this man had been Olenko's executive in Joe's abduction, and for all the potential pain and grief that Suzie Kenyon would suffer for most of her life because of this man somewhere out in the rocks close-by.

He thought of Gail then, and the cottage under the Downs in Wiltshire; the sparrows chattering in the thatch on a summer's morning. And how Gail had looked, fishing near Joe's cottage, the swing of her hips as she strode with her long legs through the high grass, and how much he loved her and wanted her.

And somewhere out in the rocks close-by was a KGB executive whose single-minded purpose was to deprive him of everything he lived for.

What will you do now, Renko? he forced himself to think.

If I were you, he thought, I would go down to that pool to see if I were there. There would be a good chance of catching a glimpse of my corpse as it turned slowly in the turbulence below the surface, perhaps a lighter patch in the dark water as a hand or face reflected in the faint light. And then you could go home to Mother Russia.

But if you couldn't see me, you would think I had survived and climbed out of the pool, and you would look around for signs. Wet rock perhaps, or a footprint—something. You might have a lighter and you could find some dry wood and make a torch, and look for signs in its flame. You would know that I am in

132

oor shape and that once you got back on my trail it wouldn't take you long to catch up with me. Where would I go? Downhill? Follow the river? Probably.

Or would I come up to the plateau where you now are, in the hope that I might pass you in the night, and make it back to the road while you yourself were climbing down to the pool?

Yes, Renko. I would watch out for that. I would wait up on that plateau long enough to make sure that if my quarry came blundering up to me I would hear him, but after a time, I would very carefully and quietly make my way down to that pool, knowing that I might meet him on the way up. Then, when I did get down, I would be *sure* that Pentland had scurried off downstream into obscurity.

What you will not be thinking of though, Salin, is that your quarry might jump you. You won't expect that, because you know you have all the cards: you have the gun, and you have the height, and you're not wounded. You have the psychological advantage of being the hunter, while I sit here shivering in the darkness like a wounded cur, with half my hand blown off and my whole body aching.

Pentland slid out of the niche and sat up against the rock. His decision allowed him to forget the pain to a large extent and poured more adrenalin into his bloodstream.

He could cover the skyline of the plateau to his right and all the darkness of the land between the plateau and the river below. He concentrated on picking out features in the darkness, forcing his eyes to adjust to their fullest extent. He practiced tracing the outlines of barely perceived buttresses and boulders, mapping the whole area piece by piece. He used his keener peripheral vision and filled the gaps with it, memorizing the layout of the slope and the features of the skyline.

The sun had been down a good time now and stars were appearing. He found that the more he concentrated on the stars, the more he saw, and the better he could pick out the shapes of the land between river and plateau. After some time he realized that the slope up to the plateau was not just a regular boulder strewn sheet of land; he saw that it was a shallow rising valley which curved up to the plateau from the pool. He had, in fact, climbed the left shoulder of this valley. The shallow cleft of its top joined the plateau in a slight dip, just perceivable on the skyline.

He thought Renko would expect him to make his way up this cleft, and probably this would be the way Renko would come down, because there would be a vestigial wash down from the plateau to the river along this route, with fewer boulders and easier going.

As he prepared his plan, he wondered what they might be doing with Joe; whether they would have gotten him out of the country yet, or whether they would wait for Renko to rejoin them. And that if they hadn't moved Joe, perhaps the place they kept him was close to the ambush point on the road. He had a feeling it was, that they expected to have pulled far enough ahead for him to have missed the turn onto the smaller road. He thought the road would probably lead to an alpine farm.

It took him ten minutes to work his way carefully across the slope. He found the softer sand and smaller rocks which confirmed the existence of the wash—a dry streambed, probably only wet after a storm or in the spring, when the snows were melting.

He began to move up the wash. His foot struck something long and faintly white; snakelike. He reached down and picked up a hardened pine limb. He could feel it was stripped of bark and had probably been repeatedly baked in the sun and frozen until it possessed a fossil hardness. He wielded it in his right hand. It felt heavy and comforting. Vestiges of branches protruded in various places; sharp little knobs. You won't like this, you Russian bastard, he thought.

He continued up the wash, carefully and very slowly. Sometimes the wash came down to meet him through open ground, but mostly between heavy boulders. It occurred to him to spit on his hand and wipe dirt into the skin of his face to dull any whiteness. He was now conscious that every step took him toward Renko. Perhaps even now, he thought, Renko was taking the same careful steps down toward him, their feet performing a synchronized silent dance toward each other through the night.

Twenty minutes later he found that the wash squeezed down between a heavy man-sized boulder to his right and another tall rock to the left. If Renko came this way, he would have to come through the four-foot gap between the rocks.

Until this point he had dreaded meeting the Russian every second, imagining the searing pain of hot metal in his flesh or hearing the sigh of Renko's rifle butt as it swung for his head. Now that he was at the two rocks he would have to wait and nourish his conviction that the Soviet would come to him.

Waiting was harder than moving.

His subconscious argued that there would be better places further up, and to keep his nerve and go on. Another voice said Renko would be too fast for him, that he was too debilitated, had lost too much blood, was too exhausted—so get out fast, and run while you can. And he wondered why he hadn't done that. What a bloody fool he was—all the doubts were flooding into his mind. He pulled himself together, and tried to clear his senses. He would need them all to reach out and listen, to feel the vibrations in the still night air.

A rock dove whirred away from a place not far above him, smacking its wings together in alarm. Not far above, he thought. Not more than thirty feet. Was it Renko coming down which had disturbed the bird? It could have been anything: wildcat, fox, stoat—anything.

But something lingered in the air.

Some additional movement lingered, some heavier vibration in the stillness. And then he heard the tiny scrape of sand compressed underfoot, the almost-no-noise of a careful footfall.

Pentland felt his heart rev up, sending a flush of blood to his head. He felt the exultation of being the hunter, not the poor bloody running animal he had been. He thought of the peregrine falcon, her big eyes dark and expressionless, and the raked-back killer form of her; her own success always the element of surprise, always attacking, never defending as she paused at the apex of her stoop . . .

One moment there was nothing. But the next, Salin Renko was there in the wash, pausing between funereal paces. He slid into view from behind the rock, like a ghost in slow-motion. Pentland could barely pick out his slightly darker shape against the masses of rock about him. He sensed rather than saw that Renko held the rifle close to his waist, with the barrel forward and ready.

It was too dark to judge distance accurately, but he knew Renko had to be in the center of the wash because of the heavy rocks to each side. He was able to fix the height of Renko's head as the Russian took his next step, the face a faint specter above the shadow of the body.

Pentland swung the pine branch for Renko's throat

136

in a wide sickle curve.

Renko must have heard the tiny rustle of Pentland's clothes or felt the compression of air in front of his face, because he got the rifle barrel up to block inhumanly fast and the pine club met the steel of the barrel with a thud, immediately followed by an ear-splitting crack as the rifle was fired, and Renko threw himself backwards to reduce the impact of wood and steel on his face.

Pentland thought fleetingly that he should have gone for a downward chop to break the Soviet's arm.

He heard Renko's body thump into the sand as he fell into the wash, off-balance, his right arm stinging with the impact of the blow. He heard Renko make a strange snuffling noise as they both struggled to shift their mass beneath them and get to their feet, and he hoped that the blow had broken the Russian's nose. As Pentland came up into a crouch he realized he was oriented with his right shoulder toward the Russian. He swung the pine branch backhanded in a sweep across the sand and hit Renko again, bringing a burst of breath from the man's lungs. With his arm now extended in a follow-through and his body twisted to the right, he brought the club back down across his body to his left in a forehand blow and broke something with a noise that sounded like a foot on a dead stick. Renko fired the weapon again and the bullet struck rock somewhere behind, whining off into the night. Pentland tucked his head down and threw himself into a forward roll to bring his heels cracking down on Renko from above, but they jarred into the sand from where Renko had moved, and he realized that the Russian had caught a glimpse of him in the muzzle-flash. As he continued the roll forward, he felt Renko's arm beneath his chin, and his head was snapped back and his spine jarred down into the sand.

Renko's breath gargled in his ear and his own breath dammed in his throat. All he could do was to straighten his legs with the full force of his thigh muscles and throw his weight backwards, snapping his head back into the Russian's face. The movement toppled them both backwards into the rocks at the side of the wash. The force of their combined impact and the suddenness of the action loosened the Russian's grip and brought his wrist close to Pentland's mouth. He bit hard into the flesh and rolled away when the grip loosened completely.

They were separated by more than four feet in the darkness. Pentland had lost the club. He wondered whether Renko still had the rifle. The last blow with the club had broken something; but not Renko's legs because he still moved fast, and not his right arm because that had been wrapped beneath his chin. It had to be Renko's left arm. Renko couldn't still be holding the weapon.

Pentland heard the Russian lunge at him from the rocks, and tried to swing himself aside, but felt Renko's boot in his ribs. The force of the kick lifted him off the sand and knocked every molecule of air from his lungs. He saw Renko silhouetted against the pale stars, a looming blackness moving in for the *coup de grace*, the Russian's breath snuffling through his broken nose as Pentland's own breath whooped back into his lungs.

Pentland kicked up for the Russian's groin, and found the mark, snapping the Russian double. Using the last of his strength as the Russian fell toward him, Pentland launched upwards with a four-fingered carotid strike at Renko's throat. The strike felled the Soviet like a heavy log.

It didn't kill him. It should have—it would have if

Pentland had been able to deliver it with normal strength. But it did give Pentland the time to get up, his breath tearing painfully back into his lungs, to kneel across the Russian's back, and find the nostrils with his fingers and jerk the head back, to snap the Russian's neck vertebrae up into his brain.

He lay over the Russian's body in a state of exhaustion. A night bird screeched in the heavy silence. He got to his knees and stared up at the billions of cold stars, his mind blank, no energy left for exultation, or regret, or nausea.

He rose painfully to his feet and found Renko's rifle in the wash. He slung the weapon over his shoulder and set off up to the plateau to find the road, holding on to the hope that Renko's people would await his return before they left with Joe Kenyon.

Briggs kept his pace casual as he walked to number fifteen. He glanced over his shoulder and saw the two boys watching him as he climbed the few stone steps to the door. As he reached for the bellpull, he saw that there was now a light glowing from behind a curtain to the left of the door. When he had looked across from the Ford there had been no lights showing. With a small sense of relief, he realized that someone must be in. He hoped that it would be Susie Kenyon. He pulled the knob and heard it ring inside.

Footsteps approached and he heard the sound of a bolt being withdrawn, then the click of a springlock. The door opened inward four inches before snapping up against a security chain. A woman's face peered out at him. He could see she wore a powder-blue housecoat and that she had blue eyes and blond hair. She wore no make-up; a woman definitely not expecting guests. Briggs began to feel a little foolish.

The woman raised her eyebrows. "Yes?" she said inquiringly. "Can I help you?" She looked at him uncertainly.

Allan Briggs knew Susie Kenyon reasonably well. They had met at functions at the embassy and elsewhere in London regularly, although he had never socialized closely with the Kenyons. It wasn't done. But Briggs knew her face well enough to feel relief that nothing seemed to have happened to Kenyon's wife during the absence of goddamned One-Five—wherever the sonofabitch was. Briggs paused for her to recognize him. When she said nothing further, he leaned closer.

"Hi, Mrs. Kenyon," he said, but she didn't recognize him. His face was in shadow from the street lights, he realized. "Allan Briggs," he added.

"Oh," she exclaimed. "Mr. Briggs! I'm so sorry—I should have known who you were, please excuse me! It's just that I didn't expect—"

Allan held up a hand and shook his head. "Please don't apologize, Mrs. Kenyon. Er—could I perhaps come inside for a moment?" Briggs looked around him, and saw the kids still watching him.

She looked uncertain and slightly bewildered. "Well," she started, "I—"

"It is important, Mrs. Kenyon," Briggs prompted.

A look of alarm crossed her face. "It isn't something to do with Joe, is it?" She unlatched the chain. "I'm expecting him back from Switzerland tonight. At any moment, as a matter of fact." She pulled the door open.

Briggs walked past her into the hall. There was a light at the end of the hall down some steps and he could see parts of a softly lit sitting room. Television voices talked out of sight.

She closed the door to the street and led him down

140

the hall.

Half a cigarette was still burning in an ashtray on a coffee table between two sofas, and a partly drunk glass of scotch in melting ice sat nearby. The room was large and well-appointed, with mixed antique and modern furniture arranged tastefully, all set off by plush red velvet floor-to-ceiling curtains drawn over the patio windows.

"Can I get you a drink, Mr. Briggs? Please sit down and make yourself comfortable."

"Thanks—no. But maybe I'll smoke if you don't mind." He sat down.

She shook her head and smiled. "I don't mind at all," she said and perched on the edge of a sofa opposite him.

Briggs lit a cigarette. "I apologize for bothering you," he said. "Joe asked me to give you a call an hour ago. But there was no reply."

Her eyebrows raised. "Oh, really?" she said. "I did take a shower earlier," she added. "That must have been when you called. Was it important?"

"Joe called in from Geneva. I guess he tried to get you, too." He paused, but she made no comment, waiting for him to go on. "He's having to catch a later plane, I'm afraid. He hopes to get to Heathrow by about ten. What he wanted you to know was that, because he was going to be late, he thought he'd better get straight out to Farnborough. He said he'd call you from there."

"Oh," she said. She looked down at her lap. "I thought he'd make it back tonight." She smiled and sighed. "Well—I guess I'll have to wait to see him at the weekend now."

Briggs caught the touch of a southern accent, and remembered Joe's wife hailed from Atlanta, Georgia. He inhaled on the cigarette.

141

"You didn't by any chance call for an ambulance, did you, Mrs. Kenyon—say an hour ago?" He watched her face. It registered surprise.

"Ambulance!" she exclaimed. "Here?" She shook her head. "No—no ambulance has been *here*," she said. She paused, frowning. "Why do you ask?"

"I—er—heard that there had been an ambulance around in the square an hour or so ago," Briggs said. "And—well, I was kinda concerned."

"Well!" she said, suddenly smiling. "That's real nice. It's comforting to know someone's watching over me while Joe's away."

"Joe would be mad as hell if something happened to you while he was away," Briggs said weakly. Of course, Kenyon's wife knew nothing about the photos. Briggs began to feel intrusive and slightly foolish. He rose from the sofa. Late evening visits from security chiefs would make anyone nervous, he thought.

"Well, Mrs. Kenyon, I guess—"

He was interrupted by the telephone ringing. She looked startled, glanced at him quickly, flashed a smile, and got up to answer it. "Excuse me, Mr. Briggs," she said over her shoulder as she picked up the receiver. She stood with her back to him, facing the red curtains.

"Hallo?" she said. "Who?—Oh, Gail!—Yes, I'm sorry. I have a—er—visitor. Could you call me back?"

"Go ahead, go ahead," Briggs called softly. "Don't mind me—"

"Thanks!" she was saying. "That'll be great—Sure, I'll be here. Great! 'Bye!"

"I'll get out of your hair," Briggs said as she replaced the receiver. "I'm really sorry to have intruded."

She seemed relieved as he stood up.

"Of *course* you haven't intruded," she said. "I'm

really grateful for the message from Joe, and your—uh—concern."

She led him through the hall to the front door. As she walked ahead of him, Briggs thought she'd put on some weight since he'd last seen her. She seemed stockier.

As the door shut behind him and he heard the locks and chain being refastened, he looked over to where the two boys had been playing. But the pavement was empty now. The two boys had been called inside. The Ford Escort still sat silently in the row of cars beyond the bushes of the small park. Briggs walked down the steps to the pavement. He glanced back at number fifteen.

Nothing added up. One-Five had disappeared—possibly in an ambulance. David Pentland had gone missing in Switzerland. But at least Susie Kenyon was okay.

Still, there was something ass-about-face somewhere.

CHAPTER EIGHT

Dimitri Olenko forced himself to sip the second vodka as the British Airways Boeing banked high over the patchwork of northern France. The first had thudded warmly to the base of his stomach in one gulp, which the blond stewardess had noticed. She had raised an eyebrow, with a smile.

"Would you like another, sir?" she'd asked, and then, noticing that her first-class passenger was sweating, said, "are you all right, sir?"

Olenko had forced himself to smile.

"I am quite all right, thank you. Yes, I would like another. The same, please."

She had gone off to get it, leaving Olenko to brood over the events that were changing his life.

On the ground it would be getting dark quickly. Up here the sun was still well above the horizon, a great orange globe lighting the tops of scattered cloud far below the aircraft in a rosy red. The fields were dark under sheets of evening mist, and lights were coming on in clusters of towns and villages. It looked like a lovely calm September evening. Olenko wished his own mood could reflect the same thing. All he could think of was Natalia—and Dzerzhinsky Square.

Never in his wildest nightmares would he have coupled the soft beauty of his wife with that forbidding complex. Never had he thought that his test-pilot career with the Soviet Air Force could someday lead him to becoming a member of the KGB, however temporarily. Gorlov had said temporarily. He hoped to the depths of his soul that the general had meant what he said.

Seven months had now passed since he had been surprisingly summoned to Moscow last February. Russia had been in the grips of a deep winter then. The plane had lifted away from Berezniky, leaving the town steaming on its frozen plain on the banks of the Karma River, under the soaring white peaks of the Urals. Olenko had been surprised to find that the plane was destined for Vnukovo, on the far side of the city from Sheremetevo. Vnukovo was the VIP airport, and the security checks there were almost perfunctory; his reception almost convinced him there and then that he was already a part of the KGB. Met by a uniformed driver, he was taken to a big black Zhiguli parked right outside the Terminal building, and driven swiftly off to the city.

Olenko had been to Moscow on numerous occasions, but never before to Dzerzhinsky Square, on business. As the car moved through the town he surveyed the drab suburbs of the city with distaste. The snow was grey and muddy at the sides of the streets, piled high along the pavements where the plows had thrown it. Pedestrians stepped around the heaps, their feet protected by rubber galoshes, looks of pained submittance on their faces as they walked, leaning forward into the ever-present freezing wind. Olenko was barely warm in his greatcoat, and he was in the back of a heated car. He planned to catch the earliest flight available back to Berezniky after his session with Gorlov.

The Zhiguli swept across the Moscow River. The pine-clad hills to the west were shrouded in thick snow, barely visible through a haze of light fog. To the left the buildings of the city rose grey and drab to a low lead-colored overcast, tinted brown by smog. The traffic was denser now and exhausts steamed in the streets as the car's tires hummed and thudded over the ice-ridged roads. As they turned into Marx Prospect and accelerated past the statue of "Iron Feliks" Olenko wondered irreverently whether the capital of the Soviet Union had looked as drab under the Czars. He shook his head. These were not thoughts with which to be occupying himself in an official KGB limousine rushing towards Dzerzhinsky Square. He allowed his eyes to settle briefly on the Lubianka to the left, and then the car was turning, before halting at the security gate, uniformed guards with a Kalashnikov on each side of the entrance watching closely. He showed his papers. They were scrutinized carefully by one man while the other searched the car with his eyes, and then they were waved through.

Olenko's pulse quickened as the car crept into the central parking square, with the great stone building crowding out the winter light on all sides, leaving a permanent gloom. Officials hurried silently back and forth. Marshall of the Soviet Union Ilyi Gorlov was Director General of the Fifth Directorate of the KGB, responsible for overseas intelligence gathering and counterintelligence operations. Most overseas embassy officials reported to Gorlov's Directorate, only the ambassadors directly to the Politburo. Now that he was actually here, Olenko's curiosity at the summons had reached unbearable heights of tension.

He was not kept waiting. He was shown immediately into the director's office overlooking the square.

A uniformed official opened one of two huge doors in the high-ceilinged building to a spacious office with deep-blue carpeting and a roaring coal fire opposite security-wired windows. The marshall's imposing desk was at the far end of the office from the entrance doors, but Olenko, saluting stiffly just inside the door, recognized from official photographs the figure warming his behind at the fire. He was a tall, thin man in civilian clothes, with greying hair parted centrally, and deep clefts on each side of a thin mouth. Grey eyes beneath surprisingly bushy eyebrows regarded Olenko for a moment.

"Come in, Colonel, come in," Gorlov's baritone voice rumbled. "Over here, where it's warm."

Olenko strode across to the marshall, halted, and bowed.

"Good afternoon, sir."

Gorlov nodded and smiled briefly.

"Make yourself comfortable. There's vodka on that table." He nodded to a table and chairs set close to the fire. "Pour me one also, please. Do take off your coat."

When Olenko had poured the drinks and handed Gorlov his glass, the marshall had remained standing with his back to the fire. Olenko sat awkwardly in his chair.

"Ah—" Gorlov breathed after taking a mouthful and tossing his head back. "Three things, Olenko. One. As from this moment you are on temporary assignment to this Directorate. You will therefore report to no other than myself. Understood?"

"Sir," Olenko said.

"Two, you will be shortly dispatched to London, where you will take up the position as the Soviet air attaché to our embassy there." Gorlov looked down at the air force colonel and raised his eyebrows. Before

147

Olenko could think of something to say, the marshall continued:

"Third, you will not be accompanied on this posting by your wife."

Olenko studied his drink. This was a bitter blow.

"I see, sir," he said quietly. "May I ask how long I shall be away from the Soviet Union, Comrade Marshall?"

"Should all go to plan you will be back at your unit in Berezniky in seven months. Not too long, eh?"

"No, sir," Olenko said. Seven months! The longest he'd been away from Natalia had been the Cuban training trip—six weeks, and *that* had been hell.

Gorlov grunted and sat down on a regency-style sofa, opposite Olenko, at the end closest to the fire.

"Pour us more vodka, Colonel, and I will acquaint you with the details of your task in England. You may smoke if you wish." The marshall lit himself a cigar and settled back in the sofa. The afternoon was wearing on beyond the window. The sky was turning to the color of slate and snow drifted beyond the panes. The low sound of traffic became more muted. The Lubianka sat like a veiled, evil ghost in stone beyond the white drift of snow. Olenko wondered briefly what poor souls screamed in its dark cellars on this late winter afternoon, while he sipped his vodka with one of the most powerful men in Russia, in the opulence of a regency-styled office on the third floor of the best-known building in Dzerzhinsky Square. He handed the marshall his drink, now feeling more relaxed as the first vodka permeated his system. However he felt about the lone posting, there was absolutely nothing he could do to change the situation. He would have to sit back and take whatever this thin, iron figure threw at him, or he would shortly find out what it was like in Lubianka himself. He would hink about how to break the news to Natalia later.

"There is an aircraft which the Americans are still testing, which they will bring to Britain for the Farnborough Air Show in September. You know, of course, the aircraft to which I refer?"

Olenko nodded.

"Their new strategic reconnaissance plane, the SR80?"

"Yes." Gorlov sipped his drink and appeared to be deep in thought for a moment. He reached for a folder on the sofa, which Olenko had not noticed previously. 'We have one photograph of this aircraft," Gorlov said. He took it from the folder and waved it in his hand. "One photograph only! They test this plane in a place in the Mojave Desert, a place they call the "ranch." We of course know where the ranch is, but their security is paranoid. The aircraft is exposed only when there are none of our satellites at an orbital position to photograph the area. It has not yet flown outside U.S. airspace. This photo was obtained when some flight problems delayed the aircraft from landing; by the time it touched down we had a satellite at the limit of surveillance. Hence this photo."

Gorlov passed it to Olenko. It was an oblique and extremely fuzzy shot of the aircraft, but as far as Olenko could see it corresponded with sketches published in U.S. air magazines—artistic impressions of what Lockheed and its genius of a designer, Clarence "Kelly" Johnson, might be dreaming up to replace the immensely successful SR71, the CIA's current reconnaissance craft. The SR80 appeared to be the shape of a long dart, with two massive tubes of engines attached close to its fuselage, and one central fin instead of the twin, canted fins of its predecessor. Something about the skin structure or paint finish seemed to prevent the aircraft from photographing well, because Olenko could see that although the desert landscape which made up the rest of the photo was clearly depicted, the aircraft itself had a fuzzy grey outline, with no visible markings. There probably *were* no markings, he thought. He handed the paper back to the marshall.

Olenko shook his head, ruefully.

"I regret to say, sir, that at present we have nothing which can touch the SR71 in the Soviet Air Force. cannot imagine what sort of performance this new aircraft will possess."

Olenko remembered his flight in the new MIG-25 Foxbat, when, for a few brief years, he had captured the world's speed record for the Soviet Union, and how the Foxbat had shaken like a derailed express train as he had held it with both hands to complete the course, the tailpipe temperatures so far in the red they had been off the scale. And then the fight to stay conscious in a cockpit temperature of 150 degrees while he slowed the aircraft and went through the cooling procedural let-down for an agonizing thirty minutes. They had to carry him from the cockpit when he landed at Berezniky.

And then the Americans in the SR71 had cruised their black, needle-shaped spy-plane to take the record at over two thousand miles an hour, and captured the world altitude record in the process. It had been reported that the pilot had been pulling back on the throttles all the time, and that any of the SR71s in the fleet could go as fast, if not a great deal faster. Since then the CIA had organized missions over the Soviet Union and China—and anywhere they chose—with impunity. No missiles or aircraft could fly high enough to touch the Blackbird, as it was now popularly called. The shape, skin finish, and ECM equipment of the aircraft were such that radar contact was rarely established with it. And if the pilot's transponder *did* record radar contact he left a trail of ghosts, electronic countermeasures causing Soviet interceptors to fire their missiles wastefully into the blackness of space. The Americans had now been using the unassailable Blackbird for seventeen years.

Olenko could not imagine the superiority of this new machine.

Gorlov rose from the sofa and walked over to the window with his glass.

"Why, Olenko," he said in a quiet voice hard with bitterness, "do we not have an aircraft capable of the performance of this Blackbird? It is beyond me." He stood at the window and looked out across the darkening square. "Why?"

"Sir, we appear to lack the technology," Olenko said. "The design and materials technology of the airframe and engine design, and also the refined computer electronics—"

Gorlov had turned at the window to face into the room, his long shape silhouetted against the remaining outside light. Olenko was unable to see the marshall's face, or to anticipate the fury of his interruption.

"*Appear?* Appear, you say! It is not an appearance, Colonel. It is a fact! Even now it is likely that one of these spy-planes is drifting across the Soviet Union, scooping up samples of our air for analysis so that the Americans will know the exact nature of our weapons testing. Yes? And photographing the warts on the face of a peasant worker in a secret missile plant in Siberia to see if he is on time for work, perhaps? Perhaps even now they regard this building and watch us with laser-operated sights, and listen to our conversations. Far-fetched, you say with your expression! Of course, but it is not far-fetched that

151

they monitor every electronic emission for analysis and decoding, and photograph this country in regular swathes in detail that a satellite could *never* manage!"

Gorlov's voice had risen. He was spitting out the words.

"They maddened Khruschev with their U2 spy-planes. They madden us now with their Blackbirds. And now they plan to introduce this new monster at Farnborough, this September. And once again the world will smirk at Soviet aircraft technology. What is the point, nations will ask themselves, of purchasing Soviet fighters and Soviet bombers, when the Americans can demonstrate such superiority? How can we argue? Eh? Even now most of the third world nations are equipping with American F-16s and Northrop F-20s. Nations which have chosen MIGs and Tupolevs and Ilyushins previously."

He paused.

"It—must—stop!" the marshall thundered.

The room was silent.

"Yes. It must stop," the marshall said again in a conversational tone, as he came back to the fire. He paused before the dying flames.

"Gometev!" he bellowed.

The door opened. A figure stood silhouetted against the lighted hallway beyond.

"Build up this fire," Gorlov ordered. "Bring us some caviar. Bring us some more vodka." He waved a hand and the door closed quietly. Gorlov sat down and lit a small cigar. It was quite dark outside now. Olenko wondered if he should say anything. Not quite seeing where all this might be leading, he was only aware that somehow it was all working toward his duties as the new attaché in London.

When the orderly had made the fire flare again with fresh coal, and had left after bringing a small silver tray with fingers of dark bread and a dish of Beluga caviar, and switched on the lights of a crystal chandelier hanging low from the middle of the high rococo ceiling, Gorlov leaned forward, his thin lips pursing as he ate.

"The American attaché is a man called Kenyon," he said. "Your opposite number in London. An air force colonel, as you are. Interesting, eh?" He nodded, then smiled.

"This man Kenyon, we understand, was responsible for the testing of the flight controls of the SR80. That is more interesting even, is it not?" He smiled. "You will have much in common with this Kenyon, I imagine. Yes?" Gorlov scooped up more caviar on a finger of bread and thrust it into his mouth. "Mmm?" he said as he chewed.

Olenko smiled.

"Yes, sir," he said. So what, he thought. Was he supposed to go and torture this Kenyon?

"The other interesting thing," Gorlov went on, still eating, "is that I am informed that so far only two American pilots have flown this new aircraft. One is Kenyon, and the other is a Colonel Lindley. It will be Lindley who flies the SR80 to England in September. The purpose, then, of your appointment to the embassy in England will be to arrange for Colonel Kenyon to fly the aircraft from Farnborough to Berezniki. Subsequently, you will be detailed to test-fly it and then to supervise its complete analysis."

Olenko had stopped breathing. His eyes searched Gorlov's face. The Marshall sat with a mouthful of caviar, his eyes glinting in the light of the flames beside him, his eyebrows raised slightly and a thin smile on his lips. Then he laughed. Crumbs flew out of his mouth. Olenko felt a wave of relief. So this was a joke, he thought. He began to smile and relax.

Gorlov wiped his mouth with a starched napkin. "And this is how it will be arranged," he said. Olenko's smile was wiped off his face.

Two hours later it was the marshall who remained seated as Olenko strode around the large office.

"Sir, I feel I am unsuited to attempt such a thing. I have had no experience in diplomacy. My whole career has been devoted to flying operational fighter aircraft, and more recently to test-flying. I feel most inadequate to accept the responsibility which this task demands. With the greatest respect, Comrade Marshall, there must be another who would be able to discharge this responsibility with more skill—"

A hardness edged into the director general's voice.

"There is no one, though, who has as much in common with Kenyon as yourself, you will admit?"

"Sir, that may be so, but—"

"Have I not also adequately pointed out to you, Colonel Olenko, that an attaché with an intelligence career in that position will be documented to his eyeballs both with the CIA and British Intelligence? He would be watched like a hawk. Any attempt, as I again point out, to befriend Kenyon and his wife would be regarded with much suspicion. But the main point, of course, is that Kenyon will be instructed to get alongside *you* to be in a position to obtain as much information of our aviation and avionics as he can. He will know your career intimately. The Americans will regard the coincidence of you both being in London in similar positions as very fortunate. Kenyon will be encouraged, not discouraged, to pursue your companionship."

Olenko came back to his chair, but remained standing.

"In consideration of the wife, sir. Would it not be better if my own wife were to accompany me? It would make it much easier to entertain the Kenyons—"

"The fact that your wife will not be in London with you will engender sympathy, particularly with Kenyon's wife. You will be required to make approaches to Mrs. Kenyon. You are good-looking, are you not? Make her fall in love with you—"

Oh, God, how could he do this? Natalia and he had married young, when he was twenty-one. He hadn't touched another woman since.

"You will have no need to worry about your wife, Colonel," Gorlov put in. "You can," he added in a voice filled with meaning, which chilled Olenko's blood, "be sure that we will watch over your little woman until you return."

Then he looked at Olenko with his grey eyes hard. "Until you—*successfully*—return."

He rose from the sofa and swung a long arm around Olenko's shoulders.

"You will be a hero, Olenko! Imagine! What will dear little Natalia think of you then, eh?" He held both of Olenko's shoulders. "You will receive instant promotion to General, my boy. You have my personal assurance of that. My personal assurance!"

And what if I fail, Olenko thought, unable to prevent the negative from invading his thoughts. The whole mission sounded impossible.

"We won't even contemplate the conditions of failure, my boy," Gorlov said, as if reading Olenko's mind. His eyes wandered to the window, where Olenko knew lights would be burning in the Lubianka across Dzerzhinsky Square.

"We won't even contemplate that," Gorlov repeated.

The plane angled down into the darkness, and soon the lights of Westminster gleamed below, the streets filled with traffic. The Houses of Parliament reflected briefly in the black Thames as flaps and wheels were lowered. The whirring and thumping ceased as the Boeing settled into its final approach for Heathrow.

The stewardess came to clear Olenko's empty glass.

KGB, Olenko thought bitterly. It stood for *Komitet Gosudarstvennoy Bezopasnosti*. He agreed vehemently with its rarely uttered nickname—"*Kontora Grubykh Banditov*," Office of Crude Bandits.

His heart thumped heavily again as he considered that the next few hours would dictate whether he became a hero of the Soviet Union—or a screaming inmate of the Lubianka prison. If the operation failed, there would be so much egg on the Kremlin's face that they would play out his new role of scapegoat with unmitigated ferocity and explicity.

Pray for me, Natalia, he breathed.

The Boeing thumped down onto the runway.

At least the MI6 man would be out of the way by now, Olenko thought. Things had gone well in Geneva. Why had he grown to like Joe and Suzie Kenyon so much, he wondered.

Because it is your job to like them so much, KGB man, a part of him sneered.

CHAPTER NINE

The air-conditioner blew cool air noisily down onto Chuck Lindley's head in the tiny officer's mess at the "ranch." Outside, the sun blasted down on the moon-scape of the Mojave Desert; but here, in the small shabby room with its brown plastic armchairs and cheap veneered tables, littered with two-month-old magazines, the air, although stale, was cool.

For the moment Chuck Lindley was alone in the mess. In less than an hour now he would be alone at more than mach three and higher than eighty thou-sand feet, fifteen miles above the earth's surface. And in less than five hours from now he would be landing in England in the middle of the night.

Chuck Lindley looked nothing like the popular view of a test pilot. To meet that particular public image he should have been tall, with broad shoulders and a square chin, blue eyes set in a bronzed face crinkled with the lines of wind exposure. He should have been wearing a beautifully cut air force uniform with the left breast bursting with ribbons—a man among men, and the idol of all women. However, anyone walking into the room could quite easily miss Lindley, who sat sprawled untidily on one of the chairs puffing on a cigarette, wearing wrinkled brown fatigues over a white T-shirt, with sneakers on his feet. Most of his hair was gone. He was on the short side, with a receding chin, unremarkable brown eyes beneath sleepy, drooping eyelids, and not-very-good teeth. He loved his wife and no other, and missed her and his two children back at Edwards Air Force Base. Chuck Lindley, besides being one of his country's top pilots, was also one of his country's top electronics wizards, which was why for the last three months he had been stuck out in the Mojave Desert with nowhere to go, except upward and very fast.

Lindley raised bored eyes to the satellite exposure-indicator on the mess wall above the door. A red light showed. Next to the red bulb was a countdown timer, currently displaying eleven minutes and a few seconds. When the green light came, on the timer would show how long the area would be unsurveyed by any Soviet satellite. In spite of the dreadful heat that he knew was beating down outside the building, Lindley wanted a breath of fresh air before he ate his high-protein meal and got suited up. After this run, he thought, as far as Dracula was concerned, there'd be no point in hiding her any longer, and she could be operated out of Edwards, or join her older sisters out of Beale, home of most of the Blackbirds for fifteen years or so. Then the ranch would be host to some other secret military aviation project.

Cigarette clamped between his teeth, sleepy eyes narrowed against the smoke, Lindley scratched idly at a plastic cuff around his right wrist. He looked down at the cuff and cursed quietly to himself. He still hated plugging into the aircraft like that. Taking the cuff off in the cockpit and exposing the disgusting little transparent tube stuck into the vein in his lower wrist, and then having to push its self-sealing end onto the needle that protruded from Dracula's special armrest was, he always thought, disgusting. Because at that moment he became part of her, and she him, and then he wasn't the same man at all. He was her man. He did things to her, he realized that, but she did a hell of a lot more to him, Goddammit! She would put him to sleep, wake him up, pep him up, slow him down; she could juice him up with amphetamines until he could read every instrument in her circuit ten times in a second, and recite the Lord's Prayer before taking evasive action from a heat-seeking missile. She could make the runway rise up to him so slowly on final approach he got bored and had time to yawn, and she could adjust his reactions to the point that he felt every progressive squeeze of compression on her tires as the hot concrete took her seventy-ton weight. If you were a student pilot, Lindley thought, and you bounced just one of her tires an inch on landing, something was wrong with Dracula's brain.

Beats me why they didn't just design the mother to goof-off by herself, Lindley sometimes thought irritably. When all was well with Dracula, he never felt so redundant. He could only comfort himself with the knowledge that *he* told her what to do. *She* just did what he told her, but used *him* to make herself do it superlatively. And on the occasions when they flew together without him being plugged into her smart-ass computer she was nothing more than a heap of titanium, Hastelloy, and Rene 41, falling about the troposphere like any other airplane. That was how good-old-Joe knew her, Lindley thought, a super SR71. He missed Joe, and was looking forward to seeing him again in England. The thought cheered him up.

Out of the corner of his eye, Chuck saw the green

light come on. The timer said thirty-five minutes, which was a good period. He bet the Russians were even now working on filling that gap. He went out into the inferno of the desert.

Light, heat, and wind beat at him simultaneously. So much light that at first he was unable to see, his eyes automatically closing against its onslaught, and for a few moments he stood just beyond the doorway of the mess. The heat dried his nostrils, and his first few breaths made him cough as the dry, hot desert wind scurried around the buildings in mad gusts, whipping at his fatigues. The sun was a white glare filling the cloudless sky.

Sand shifted constantly across the ground around Lindley's feet as he shaded his eyes and looked around him at the horizon of this flat bowl in the Nevada desert, distantly ringed by spiky piles of boulder-strewn hills, its surface shimmering into white mirages in all directions. Only sparse patches of sad-looking sage and brown tumbleweed grew, with a scattering of withered yucca trees doing their best to hold their own. The rest of the landscape was stones, and more stones, and sand, all of it a pale beige merging into lighter tones in the distance, and finally into white, as the sun leached the color from the land with its fierce radiation.

Three buildings crouched close-by. They were low buildings, hugging the flat contours of the land, their roofs littered with rocks and painted the same color as the desert. From above, they cast the same ragged shadows as the wind-eroded landscape. Two of the buildings were fairly close together. One housed pilots and the officers' mess, and the other contained quarters for the contingent of highly trained Marine security guards. The third was a very large rectangular structure with a wide ramp sloping down to its entrance—Dracula's hangar and maintenance base. There were no roads or tracks; no marks of vehicles on the desert's surface. Any such marks were quickly erased by the Marines. There was a security fence for the ranch five-miles away in each direction marked: "DANGER. HIGH EXPLOSIVE. GOVERNMENT PROPERTY. KEEP OUT," in red-on-white boards at twenty-yard intervals. Helicopters patrolled the perimeter, and air charts marked the area for thirty miles in each direction as prohibited air space with no ceiling limit.

As Lindley's eyes adjusted, he became aware of a Marine standing close-by, a machine pistol hanging across his waist. The Marine wore desert fatigues, and with his nut-brown face was barely distinguishable from the background. Lindley cupped his hands around his lighter and lit a cigarette, then squinted his eyes to look down the "runway" which stretched into the distance. The runway was concrete, but was painted the color of the sand and streaked with white like the salty residue of a dry lake, which is what it resembled from the air. Any tire marks from landings were quickly painted over by a mobile road-spraying machine.

"Lovely weather we're havin'," Lindley remarked.

"Shit," said the Marine, disgustedly.

"Yeah," Lindley grinned. "I'm walkin' over to the hangar."

"Good luck, sir," the Marine said, standing with his feet in the shade of the building.

"You just keep on your toes, there, soldier," Lindley murmured.

As he walked off he recalled that the only action they'd had from a security point of view was when some asshole of a light-plane pilot had come volplaning down in a Piper Cherokee, out of gas, last month.

He'd been off-course and lost, and thought he was in for a really long walk. They still talked about the look on his face when he'd found himself surrounded by heavily armed Marines who seemed to come from nowhere. He'd been searched, his plane searched, and then told to stand facing the hills away from the buildings while the base commander told someone to go find some gasoline, and when the Cherokee was fueled they ordered him to get the hell out and say nothing—or lose his license forever. The only thing the guy had learned, Lindley knew, was course and distance to the nearest civilization. Lindley had been on a "local" flight of 5,000 miles to Florida and back, which had kept him away from the ranch for nearly three hours. They'd told him about it when he got back.

After showing his pass to another Marine standing outside the small side-entrance door of the huge squat building, Lindley walked into the apparent pitch-blackness of Dracula's hangar. His eyes adjusted to the neon lighting as he spiraled down the iron steps, using his hands for guidance. By the time he arrived on the plastic-coated hangar floor he could see again, and the sweat was drying on his face in the contrasting cold of the hangar's air-conditioning.

In spite of powerful overhead lighting, the SR80 reflected nothing from her blue-black surfaces. She seemed to absorb the light in her skin; her shape was difficult to determine because of the lack of shadows. When he had first walked into this hangar, Lindley had only been aware of something long and high occupying most of the floor space; something very long and pointed, bulkier to the rear. On closer examination, the skin on her fuselage and wings appeared bumpy and badly formed, like the cotton fabric of early cloth-covered aircraft with the ribs showing through, until he remembered that at the speeds the SR80 flew, her skin temperature rose close to a thousand degrees, and then everything would smooth out and her surfaces would be perfect, precise curves of titanium planing down to knifelike trailing edges.

In design she was a long needle-shape, fanning out into a delta, an extended dart, stretching a hundred and thirty feet from nose to tail, as long as a DC9 or Boeing 727. The leading edges of her delta wings were carried forward to the tip of her nose like the narrow webs of an eel's body, giving her lift over the full length of her fuselage, holding her nose up as her speed increased and the center of lift moved to the rear.

Now, the aircraft was being fueled and her fuselage and wing skins steamed in the cool climate of the building. As Lindley walked to a position below her nose, the crew chief approached.

"She's all ready to touch flesh, Colonel," he said with a leer. "Look at her—panting for it!"

Both men looked up at the steaming surfaces.

"Where you goin' today?" the crew chief asked.

"Shit, Chief, you know better than that," Lindley said lazily. "But I won't be back for a week, if that satisfies your curiosity."

"Yeah?" said the master sergeant. "Well, who in hell's goin' to take care of this airplane when you get where you're goin'?"

"There'll be a '71 crew on hand. If anything goes bad we'll send for you."

"Damn right, you better."

Chuck smiled and began to do the walk-around he always carried out on any aircraft he was about to fly. It was more traditional than necessary to carry out a pilot's check, but he knew that the half-hour it took put him in the right frame of mind to go flying. It served as a transitional period for adjustment and started the adrenalin creeping into his system. The crew chief left him to it. As Lindley walked around the aircraft, someone sang like Caruso, his voice echoing in the hangar.

He started below her nose. From this viewpoint she resembled a cross between a rattlesnake and a swan, the flared fins on each side of the oval fuselage flattening her nose with the jaws of a rattlesnake, her cockpit like two malevolent eyes above. The rest of the fuselage was swanlike, tapering away to her wings and engines in the hangar's distance. Lindley walked slowly down her starboard side, back to the massive twenty-three-foot-long Pratt and Whitney turbo-ram-jets which drooped down from the leading edge of her short wings, close to each side of the fuselage. From their inlet nacelles protruded conical spikes, adjustable fore and aft, to capture the supersonic shock wave and turn it into turboboost for the afterburners. Each engine, by itself, could produce more thrust than the engines of the Queen Mary. Pushing on full throttle was like a sustained kick in the ass, Lindley mused.

There was nothing shiny about her skin. It had the texture of shark skin, like sandpaper, which someone had explained increased boundary-layer control, and at the same time reduced radar reflectivity and provided maximum skin-cooling properties. The rear of the fuselage was stuffed full of electronic countermeasure systems. The rest of the fuselage, except the ejectable cockpit module and radar in the nose, was fuel tank. The SR80 could sustain herself for eight hours at more than four times the speed of sound, during which time she could fly around the globe on latitude forty north at her cruising altitude of ninety thousand feet. With everything switched on, she could ook at one hundred thousand square miles of territory per flight hour.

If you had to leave the aircraft for any reason, the whole cockpit module, complete with all onboard computers and main systems, was ejected. Then you sat where you were until you hit the deck, and when you got out, if it was enemy territory, you hit the button and blew the whole shebang to pieces. After ejection the whole aircraft would self-destruct, shedding minute pieces over a twenty-mile area. If the Russkies ever managed to get something up high enough and fast enough, Lindley thought, to knock an '80 out of the upper atmosphere, there wouldn't be much left to examine by the time it hit the ground. A few tiny, burnt pieces of titanium, that's all. And we bought most of that from the Soviet Union, anyway, he grinned.

Twenty minutes later he braved the outside conditions again and went back to the mess for a meal of very lean steak and two eggs with a glass of orange juice, and no coffee.

The pain in Pentland's hand shrieked for attention. Holding the hand above the level of his shoulder as he trudged up the rocky wash back to the plateau provided some measure of relief, reducing the pounding bloodflow. But most of all, it reduced the possibility of another explosion of pain from an accidental bang against a rock in the darkness.

Until now there had been little time to think, and now that he had the time, Pentland found it difficult to drag his mind from the focus of the pain. His energy level barely provided him with sufficient power to place one foot before the other in the darkness, and with the anticlimax of ridding himself of his pursuer came dejection and hopelessness. He realized that morbidity was an inevitable sequel to homicide. It had been a long time since he had been driven to such a measure on any operation, and he knew that somehow he should have found a way of avoiding it this time, even if only to find out from the Russian where they would have taken Joe Kenyon. But it had clearly been kill, or be killed. The Russian had given no quarter, had never let up in his relentless pursuit. Pentland knew that he should have been stepping up this pale starlit wash with a glad song of survival in his heart. But instead of elation, the black rock pressed in from the sides like monstrous black figures of judges, reminding him of the Russian's spirit back there, mourning over its broken body.

He found he was shivering again as he felt his painful way through the jumbled rocks, sliding and cursing on the loose shale. But his face felt hot, and he knew he was feverish; he tried to fix his concentration on reaching the road ahead. It would be a triumph to reach the road, he thought numbly. If he failed, he knew there was a strong possibility that with the loss of blood and the shock he could die of exposure in the chill wind that was stirring with increasing strength around him, moaning and sighing in the peaks above.

The loom of the silent boulders brought an old memory to his mind. The time when he was thirteen and he had taken on a bet, for five pounds, that he would dare to spend the night alone in the ancient ring of Stonehenge. They had dropped him off there before sunset one summer night, and he had pitched his tent in the center of the ring of ageless monoliths, and had watched the sun go down behind them and the darkness creep up over Salisbury Plain. With it had come a night wind. The stones had seemed to grow taller with the darkness, black against the fading rosiness of the deepening sky. And later the moon had loomed up over the horizon and enveloped the tiny tent in the black shadow of the altar stone. He had crept into the warmth of his sleeping bag and waited. The wind played strange fluting descants around the unseen stones, which now sounded to his raw imagination like the crooning of the dead. It had plucked at the thin nylon walls of the tent from all directions, as if trying to get in, and he remembered burying his head and waiting fearfully for the dawn.

Perhaps we never really grow up, he thought. Perhaps we just build walls, and if we should find it necessary to kill someone, we find the walls we build are thin, like the tent, and he's still with you for a period, because you're the last one he's been with, and he hangs on . . .

When Allan Briggs got back to his office, Jerry Anderson told him that two calls had come in. One from Joe Kenyon in Geneva, saying that the flight had been delayed by fog and was now estimated to arrive at Heathrow not earlier than eleven-thirty, and the second from the duty officer at MI6 asking him to call back.

"Okay, Jerry," Briggs said tiredly, slumping down at his desk. "Get down to Brompton Square, will you? I've got a funny feeling about the place. I can't pin it down, but watch the Kenyons' house like a hawk. Keep your eyes glued to the door. I want to know if anyone arrives, or leaves, right when it happens. Mrs. Kenyon's inside waiting for her husband." He told the agent about the kids and the ambulance, and shook his head.

"I can't figure it out," Briggs said. Then he nodded

at Anderson in dismissal, and as the agent left he reached for the telephone.

"Duty officer," a voice said on the other end.

"Hi. Briggs here."

"Ah, Briggs. As you know, because he called your office, your man is at Cointrin. He's currently waiting for the flight to depart. They have fog there. He's through immigration and we have a man close to him. I think he'll be all right."

"Great. What news of David?"

"Not a lot at the moment. There was some disturbance in the lobby of his hotel and the last anyone saw of him, he was driving out of the car-park like Fangio in a blue Peugeot. No one seems to know why. The Swiss police had a couple of reports of a similar car going like a bat out of hell near Thonon, and later near Monthey. The report from Monthey indicated that a Mercedes and a Peugeot went through the town like they were on the Alpine rally. Apparently the Mercedes was about a mile ahead. We have a man checking from there. When I get anything else I'll call."

"Okay, thanks. I really appreciate it."

"That's beside the point, old boy. He's our man, you know."

Briggs smiled.

"Yeah, I guess he is. I guess he is," he repeated absently as he drew on a cigarette, and remembered the telephone call at the Kenyons' house. Someone called Gail. "Doesn't he have a girl called Gail something-or-other?"

The man on the other end laughed.

"Yes, that's right. An absolute smasher. Gail Seldon."

"You wouldn't know her address, I guess?"

"I say, that's a bit unsporting, isn't it? I mean—"

"Come off it, Simon," Briggs groaned. "Business!"

"271-3053."

"Thanks. Talk to you later."

Briggs looked at his watch as he replaced the receiver. It was nearly ten-thirty.

He dialed Gail's number. She answered on the sixth ring, and he knew he had got her out of bed. Her voice was slightly husky. It occurred to him that he would like to listen to that voice off-duty sometime. Voices could be very misleading, he thought. How many times had he heard the most provocative tones on the other end of a telephone, only to find out subsequently that its owner was either sixty-five, or fat and pimply. However, Simon had said she was an "absolute smasher." Knowing David Pentland, he could easily believe that.

"Miss Seldon?"

"Yes, who is this?"

"I'm a friend of David's."

"Oh?"

She was certainly no blabber, Briggs thought.

"Er—we sometimes work together. My name's Allan Briggs—"

"Yes, Mr. Briggs," she said, with a trace of impatience.

Briggs had no idea whether Gail Seldon was familiar with Pentland's work. She probably wouldn't be, he thought, in which case his own name would never have come up.

"If you're calling for David, I'm afraid he's not here at the moment."

"I know that," he said, meaning to go on.

"Really," Gail Seldon murmured. "How interesting. Then perhaps *you* can tell *me* where I could contact him. We had arranged to meet tonight."

"What I would like to do, Miss Seldon, if it's at all

169

possible, is to meet with you. I realize it's late, but I have something important to discuss with you. Would that be possible?"

"Are you with the embassy?"

The American accent, he thought.

"Yes, I am."

"And would this discussion concern Joe Kenyon?"

That surprised him. Beautiful *and* sharp, he thought.

"It would."

She gave him her address.

As Allan Briggs walked out of the elevator door into the dim lighting of the car-park below the embassy, the phone rang in Dimitri Olenko's apartment in Holland Park Road.

Olenko had changed and showered, and was packing an overnight bag with fresh clothes, ready for the drive out to Farnborough. He had arranged to stay at the same hotel as Joe Kenyon and he planned to arrive there at eleven-thirty. It was now ten-forty and he had allowed forty-five minutes for the drive at this time of night. The roads would be clear and it would amuse him to keep absolutely to all the speed limits, which he knew would bore the daylights out of the British agent assigned to follow him wherever he went.

After the vodkas on the plane from Geneva and a couple more since he had gotten back to the flat, he felt more relaxed, although his mind continued to race over the details of the plan; and each time he looked at his watch, unable to believe how fast time seemed to be passing, his heart would thump and the blood would rush to his head.

When the telephone rang he stiffened at his position by the bed, in the act of laying a sports coat into an open case. He was expecting no calls, unless it should be an unnecessary one from Switzerland to advise him that Renko had returned to the chalet after dealing with Pentland. At the fourth ring he threw the coat onto the bed, strode through to the sitting room and snatched up the receiver from the cradle, which was plugged into a scrambler box.

"Yes?" His voice was hoarse, and he coughed. "Yes?" he repeated.

"The man Briggs has just talked on the telephone to Pentland's girl," a voice said. "Briggs has arranged to go to her place in Chelsea."

Olenko thought hard.

"Do you—?" the voice started to say.

"Be quiet," Olenko snapped. "Wait."

The woman had reported that Pentland's girl had called while Briggs was there. Did Briggs suspect something? The CIA man had been quite satisfied, the woman had assured him, when he left. Now Olenko wondered whether the woman had made a correct assumption.

"Read me a transcript."

He listened carefully, and then with alarm, as Gail mentioned Kenyon's name. Thank God he had had the foresight to have the girl's place wired. If she had detected something wrong with the way her call to Brompton Square had been answered, it was very possible that Briggs would put two and two together and come up with ten.

"You can hear conversation from inside her place, can you not," Olenko asked.

"Yes, Comrade. Unless there is any other loud noise which might smother it."

Olenko thought again. He had made a vow with himself to minimize violence. If this operation was concluded successfully it would be necessary to live

171

with his conscience for the rest of his life. One British agent removed in Switzerland did not worry him. Such people lived with that risk. They chose their occupation knowing that a very real war existed below the strata of normal existence, just as he had regularly risked his own life to test new Soviet aircraft. And, besides, this Pentland had dealt very briskly with the man sent to Queens Gate. The Englishman certainly had not pulled his punches that night. And subsequently he had proved to be very disrupting.

But there must be no violence with the girl.

"Then place yourselves to listen to their conversations. I will stand by this phone."

He looked at his watch. This would make him late for Farnborough, but not too late.

"You will only take appropriate action *after* he leaves the girl. Do you understand? And only then should his discussion with the girl develop a dangerous drift, do I make myself clear?"

"Yes, Comrade Colonel."

"Be very careful. You must do whatever has to be done with no one to witness it, yes?"

"Of course," the voice replied, with a hint of sarcasm, "Comrade," it added.

Olenko slammed the receiver down and lit a cigarette, his fingers shaking. Filthy KGB night-dogs, he thought. He hurried to the drinks table, poured another vodka, and threw it back with a gulp. Careful, he told himself.

Gorlov would be in his office tonight. The marshall would have one eye on the clock—his hand ready to answer the telephone—and the number of the senior Soviet military air traffic controller at his fingertips. Squadrons of interceptors would be standing-by throughout the Soviet Union, and his own comrades at Berezniky would not sleep tonight, he knew. They would remain at the base, their wives told that a night exercise was in progress. He wished he was with them. He wished it was only an exercise.

The phone rang again.

Olenko cursed loudly and snatched up the receiver. What now? There was the familiar sinking feeling in his stomach.

"The flight from Geneva is delayed until eleven-thirty," the man at the airport said.

"Oh, *shit*," Olenko exploded. "Why?"

"Fog there, Comrade Colonel."

"What are conditions at Heathrow?"

"Good."

"All right. Contact me from now on by radio. Tell me as soon as the aircraft leaves Geneva, and tell me its ETA immediately you know. It is of the utmost urgency, you understand?"

"I will, Comrade Colonel," the voice assured him.

As Lindley walked across the plastic-coated hangar floor he could see that Dracula was bursting with fuel. Her oleos were compressed and she squatted down on her rear gear with her long neck canted up at a perceptible angle, her needle-nose seeming to point longingly at the hangar doors.

The G-suit Lindley wore was a tight fit. He knew that it displayed his body shape as if he had been nude. The suit's shiny reflective surface and its horizontal ribbing gave him a reptilian look. The ribbing would hold his guts together should he have cause to adopt evasive maneuvers, or if one of Dracula's engines ate a shock wave at max cruise and flamed out. If this happened he would be slammed sideways with colossal force as the asymmetrical thrust of the other engine continued to shove out fifty thousand pounds

173

of propulsive power. The live engine would be automatically shut down within microseconds, but there would still be plenty of time for Lindley's helmet to smash against the transparent sides of the cockpit capsule. And then all hell would break loose as the bird decelerated; and his guts would be up against the suit and straps, with the force shoving his head down onto his chest as he lowered her nose and groped with his left hand for the restart contacts.

Yeah, he thought, she got real wild with an unstart.

Maloney, the crew chief, grinned at the pilot as he approached Dracula's ladder.

"Hey!" he exclaimed in mock admiration at Lindley's displayed physique. "Are we losing a little weight, Colonel?" he leered.

Lindley paused with one hand on the ladder.

"You wanna know the secret, smart ass?" he drawled with a grin, focusing his eyes on Maloney's own ample belly.

"Sure! Tell me all, Colonel."

"Heave your ass up into that black bucket," Lindley jerked his head up at the SR80 hanging over them, "and go through an unstart—just one unstart, Chief, and you'll come back twenty pounds lighter. However," he went on, without pause, "nobody would notice just twenty pounds, would they? You'd have to do it every day for a week, right? How do you think I stay so trim, eh?" Lindley patted his small potbelly and stuck it out against the suit, tucking his already receding chin into his chest and rounding his shoulders. "Think! You could look like me!"

Loud laughter rang out from the maintenance and preflight crew who were removing the aircraft's pitot and transducer covers, and the big red nacelle bungs. At the laughter, Lindley adopted a hurt look. He shook his head as he climbed the ladder to the cockpit, trailing his bone dome in one hand, the other gripping the rungs. At the top he turned to look down on the crew below him.

"You people," he grumbled, "have no respect for one who heroically challenges the very boundaries of space." He ducked his head below the canopy frame, poised like a jaw above him. "No appreciation," he cried, "for those who go forth to conquer the elements, who seek to defy Newton's inimitable force!" He sank down onto the contoured couch.

"Hee, hee, hee!" Maloney laughed below.

Lindley peered down at the chief over the side of the cockpit.

"You giggle at outright bravery, you cur." Lindley swiveled his head to take in the rest of the crew who were peering up at him, laughing. Then he pointed dramatically down at Maloney.

"He cares not," Lindley cried, "that he mocks the fastest ass in the world—"

"We got one and eight," Maloney shouted, wiping his eyes.

Green in one minute, then eight minutes before the next Russian satellite orbited into range. Lindley knew that the ranch would be five hundred miles to the rear by then.

"Good enough, sergeant," he said, businesslike now. "Roll out on the green."

"Good trip, Colonel," Maloney called up.

"See you in a week," the pilot called back.

"Yes, sir!" Maloney waved.

The control panel before Lindley was a series of blank vertical and horizontal rectangles with only a few analog instruments. All, at the moment, were dead patches of translucent grey material set in a matte-black surface. Lindley settled his body in the reclining, oil-filled couch, which molded comfortably and fluidly to the shape of his body. He looked down, and removed the wrist-cuff to expose the sealed catheter protruding from his arm, then took off the plastic cover from his link to Dracula: a short, shining, steel needle, now protruding from a molded recess in the right armrest. With a small grimace of distaste he slid the end of the catheter onto the needle, and immediately became linked physiologically to the systems of the aircraft, and its own brain, the onboard computer that incorporated the Physiological Control Monitoring System—the heart of Dracula. As the PCMS tasted his blood, the panel before him came alive, all six hundred or so of the verniers and dials, digital readouts, sensory equipment, and radar screens lighting up in soft reds and greens and matte areas of silver-grey. The PCMS clacked quietly as it made its own decisions about Lindley's psychological and physiological state, and he felt the familiar slight buzz as Dracula fed a tiny, measured amount of amphetamines into his system.

From that moment, Lindley's hands were a blur of movement as he checked all instruments and rapidly completed the engine prestart check procedures. Moments later he had checked all the hydraulic systems, electrical breakers, onboard surveillance equipment—including infrared, ultraviolet, topographical lasers, telephoto visual sights, and the Terrain Avoidance and Search and Detection radars, then the full inventory of electronic countermeasure systems: a bewildering display of test lights, audio and visual alarms, and circuit breakers. He then checked his own mental and physical condition on the PCMS screen: blood pressure, acid-base balance, EKG and renal functions, p-co-2, p-o-s—which were all, as expected, in the green.

When he had completed these checks and adjusted the acceleration couch to a semi-sitting position, he reached forward and touched the pressure-sensitive switch to bring the open upper jaw of the canopy sighing down with a soft whine, hermetically sealing him in the aircraft and insulating him completely from the outside world. The cockpit was now an independent module with its own oxygen, recycling, air-conditioning, and pressurization systems separate from those required to service the rest of the SR80.

Through the light-sensitive transparency of the cockpit skin he saw the hangar's satellite warning lights change from red to green; the massive hangar doors immediately began to roll open, exposing a widening vertical rectangle of brilliant outside light. Like sensitive sun-optics, the canopy darkened proportionately to allow only a comfortable amount of light through to his eyes.

Maloney's voice then rumbled in his ears.

"Ready to roll, Colonel?"

"Roger for roll-out," Lindley murmured back.

There was a slight jolt as Dracula rocked on her gear before slowly moving forward, pulled by the ground tractor, toward the ever-widening rectangle of light. As the plane moved, Lindley's fingers keyed the flight plan into the computer together with previously computed details of the course-plot, then settled the palm and fingers of his right hand lightly on the short, immovable control stick protruding from the armrest just forward of his wrist. The stick was pressure-sensitive to his hand in any direction. Lindley now felt a heightened sense of awareness as the tractor towed the aircraft up the ramp and clear of the hangar doors to ground level, facing the glaring desert.

By now the symbiosis between the great black aircraft and its pilot was complete. Chuck Lindley did not just *feel* part of the SR80; he *was* a part of it.

Dracula, for a moment at rest as the tractor was disconnected, lurched gently from side to side on her long landing gear in the desert wind.

"Clear to start, Colonel," came Maloney's voice again.

Only thirty seconds had elapsed since the green light came on.

"Roger to start," Lindley confirmed as he flicked the switches that brought Dracula's massive twin Pratt and Whitney turbo-ramjets to life. They spooled up one hundred feet to his rear with a faintly heard ascending whine as he kept the balls of his feet on the brakes.

"Wind two six five, at three three," another voice said. "Altimeter two niner decimal niner three—clear to go."

Lindley selected takeoff flaps and trim, and with his left hand moved the twin power levers to full-forward. With a tympanic howl the ramjets kicked in, shaking the airframe savagely as the pilot released the brakes. Then with a great surge which pushed Lindley hard back into the couch, and an ear-splitting roar which sent gophers and lizards panicking for their holes over a five-mile radius, Dracula leapt forward.

Lindley's helmeted head was thrust heavily back into its padded cradle and his guts flattened in the G-suit as the great black aircraft, ejecting hot plasma with a force in excess of a hundred thousand pounds of thrust, tore down the ranch's camouflaged runway. Red digits of compounding velocity flickered ever faster in a head-up display in front of his face, and as the digits blurred past one hundred and forty knots, the pilot pressed back lightly with his fingers and Dracula's needle-nose lifted smoothly upwards. Lindley held a slight amount of right rudder to keep

178

the aircraft straight in the crosswind, and as the digits sped past one hundred and sixty knots he increased backpressure smoothly and the SR80 pointed at the deep blue of the sky to leave the runway in a rocketlike trajectory. Quickly, Lindley retracted gear and flaps and trimmed the plane into its climb. Three seconds later, Dracula gave an almost imperceptible shudder, which was all the pilot felt as the aircraft burst through the sound barrier to rattle the rocks below in a massive sonic boom. Her afterburners split the receding air like thunder as she tore for the troposphere at three times the speed of sound. Thirty seconds after her wheels left the hot concrete of the desert runway, she was thirty thousand feet above the surface, and two minutes after that Lindley trimmed-out at ninety thousand feet and pulled the levers back as she accelerated quickly to mach four, already a hundred and seventy-three miles north of the ranch.

Now her engine inlets trapped the shock waves generated by her supersonic speed through the atmosphere, and used the enormous pressures to feed the afterburners, which from then on would supercede the power of her engines as the primary source of thrust. The outside skin temperatures rose to eight hundred degrees in spite of the ambient temperature of minus sixty degrees, then stabilized as the air-conditioners blasted minus forty degree air through spaces in her fuselage and piping in her fuel tanks to maintain her vitals at a comfortable temperature.

Once established at cruise, Lindley reached forward and cranked out the limits of the ECM antiradar to a range of sixteen hundred miles around him, and as far as equipment on the ground or in other aircraft was concerned, Dracula ceased to exist: a mach-four ghost of the troposphere.

Once these tasks were complete, the PCMS fed

Lindley's bloodstream with a measured quantity of tranquilizers and he settled back in the acceleration couch at full-recline and studied the distant browns and yellows of the earth below, occasionally gazing into the black, star-strewn sky above him as the aircraft skimmed through the outer limits of the atmosphere on a diagonal across the United States and Canada toward Greenland.

CHAPTER TEN

Allen Briggs drove slowly along Stanton Street and searched for the small mews, looking from side to side. This was a quiet residential area and good-quality cars were parked nose to tail on each side of the road. Old-fashioned, painted-iron gas lamps, converted to electricity, spread yellow pools of light, leaving dark areas of shadow between. Quiet terraced houses stood back from the pavement with light peeping past drawn curtains. There were very few people about. As he spotted the white painted sign fastened to a corner wall announcing HEATH-STEAD MEWS, Briggs saw an empty slot and quickly drove up to it and parked the Ford. He locked the car and walked into the mews and across the narrow cobbled area to number nine. Gail Seldon's cottage was toward the end of the small cul-de-sac on the left side. Briggs heard someone working in a lighted garage opposite, otherwise the mews was quiet. He looked around him quickly, then pressed the bell.

Just before the door swung open he was thinking how remarkable London was, with these old parts of it where you could kid yourself that you were in some small country village. No sound of traffic, very few people on the streets. Very peaceful—like a quiet backwater of some raging torrent.

"Smasher" wasn't the right word for this girl friend of Pentland's, Briggs thought, as Gail opened the door. He would have used "stunning," or perhaps just goddamn beautiful—

"You must be Mr. Briggs," she said. "At least, I *hope* you are!"

He took in a fairly tall girl with long, somewhat tousled hair, perhaps auburn, thick on each side of a longish face. Dark eyes and full lips smiled at him.

"Er, yeah!" Briggs said, gathering his wits. "Hi, Miss Seldon. I'm real sorry to bother you so late at night, but—"

"Please don't worry." She stepped back from the door so that he could enter. "Come in." Her voice was deeply pitched and husky. She was dressed in a dark-blue housecoat and had nothing on her feet.

Briggs walked past her into a small sitting room. Most of the wall area of the room seemed to be bookcases. There were flowers before the fire grate and some low comfortable-looking easy chairs and a sofa. A writing desk stood below the window to the street and a small dining table sat by the wall below a line of framed prints, opposite the fireplace. It was a tiny room, with thick wall-to-wall carpeting in dark grey, which set off the warm autumn colors of the seat coverings. A pool of light from a standing lamp lit one end of the sofa and part of the carpet, presently occupied by a black cat which regarded him with its tail pointing straight up.

"Shoo!" Gail said to the cat, which retreated to the kitchen. She turned to Briggs.

"I've just made myself some instant coffee. Would you like some?"

"Thanks. I would."

Gail went through the door into the kitchen.

"Do make yourself comfortable," she called.

He sat down on the sofa and the cat came through and leapt onto his lap. Gail came back and handed him the coffee. "Get off!" she said to the cat, which climbed down to the carpet, curled up and went to sleep. Briggs stirred the coffee and turned to her at the other end of the sofa.

"You know Joe Kenyon's wife pretty well, don't you, Miss Seldon?"

She nodded. "I suppose I do. We're quite good friends."

"Yeah. I was with her at Brompton Square when you called. It *was* you who called, right?"

"Yes. I called her—let's see, about nine o'clock, I suppose. She said she had a visitor and asked me to call back. Why? Is something wrong?"

"Did you call her back?" Briggs asked quickly, his cup poised below his mouth.

"Yes."

"Ah—"

"She wasn't in, though. You didn't answer my question."

Briggs sipped the coffee. He shook his head. "I don't know," he said. "Did you try again, later?"

Gail frowned. "Well, that was the funny part about it. I did try again twenty minutes or so later, and again half an hour after that, but she still wasn't in. At least no one answered. We often call each other and it isn't like her to ask me to call back, and then just not be there." She thought for a moment, staring down at the carpet with her chin in her hand, and then she turned to face Briggs.

"As a matter of fact, I remember thinking that she sounded a bit odd. She didn't seem to know my voice

183

at first." Gail frowned. "Anyway, please, Mr. Briggs, why the questions?"

Briggs sipped his coffee again and sighed.

"You mind if I smoke?" Gail shook her head and accepted one of his cigarettes.

"It's kind of a long story." Briggs lit their cigarettes. "I won't bore you with it, except to say that, as you might well know, we keep a careful eye on our people overseas. There's a lot of terrorist activity about the world, particularly around embassy people. Joe's a valuable man."

He paused and blew smoke.

"Well, Joe's away at the moment. He's expected back tonight, matter of fact. While he's away we keep a man close by to kind of watch over things." Briggs raised an eyebrow and glanced at Gail with a small smile. "You know?"

"Yes, I think so."

"Yeah." Briggs nodded almost to himself and said nothing for a couple of seconds. Then he turned to her.

"Our man—well—kinda disappeared from his post, Miss Seldon." Briggs looked down at the cat, frowning. He ran a hand through his hair, then sat back. "His car was there, but he wasn't. We've no idea where the hell he is."

She was sipping her coffee, her eyes slightly narrowed at him above the cup. He smiled to himself. What the hell would she care, here, in the middle of the night, he thought.

"Funny thing was," he continued, "some kids said an ambulance pulled in and that some guy from the ambulance talked to him—then they saw him go with the guy to the ambulance." He smiled at her for a moment and took a sip of the coffee. "Then the kids said their mother called 'em in, and when they came back out he was gone. So was the ambulance." He paused and stared at some pictures on the wall for a moment, then turned to look at her again. Christ, she was really something. "That's how it was when I got there," he said.

She placed her coffee cup in its saucer on a small table at her end of the sofa. The dressing gown opened as she turned back and he saw the beginnings of the swells of fine-looking breasts. He forced his eyes upward to meet hers. His mind considered Pentland for a moment. What was it about these English women—the classy ones? Pentland knew, the sonofabitch. He'd ask Pentland when he got back from Switzerland. Where the hell *was* Pentland, anyway?

"You're not leading up," Gail Seldon was saying, "to telling me that something has happened to Susie, are you, Mr. Briggs?" she asked. Her big eyes had widened a little and she was sitting very still.

Briggs leaned back in the sofa and stretched his neck. He shook his head.

"I guess not. I went to the house soon as I finished talking to the kids." He looked back at her, smiling apologetically, and saw the relief on her face. He searched for somewhere to put the empty coffee cup, and she took it from him and took it into the kitchen.

As she came back in, he said, "There was something kinda odd about her, though, Miss Seldon," he paused. "You said she didn't recognize your voice at first on the telephone, right?"

She nodded.

"Well, she didn't recognize me right off, either. She must know my face pretty well. My work brings me into contact with her quite a bit, when she's with Joe at various goings-on around town." He glanced down at his watch. Jesus—it was nearly eleven. Joe was getting in any time, and he should be on his way out

185

to Heathrow. "See," he continued, looking up at her again, "at all the functions I've seen Mrs. Kenyon at, I've never seen her smoke. And—"

"She doesn't," Gail said quickly. "She never smokes."

"She was smoking when I saw her tonight, Miss Seldon," Briggs said quietly.

"You're not suggesting," Gail said, leaning slightly forward and opening the front of the gown again, "that it *wasn't* Susie you saw there tonight—are you?"

"When she has a drink—what does she drink?" Briggs asked quickly.

Gail raised an eyebrow. "Oh," she said, "either white wine, or sometimes a screwdriver, if she wants something stronger—"

"Well, this lady was drinking scotch on the rocks—"

"What! She *loathes* Scotch. She can't stand it. Joe drinks it, but Susie—"

Briggs was rising quickly from the sofa. Gail stood up with him.

"Mr. Briggs," she said, her voice betraying her fear, "I don't think that *was* Susie Kenyon you saw there tonight. It couldn't have been—" She stared at him for a moment. "Oh, my god. The ambulance! Do you think—?"

Briggs was walking quickly toward the door.

"Yeah," he said as he opened it. "That goddamned ambulance."

His shoes thumping an urgent tattoo over the cobbles of the dark mews, Briggs sprinted for the lights of Stanton Street in an agony of realization that his instincts had been correct in Brompton Square.

He scrabbled awkwardly for the car keys in the pocket of his trousers as he ran. He would radio Anderson when he got to the car; tell him to alert Pentland's boys and then get into the Kenyons' place and hold the woman.

The woman would be the link with whoever had taken Susie Kenyon. If Anderson missed her there would be nothing to go on—no way they would know where Susie Kenyon would be. It had to be the Soviets, he thought. But why leave a look-alike in Susie's place? Did that mean that they needed time? Time for what, for Christ's sake?

Briggs swerved around the corner from the mews into Stanton Street and raced for the Ford.

An elderly couple blocked the pavement ahead of him, between him and the car. The man, dressed in a raincoat and wearing a trilby hat which left his face in shadow from the overhead street lights, held a lead in his left hand attached to a spaniel dog, which was in the process of littering a bare patch of earth below one of the plane trees growing at intervals along the side of the pavement. Briggs appeared to startle them both as he raced toward them. The dog dragged its lead from the old man's hand and leapt into a space between two parked cars. The woman raised both hands as if to ward off the running figure, and the man raised his walking stick horizontally toward Briggs as the CIA man slowed and aimed to pass between them. Briggs heard a tiny click above the noise of his skidding shoes, and saw with horror the tiny flashing reflection of a needle blade snick out from the end of the walking stick. He brought his hands across his body in a desperate effort to thrust the stick aside before his momentum impaled the needle in his stomach. He gasped at the impact as the old man stepped aside like a matador, while his momentum carried Briggs lurch-

187

ing between the couple, his feet already stumbling out of control as the poison was pumped quickly to his heart by his racing pulse. Then the end of the walking stick, still impaled in his intestines, fell between his legs, ripping at his guts and tripping him to sprawl full length by the Ford. Briggs's mouth opened wide but no sound came as the chemical paralyzed his body in a rictus of agony and forced him to draw his knees up to his chest. The final images to blearily reach his dying brain were minute yellow reflections from the sandpapery surface of Stanton Street below the shadow of the parked Ford.

The old man quickly stepped over and retrieved the walking stick. There was another tiny click as the blade sprang back into its sheath. He turned to his companion who leaned against the sidewall, a picture of shock as she held her hands across her bosom.

"Oh, these dreadful young men!" she cried. "They have no consideration!"

The old man took her arm solicitously with one hand and adjusted his hat with the other.

"Are you all right, my dear?" he asked.

She smoothed her coat and nodded weakly.

Someone across the street opened a front door and light spilled across the road.

"Are you two okay?" called a cultured voice.

"I think this young man's drunk. We're all right, thank you. But perhaps you would be so kind as to phone the police. He seems to have collapsed." They stood for a moment looking down at Briggs's stiffened figure.

"Wretched drunks!" the man at the door muttered. "The streets," he said, "are not safe these days. Where are the police when you need them, dammit!"

"Quite," agreed the old man. He was stooping to grasp the lead as the dog reappeared from between the cars. He straightened and shook his head. "Dreadful!" he said and side by side they began to walk away into the gloom between the streetlights.

When Pentland finally reached the road, the night sky had settled into a brittle black clarity, faintly lit by a billion sparkling stars. The high peaks of the Alps were still covered with snow—which gave them a disembodied look as they floated above their dark lower slopes like faint, white ghosts—looming above him. The thin cold wind which keened around the rocks had, by now, chilled deep into every bone in Pentland's body as he scrambled stiffly and weakly over the broken parapet onto the road's unfamiliar smooth surface. For a few minutes as he trudged along the road, choosing the uphill direction, he felt like a sailor who had just stepped ashore after a long voyage, no longer needing to deal with the ever-moving sea, but with nerves so accustomed to the perpetual movement that they refused to give up their compensatory instructions to his muscles.

He had turned uphill against his survival instincts, knowing that he would be more likely to come across human habitation more quickly the lower he went down the mountains. And he desperately needed human hospitality. His body felt as though he had been incessantly beaten, his muscles aching and raw, with a weariness so deep that it felt to him like a cancer eating into his bones. Overlaying the weariness was the constant ball-peen hammering in his hand which, as he walked slowly up the slope of the road, he still held above his left shoulder to reduce the rhythmic pain caused by the beat of his own heart as it pumped blood around the tiny capillaries of the stumped fingers and kept the shattered nerves alert.

For the last two hours, as he had made his painful and pitifully slow progress through the rocks and the darkness from where he had left Renko, he had tried every mental effort to hypnotize his brain's focus from the dogged pounding in his hand. He had told himself repeatedly that it was not pain he felt, but sheer pleasure, something to be enjoyed and relished; an attempt to fool his system, which had been totally unsuccessful.

At one point, when he had stumbled across a low unseen rock and fallen onto his left side, bringing the hand crashing unavoidably down onto the shale, he had screamed with the searing impulse of the pain, and then lain with his legs drawn up to his chest in a fetal position while tears of frustration and fear and weakness and pain had squeezed from his eyes, and his lips had moaned like a dying animal. He had no idea how long he had lain like that while the wind chilled him to the marrow and sucked the sweat from his body, leaving him so cold and stiff that when he did manage to struggle to his knee he could hardly move at all for many minutes.

Then, still on his knees, he had heard himself screaming for help like a snared rabbit, and heard the mountains throw back his voice hollowly and mournfully; and when at last he had stopped, his voice hoarse from his parched throat, the silence seemed deeper and menacing, and it had occurred to him that somehow the stillness waited for his death—a pregnant silence full of expectancy, and certainty, that shortly his soul would join the ghosts glimmering whitely high above him against the black infinity of space. And then even the whisper of the wind, his only unwelcome company in the high Alps, chided him to hurry up and let go, to lay back and fall asleep in the numbing coldness while his life seeped from him, whispering to his tortured brain that then the pain would leave, and his sensations would be equalized to a common denominator of nothing. And nothing was a paradise compared to what existed now; Nothing was warm and welcoming compared to this existence of pain, and hunger, and weariness and loneliness.

But he had found himself wobbling to his feet again, even while his mind was preoccupied with these considerations, and his right hand still clutched Renko's rifle, and he had shuffled on toward the road with his mind clearing, as the movement once again consumed carbohydrates stored in his body and sent the warmth of the fuel into his blood. During the rest of the time it took him to reach the road he had conducted an argument with himself about which way to turn when he got there—uphill to find Joe Kenyon, or downhill to find someone to feed him, and warm him, and dress his hand and give him morphine to kill the pain. Between the moments of sentient logic he dreamed of morphine, trying to imagine how it would feel when the pain was banished, trying to remember the odd times when an injection had killed the hysterical throb of an abscessed tooth, and remembering as a younger man the enormous relief from the gas which had changed him from a knotted victim of appendicitis to a relaxed smiling figure just before the blessed light of his brain went out on the operating table.

Somehow he had made the decision to turn uphill to find Joe, having scrabbled around in his mind for the rationale that if he did not find him, then none of this effort could ever be worth anything—not the pain, or Renko's death, or his career to date. And it was Gail, his thoughts of her, and what, if he survived, he would say to her, who finally cemented the decision in his mind, so that by the time he clambered up onto the road there was no thought of turning left and down-hill, only a dumb unreasoning urge to turn right and climb, and to look for the telltale light of some cottage, or cabin, or farm, which had to lie some-where up this road—or why the hell would anyone have bothered to build the road in the first place? All roads led somewhere.

He plodded on with his left hand still raised in a weary salute to the darkness, the gun held in his right hand by the barrel, its butt banging along on the road beside him.

The even road surface gradually allowed his body to adopt a rhythm of movement, rather than the lurch-ing, tripping, staggering progress through the rocks and rough ground of the mountains, with a resulting decrease in the requirement for energy, and gradually Pentland became aware that he was thinking again, instead of reacting. There was some surplus of energy in him, to feed his brain in addition to keeping his legs moving heavily in the slow ascent of the steep moun-tain road, and for the first time in a long while he looked at his watch, raising the hand with the rifle to the level of his chin to make out the small, lighted digits. He was surprised to see that it was a little after eleven-thirty. He had thought that most of the night had passed, and a part of him had been expecting to become aware of the dawn at any time. As he lowered his arm and started to move forward again with an inward groan of effort, the deep blackness of the cliff close to his left side gave way to the starlit sky as he rounded a turn in the road, and light from somewhere up the mountain to his left faintly lit some pines on a dark slope. He became aware that a steep valley led up from the road into the mountains to his left. If there was light up there, he thought, there should be a house of some sort. Light meant people, and people could include Joe. The light could conceivably be shining from the refuge of Joe's captors. He hoped the road would lead to the light, but, he found ten minutes later, that he seemed to be passing the faint glow. He had hoped that as he progressed, the glow would become a definite source, but the pines continued to hide it. Perhaps he had missed a track off the road in the darkness, he thought. Reluctantly he decided to retrace his steps for a hundred yards. He would count the paces, and if he found no track, no path by then, he would once again turn and continue up the mountain.

For the first time in what seemed an eternity he felt elation, a quickening of his pulse, as he found the opening: a track leading off the road at an angle, not more than a dirt track one vehicle's width, but in the faint starlight he thought that he could make out fresh tire marks. The track seemed to lead upwards steeply toward the source of the faint glow of light. Pentland staggered up the track toward it.

Thirty minutes later the track wound up through dense pines into a clearing, a small plateau on the side of the mountain. Through the trees the light glimmered sharply, and gradually he made out the shape of a cabin. Light glowed from two equal-sized windows on its ground floor. Pentland pushed carefully through the trees to the edge of the clearing.

If this was where they had taken Joe, he expected to see vehicles, or at least the Mercedes he had chased from Geneva. But there was no sign of a vehicle, and no other structure which might contain one. The cabin sat in its clearing, alone, the light from its windows reflecting from the needles of the dense pines surrounding it. Pentland experienced a surge of disappointment. After all, he thought, the road could lead to a plethora of houses or cabins, winter and summer retreats for those who liked to get away from the cities to the wilderness of the mountains. This place could be one of fifty others like it.

He was thirty yards from the building, still hidden in the trees, the only sound now his own breath and the muffled thumping of his heart, slowing as he stood watching. The trees killed the sound of the keening wind, and it was now very dark beneath the canopy of pines. At one point as he watched, a shadow passed across the left window. So there *is* someone in there, he thought. But there was no sound, no noise of a radio, no distant sounds of conversation. Pentland lifted the rifle clear of the ground and ran across the exposed plateau. His feet made no sound on the thick carpeting of pine needles covering the open space between trees and cabin. As he approached, he distinguished a door between the two lighted windows, and he made for the darkness of the wall between the door and the left window where he had seen the shadow move across the light. He halted with his back to the horizontal logs that made up the walls of the structure, and listened. Pentland stood still for two minutes before he heard someone cough, a male clearing of the throat. He slid across to the window and slowly moved his head into the light, and what he saw nearly made him exclaim loudly with intense relief. Joe Kenyon sat comfortably in a chair close to a log fire, smoking a cigarette. His feet were raised on a couple of large logs, crossed in a relaxed position as he sat in profile to the window.

There appeared to be no one else in the room. The glow of the fire flickered warmly on the pilot's figure. An oil lamp sat on a table behind Joe's chair, emitting an intense light, no doubt hissing quietly and delivering its share of warmth to the room, Pentland noticed, shivering.

Why would Joe Kenyon be sitting unconcernedly by a comfortable log fire in a cabin in the Swiss mountains, when a few hours ago he had been violently abducted? If there was no one with him, why did he not leave, for Christ's sake? Pentland moved to the door. By the time his hand had found the latch and he had thrown the door open and stepped into the room, he felt anger rising at the apparent nonchalance of his friend.

Joe's face turned quickly toward him as the door flew open. The attaché's eyes were wide as they settled on Pentland, a look of fear spreading across his features.

"What the hell, Joe!" Pentland said angrily, his voice hoarse. "What the hell are you doing, for Christ's sake!"

There was no answer from Joe Kenyon. He sat, eyes wide, his body seeming to shrink down into the chair.

"Who—?" he quavered.

"I've been chased halfway over the fuckin' Swiss Alps," Pentland swore, "on account of you, my friend, and you tuck your ass into a comfortable chair and contemplate your navel! By now the whole world'll be out looking for the lost bloody diplomat, and you apparently don't give a shit. Excuse me if I should sound a trifle overwrought, but I hope you'll concede you owe me an explanation!" Pentland leaned tiredly against the wall with Renko's gun trailing in his right hand. As he finished speaking, there was a flurry of movement through a doorway, which Pentland now noticed led into the other room, and much to his surprise a woman in a dressing gown stood in the doorway with her mouth open in surprise. As she appeared, Joe Kenyon began to rise from his seat.

Several things then happened in quick succession.

The woman disappeared back through the doorway out of Pentland's view, and Joe Kenyon rose quickly from the chair. As the attaché stood up it dawned on Pentland's tired brain that there was something different about his friend, something indefinably different about the set of his features and the shape of his body. Before he could react, the woman appeared again in the doorway with a heavy shotgun cradled in her arms, the twin black barrels pointing at Pentland's belly.

The full implication hit Pentland like a blow. The chase from the hotel, the loss of the car, the desperate run for survival through the Swiss mountains, the loss of his fingers, and the killing of the Russian, had been for nothing. His efforts had been totally in vain. The man who stood on the far side of the room before the log fire was not Joe Kenyon.

Pentland felt his remaining strength dwindle in a wave of defeated hopelessness as he slumped against the wall beside the door of the cabin. What, by now, had they done with the real Joe Kenyon? Had this all been an elaborate red herring to draw him away from Joe, so that they could get their hands on him easily, without risk of interference? Pentland experienced the leaden heaviness of failure as he stared at the figure opposite; the woman with the gun stared at him. The fire crackled in the silence, and the oil lamp hissed on the table.

A telephone, he thought desperately. He had to find a telephone, and alert Briggs. As he was thinking this, he was unable to prevent his legs from folding, and his body began to subside against the wall, Renko's gun falling from his unfeeling fingers to clatter on the pine-planked floor of the cabin. The pain washed over his brain to further dull his sensations, and as if from an independent observer, he took note of the fact that he now sat sprawled against the wall, one leg bent below him and the other stretched forward, barely able to prop his heavy trunk upright with his right hand. He was dimly aware of the woman saying something to her companion, and the image of the man who looked like Joe was advancing toward him, stooping over him. He raised his right arm to ward off the approaching figure, and without its support his body sagged sideways until he lay on the pine planks with the room swimming lopsidedly in his vision.

"He has lost much blood," he heard the woman say, her voice distant and ringing peculiarly in his ears.

He felt hands beneath his shoulders and the room lurched, and for a few moments his vision blackened completely as he was hauled upright and the blood ran from his brain. Then he was aware that he sat sprawled at a rough table, with the bright light of the lamp hissing in front of his face. The faces of the man and woman swam back into focus.

Pentland lifted his head and concentrated on the man who looked like Kenyon.

"If you're not—Joe Kenyon—who—are you?" he asked.

"My God, his hand!" the woman exclaimed from behind him. "Get him some brandy, Ernst!" She came from behind him to peer into his eyes. "What has happened to you? What happened to your hand?" she said, her voice low and husky with concern.

"I want to—know—who—?"

"Here!" Ernst was back at the table. "Drink." He held a mug below Pentland's mouth. Strong fumes crept into his nose. Pentland took the mug shakily and drank the brandy quickly. He coughed and closed his eyes briefly as the spirit sluiced down his throat. Its sharpness made him gasp, but began to clear his head.

"You are the one who followed in the car—yes?" Ernst said. "They said Renko had gone to kill you—"

"Renko," Pentland breathed. "The others. Where are the others?"

"They will come back. Soon." Ernst looked worriedly at his watch, then across Pentland's head to the woman.

"Olga! What should we—?"

"Why are they coming back?" Pentland said. "You mean the Soviets. Renko's men. Why are they coming back here?"

"He must stay here," the woman called Olga said.

"Yes—" Ernst agreed, nodding heavily. "Yes, you are right."

"What time are they coming?" Pentland asked quickly.

"One hour," the woman said. "Possibly less. You must stay. Anyway, you are in no condition to leave. We must see what can be done with that hand. Fetch my bag, Ernst. From the bedroom." She jerked her head toward the door from which she had appeared with the shotgun.

"Is there a telephone?" Pentland focused on the woman's face as Ernst disappeared through the doorway opposite the table. "I must get to a telephone—"

"There is no telephone. There is no telephone until Monthey. Monthey is fifteen kilometers. There is no car. You will have to wait."

Ernst came back into the room holding a heavy black case. He placed it on the table in front of Pentland, and Olga opened it. It was full of medical and surgical equipment. Pentland looked up at the woman's face as she took a hypodermic from a plastic case. Her face was heavy-set with a full mouth, which turned down at the corners. There were lines around her eyes. She appeared to be in her early forties, and had been attractive once, Pentland thought, but looked as though she was jaded by a hard life. Mousy blond hair dropped across her face as she leaned over the bag. She came round the table back to Pentland's side and began to clean the inside of his arm near his elbow with some gauze soaked in spirit.

"What is in the hypodermic?" Pentland asked. "Are you a doctor?"

"I am a nurse," she said. "This is to kill the pain. I must clean your hand. What happened to it?" She finished cleaning the skin and bunched a portion of the flesh between her fingers.

"Two of the fingers are gone," Pentland said as she inserted the needle.

Pentland was torn between stopping her, not trusting her, not trusting what might be injected into him, and the look of honesty in both her's and Ernst's features and her genuine concern about the state of his hand. The longing for relief from the throbbing pain won the day, and he remained still as she slowly plunged the fluid in the syringe into a vein in his arm. Seconds later the throb of the ball-peen hammer subsided to a distant rhythm and he leaned back in the wooden chair with relief, realizing that he had dreamed of this moment for so long it seemed like most of his life. Gradually, with the retreat of pain, his thinking became clearer, his brain now able to cope with sentience, released from its preoccupation with survival.

He felt desperately hungry then.

"Do you have any food?" he asked Ernst, as the woman left to fill a large bowl with hot water. "Some cheese, perhaps. I'm very hungry. Some milk and cheese would be perfect."

Ernst nodded and smiled, looking so peculiarly like

Joe Kenyon.

"I bring some," he said.

"You are Swiss?" Pentland asked as Ernst went across to the small kitchen.

"We are from Zurich," Olga called.

"You're not Soviet. Not KGB," Pentland stated.

"We are not," Ernst said with emphasis, as he came back with a hunk of cheese and part of a French roll on a plate in one hand and a glass of milk in the other. "Here," he said, placing the food in front of Pentland.

"Then why are you with them? Why are you impersonating an American diplomat?"

Olga had come back to the table and was placing Pentland's left hand in a bowl of steaming water into which she poured some blue liquid. She began to gently soak the filthy handkerchief from the mess of the hand.

"Do not look," she said.

Pentland concentrated on Ernst who now sat at the table, also keeping his eyes averted from the mess Olga was revealing in the bowl.

"For money," Ernst said simply. "They offered me money—"

"Ernst, are you a fool?" Olga hissed. "Tell him nothing. Nothing. He is British. They are Soviet. It is their affair. We must do just as we are told, no more. We are not instructed to discuss this with strangers."

Ernst nodded. "You are right. I am sorry."

"Sometimes you are not good with your brain, *nicht*?"

Ernst smiled sheepishly.

Pentland had been wolfing the cheese. He drank the milk, then made the mistake of glancing down at Olga's work. She had peeled off the remains of the handkerchief, revealing pieces of shredded white skin through which the splintered bones that were once the two end fingers of his left hand protruded.

"Ah, God—" Pentland gasped.

"I told you not to look."

The food grew heavy and cold in Pentland's belly, and for a few moments he thought he would throw up. With an effort, keeping his eyes well away from the bowl on the table before him, over which Olga bent, he contained the feeling and felt the sweat grow cold on his brow. The shock of the sight of his hand caused anger to well up, bringing with it a new surge of energy and determination. He would let her finish, and then he would have to get out. Get to Monthey, and find a phone and call Briggs. Get hold of the MI6 people in Geneva and trace Joe.

"Isn't your job finished?" he asked. "What more could there be to do? You have successfully lured me away from the American. Why don't you leave and go back to Zurich?"

"No *questions*," Olga put in quickly.

She was wrapping his hand in clean bandage, which she secured with tape. She then produced a plastic mitten which she carefully drew over the lump and fastened at his wrist. It was a very professional job.

Then she quickly cleaned his face and secured a plaster across the gash in his cheek.

"You should rest now," she said.

"Thank you, Olga. Thank you very much," Pentland said, rising from the table.

"Why do you get up—?" Olga started, concern and a little fear coming into her expression. "Sit. I will prepare something hot, then you should rest—"

"I have to find a telephone," Pentland said quietly.

Both she and Ernst got to their feet.

"You cannot leave," she said firmly. "I have told you this."

"I must. You don't know what's at stake. Your involvement is very small. No one will know I've been here if you do not tell them. I'm very grateful for your help, Olga. You are both kind people. You should not have allowed yourself to become involved with these people. The money is not worth it. You should also leave, before the Russians return. While you can—"

"But then we should not be paid," Ernst said.

"Quit while you can, Ernst."

"Do not listen to him, Ernst." Olga stepped back, bent down, and came up with the shotgun. "You will sit down. You will not leave," she said, her lips compressed. "You are ungrateful."

"Leave, and I will see that you are paid whatever they promised," Pentland said.

Ernst turned to her.

"Olga—" he began.

"Why should you trust him?" she cried. "No. We do not know you. We have a contract. Money is in an account for us. Waiting. Why should we risk this? We are poor. We need the money—"

"In my view you are foolish to trust the Soviets, Olga. You have done what they asked. Leave now," he urged. Something flitted across her expression as he said this. Something he did not register in his preoccupation to leave.

Pentland walked slowly across to where he had dropped Renko's gun by the door.

"Stop!" Olga cried. "You will *stop*!"

Pentland turned.

She stood with her legs planted apart, pointing the shotgun at his chest. She had raised it to her shoulder and her eyes flashed with anger at the far end of the twin barrels. Ernst stood a little behind her looking uncertain, his eyes flicking from Pentland's to the back of her head.

"I've never known of a nurse who would cold-bloodedly blow a man apart, especially with a weapon as coarse as a shotgun," Pentland said evenly. "At this range, that thing would blow my guts all over this cabin. I don't think you have any idea what kind of disgusting mess it would make. There would be no patching me up after that."

He reached for the door latch.

"Thank you again. I must go. I am sorry to be so difficult."

And then he was through, closing the door quietly behind, feeling the cold bite immediately through his torn clothing. A minute later he was deep into the pines, half-running, half-slithering down the slope back to the track that led to the road to Monthey.

When he reached the road he turned right, downhill, easing into a steady loping run, hoping that the small amount of energy he had recouped would be sufficient to sustain him until he came across a house or made it to the small town at the junction. There was no pain now, but he knew that it would not be long before the effects of the injection wore off, and then the pain would be back with a vengeance. But it would not be so bad, he thought, now that the concern with infection was eliminated. And the cheese and milk would supply some much-needed protein to sustain him.

As he ran he tried to make sense of the period since the bogus Joe had been abducted from the hotel. It appeared that it had all been a red herring to get him from the real Joe's side, to leave the way clear for the Soviets to carry out whatever plan they were following. But if they wanted Joe Kenyon, as he had been convinced all along since he had first noticed the photographing operation, then why on earth hadn't they just taken him? If they could abduct the bogus

Joe so convincingly, then why not the real Joe? He had to assume that they had not been willing to attempt kidnapping Joe until they had managed to separate him from the constant attention of MI6—in which they had been more than successful. They now presumably believed me to be dead, he thought, and had probably taken Kenyon while he was on his way to Cointrin, in which case there would be no hope of catching up with them before they removed Kenyon to the Soviet Union. Olenko had been clever and thorough, his timing faultless. They had most likely had a plane waiting at Cointrin, and Joe would have arrived in the Soviet Union hours ago.

Pentland loped around a corner of the twisty road and saw the glimmer of lights moving across to his left, swinging and illuminating the pine-clad slopes dimly. A vehicle was winding up toward him, still some distance off.

For a moment he felt elated. He would flag it down, get them to take him to a telephone, plead emergency. Force them with the gun, which he still carried, if he had to. Then it occurred to him that the vehicle could contain the Soviets returning to the cabin he had just left. He slowed his pace, breathing hard, and looked around in the darkness to find somewhere to conceal himself. He could hear the vehicle's engine now, in low gear, as it strained up the steep, twisting road. Its headlights lit parts of the rock cliff to his left brightly, swinging from the cliffs to the black void below the road to the right, the beams slicing through the clear, cold, night air, to light up the rocks and pines of the mountains.

Pentland noticed a deep fissure in the rock face. He quickly slid his body into it as the lights grew bright and the engine roar approached.

As the vehicle swung past him, grinding up the

road, he saw that it was a van, its interior softly lit behind the darkened glass of its side windows. There was a driver and passenger in front. As it swept past, the red taillights illuminated a red cross on its rear doors. An ambulance, he thought. He wished now he'd stepped out into the road to stop it. He found himself standing in the center of the asphalt shouting at the retreating lights, which were almost immediately hidden beyond the breast of the cliff as the road wound back on itself. The red glow of the lights faded into the blackness and the sound of the engine was quickly swallowed in the hills. Once again there was only the sound of the wind keening in the high peaks, and the blackness of the night was deeper after the brief brightness.

Damn, he cursed to himself, then set his stiffening, tired legs to adopt their previous rhythm.

The lights had revealed that he was close to the place where the car had burst through the parapet. Briefly he had recognized the shapes of the land, the peaks rising high above the canyon down which he had run earlier in the night, with the bullets from Renko's gun whining past his head. The thoughts reminded him that he was lucky to be alive. There had been too many occasions during this night when he had been convinced that the Horseman had focused his orbless gaze on his running figure. The effects of the brandy and the painkiller were wearing off quickly as his pace pumped the blood around his system, and his blood once more pounded in his ears. A part of him insisted that nothing he could do now could prevent the Soviets from doing whatever they liked with Joe Kenyon, so what was the hurry? Another part argued that while the facts were concealed, before he knew irrevocably that they had Joe, it was essential to do all he could, to put out his best effort.

If it meant running to Monthey so that he could alert Briggs, and there would be some chance that Briggs would be able to intervene, then he would run, keep going until he was unable to run a step further, in the meantime hoping that someone would drive up this road, someone else who he could flag down.

Something about the pounding of his blood in his ears was wrong. There seemed to be a double pounding, like an echo in his head. His breath rasped from his mouth noisily, and his feet slapped on the asphalt of the road. But above these rhythms he became conscious of a new thudding, distinct from the noises of his progress. As he became aware of it, the noise echoed hollowly in the peaks and it was impossible to pinpoint the direction. He slowed to a halt, and listened, trying to restrain his noisy breathing.

Pentland's legs trembled with fatigue and sweat ran off him in spite of the cold air, while his heartbeat pumped perceptibly slower in his chest as he swung around in the road, eyes and ears questing for the direction of the increasing, rhythmic, knocking sound. The noise grew and once again he saw the loom of lights beyond the next corner. A few seconds later he identified it. A helicopter was flying up the valley toward him, low above the road. It came into view as it swung out over the valley to his left, perhaps half a mile ahead, a beam shining down from its invisible fuselage onto the rocks below.

As he watched, once again wondering whether whoever flew the machine was friend or foe, the light picked out the remains of the Peugeot. The car was lit in bright relief as it lay on its back in the rocks down the slope, its wheels seeming to appeal to the source of the light above. Pentland told himself that whoever flew the machine was not likely to be one of Olenko's people—they already knew about the car—that it could be a Swiss police helicopter, dispatched as a result of a report of some road user who had noticed the wreck of the car before darkness, or someone who had heard shots.

Pentland ran forward, shouting, before he realized that there was no chance of being heard. He slid to a halt and watched the machine hopelessly as it hovered over the car. For Christ's sake, land, he groaned to himself. Land! Cut the engine so that you can hear! He ran forward again, sprinting for the place where the car had holed the retaining wall. From there he could pick out the vague shape of the machine. It was not much higher than him as it hovered fifty feet or so above the car out in the valley. As he watched, the light beam began to quarter the rocks in the immediate area of the car. Half a minute later, the machine slid sideways away from where he stood, toward the cliff he had climbed down, where the Russian had shot him, and he raised his hands in a useless gesture of despair as its clatter lessened and the light grew smaller.

Pentland swung himself through the broken gap and began to climb desperately and incautiously down to the car. Getting to the car was his only thought. They might come back this way and give it another look. He could think of nothing else to do. He forgot his hand until he reached for a sharp rock and felt the searing pain run up his arm. He heard his own voice cry out and the experience steadied him as he continued downward with more care. Eventually he slid the last part to the car, and stood breathing hard, leaning on its broken bodywork as he watched the machine sink for a moment beneath the level of the cliff above the river. Come back, he breathed. For Christ's sake, come back!

The helicopter rose above the level of the cliff and

the noise grew as it came toward him, the light still sweeping back and forth below it. Pentland ran clear of the car, now shouting and waving his hands above his head again in the darkness. He tried to anticipate the wide swing of the beam, to estimate its position when the machine would be more or less overhead. He ran to one side, then changed his mind and ran to the other, tripping and falling over unseen rocks, his breath coming in sobbing gasps, desperate to be seen.

The machine passed overhead with a deafening clatter. Dust whirled up into Pentland's eyes and the light swept past, feet away, missing him. He swung Renko's gun into the air and fired again and again, the sharp sounds of the shots cracking above the beat of rotors and the steady roar of the engine. Then the light swung back toward him, and the machine reversed its course. The beam hit Pentland's eyes and he wobbled to the ground exhausted as the dust once more whirled up around him. He had no idea that he knelt in the shale, brightly illuminated as he held up both hands, the one clublike, bound in its white bandages, the other clutching Renko's gun, the barrel waving in the direction of the descending machine.

A loud voice bellowed something in French; a voice that filled the valley and echoed off the slopes, repeating the message twice before Pentland realized that they were telling him to place the weapon on the ground and walk away from it. He threw the gun down and staggered to one side, holding up his hands. The machine landed carefully on the sloping shale while the pilot kept its power up, practically hovering. Someone came from its door toward him.

A light shone into his face, held by someone who he could not see.

"David!" a voice exclaimed, with a mixture of disbelief, concern, and perhaps a trace of amusement;

a big, deep voice with a strong French accent.

Pentland felt even weaker with relief.

"Maurice!" he croaked. "Christ! Maurice—is it really you?"

There was a stentorian laugh from behind the flashlight.

"It is just Maurice, David, but per'aps it would be better for you if it was the Other, *hein*? Where 'ave you been?"

Pentland walked forward on tottering legs.

"Am I glad to see you, Maurice. You've got to get me to a telephone fast." He waved at the helicopter, still whining and clattering as the pilot held it lightly on the sloping shale. "Where did you get this?"

"I—'ow do you say—happropriated it from the Swiss Police. On the 'ighest authority, of course. Mount yourself in to the be'ind." Maurice opened the door of the helicopter and helped Pentland get into the rear bench seat, then heaved his bulk into the front with the pilot. Judging from the fact that the pilot was dressed in civilian clothes, he was one of Fennel's men.

" 'It the button!" Maurice shouted to the pilot in his hopeless imitation of the American Mafia.

The helicopter lifted away from the slope in a blast of dust. For a few moments as the machine ascended it was impossible to speak over the clatter of the rotors and the roar of the engine. Once back over the road and facing the valley that wound down to Monthey, with the machine still rising, but now making good progress forward as the nose lowered, conversation was once again possible.

"Your people in London 'ave much concern for you, David," Fennel bellowed. "What on earth 'ave you been doing, *hein*?" He gesticulated back down into the darkness behind, where the smashed Peugeot lay.

Pentland was leaning back in the seat, exhausted. Fennel had twisted round to half-face him.

"Joe Kenyon," Pentland said. "They snatched someone the splitting image of Joe from the hotel. I followed. They shot my tires out back there. Afterwards, that bastard Renko chased me halfway across the Swiss Alps—"

"What 'as 'appened to your 'and?"

"One of the Russian's bullets. I'm lucky. Anyway, I sorted him out, got back to the road down there, and found the place they took Joe to—only it wasn't Joe, of course. A woman there, who says she trained as a nurse, fixed the hand. I saw the chopper on my way back down the road. I guessed you might not pick me out, so I got down to the car and hoped you'd see me."

Pentland leaned forward urgently.

"Now look, Maurice, Christ knows where the genuine Kenyon is at the moment. I must contact Briggs. I only hope Joe caught the flight and Briggs met him. But while I was out of the way, the Russians had an ideal opportunity to snatch him. I'm sure that's what they were working up to. It's probably why they used this Kenyon decoy—to lure our attentions elsewhere. Can you put this thing down at Monthey?"

"But David, London contacted me after you disappeared. Briggs 'ad been on to them to say that Joe Kenyon phoned from the 'otel when you failed to meet 'im. London asked me to search for you and to supply someone to cover Kenyon to Cointrin. There was no problem. The plane was delayed by fog, but Kenyon eventually left for London on it."

Pentland felt enormous relief. Briggs would have met Joe in London, in that case, and escorted him to Farnborough. Thank God for that. Then what the hell had the Soviets been up to, using a look-alike, and abducting him, if it was not to create an opportunity to snatch Joe? The only reason Pentland could think of was that the Russians had devised a red herring, to keep MI6 occupied in Switzerland while they did whatever they were planning to do back in the U.K. But if it *was* their intention to snatch Joe, why had they missed their prime opportunity—when the attaché was defenseless immediately after he, Pentland, had followed the bogus Joe up into the mountains? And Briggs would have no idea yet about this decoy operation. If the Soviets still had something up their sleeves, were they for some reason waiting for Joe to get to Farnborough? The whole thing still made no sense, as Pentland saw it.

"You're sure that Kenyon got on that plane?"

Fennel spread his big hands with a grin. "My man was there until they closed the gate. I am sure. You wish to go to the airport? We can go there directly. If necessary you could 'ire a plane for Angleterre, if it is urgent." Then Fennel raised his heavy eyebrows with a wide grin. "But why don't you stay? We could 'ave a few little drinks, *hein*? There are some good places you 'ave not seen. There is one with, mmm, the *most* beautiful girls, David, you 'ave no idea! We could 'ave—"

Pentland smiled and shook his head. He raised his right hand and waved it tiredly.

"There'll be another time, Maurice."

Fennel shrugged good-humoredly.

"You are getting old, David. No stamina!" Then he roared with laughter.

"You'll die of drink and women one day, you mad bugger," Pentland retorted.

"But I will die 'appy!" Fennel said, and turned to peer forward.

"Go for the airport, Maurice."

Fennel spoke to the pilot, who nodded.

Pentland sat back to think as the helicopter roared through the darkness. Were they waiting for Joe to get to Farnborough? This question plucked at Pentland's mind. Farnborough; the SR80—were they after all somehow after the SR80? But he and Briggs and Joe had already thrashed that one out, back in the safe-house in Battersea. Joe had been emphatic that there was no way for the Soviets to hijack the aircraft, because of the PCMS connection. But Allan Briggs had remained concerned about the possibility, he remembered. Was there, then, any way they might get at Lindley? Any possible way they could somehow intercept Lindley as he landed, and persuade him to leave again for Russia? No, he thought, it wasn't possible, and anyway the thrust of their attention had been directed at Joe, not Lindley. They had had no way to get at Lindley previously, incarcerated as the pilot had been for so long in the depths of the Mojave, surrounded by the best security the Defense Intelligence Agency could devise.

Joe—Farnborough—the SR80.

Pentland passed a weary hand through his hair and stared out into the darkness. Briggs, he decided; he must speak to Briggs. He had to know from Briggs that Kenyon was securely ensconced in the hotel at Farnborough, where the CIA man would be close by. Once the SR80 landed it would be well-protected by Farnborough security, and so would Lindley. No doubt the pilot would be whisked away to quarters at Greenham Common, where no one would have a hope at getting at him. But unless Joe was safe at Farnborough, who knew what the damned Russians were up to? He reached forward and tapped Maurice Fennel on the shoulder.

"Maurice, we've assumed that Kenyon got to London okay, but I need to be sure. Can you get this thing down somewhere so that I can make a call? I must talk to Briggs."

"But David, we shall arrive in Cointrin in twenty minutes."

"A lot can happen in twenty minutes."

"It is better I contact my office on the radio," Maurice said. "They can patch us through to London. The police, they are not pleased with you!" Fennel gave an explosive laugh. "They are *mad* with your driving. 'Ow else is it that I can find you 'ere in these mountains? Also, Avis—they wish to 'ave their car returned." Fennel shook his head. "*Non*, I think it is better not to be near the cops." He held up a hand briefly. "*Attendez un moment*, David."

Fennel turned away and fiddled with the radio on the console between him and the pilot, donned a headset, and for a few moments Pentland could see his lips moving. At one point he turned his head briefly, nodding enthusiastically, and a few moments later whipped off his headset and passed it back. Pentland quickly placed it over his head and adjusted the boom-mike.

"Who is this?" Pentland asked.

"This is the United States Embassy in London," the speaker replied.

"Put me through to Briggs, this is urgent. Over."

"I'm afraid Mr. Briggs is not in the office, sir." The male voice which crackled back over the radio on the patched-in telephone connection was faint, clear, unemotional, and uncommunicative.

"My name is David Pentland. I'm with British military intelligence. I have to contact Mr. Briggs on a matter of urgent national security—over."

The helicopter clattered on through the night, heading for Geneva, while Pentland fumed over the delay. Static hissed and crackled faintly in the background. Pentland pressed the earpieces close with both hands.

"Mr. Pentland, what is the subject of national security about which you are concerned? You will appreciate this is an open communication—over."

"I understand. I am in an aircraft in Switzerland. This concerns your attaché, Colonel Kenyon. I must, repeat must, speak with Allan Briggs. This is most urgent—over."

"I am afraid it will be impossible for you to speak with Mr. Briggs, sir. Mr. Briggs met with an accident a short while ago. He is unavailable. Over."

"You mean short-term—or long-term unavailable—over."

"Er—long-term, sir."

Oh my God, Pentland thought. He felt the blood run from his face and the hairs on the back of his neck prickle. Oh no, he thought, not Allan. Pentland knew he'd get nowhere with whoever this was on the other end. Briggs, if he could have talked to him, would have recognized his voice, but this official would probably already be kicking himself for giving away the information, such as it was, about Allan Briggs.

"I most urgently request you to contact my department on this number." He gave the number in Whitehall. "Tell them that I will be in touch with them immediately. Remain on the line with them and get hold of the next most senior official to Mr. Briggs. It will be necessary to discuss matters in a conference call, do you understand?—Over."

"I understand, sir."

"Good. Thank you. Over and out."

Pentland whipped the headset off and tapped Maurice on the shoulder. The lights of a few cars snaked along a road below them. The sky seemed lighter up ahead and Pentland realized that they were now out of the mountains and approaching the city.

"Maurice, that was useless. Except that something serious has happened to Allan Briggs. Can you get us patched through to MI6 in London? I've asked the U.S. Embassy guy I spoke with to phone the DO at Whitehall and stay on the line." He passed the headset back to the big Swiss, then looked at his watch.

It was just before one-fifteen.

CHAPTER ELEVEN

Joe Kenyon fell asleep in the hotel room at Farnborough in an irritable mood. Twice, while waiting for the fog to clear back at Cointrin Airport outside Geneva, he had phoned the house, and twice there had been no answer. Between the calls to Suzie he had expected Pentland to come hurrying in to the Departure Lounge at any moment, with some reasonable explanation of why he had so precipitately and inexplicably disappeared from the hotel. Not that the attaché had been overconcerned; he was used to these secret-service bodies behaving in what often amounted to unusual and peremptory fashion. But the fact that Suzie had not answered had worried him, until he realized that after Allan Briggs would have called her, she had probably telephoned Gail and arranged to go to a show, then stopped somewhere for a late supper afterwards. Still, he had nevertheless dropped to sleep uneasily, because of on top of that, the Bureau office at the embassy had told him Briggs was out, but that they expected to hear from him at any moment. Kenyon had called first from Heathrow, and then later from the hotel at Farnborough when he had arrived there by cab. But still no Briggs. It was unlike Briggs not to keep in touch, especially considering his concern with the Soviet photographing business. The whole thing left Kenyon feeling vaguely uneasy.

The plane from Geneva had eventually touched down at London after midnight, and although Joe had felt tempted to go home for the night, it would have meant a very early start the following morning to get to Farnborough early enough to catch up with things, and all in all he had decided to get to the airshow site, and sleep there, leaving word for a call at five-thirty, so that he would have time to get into the paperwork before the morning planning meetings. And he was hoping to squeeze time to have breakfast with Chuck Lindley, who would soon be sliding out of the night sky to land at Farnborough. It was going to be a short enough night as it was. The next few days were likely to be real hectic, Joe Kenyon thought wearily as he drifted off to sleep.

The next sensation of which Joe was aware, was that of lying in the sun on a very hot beach during a cloudless summer day, but he was painfully unable to shut his eyes. He was on his back and the sun beat down on him, searing his optic nerves, and he tried desperately to close his eyes, to no avail. He felt all the sensations of squeezing his eyelids shut, but it made no difference, and although he desperately tried to get his hands up to them to shade them, he was unable to move, and unable to tell anyone; and as in dreams of this kind, his limbs would obey no command of his brain and he felt a rising panic that the sun would burn through and fry his brain, shriveling the life from him in a dreadful agony. He tried to scream, but no sound issued from his mouth, and he woke up with sweat pouring from his body.

He knew he was awake now, realizing foggily that

the experience had been a dream, and that he was in fact in his hotel bed at Farnborough, but, unaccountably, a fierce light was still there, burning into his eyes, which were now squeezed shut in an instinctive reaction as his mind vacated the sensations of the dream.

And then a voice said, "Just lie still, Joe."

Someone was in his room, shining a powerful light directly into his eyes. For a brief moment Joe Kenyon did lay quite still with shock as he recognized the voice of Dimitri Olenko.

"The life of your wife is in very real danger, Joe," Olenko said, in what sounded to Kenyon a heavy, but convincing, monotone voice. Olenko continued before Joe could speak.

"There is with me here," Olenko continued, "a person employed by section thirteen of the KGB. As I am sure you will know, those employed by this section are a law unto themselves—"

Still Joe said nothing. However, he knew what Dimitri meant. Dimitri was telling him that there was a *mokrie dela* man in this room, who would have no compunctions about ending his life if he should think this necessary.

Joe tried to keep his eyes open, but was forced to close them again against the searing impact of the concentrated beam.

"For the moment, lie still, Joe, while I explain why it is that this man and I are in your room at this time."

"Get that fucking light out of my eyes, Dimitri, for Christ's sake, will you?"

"Joe, I regret to tell you that Zuzie is being held by other members of the same section of the First Main Directorate, and she will be severely harmed unless you do precisely what I tell you to do."

"*What!* Dimitri, what the fuck do you think

218

ou're—?"

Another voice, heavily accented, came out of the darkness behind the brilliant light shining in Joe Kenyon's eyes.

"Is necessary you remain still, as Comrade Olenko has instructed," the voice hissed. "If you do not, within minutes very painful thing will occur to your woman—"

"Dimitri!" Joe cried. "Get this hoodlum—"

"Joe, please! You must be quiet. You must *listen*. I want no harm to come to you or Suzie. But I can assure you great harm will be done to her unless you cooperate—"

"Cooperate! Olenko, you've just talked yourself into a pile of shit which is likely to result in serious repercussions for you, my friend—"

"Joe, you may not believe it, but I am your friend. I am also an instrument of my government, however, and my career and the life of my own wife are at stake. You *must* listen to me, because I *am* your friend."

"What have you bastards *done* with Suzie? Where is she? You talk of cooperation! Shit, I'll have both you sons of bitches thrown in *jail*—"

"It is nearly one o'clock in the morning, Joe. At one-thirty the SR80 is due to land. You will go over to the airfield to meet it, and your friend Lindley, and you will ask Lindley if you may sit in the aircraft for a moment for old time's sake, and then you will start the engines and fly the aircraft to the Soviet Union—to my base at Berezniky—"

"Dimitri, Dimitri! You goddamned, fucking stupid Russian," Joe half-laughed, half-sneered. "I couldn't even get the *canopy* shut, let alone start the engines! Jesus! I wouldn't have a chance of getting *close* to the aircraft. The place will be stiff with security, don't you understand? Now, look, you've made an impossible goof, Dimitri. Back out while you still can. The worst that could happen after this is a quick trip back to Mother Russia, right? Now, what the hell do you *mean* Suzie's in danger? You must be *nuts*, Dimitri. You've made a massive error of judge—"

"This man here is holding a telephone connected to the place where your wife is being held by the KGB," Olenko said quietly. "If he should choose to give the order, they will start on Zuzie's fingers. The beginning, only, after which they will do much worse things, do you not *understand*! Please, Joe, do not *risk* these things for only an aircraft—"

"For *only* an aircraft! Dimitri, the SR80 represents the highest state of the art in aircraft and systems technology that my country is capable of, and you laughingly suggest that I get out of bed, climb in, and fly it to fucking Russia! I mean, am I dreaming, or something? Do you—"

Joe was interrupted by a tiny scream from the darkness. A woman's voice in a ululation of pain, a tiny little sound as though made by a Tom Thumb-sized figure, but in its way a shocking, paralyzing noise in the room.

"What was *that*? What the fuck was that! Oh, no, Dimitri, that wasn't *Suzie*—it couldn't have been Suzie—" Then he remembered that there had been no answer from the house, no answer from Briggs—and Pentland had disappeared—

"Dimitri!" Joe whispered, and then he came out of the bed like a madman, his mouth wide open to begin a scream of abuse, reaching for the Russian, but before he was able to make a sound the fist of the section-thirteen man drove accurately into his plexus and evacuated every morsel of breath from his body;

220

he collapsed in a writing, pajama-clad, breath-whooping heap back onto the bed in the glare of the powerful light. Then, seconds later, he heard Olenko start to talk again.

Joe could only lay doubled up and listen, as he struggled to fill his lungs with air and tried to prevent himself from vomiting on the bed.

"All will be lost, Joe, if you should attract attention to this room. I must assure you your wife will die. You will *never* see her again. You must believe me." He paused, unseen in the darkness. Joe had seen neither man since he woke from the dream in the beam of the flashlight. Something about Olenko's voice chilled him. Olenko seemed to be pleading with him, also terribly concerned about what might happen to Suzie. Oh God, Kenyon thought. And she's pregnant! If they abuse her she could miscarry, and their hopes for the future would once again be dashed. Was it really his wife he had heard scream over the telephone line?

"You prove it, Dimitri," he at last managed to past. "How—do I—know that's my wife—you—bastards have on the other of that—phone. Jesus! I thought you were a decent—man, you fucking Soviet *savage*—"

"It *was* Zuzie, Joe. It was—"

"*Where?* Where *is* she? For the sake of all that's *human*, leave her out of this. Dimitri, you *know* her, you *like* her, for Christ's sake. She likes *you*, man, don't you realize? How could you involve yourself in such—"

Joe felt himself beginning to break, and made a massive effort to pull himself together.

"Where is she, Olenko?" he asked eventually, in a monotone.

"I cannot tell you that. But if you do as I ask, I can assure you that she will be unharmed, and will be safely conducted to London as soon as you arrive in Berezniky."

"You and Natalia have two little girls. Two daughters. That's right, isn't it, Dimitri?"

Olenko coughed in the darkness. His voice was husky as he replied.

"Yes," he whispered. "Yes," he repeated more strongly. "But—"

"Suzie and I have no children, Dimitri. We have been trying to have a child since we were married. Oh, Christ," he whispered. "And now, at long last, my wife is pregnant. Three months pregnant. If she is badly treated she could have a miscarriage. If she has a miscarriage again, the doctors say, she will never have a child. Never, Dimitri." Joe's voice broke. "Never—"

"Then, for her sake and your sake—and yes, for mine, too—please do as I ask." There was a short silence in the room. The beam of the light held by the *mokrie dela* man never wavered from Joe's face as he stared in the direction of Olenko's voice.

"I want to talk to her," Joe said, finally.

Olenko said something in Russian to the unseen KGB hitman. There was a muttered reply and scuffled movement.

"Reach out your hand, Joe," Olenko said.

Joe felt the cold plastic of the telephone receiver. He took it and placed it to his ear, his lips resting on the mouthpiece.

"Suzie?" he said. But the word came out as a husky whisper. He cleared his throat. "Suzie?" he said again.

For a moment there was only the hiss of the carrier wave in the earpiece, and then he heard his wife's voice, tiny and distant on the line.

"Oh *Joe*," she cried. "Joe, is that you? Joe, I don't

know where I am. They've got me—" her voice was muffled, then he heard her cry out.

"Joe, they won't let me *tell* you—" her voice came back, broken and tearful.

"Suzie, Suzie," Joe said, trying to calm her, clutching the instrument with both hands. "Do as they tell you. Don't give them cause to hurt you. We'll have you out of this soon—"

"Joe, what's going *on*? They came to the house and—" Her voice was smothered again. Seconds later she was back. "I feel bad, darling," she cried. "I'm so worried about—about—about—" She couldn't get it out. "Oh, *Joe*, please do something—"

The phone was snatched from Joe's hands. He lashed out and felt his fist land on someone's body. There was an answering gasp and a hiss of invective in Russian, which he heard a microsecond before he received a blow in the mouth, which brought blood from his lip and slammed him back onto the bed. Once again, Joe Kenyon found himself gasping with pain and lying on the bed, dazed. He heard Olenko's voice hammering away at the KGB man, and knew enough Russian to realize that Olenko was telling the other man that to beat Joe up would be to risk the whole operation.

Then Olenko was speaking in English again, addressing him.

"Joe, no one is aware of this. Your MI6 friend is still in Switzerland. I am afraid he is dead by now. Your CIA man is also dead. No trails lead to you here. The deadline is two o'clock in the morning. Oh-two-hundred," he repeated. "If you are not in the air in the SR80 at that time, the people holding your wife have instructions to terminate her. Or, I should say, unless they hear from me that you have done as we have asked, they will obey instructions from my

223

masters, who have no consideration for Zuzie's well-being. It is beyond my control. There is nothing I am able to do that will change this, you must understand. You must choose between your wife, and this *Americanski spion samolot*," he finished, lapsing into Russian. "Now, it is one o'clock. Lindley will land in thirty minutes. Then you must be there. You must be there so that you can climb into the cockpit while the ladder is still there for him, and you must move the aircraft before they put the covers on and put the chocks at the wheels."

"I can't fly the fucking thing," Joe said hopelessly. "To fly it, I need a special catheter inserted into my wrist vein. How the hell do you think I can get that fitted without giving the game away, huh?"

"What do you mean, a cath—cath—?"

"Catheter. I must be connected to the PCMS computer intravenously. Or I couldn't even close the canopy. Like I told you, it won't work, Olenko. There's no way. No hope. This thing is like no other airplane. You've failed, and if what you tell me about what is arranged for Suzie is accurate, and any harm comes to her, I will kill you slowly, Dimitri, and afterwards I will find a way to go to Russia, and then I'll kill Natalia. You better *believe* me, Dimitri Olenko. You destroy my life, and I'll sure as hell destroy yours."

No one spoke. Noises occasionally came from the still-open line connecting the room to wherever they had Suzie. Joe was conscious of the breathing of the three of them. Then the KGB man asked Olenko a question in Russian. Olenko told him to shut up in a bitter tone.

"Joe, what is the connection in the plane? What instrument accepts the tube from your vein?"

"A small needle in the armrest."

"Then you could insert this needle directly into your own vein, could you not?"

It would be possible, he supposed, he'd already thought of that. But he was using the hiatus as an opportunity to try to find a way out of the horrible choice he would have to make in the next few minutes. Once they had the SR80 in the Soviet Union, and with it, they would take the plane to pieces, and they would take *him* to pieces, or certainly his mind. If he ever got back to the West he'd be little better than a vegetable, and a trial for treason would await him, with execution an inevitable result for such a transgression. The United States had every right to expect him to say "no" and sacrifice his wife. He was an air force officer with the highest security clearance possible, a very valuable man in his country's armed forces, with knowledge of supreme value about a number of matters of even greater value to the Soviets. What a prize, he thought. But how in hell could he face himself if he sacrificed his wife? It was *impossible* for him to even address the thought in the first place. Even as he asked himself, he knew it was an academic question, because he also knew—despite whatever oath of allegiance and secrecy he had signed—he would rather lose his life than give Suzie up in exchange for the secrets of the SR80. His life, if somehow he sacrificed her, would be a continuing self-recriminating hell, during which he was sure he would become mad. A hell on earth.

"It is possible," Joe said finally in answer to Olenko's question, "unless they've changed the hookup since I last flew the aircraft."

"Ah! Good!" There was enormous relief in Olenko's voice. "So, you will enter Soviet air space only at Murmansk. You will fly west of the Scandinavian Peninsula, turning south when you are beyond Nord Kapp in Norway. Then, you will fly directly southeast to Berezniky. This course will allow you to stay reasonably clear of NATO aircraft, and of course you will use the aircraft's ECM equipment to avoid any attempt they may make to shoot you down. You understand of course they *will* attempt this?"

"Yes," Joe said dully.

"You will use every feature of the aircraft to avoid contact, of course. This should not be so difficult. Predecessors of this aircraft are able to transit the Soviet Union with impunity. Therefore, it is not possible you will have a problem with NATO aircraft, I think."

"How the hell would you know?" Joe retorted.

"Joe, you are a good pilot. You know your aircraft, and all the tricks. I am confident. And you will make a strong effort, yes? To save the life of Zuzie," he finished quietly.

"What guarantee do I have that she will be brought home and set free?"

"You have my word, Joe."

"Shit, Olenko! Your word means nothing to me. Nothing!"

"You and I will be together for a while at Berezniky, Joe. I will bring you proof that Suzie is safe before you answer one question there. When the aircraft is on the ground safely at Berezniky, she will be immediately released, and in the meantime, good care will be taken of her."

Joe desperately forced his mind to work. Olenko had mentioned nothing about a deadline for arrival at Berezniky. How long would it take him to get there? His mental picture of the route—due north to Scotland, then across to Norway, around the North Cape,

and then to Murmansk and southeast to the Urals—
worked out to about two thousand five hundred miles.
Flat-out with no problems he could do that in an
hour, for Christ's sake! But he could loiter, he
thought. He could stretch that, perhaps to three or
four hours. The Soviets would expect NATO to make
an all-out effort to shoot him down before he got to
Soviet airspace. The powers would order it. So he
could reasonably claim time wasted in avoidance.

What it boiled down to was that he had less than an
hour now to hope for some possible change in the
situation. There was no way that he could foresee the
situation *could* change, though. But time was his only
ally at this point. Once he left the ground, if he should
be so lucky as to even manage that, at least he would
then have four hours in which to think, and *something*
could change to his advantage in that time. There had
to be something . . .

"Once you are in the air, of course, you are forbid-
den to cry for help. The minute you do so, it will be as
if you have broken this agreement. It is possible that
we shall not know this, but if it appears to us that you
have made contact and that our safety is in jeopardy,
or our current situations or relationships as diplomats
in London change in the slightest, you will be blamed,
and your wife will die. You understand?"

Olenko looked at his watch.

"I sincerely wish you luck. It is time, I think, that
you should prepare yourself and go to the airfield. We
shall leave you now. I will see you next at Berezniky,
yes?"

"I'll be glad to see the back of you, Olenko. It is
little wonder to me that your administration sees the
necessity to build walls around your country to keep
people in. If you took your walls down you'd be left
with a wilderness. After meeting you, I was prepared

227

to revise this cliché. I'm not now. Good faith seems to be a meaningless term in the Soviet. You live in fear of people like this thug you brought into my room. You're no better yourself. Get lost, now."

"Joe," Olenko started quietly. "Joe, I—"

"I said, get lost. Get out. Leave while you're ahead. Leave."

The beam of the flashlight retreated to the door, still shining directly into Joe Kenyon's face. There was a small click as the door opened, then the light went out, and another click as the door closed, then silence in the room.

"Oh, my God," Joe said to himself.

After the door clicked shut and silence descended on the hotel bedroom, Joe Kenyon sat slumped on the side of the bed in his pajamas. He was unable to move, even to reach across to switch on the reading lamp at the side of the bed. And so he sat in darkness, pitch-black and soundless, while the hotel slept around him. His mind raced, but with all the effectiveness of a beam of light trapped inside a diamond prism. He felt drained, paralyzed, only able to remember with any clarity the sound of that tiny scream as the flashlight beat at his eyes, and the timbre of Olenko's accented baritone voice. A part of him realized that his lip had swollen and his stomach was sore deep inside from the blows of the section-thirteen man. But another part of his mind kept visualizing the tiny fetus deep and warm within his wife, which one day would grow into perhaps a son of whom he could be proud; who he would take fishing in his later years, and watch him grow up and learn, and become accomplished, while he and Suzie settled into the warm autumn of their lives.

Now, at a stroke, those dreams were ruined, smashed into a thousand shards, never to be reassembled, because if he took the aircraft to the Soviet Union the Russians might keep their promise to return him to the United States, but as what? No more than a human vegetable to those who knew him, stripped of self-respect, and confidence, shunned by his friends in the service as a traitor. And there would be the endless interrogation by his own people, so they could know what information he had released to the Soviets, and what information, little though it would be, that he might have learned from his experience. And it would be a short, miserable existence, because then would come the trial for treason, and it would be a miracle if he was not executed At best, he would serve years in prison, to be released in his old age to the winter of his life.

On the other hand, he could walk away, remain loyal to the Service to which he had given his efforts over all these years, which had rewarded him with its trust in his test-flying years, and then as a senior diplomat to the air force, and the strong likelihood of general rank when the term was concluded. What would he be then, he wondered? A cold hero about whom it would be whispered that he had somehow managed to put his loyalty to his country before his wife, choosing to *sacrifice* her to prevent the transfer of secrets to the enemy of the United States. Yes, he thought, his country would reward him well for that. From then on he would be trusted like no other man. No other in the Service would have proven his loyalty and trust to such an extent.

But his wife would be dead, and the fetus would be dead—and he knew he would be dead. As good as dead, and how much better than death could that be? Worse, because there would be no forgetting.

The only choice was to allow his wife to live, and bear the child. It could only be that which he could rely on over the next hours. He lit a cigarette with trembling fingers in the darkness and concentrated on his memory of Suzie's face, and how he imagined his son would look in her arms. Olenko was right. He could not risk her.

He stood up from the bed, realizing that his only remaining asset was time, and only then if he was successful in leaving the ground with the SR80. The thought forced him to look at his watch. It was nearly ten minutes past one. Lindley would arrive in twenty minutes. They would have phoned him if there was going to be any change in schedule, he knew. The great black aircraft would slide out of the night sky over southern England in twenty minutes, and Chuck Lindley would set her down like a feather on Farnborough's long runway exactly on the half-hour, because Lindley was that way, the way all test pilots were: exact. Lindley could be absolutely relied on, Joe thought.

He laid the cigarette in an ashtray and pulled on trousers, soft shoes, a T-shirt, and a wool sweater. The night air was warm. He went silently from the hotel.

Since he had no car, it was fortunate that the security area for the Farnborough Air Show was on the side of the airport nearest the village. The guarded entrance gate was no more than ten minutes walk from the hotel. The small side street by the hotel was dark and silent; there was no traffic at this hour. Between the biannual shows, the small town was ordinary and unnoticed, clustered close to the famous airfield where so many new aircraft over the last couple of decades had shown their paces to astonish the world.

Joe turned out onto the main road, which ran along

the boundary of the airfield. The high, wire security fence was hidden from the road by higher hedges, which now loomed up beside him. The main runway paralleled the hedge, with the hangar buildings, public enclosures, and empty grandstands visible in the darkness on the far side of the field.

As he walked, Joe thought of when it had started, with the night photography from the wood below David Pentland's cottage, during the weekend when they had all gone down to Wiltshire and had such a good time. He groaned aloud as he realized there would be no more days like those. Why hadn't he taken David more seriously? And later, both Pentland and Allan Briggs in the safe-house. He had resisted them, considered them melodramatic, had even convinced himself, in spite of their warnings, that it was Olenko who was vulnerable in London, not him. And what on earth had happened to David in Geneva? He remembered then with fresh shock what Olenko had said—that Pentland was dead, and so was Briggs. Until this moment he had not believed Olenko—believing it to be some subterfuge of the Russian to persuade him. But now he realized that there would be no advantage to the Russian in telling him unless it were the truth.

As he approached the security gate he felt like a condemned man. But that's what I am, he thought, a condemned man.

"Yes, sir." The security sergeant stood before Joe at the small gate in the high fence, the guard building looming beyond with yellow light showing in the windows. He wanted to blurt out to this English army sergeant all the details of his dilemma. He wanted to go with the man inside the warmth of the guard hut and sip tea, and tell them all about it, so that they could swing into action and arrest Olenko and the *mokrie dela* man, and then he could be left alone to get on—Christ. What was he thinking?

"Sir?" the sergeant inquired again, a sharpness in his tone.

Joe fumbled for his security pass and ID.

"Sorry, sergeant," he said hoarsely. He forced a grin. "Still feel sleepy. Had to get up to meet the aircraft."

The guard looked the pass and ID over carefully in the light of a torch.

"Pass on through, Colonel Kenyon, sir," he said, coming to attention and saluting.

"Thank you sergeant," Joe murmured, and walked through into the security enclosure.

As he approached the open side facing the runway, close to the refueling pits and maintenance sheds, he noticed the place was stiff with U.S. Marines strolling unobtrusively and standing in the deep shadows of buildings, heavily armed and wearing full battle dress.

He heard the growling voice of the crew chief, a man who was well known to him, and whose team had been a permanent fixture at Farnborough over the years.

"Good evening, Sergeant Harris," he said as he walked clear of the buildings.

The sergeant peered at him in the poor light from lamps scattered on the sides of various buildings. They cast more shadow than light, Joe thought.

"Colonel Kenyon, sir!" the chief exclaimed. "Come to see our boy arrive, have you, sir?"

"Yeah," Joe said. "He's an old friend. Where you parking him, huh?"

"This side of those two F-16s, sir. We'll leave the aircraft outside for the night. That way we can keep a better eye on her. There's enough men here to hold hands all the way round her." Thank God for that, Joe thought.

"Maloney's not coming across, is he?"

Joe was glad that Maloney did not appear to be around. The SR80 chief knew too much about the bird, and Joe was counting on complete surprise to get him away from the security area before anyone realized what was happening. He felt the adrenalin begin to course into his bloodstream at the thought. The September night air was cool, but he could feel sweat on his brow.

"No, sir. Only if we have a problem we can't beat. And that's never happened yet, sir," Harris smiled.

"Okay," Joe said. "Good to see you, sergeant."

Harris saluted. "And you, sir. No flying this year, I guess?"

Joe forced a grin. "Only a goddamn desk," he said as he walked away.

Two hours after leaving the ranch, responding to the programmed course-plot, Dracula's computer clacked quietly to itself, initiating the PCMS program to sip Lindley's blood. The curve of the earth's horizon, pronounced at this altitude, was lighting up brightly in anticipation of an approaching dawn that had only given way to night an hour ago.

The SR80 was dawdling at mach three, one hundred and twenty thousand feet above the surface, with the ECM antiradar extended to a radius of seven hundred miles. The ident lights on the immensely sensitive bank of transponders had not reacted once to any probing radar emissions from friend or foe. As a result, while the great black aircraft slid through the thin upper atmosphere guided by its autopilot, there had been nothing for Lindley to do. However, he had instructed the computer to alert him every thirty minutes just to be sure that Dracula understood there was a human aboard who was ultimately responsible, and now, as the PCMS solicitously touched his blood with a tiny dose of benzedrine—no more stimulation actually than Lindley would have received from a good strong cup of coffee, which he craved—the pilot adjusted the acceleration couch to semi-sitting, yawned, and peered from the cockpit at the white landscape of Greenland passing below.

As he looked out, the engines changed their note in a subtle way to a shade-lower pitch and Dracula's needle-nose lowered slightly down to the horizon. At the same time the aircraft banked gently but steeply to the right, and over a distance of nearly fifty miles, altered course for a point well south of Iceland, well clear of the Air Defense Identification Zone of the volcanic island. Not that anyone on duty at military radar screens in Keflavik would have seen anything, but why lope into someone else's airspace if you didn't have to, Lindley thought. In fact, Dracula was beginning her descent, activated by the computer, for the British Isles.

Lindley glanced at the chronometer in the panel, which had automatically adjusted for British summer time on its outer local-time scale. It read nine minutes to one o'clock in the morning, which left thirty-nine minutes to get to England and slide down the approach to Farnborough. Echoing his own thoughts, the computer reduced the power settings even further, and the mach scale dropped back to a little over twice the speed of sound. There was no point in an early arrival. They wouldn't be ready for him, and if he'd said that he'd touch down at oh-one-thirty, then by gosh that was when the tires would burn Farnborough's runway. "Pre-cisely," Lindley said to himself by way of diversion, his voice strangely loud in the almost-silent cockpit.

The east coast of Greenland rapidly slid to the rear, giving way to dark ocean liberally sprinkled with patches of ice, looking like unmelted snowflakes from this height, but undoubtedly large icebergs drifting down to the southern limit of the ice pack for this time of the year. In another month, he thought, this whole ocean would be a white waste cowering below the great katabatic storms that swept down from Greenland's icecap, snarling into the low troughs of the warmer Atlantic and bringing the first cold storms of approaching winter to the European continent. The thought made him shiver.

Fifteen minutes later, the coast of Iceland showed on the screens, eighty miles or so to the north, and once again, in accordance with the great circle route, and smack on the twenty-second meridian, Dracula banked steeply to the right and headed southeast, now on a beeline for Northern Ireland. From there she would slip south between Ireland and England, down across the Isle of Man, over the mountains of Wales, before making a shallow left turn to approach Farnborough from the west.

Lindley eyed the outside skin temperature, which had begun to drop with the reduction in airspeed. Twelve minutes after leaving Iceland, the aircraft came up on the Shanwick ADIZ, still at an altitude of eighty thousand feet and a speed of mach two, and Lindley was obliged to report his position.

"Shannon, Shannon, Shannon," he murmured into the tiny microphone, a hair's breadth from his lip. "Shannon, Shannon—Blackbird—position." "Blackbird" was a lie, but how could he explain? He smiled as he waited for the reply.

"Blackbird, this is Shannon; go ahead your

235

position."

"Blackbird—position six one zero zero North, one eight zero zero west, at zero one zero nine, flight level eight zero zero. Estimate Belfast at zero one one eight, over."

"Blackbird, say again your flight level?"

Lindley grinned.

"Er, eight zero zero, sir."

"Jesus, what are you, Blackbird?" Then, before Lindley could reply, the man at the radar facility in Shannon gasped over the air and said, "Say again your speed, Blackbird!"

"Estimate position Belfast at oh one one eight. Er, speed approximately one six seven five knots, over. Aircraft description classified until Farnborough tomorrow," he added with another grin.

"Roger, Blackbird, er—have a good trip, sir."

"Thanks, Shannon."

Lindley now switched off the ECM and extended the contact radar search to maximum, turning up the audio warning system and, as a precaution, keying the computer to advise of any signals that might appear on an intercept range. The PCMS immediately cranked up Lindley's awareness, construing from this instruction to the computer that he expected trouble.

As the aircraft dropped lower, night fell again, the high dawn dropping back below the curved rim of a dark-blue earth, and in sympathetic reaction the rheostats on the instrument panel raised the intensity of the lights.

A hundred miles north of a dark Ireland, Lindley reported his position to Belfast, then contacted London Control, at the same time reducing his speed to mach one point five and dropping down to forty thousand feet to further cool the aircraft in preparation for landing.

In quick succession, Northern Ireland passed unseen to his right, then the Isle of Man below, and Lindley reduced speed to subsonic. London then contacted him and vectored him for an approach to Farnborough from the west, and he swung to port over the Bristol Channel, loafing along at four hundred knots and dropping down to twenty thousand feet. At Bristol he began the descent to ten thousand and cut the speed to three hundred, and ten minutes later rolled out some flap and slowed the aircraft for the final approach.

It was one twenty-six.

CHAPTER TWELVE

Gail strode restlessly around the small sitting room of the mews house. She felt anxious, tired, and not a little angry. Speedy Gonzales received short shrift as he followed her, trying to rub himself against her ankles.

What a bloody awful evening, she thought.

First, David doesn't show up, and no word from him; then Suzie Kenyon behaves strangely, to say the least. An American agent descends on her and rushes off leaving her with the ghastly thought that there could be an impostor at the Kenyons' house. He had promised to call.

Why *didn't* he call?

She kept eyeing the telephone with an urge to call Suzie. Don't call her, Briggs had instructed, wait until you hear from me.

By now she was no longer prepared to believe that Suzie Kenyon was missing and that whoever had taken her had left someone who looked like her in her place. It was too preposterous. After all, perhaps Suzie *did* enjoy a scotch when she was by herself—and perhaps she *did* smoke then. Sometimes people did things and behaved not as you would expect them to, she thought. Who really knew what went on deep in someone's mind? And she reminded herself that Suzie *was* pregnant. Women developed odd obsessions during pregnancy. Perhaps scotch and cigarettes were Suzie Kenyon's pregnancy obsessions, and she and Briggs had overreacted.

But these thoughts provided no real relief from her anxiety.

Just before one o'clock she decided to phone Briggs. She hurried to the telephone and dialed the embassy, asking to be put through to the CIA man.

"May I say who is calling?" a female voice answered.

"Tell him it's Gail Seldon. He was with me earlier."

"Just a moment, please."

"Mrs. Seldon?" a male voice said.

"*Miss* Seldon," Gail corrected. It wasn't Briggs.

"Did you say that Mr. Briggs was with you this evening?"

"Yes. Who am I talking to, please?"

"My name is Anderson. I work in the same office as Mr. Briggs."

"Good!" Gail said. "Then perhaps I could speak to him."

"I'm afraid not. Mr. Briggs has had an accident."

"What! Is he all right? He was here only an hour or so ago. I was expecting him to call."

"On what subject, Miss Seldon?"

"Well, as a matter of fact it was about Mrs. Kenyon, the attaché's wife. I—Mr. Briggs—is he all *right*?" Gail felt a cold feeling in her stomach. Could the accident have happened to Briggs in connection with Suzie Kenyon?

"Miss Seldon, would you mind if I came by? It's very important."

"Well, I—when?" she stumbled, now very alarmed.

"Right now," Anderson said.

"All right," she said. Oh God, she thought. What

was happening?

"Your address?"

She gave it to him. "Mrs. Kenyon," she said, "is she all right?"

But only a dialing tone answered.

Damn, she thought. She stood still by the telephone for a few moments while Speedy Gonzales wrapped himself around her ankles and purred; then she went to make some more coffee.

Anderson was a tall, spare American with short-cropped hair, in his early thirties, with blue eyes and a freckled complexion. He looked very tired, even in the shadows outside the open door to her mews cottage. She felt bloody tired herself, she thought, as she asked him to come in. It seemed to be an evening for playing hostess to American security people, and being stood up.

"Come in, Mr. Anderson. You rang off before I could ask you if Mrs. Kenyon was all right. Is she?" she asked anxiously as Andrews walked past her into the sitting room.

"Yes, I'm sure she is, Miss Seldon," Anderson said. "Until half an hour ago, just before you called, I was sitting in a car outside the Kenyons' house. No one left, and no one arrived. Mr. Briggs saw her earlier, and she was all right then. The reason I am here is that—"

"But Mr. Anderson. Didn't Mr. Briggs *tell* you about Mrs. Kenyon!"

"Miss Seldon, Mr. Briggs is dead," the agent said tiredly. "He was murdered very close to your place, in Stanton Street. I assume, now that we know he visited you, it happened just after he left you."

Gail sat down heavily on the sofa, her face white.

"Somebody *knew*," she whispered. "Somebody

240

knew that Mr. Briggs had found out about Suzie, and *killed* him for it! Oh my God!''

"Miss Seldon," Anderson leaned toward her. "What's this about a Suzie? What are you talking about—?"

"Suzie *Kenyon!*" Gail shouted in frustration. "I've been trying to tell you! Briggs came to see me because he thought there was something odd about Suzie Kenyon when he saw her earlier!"

She stood up and paced jerkily around the room, her robe flying out as she told Anderson about Briggs' visit and how he'd left in a hurry to get to Brompton Square.

"Something *has* happened to Suzie! Someone's taken her. And—oh my God—she's pregnant! Why didn't I *go* there? I should have *gone* there—"

"Jesus!" Anderson breathed. "Oh, Jesus!"

He whipped a small radio from beneath his jacket.

"Zero-Two—Base," he said with his mouth against the small black instrument.

"Go ahead Two," a tinny little voice replied.

"Contact One-Two, tell him to penetrate the Kenyon place to confirm the status of Mrs. Kenyon. There is reason to believe that some woman is substituting for Mrs. Kenyon. Hold her. I'll be there," he glanced at his watch, "in ten minutes. Confirm."

"Will do. Stand by Two," the voice added. "We just had a contact from Switzerland. Someone called Pentland—says he's with the Brits, matter of national security. Wants us to contact the Brit DO for a conference."

"Did he say *Pentland?*" Gail blurted out.

"Just a moment, Miss Seldon," Anderson said irritably. He turned his face back to the machine. "Say again—after 'contact.'"

"He asked us to contact the MI6 DO for a conference call—over."

"Base, get One-Two moving, then standby for me—over."

"Will do—out."

Anderson turned to her. "What did you say just then?"

"I'm sorry—" Gail pushed a hand through her hair. "The person you were talking to mentioned someone called Pentland, in Switzerland. I was expecting someone called Pentland to return from Switzerland, tonight." She smiled. "It was just a coincidence, I expect."

"Does he work for British intelligence?"

She looked startled. "Well, he never *said* he did. He said he worked for the government, though."

"Christ," Anderson said. "Something's moving. I'd better get hold of Colonel Kenyon. Excuse me for a moment." Andrews turned back to his tiny transmitter.

"Zero-Two—Base."

"Go ahead, Two."

"Get hold of Colonel Kenyon. He'll be at Farnborough. Tell him—*Jesus!*—tell him we might need him to identify his wife!"

"You have a number?—over."

"Negative. Check Briggs's desk."

"Will do."

"And Base!—check tonight's contact code for a call to the MI6 DO, and advise. I'll contact from here—over."

"Stand-by Two. Out."

Anderson took a packet of cigarettes from his suit pocket and lit one absently, not noticing that Gail was doing the same thing. She sat on the sofa, while the CIA man leaned on the back of a chair opposite, looking thoughtfully at his machine. She was desperate to hear news of Suzie Kenyon. And *could* it have been David who had contacted the Americans from Switzerland? What on earth was going on?

"Base—Two, come in."

"This is Two, go ahead," Anderson said quickly.

"The Brit DO code name this date is Simon, repeat, Simon. The number to call is three seven one, one two one six. Item. One-Two reports Mrs. Kenyon missing. The house is unoccupied, repeat, unoccupied. One-Two is returning to base. Over."

Anderson swore.

Gail rose from the sofa, about to exclaim. Anderson waved her quiet and she subsided. Anderson was talking on the machine again.

"What about the Colonel?"

"He's not in his room, but the hotel confirms he checked in at twelve-fifteen. Over."

Gail saw that Anderson's face was now white with strain. Everything was happening at once. First, Suzie missing, now Joe. And poor Mr. Briggs. God, she thought, I wish David was here.

Joe found himself close to the open doorway of the maintenance crew room. Light spilled from the doorway and he could hear a murmur of voices. There was enough light where he stood for him to check his watch. It said one twenty-six. Four minutes. His heart began to pound. There was a VHF transceiver in the crew room so that the crew chief could monitor aircraft movements, particularly Farnborough Ground Control, and the radio crackled now as Chuck Lindley's laconic voice contacted London Approach Control.

"London—Sierra Romeo Eight-Zero at nine thousand, DME four three west."

Forty-three miles, Joe thought. A few seconds now. He tried to work out the exact time in his mind. It

243

wouldn't make any difference. Lindley would touch down at exactly one-thirty.

London Approach switched Lindley to Farnborough Tower.

"Eight-Zero, contact Farnborough Tower on one eight decimal five. Good evening."

"Evening and thanks, London," Lindley murmured. There was a pause as he switched frequency and spoke to Farnborough.

"Farnborough Tower, Sierra Romeo Eight-Zero is two six DME west for landing."

"Evening Eight-Zero," Farnborough replied. "This is Farnborough Tower; you are cleared for a straight-in to runway seven, QFE one zero one three millibars, wind calm, no other traffic, report final."

People began to move out of the hut toward the open area near runway seven, and a few seconds later Joe heard a distant high-pitched whine above a muted roar in the calm night air.

Panic clutched at his chest at the sound, and he found it difficult to breathe. Now that he was here, waiting, he believed it impossible to step into the SR80's cockpit, ram his wrist onto the PCMS needle, hit the start buttons, and roar off into the night. The place was buzzing with people: American and British air force officers and men, maintenance crews, and armed marines. What the hell would they do, he thought with horror, when they realized he was in the process of stealing the most closely guarded secret of the United States perhaps since the Manhattan Project—the ultimate in America's aeronautical and electronics technology? Would they shoot? Would they became desperate and ram a vehicle into the aircraft's landing gear as he blasted away from the apron? There were any number of possibilities.

The only faint chance he might have, he told himself

in an effort to boost his thin morale, was that no one would expect a test-pilot of the United States Air Force, who was also an American attaché to England, to steal the aircraft. It would be impossible for them to conceive that he would plan to depart for the Soviet Union in order to hand the plane to the Russians on a plate. That factor alone might give him a small period of time to get clear. They would wait to talk to him on the radio, try to talk him back down; assume that he had gone off his rocker, and that they would be able to make him see sense—perhaps, he thought. And that presupposed he could even get the canopy shut.

Then a new thought gripped his guts like cold steel. Supposing the chief advised Lindley to switch-off well clear, with the intention of towing the aircraft in, or alternatively, Lindley might switch-off with the nose close to some obstruction. Dracula possessed no reverse thrust—there was no way to back her up.

Oh God, he thought, there were endless possibilities to prevent him from getting clear. He should have thought of these things back in the hotel room, and used them to persuade Olenko that the whole thing would be a disaster. But then he realized that Olenko would have considered these factors. And Joe remembered that the Russian's own career was on the line. Olenko had told him this—had told him that if he failed, Natalia would be lost to him. So, like Joe, Olenko was forced to trust to Joe, and luck, as much as he, Joe, was now in the hands of fate.

Joe's agonizing thoughts were eclipsed by an ear-splitting whine and a vibrating roar that shook the ground beneath his feet as his friend Chuck Lindley brought the SR80 over the fence from the west and goosed the throttles momentarily to kill the descent and touch Dracula's wheels down on the numbers as light as thistledown.

It was exactly one-thirty.

The long black aircraft hurtled past from right to left, her needle-nose dropping toward the runway. She disappeared from view with her tailpipes glowing plum-red in the darkness, the rest of her already invisible.

People around Joe cheered and broke out into excited conversation, splitting into small animated groups as they anticipated the reaction to the aircraft on her first showing to the public the next day.

Then Sergeant Harris was barking orders.

The rolling, extended ladder was pushed out by ratings toward the two F-16s squatting silently fifty yards to the left, and a military Land Rover departed with lights blazing to intercept Lindley on the taxiway and lead him back to the apron. The red, flashing FOLLOW ME was visible constantly as it grew smaller toward the end of the field.

Now Joe could hear the massive Pratt and Whitneys distantly spooling up as the pilot stroked the long aircraft back down the taxiway toward the maintenance area, toward him.

Joe lit a last cigarette with trembling fingers, quickly killing the lighter flame to prevent anyone close-by from catching a glimpse of the sweating agony of his features.

He still desperately hoped to wake up from this appalling nightmare—but the seconds sped past, and the noise of the aircraft rolling toward the pool of light on the apron grew increasingly loud, underlining the harsh reality.

Joe found himself willing Lindley not to close the canopy, willing him to park the aircraft with her nose pointing to the open darkness of the airfield, willing Harris not to be too keen to place the chocks quickly, or to order the pitot and engine covers to be secured. There was hope that Harris might be just a little too keen to identify himself with Lindley and the aircraft—Harris

246

was that sort. The chief might delay enough to pose for photographs with Lindley and Dracula in the background; he would want to be seen with some of the VIPs who were now clustered close in front of Joe, as the attaché leaned weakly against the shadowed concrete side of one of the buildings.

Joe willed these favorable factors to occur while he waited, and sweated; his stomach churned, and wispy images of Suzie appeared in his mind: sometimes serious, sometimes with her blue eyes laughing, sometimes talking animatedly with her light southern accent, always beautiful . . .

Joe touched the cold concrete of the wall close to him, yearning to feel as immovable and solid as its rough, damp, enduring surface.

Dracula now loomed out of the darkness like a great, black elongated bat, pointing her long nose straight at him, somehow as if she knew. Her rattlesnake eyes reflected in the lights of the apron atop her flattened oval fuselage, peering directly at him, growing larger as she swayed closer on her tall landing gear. The huge open maws of the turbo-ramjets sitting on the top surfaces of her dartlike wings shrieked like banshees.

Joe shuddered. Once he had loved this immense tribute to American technology and aerodynamics. Now the sight of the machine nauseated him as it came shimmering out of the darkness, wobbling in its own mirage of radiating heat.

With his heart thumping madly in his chest, Joe Kenyon threw down the half-consumed cigarette, and slowly, reluctantly, moved out into the pool of light to welcome his long-time friend and colleague.

Maurice Fennel worked at establishing contact with London. Pentland could see his jaw moving from the rear of the clattering helicopter. The pilot glanced at

Maurice occasionally, no doubt wondering what was going on. He was lucky, Pentland thought. All he had to do was fly the machine. They were well into the flat plain which stretched between the Alps and Geneva. The sky was mostly clear of cloud; there were just a few wisps remaining of the heavy thunderclouds that had lurked gloomily overhead during the day. Ahead, the lights of the city reflected peacefully in the still waters of Lac Leman, and the headlights of cars crept through the darkness along the Route de Chene below them.

Pentland found it difficult to keep his eyes open as he waited for Maurice to pass him the headset. Reaction from the rigors of the night was settling in with the diminishment of shock, and the pain in his hand throbbed ryhthmically again. He tried to remember how it had felt without pain, the memory of the release from it after the injection back at the cabin now dreamlike. He was beginning to think it would be with him for the rest of his life, and that he would have to get used to it like Bunyon's burden. Clatter, clatter, clatter, went the blades overhead. Bang, bang, bang, went the ball-peen hammer. And the helicopter's engine beat steadily behind his back.

Now something beat on his shoulder. His whole existence seemed to consist of rhythmic beating. What kept dragging him out of the warm supportive water? Why couldn't he lay back and immerse himself in it? The pain went away in the water, and it was peaceful, and warm, with the water lapping soothingly over his face . . .

"—vid. David! This is not an occasion for sleeping!" someone shouted. "London. It is London, David! 'Ere, take this contraption, *hein*?" Mount it on your 'ead—"

Pentland shook himself and reached for the headset which Maurice dangled before his face.

He adjusted the earpieces and cleared his throat.

"It is someone 'oo calls 'imself Simon," Maurice bellowed. "It is the DO—"

Pentland nodded at Fennel.

"Simon, this is Peter—how do you read?—over."

"Five five, Peter," the DO's familiar voice crackled back, faintly. "We're on conference with Anderson, one of the cousins. You're patched in with Foxtrot's equipment but you're open locally, and Anderson is on an open telephone line, so we're clear in the middle, but not at the ends, if you see what I mean. This is most irregular! Ovah!"

Pentland smiled at the DO's Cambridge tones and his indignation at this irregular manner of communicating. In the DO's position he would have felt the same himself. But what else could he do, he thought? He had to know if Joe was safe and what had happened to Briggs.

"Understood," Pentland acknowledged. "Mother snatched a look-alike of our family from a hotel here. I followed. Foxtrot picked me up twenty minutes ago. Please urgently establish whereabouts of friend. It looked like a red herring this end—over."

"We have problems here, Peter. Our friend is not available. Nor, we learn, is his wife, and I regret that Cousin One is out. Ovah."

Pentland went rigid, staring at the fast-approaching lights of Geneva through the windscreen between the pilot's and Maurice's shoulders. Had he heard correctly, he wondered in desperation? Had the DO just informed him that not only was Briggs dead, but that Joe was missing, and so was *Suzie*?

"What was friend's last known location?—over," he asked urgently.

"Room fifteen, Swan Hotel Farnborough—ovah."

"Time last observed?—over."

"Zero zero one five, when he checked in—ovah."

Pentland quickly checked his watch. It was one forty-two. The static hissed in his ears, the noise of the helicopter subdued by the sound attenuation of the earphones. He had no doubt now that the Soviets had gotten at Joe Kenyon. He was also convinced that the night's activity in Switzerland had been an elaborate red herring. But were they also responsible for the disappearance of Suzie Kenyon? What conceivably could they *want* with her?

"Simon, give me basics of Cousin One's situation—over."

"He had just talked to your friend Golph about wife. Golph confirmed that wife in residence was unreal. One was on his way to check—ovah."

Golph! Who the fuck was Golph? Did Simon mean that there was a look-alike at Brompton Square? Golph—Gail! Briggs must have seen something odd about Suzie Kenyon and somehow used Gail to confirm it. The Soviets had stopped Briggs, was that it? In which case taking Suzie had been part of the plan. Why, for Christ's sake!

He leaned forward.

"Simon, you mean there was a look-alike wife?—over."

"Affirmative—ovah."

"Oh shit—"

"Say again, Peter."

"Ignore that. Standby."

They were leaving the city behind and crossing the suburbs towards Cointrin. Pentland could see the pilot's lips moving as he communicated with Cointrin Tower. They would land soon. He tried to make sense of events. The wild-card was Suzie. *Why* had they taken Suzie Kenyon and killed Briggs? Because he had presumably threatened to interrupt them? Why would a wife be

250

kidnapped unless it was to put the husband over a barrel?

And then it hit him with stunning clarity.

"Oh, *Christ!*" he yelled aloud, unable to prevent himself. Maurice turned to peer at him. Simon's voice said something in his ears, but it did not register. What time had Joe said that Chuck Lindley was due to arrive in the SR80? Hadn't he said one—*Jesus!* He peered down at the watch on his wrist, hoping somehow that he would not see what he knew he would see, hoping that the last time he had checked he had been mistaken, and that it hadn't been one forty-two, because if it had, they might be too late . . .

"Simon, Simon, do you read?—over."

"Fives, Peter—ovah."

"Get on to security at Farnborough," Pentland said, his whole body trembling. "Joe Kenyon is going to steal the SR80, do you *understand!* He's over a barrel. They're using his wife to make him do it. Stop him somehow, for Christ's *sake!*"

"Peter, what—"

Pentland cut the transmission out as he bellowed: "Fucking well do as I say, *Now, Now, Now!*"

It was one fifty-three.

Pentland slumped back in the seat as the helicopter descended into the pattern of blue and white lights that was Cointrin Airport.

CHAPTER THIRTEEN

A pilot has a natural tendency to park his aircraft in line with others close-by, just as a motorist would inch his car into line with the one closest to him in a car-park. It reflects a natural urge to conform.

"Swing her around, Chuck," Joe Kenyon whispered. "Swing her *round*—"

The SR80's nose still pointed straight at him, straight at the buildings behind him, as it crept abreast of the two F-16s. But then it started to swing to the left and Joe watched the nose-wheel turn. For a few moments the great length of the aircraft was profiled for the watchers, then it began to foreshorten again and the tailpipes swung into view, still glowing. Lindley was obeying convention as he lined the plane up with the two F-16s, facing out toward the open field.

Joe Kenyon released pent-up breath and trembled with relief.

The loud whine and roaring blast of the ramjets died with a mournful moan as the pilot switched off. The ratings pushed the steps into position. The watchers surged forward, Joe now with them, excited voices all around him as people discussed their first impressions of the aircraft's enormous size and shape.

People were now keen to see the man who had flown the machine from Nevada to Farnborough in a little over three hours.

"Phenomenal!" Joe heard. "Unbelievable!" English and American voices talked excitedly in the darkness. Bright light now played on the SR80's cockpit, most of it absorbed in her nonreflective coating. Joe felt the heat still radiating from skin and tailpipes as he drew close to the steps. By the time the small crowd reached the foot of the steps, Joe was in front. Recognizing him, officers deferred to him. Most people there knew he was the only other man to have flown this marvelous black dart, now quiet before them. For the moment everyone was hypnotized, in awe; content to stand and gape. Those who flew, or had flown—and most of them who had bothered to make this rendezvous in the middle of the night were pilots or ex-pilots—were content for the moment to allow their imaginations free rein while they waited for Lindley to emerge.

Harris was about to climb the steps.

"Just a moment, chief," Joe said, stepping forward.

Harris turned, one hand on the rail.

"What's that, now, sir?" he responded with a trace of impatience.

"Keep those people back from the steps, chief." Joe pushed past the sergeant. "I don't want anyone looking into that cockpit until Lindley's clear. You and I know why, right?"

Harris looked puzzled for a moment. He had no idea why, but he thought he ought to look as though he did.

"Very good, sir," Harris said.

Joe climbed the steps. As he went up he heard the whine of the cockpit canopy opening and saw the upper portion lift upward to reveal Lindley's helmeted head. As Joe arrived on the small aluminum platform at the top of the steps, Lindley was removing his helmet. Joe reached down and took it from his friend.

The trembling had stopped. Joe's heart still thumped hard, flooding his system with adrenalin, but he felt no emotion. It was the same as it had been in Vietnam—all piss and wind until the action began, and then a peculiar cold detachment as you locked the target onto the screen. Training and experience took over then. Cold balls to the wall after that, as you kept the target locked-in and closed the range, perhaps a muttered expletive as you punched a Sidewinder loose, and watched it track in, pulling up and away, but keeping your eyes glued to the contact radar until the image spread, and diffused.

"What kept you, Chuck?" Joe smiled down on Lindley, sitting in the cockpit.

Lindley looked up with a grin.

"No one told me to hurry," he said. "How ya doin', Joe?"

Dracula was still alive. The panel glowed with soft light. Gyros hummed quietly. Lindley bent his head to concentrate on his right wrist.

"Bedtime, motherfucker," he murmured as he drew the wrist catheter back off the PCMS needle. He looked briefly up at Joe, his forehead wrinkled in a quizzical smile, as the panel blanked out in front of him.

"I don't think she likes this bit," Lindley said.

"You flatter yourself," Joe murmured. He was keeping one eye on the ground crew below. Harris stood at the base of the steps looking up, his face a bright moon in the light. They hadn't started with the covers yet, and Joe hadn't seen anyone move below the fuselage to place chocks. They should have done that already. They would have, normally, but they were too interested in staring for the moment.

Lindley slid the leather cuff on his wrist and placed the plastic cover over the PCMS needle. He sighed as he prepared to heave himself from the acceleration couch, which he had operated to its upright position before he disconnected from the computer to shut the aircraft's systems down.

"I hope someone brought coffee, Joe. You got 'ny smokes?"

"Sure!" Joe smiled, and took a pack from his pocket. He handed them to Lindley with his lighter. "You know what, Chuck?"

"How's that, Mr. Diplomat?"

"It's been a long time since I sat in this bucket. Never thought I'd want to, after what she put me through. But it's kinda like meeting up with an old flame, right? You wonder if she still turns you on the same?"

Lindley looked at Joe quizzically for a second. Joe felt a flash of fear that he might have sounded obvious, but submerged it instantly with the realization that Lindley could have no idea of his intentions.

"Shit, you can sleep with the bitch for all I care, son!" Lindley laughed as he lit his cigarette. "Who's that guy down there, Joe?" he said, turning to look down to the base of the ladder.

Joe followed Lindley's eyes.

"That's Harris—your crew chief."

"Hey, chief!" Lindley called. "You wanna put this baby to bed, and tell me where you all 're hidin' the coffee?"

Some of the group below laughed.

"Glad to see you, sir," Harris called back. "We got fresh coffee in the crew room." Harris turned away for a moment. "You hear that, Stevens? Fetch Mr.

Lindley a cup—on the double!"

Joe slid into the cockpit holding Lindley's bone dome.

"Now ya talkin'!" he heard Lindley call.

With a small grimace of pain Joe positioned his wrist over the PCMS needle and hoped it would connect with the big vein that ran up the center of his arm. Lindley's back was toward Joe as the pilot finished shouting down to the crew chief, and he was not immediately aware that Dracula's panel had sprung to life the instant the needle had penetrated Joe's skin and the computer had tasted his blood. In nanoseconds the computer checked the chemical composition of the new blood, registered the unusually high level of adrenalin, and shot this new but recognized organism an instant dose of amphetamines as it decided to respond to an anticipated emergency.

Joe's resulting movements in the cockpit became a blur of speed as he and the PCMS resolved into a scramble-mode combination. The open clamshell upper cockpit came slamming down with a screaming whine, and at the same instant the huge Pratt and Whitneys moaned fast up their ascending scale.

Lindley whirled around on the boarding platform with a startled look, which changed to one of incomprehension and horror as he saw the cockpit clamp shut with Kenyon inside wearing his own helmet.

"Jesus H. Christ!" he yelled. "Joe! *Joe*, what in the fuck you *doin'*!"

Inside the cockpit, Joe Kenyon heard nothing.

From the control tower halfway up the field on the left a siren began to wail urgently in the darkness, and lights appeared everywhere, as security forces reacted to the emergency call from MI6 London Center. Vehicle lights converged toward the ramp area like baleful eyes, engines howling at full throttle in the darkness. The watchers at the base of the ramp scattered in confusion, a sea of anxious white faces peering up at the black aircraft as the turbo-ramjets spooled up into a scream and the SR80 lurched.

Dracula lurched—but failed to move forward.

Joe's left hand slid the throttles full forward to afterburner and the SR80 strained and vibrated, but still failed to move. He could hear the enormous cacophony of sound from the rear as the engines bellowed hot gases from the tailpipes at full throttle. He was unable to see that the force of the enormous exhaust caught a military jeep as the driver sped past the rear of the aircraft. The jeep was blown into the side of a concrete hangar like a piece of garbage.

In his heightened state of mind, Joe quickly realized what had happened. Someone *had* put a chock below the nose-wheel. He pushed in full-right steering and heard the hydraulics scream on overrun as the wheel deflected fully. Dracula lurched forward and gathered speed toward the group who had been watching her. People ran for their lives as Joe reversed steering to full-left and straightened the aircraft toward the darkness masking the taxiway.

At the first lurch, Lindley sprang down the steps and cleared them a second before Dracula's fuselage toppled them over. As she spun to the left her right main wheels crumpled them. The blast from the engines as she swung demolished the interior of the crew room, and set fire to paperwork clamped to clipboards placed on hooks above the chief's desk. The rating who had run for Lindley's coffee was shoved against the far wall and screamed as his clothes and hair caught fire. A marine quickly used a fire extinguisher on him.

Marines sprang forward with ready weapons. Harris howled at them not to fire, knowing that one lucky shot could reduce Dracula to a ball of explosively igniting titanium and fuel.

"Block him! Block him!" Harris shrieked at the drivers of jeeps and personnel carriers milling about the scene. "Get in front of him, goddammit! Surround him!" The sergeant leapt up and down in agitation. "Cut him *off*!" he bellowed.

The air was a typhoon of hot gases. Hats, paper, and people blew around in the blast as Dracula merged away into the darkness. No one knew what to do. Harris could not be heard above the banshee shriek of the engines. Other officers bawled commands which no one heard. It was utter chaos.

Insulated in the cockpit module, Joe only heard the whine of the engines and a voice in his ears from Farnborough control tower as his eyes and left hand sped through the pre-takeoff checks.

"Eight-Zero, Eight-Zero—Abort your movement and return to the maintenance area. Eight-Zero, Eight-Zero—do you read? Come in, Eight Zero—"

Dracula reached eighty miles an hour on the taxiway during the quarter mile to the end of the runway. She lurched and pitched on gear not designed for taxi speeds this high, and Joe tightened the harness, feeling like a rodeo rider. He was conscious of vehicle lights in back of him on both sides, bumping along over the grass in an effort to catch up. He hoped no one would drive onto the runway and try to stop him during the takeoff roll. The gear would collapse, and considering that the aircraft was mostly fuel tank, it would be the end of him *and* Dracula.

The beam of the single landing light picked out the hold area before the fence, and Joe pressed the brakes progressively to arrest Dracula's momentum. He swung round into a hairpin turn at nearly twenty miles an hour. As the aircraft lurched straight on the centerline he rammed the throttles full-forward through the gate into afterburner.

Dracula shook with a vibrating roar from the rear. The turbine RPM spooled up to an almost inaudible pitch and the aircraft leapt forward, accelerating like a bullet. Farnborough Tower screamed over the radio for Joe to abort. Lights approaching from the left, cutting toward Joe from the side, began to blur with speed, and within seconds there was just the black runway ahead reeling toward him between streamers of white marker-lights and a river of white light blurring down the centerline. Joe pressed back with his captive wrist and Dracula bounded into the air, rotating nose-up to nearly ninety degrees as the great turbo-ramjets thrust her upwards in rocket mode.

The sonic boom as she cleared the fence at the end of the runway broke most of the windows of the airfield structures and woke every inhabitant in Farnborough.

With his head pinned back and cheeks sagging with the increasing force of acceleration, Joe sped for the troposphere, the radio blaring in his earphones.

The hotel room was pitch-dark. The window showed as a slightly lighter patch, and a small breeze rustled the curtains.

Dimitri Olenko sat on a cane chair with his forearms leaning on the room's circular writing table, facing the window, hardly daring to breathe. Olenko was stiff with tension. The next minutes would have a marked effect on the rest of his life. They would, in all likelihood, determine the survival of Natalia and their two little girls, whom he loved deeply. Natalia and the girls would be asleep at this moment, home in Berezniky, nestling below the Urals. It would be a hot night, and the windows of the house would be open, allowing entry of the warm outside air. Olenko could picture the form of his wife sprawled across the bed in her usual fashion, probably only half-covered with a sheet.

Tomorrow night he would either be with her, or he would be in a small room in the Lubianka.

He heard the American spy-plane land, the great roar as the pilot gave a burst of thrust to break the descent, and then he had heard the aircraft taxi back, and her engines die, leaving the night once again silent. The hotel creaked a little like all old buildings did during the night. The *mokrie dela* man was in the next room, also silent. Hateful animal, Olenko thought.

What was Joe Kenyon doing at the moment?

Perhaps he was talking to the chief of security. Perhaps he would sacrifice Suzie in the interests of protecting his country's military secrets. Often, Olenko had tried to decide how he would act faced with the same terrible choice. One moment he would be adamant that he would act to protect Natalia, but the next he could not be so sure. In Russia things would be different than America. Whatever he did he would lose. If the situation was reversed, and this was Russia and it was he who had to decide, whichever way he decided he would lose. If he stole the aircraft the KGB would take revenge on his wife, and if he didn't he would lose her anyway. That was the difference between the two states. It was a very fundamental difference, he thought.

It was still silent. What was happening? Olenko glanced toward the door, expecting at any moment that he would hear the thump of feet in the corridor—and the door would smash inward and then he would bite the thing he had resolved to carry in his mouth after he had completed the interview with Joe. Oh, no, he thought. There would be no solitary confinement in some hell-hole of an intelligence keep, deep somewhere in the British countryside for him—and certainly no little room in the Lubianka. He would at least deny both sides that satisfaction.

An owl hooted.

Olenko willed that he would hear a roar of ascending turbines.

If he did, it would mean he had won.

And Joe would have lost.

Olenko wished he hadn't grown to like Joe Kenyon so much. He saw so much of himself in the stocky, likable American colonel. They had each progressed through similar careers, and somehow the years of flying and service life had provided a mold from which they had matured into similar types. In so many ways, they thought alike and looked alike. Zuzie had often said so.

Zuzie.

Oh, God, what had he done to Zuzie? The thought of her sent an almost-disabling stab of guilt through his chest. She was so beautiful. So sweet. And when the team had found out that she was pregnant, after following her to the clinic, he had almost taken the capsule from its secret place and bitten it there and then. How could he go on planning the operation when he knew that Joe and Zuzie had waited all their married lives for a child? And that what he planned for them would wreck their lives and that of the child—should it ever be born.

But to his inner disgust he still found the motivation to carry on. He was Russian. Joe was American. They were enemies of each other. It was his duty.

And there was Natalia.

The night became filled with an ascending shriek

and then an ululating roar, and the sound grew.

Olenko leaned forward, his breath stifled. Could it be? *Could* it be?

Yes! he thought exultantly. What he heard was not taxi power.

It was *take-off* power.

Had he won, then? Had he *won*?

The sound grew to enormous volume, a shattering, thunderous noise, which rattled the windows and seemed to vibrate his guts, and then the air was split with a hideous cracking boom and the window glass fell into the room and the sound quickly died.

In the afterquiet, Olenko heard sirens and engines. Lights flashed across rooftops.

"Oh, Christ!" he whispered. "It's worked. I've won. I've *won*!"

It was one fifty-five.

CHAPTER FOURTEEN

Joe Kenyon felt no exhilaration, just a deep sense of loss, as the SR80 sped upward through eighty thousand feet, still accelerating. The sun had followed him up and was now a glaring ball over the eastern horizon, the sky a blaze of orange, fading to azure blue above. The curve of the earth's surface was a scimitar of white light to the east, giving way to a gradual darkening to north and south until it became, in each direction, once again night. Below, England still slumbered in darkness, as it would for the next four hours or so. Large tracts of land were covered with pale cloud which, from this altitude, appeared like uniform layers of lace.

Normally Joe would have spared a few moments to appreciate the magnificent solitude and purity of flight through the thin upper atmosphere; but not this time. He throttled back to mach one point five and switched in the autopilot interface with the course monitor, having programmed the computer to take the aircraft northwest, out into the north Atlantic. The SR80 banked steeply to the left, and the engines spooled up in a slight murmur to the rear as they adjusted speed in the turn.

So what next, Joe thought?

He reached forward and extended the ECM counterdetection range to its full extent, which would blank him from questing radar beams over the whole of the British Isles. Then he warmed up the contact readout screens and instructed the computer to search for possible intercepts.

What he saw gave him a shock.

There were at least a dozen rising blips. Some were fanning out from east of London, more from Cornwall back to his left, and half a dozen rising up and spreading out across his course from Scotland. He could discount the first two batches, but the Scottish group up ahead could be a problem. As he concentrated on the contact screen, it printed the data that the aircraft were F-16s. At this speed and altitude, Joe thought, they'd have him visually in less than two minutes.

There could be no trifling with F-16s.

He saw that the six interceptors were going for altitude like scalded cats. Of course they would be, he thought. They would expect him to use the altitude potential of the SR80 for avoidance. Once over and past them, they wouldn't stand a chance. Whoever was in command down there knew that. So what they were doing was throwing a screen up in front of him, in the hope that the distance would not be sufficient to allow him to climb high enough. Consulting the computer in a blur of fingers he found he could get up to one hundred and forty thousand by the time he reached their positions. But that wasn't high enough—not by far. He would be a sitting duck for their missiles.

Joe made his decision. They were expecting him to go high—so he would go low. He was not within their visual range yet, and they had no idea where he was.

264

They were, at the moment, just a picket fence.

A sweater and slacks were not going to be much help if he got himself involved in violent evasive maneuvers, he thought.

Joe took over manual control and pointed the needle-nose steeply downward, building speed to mach three. He flicked on the ground-map readout as Dracula plunged toward the darkness, and altered heading to the left, diving toward Anglesey on the northern tip of Wales. As he passed down through forty thousand feet, he throttled back and reduced speed to subsonic to avoid the telltale boom at ground level.

Dracula came out of the descent five hundred feet over Caernarvon Bay to the west of Anglesey Island, and leveled out to loaf at three hundred knots out into the Irish Sea. Joe cranked back the ECM range to fifteen miles; no point in advertising, he thought. The device caused an electromagnetic disturbance on radar screens, and if they were clever and plotted the extent of this disturbance, they could fix its radius and know he would be at the center. He now cut a blank, only thirty-miles wide across the dark ocean below, aiming for the narrow channel between Northern Ireland's Belfast Lough and the Mull of Galloway.

As he settled into the new mode he saw that the F-16s were still climbing for altitude up ahead.

For the moment Joe thought he could relax. The engines, now in their turbofan mode at this low speed and altitude, whined soothingly behind him. The PCMS administered a relaxing touch of tranquilizers and Joe settled back in the oil-filled couch. He watched the outlines of the Irish and Scottish coasts creep towards him and the Isle of Man slide past to his right.

The drugs reduced the severity of his sense of loss,

which had been like a sharp pain in his chest since he had made the decision to fly to the Soviet Union, and leave Suzie behind. His depression, after the rigors of the night, now left him feeling dog-weary. The computer had reduced the intensity of the panel's system lights, and Joe had set the ambient cockpit temperature at sixty-eight degrees, which he found a comfortable level in his sweater and slacks. He set the computer for audio alarm to warn him of any threatening change in the radar bearings of the interceptor screen fanning out ahead, now a hundred and twenty thousand feet above him.

Joe refused to allow his mind to dwell on what would happen when he landed the aircraft in the Soviet Union. The only thing he had irrevocably determined to do was to kill Dimitri Olenko at the first opportunity.

Joe regarded the killing of Olenko as his one remaining goal in life. A goal he was determined to achieve.

"Peter, do you read? Ovah."

The pilot had switched off and the blades were turning ever more slowly overhead. Simon's voice in the earphones was peculiarly loud and clear. Maurice opened the door a little and a cool breeze played around the inside of the small machine. They were parked close to a bunch of general aviation aircraft, Cessnas and Pipers, and some business twins and executive jets. At this hour—two in the morning—Cointrin was quiet. Blue taxi-lights stretched away across the airport in random patterns, and the white and green light on top of the control tower pulsed its beam regularly into the darkness.

At the sound of the DO's voice, Pentland felt his

heart thump. Had they been in time? Was his theory correct—that Joe was being forced to hijack the SR80? Perhaps, Pentland thought, he was overreacting and going a little nuts with the strain. He didn't think he was, but he hoped he was. If that was the case, he could go back to Maurice's place and sleep. He was desperate for sleep. Dreading what he might hear, he cleared his throat.

"Fives, Simon—go ahead," he transmitted.

For a few seconds the airwaves hissed in silence.

"We were—ah—too late, Peter—The—ah—bird has flown—Ovah."

"Oh my God," Pentland groaned. "What action have you initiated—Over." So he wasn't overreacting, he wasn't nuts—and the nightmare was real.

The DO's cultured tones crackled back.

"I have, of course, handed over to "C," who informed the defense minister, who in turn contacted the United States ambassador. The DIA has requested the cooperation of British forces to ensure that the—ah—bird is prevented from penetrating Soviet airspace—Ovah."

Which meant, Pentland knew, that the Defense Intelligence Agency of the United States had ordered that Joe Kenyon be shot down!

There *had* to be another way! The DIA would not risk the aircraft falling into the hands of the Soviets, that was obvious. But had they tried contacting Joe? Had they tried to talk him out of it? The tiredness disappeared as Pentland's adrenalin pumped again and he found himself sweating with fear for his friend.

"Simon—advise "C" to get hold of Lindley. Get Lindley talking to Kenyon. They're the best of friends and Lindley knows the aircraft's performance as well as Kenyon. He'll know if there's any way to talk to Joe. There must be some sort of priority system on board by which he could be contacted, even if he's shut the radios down. That plane's equipped with a real high-tech computer—Over."

"Roger, Peter. But who is Lindley?—Ovah."

"He's the fucking pilot who flew the thing to Farnborough, for Christ's sake!—Over!"

"Ah!—affirmative—please advise your disposition regarding further contact—Ovah."

"I'll contact you from the United States embassy in Geneva. Over and out."

Pentland wrenched the headphones off and threw them onto the seat beside him.

"You heard that, Maurice—let's go!"

The pilot's car was in the car-park. The three men ran across the tarmac to the wire fence surrounding the airport. Maurice puffed heavily beside Pentland.

"Somehow—Maurice—we've got—to find—a way—to stop them—shooting—Kenyon down—and we've got—to find—the poor bugger's—wife!"

Two minutes later the pilot was driving flat-out down the quiet auto-route back to Geneva.

Sitting in the back of the speeding car, Pentland tried to sort out the information in his mind. What were the influencing factors?

The most important, as he saw it, was: How long would it take Joe to get where they would have told him to go in the Soviet Union?

This immediately raised the question of what route Joe would decide to take. Would he realize that the Americans would use their influence to direct the whole of NATO against him? Christ, what a thought! Yes, Joe would work that out quickly. *He* might be expendable, but the SR80 sure as hell was not. The Americans would do all they could to prevent the aircraft landing anywhere, let alone the Soviet Union. If it had to go down, it would go down in tiny incinerated pieces; and if that should be anywhere in the West, the Americans would be on-site within minutes. By the time they finished, not one piece of metal would remain on the crash sight. Not one. So, how would Joe avoid the brunt of NATO interceptor aircraft? Get the hell up into the Arctic, Pentland thought. As far away from Britain and Western Europe as possible—as quickly as possible. Then come down on the Soviet Union from the north—over the Barents Sea.

Fuel—how much fuel did he leave with?

Lindley would know that. Fuel quantity would dictate the route to a major extent. Pentland thought that the aircraft would have an endurance of around eight hours at cruise—less than that should there be need to conduct avoidance maneuvers. Say, seven hours—and Lindley had used up three on the way across from Nevada.

Four hours would be all Joe could rely on. He could go a long way in four hours, though. How far *would* he have to go? If he went north, say, up into the Norwegian Sea and then on into the Barents Sea, past the North Cape of Norway and down into Russia, it might be—what—three to four thousand miles? Oh God, he thought, he could do that easily in *two* hours!

But Joe would conserve fuel. Joe would work out that the only advantage he could milk from the whole situation would be time. He would have no idea what would be happening on the ground, except that he would assume that by now it would be known that his wife was missing. And he would also know that the police would be turning the country upside down to find her before he was forced to land. So he would do his best to loiter, to drag it out. The Russians would be furious, but there would be nothing they could do.

While he was in the air, they could only grit their teeth and wait.

It all revolved around Suzie.

Where in hell would they have taken her? He should have asked—what was his name—Anderson— the man on the conference call with Simon, Briggs's number two, if there were any leads. He would do that once they got to the embassy.

They were belting through the city now. Pentland had no idea where the United States embassy was located, but the pilot seemed to know. And, of course, Maurice would. The pilot shot the small Renault around corners with the tires squealing like little pigs in the quiet streets. Thank God it was after two in the morning, and not rush hour.

"Do you know anyone from the embassy?" Pentland leaned forward and asked Maurice.

"I do not know the *ambassadeur*," Maurice replied. "But the CIA man there is called Stenning. I 'ave bumped into 'im on occasion."

"Ask for him, then. Where *is* the bloody embassy? There's so little time—"

"*Un moment*—we are nearly there. It is close now."

Thank God for Maurice.

The Renault heeled around a right-hand turn into a cul-de-sac of heavy, opulent-looking, three-story stone houses, separated by high brick walls. The sides of the cul-de-sac were lined with big trees, heavy with foliage. The Renault sped toward an imposing building at the end of the cul-de-sac behind high scrolled iron gates.

"We are 'ere," Maurice announced.

It was two-twenty.

Thick vapor engulfed Dracula. On the infrared

270

screen, the scattered population of the Mull of Kintyre appeared as dark spots. Lighthouses pulsed heavily on both sides: Rathlin Island to the left, the outpost of the extreme northeast coast of Northern Ireland, and the Kintyre light to the right. The black cloud he had penetrated a few minutes ago extinguished the lights of Belfast as he slid past the Northern Irish capital. The fan of F-16s leveled out at one hundred and twenty thousand feet, and then adopted a covering patrol routine across his flight path from west to east. There was nothing to indicate from this routine, however, that he had been spotted, or even that they suspected he was in the area. In another ten minutes, Joe calculated, he would be north of them, and at the right moment he would kick the SR80 up to maximum altitude and crank out the ECM to full range again.

He had four-and-a-quarter hours of fuel at mach three cruise, and he was going to do his best to make the goddamn flight last for four hours and ten minutes. A lot could happen in four hours, but he had no specific ideas of what that could mean. He was alone, with only hope to keep him company. Hope for what? he kept asking himself. That someone would find Suzie? How *could* anyone find Suzie? Briggs was dead. Pentland was dead. Who, back down there, had any idea of what had happened? There would be no one to pick up the threads.

Everyone had screamed at him—until he had later switched off the radios: London Center, Farnborough, Greenham Common—a guy with his own accent there. Something about the American voice had brought a lump to his throat. It reminded him of what two hundred million Americans would think of him when it was disclosed that he had flown this very special plane of theirs over to the heart of the enemy.

Most of them would think he was a defector. He smiled grimly to himself.

They would *all* think he was a defector—he *was* a defector.

The audio alarm blasted in his ears and Joe's eyes shot to the contact readout. They opened wide as he took in the plot. Two blips showed on the same course as Dracula, two hundred miles to the rear at forty thousand, closing fast.

The point was—were they after him, or was this a south-to-north patrol someone had initiated on the off-chance he might be tooling up the west coast of the British Isles?

The readout identified two Tornados at one point five mach—probably out of St. Mawgan in Cornwall, he thought. Up went his adrenalin secretion together with his pulse, as Dracula nudged him into an alert physiological condition. Joe immediately pushed the throttles forward to match the Tornados' speed. He knew that at mach one point five at this low altitude Dracula would now be gulping fuel at a ridiculous rate. He would have to jump up high or, alternatively, slow down very soon, he thought. But first, the thing to do was to find out if these two boys knew he was there.

He switched the range for a second to bring in the F-16s, which he saw had not altered their pattern. He began to feel uncomfortably pincered, with interceptors high at twelve o'clock and to the rear at six o'clock.

Joe banked Dracula thirty degrees to the west and headed straight out into the north Atlantic.

The two Tornados immediately altered course to intercept.

"Oh, shit!" Joe said to himself, his voice strangely unfamiliar in the almost quiet cockpit.

Dracula instantly sensed the change in his attitude and fed his blood with lysergic acid, to urge his thinking processes up to phenomenal speed, and amphetamines to tune his body for the anticipated reaction load.

He saw that the F-16s had reoriented themselves into a north-south line over central Scotland, forming a barrier to the east, and Joe now thought he understood the basis of their tactics. They were going to fence him off from the east, and the north. They were going to herd him out into the Atlantic—and they were going to keep on doing this until he no longer had fuel to make it to the Soviet Union. In this way, they would hope that he would finally be forced to land somewhere back in British territory—or bail out over the ocean. They would of course prefer anything to letting him through the net to the Soviet Union.

Someone was thinking real fast down there, he thought.

As he considered his next move, more blips rose up from the east coast of Scotland and the same number of patrolling F-16s dropped down the screen. Fuel relay, he thought. Some of the high patrolling interceptors would be running short of fuel.

But how had they got onto him? The range was too far for the Tornados' IR gear to have picked him up. It had to be some electronically equipped boat, he thought, or perhaps an ECM-equipped AWACs aircraft.

Joe warmed up one of the ECM "cubs." The missile was designed to duplicate his image. At the point of launch, he would program the cub's own ECM, fire it off on his present course and speed, crank out his own gear to full range, and split for the Herbrides.

Joe punched the switch and pulled hard right,

instructing the computer to go to full antidetection range. The cub and Dracula quickly diverged as the cub ran on for the Atlantic. The SR80 sped at mach two for the Firth of Lorn, which opened up just south of the Isle of Mull. Joe leveled out at one hundred feet, now below the cloud cover; the Island of Colonsay whipped past, a dark hump to his right.

There was no change in the Tornados' course as they continued on an intercept for the cub. So far, so good, Joe thought.

Quickly he consulted the rolling terrain map. Dracula was hurtling into Loch Linne, the start of the diagonal rift valley that practically cut Scotland in half in a straight line from southwest to northeast. Loch Linne was separated from Loch Ness by a low-lying valley with Fort William at its southern end and Fort Augustus to the north. Beyond Loch Ness he would burst out into the Moray Firth on Scotland's east coast and streak for altitude over the North Sea. However, once the Tornado pilots discovered they had followed the cub, and at the same time it was reported from the ground that something was blasting up the rift valley at zero feet and mach two, the F-16s would pounce on him before he could gain altitude, and that would be that. Then over the North Sea they would have no hesitation in going for a maximum effort to shoot him down, and the sky would be full of heat-seeking missiles.

Joe decided to launch another cub. He pulled Dracula up and released this one, programmed to traverse the rift valley at mach two, its ECM contracted to a five-mile radius.

He racked the SR80 round to a heading of three fifty degrees which would take him northward again towards Iceland, then punched on the afterburners, and sent Dracula hurtling for altitude at mach three, while the ghost sped on into Loch Linne.

"Yeah, this is Chuck Lindley," said a laconic voice with a southern accent.

The voice issued from a speaker close to a bank of telephones in the stuffy communications room of the embassy in Geneva. The radio operator, a ferret-faced little man with a cigarette drooping from his lips, sat in front of a bank of radios and encoders, which filled one wall of the small room.

Three, grey, steel government-issue chairs stood close to a folding-legged formica-topped table on which sat the telephone equipment. The United States ambassador to Switzerland sat on one of these chairs facing the chair's back, with his arms resting across the top as he listened. The portly figure of Henry Stenning leaned against the edge of the table with his arms folded across his chest, wearing a worried look. Sweat gleamed on his bald head beneath the harsh glare of a single, 150-watt overhead light bulb. Pentland was leaning his back against the wall, and Maurice Fennel's bulk flowed over one of the other chairs near the ambassador. The pilot had been told to find himself a cup of coffee, and stand by.

At the sound of Lindley's voice, the five men straightened a little.

"Ah!" Pentland said. Then, without preamble, "Chuck, what was his fuel state when he left?"

"At efficient cruise—eighty thousand and one point five—five hours max," Lindley replied. "But judgin' from what I hear this end he'll be drinking it by the tankerload."

"What do you mean?"

"Well—the whole of the goddamn Brit air force is up there chasin' him around like a bunch of fuckin'

275

Indians," Lindley said. "As likely as not they won't catch old Joe, but the last time I heard, he was down on the deck somewhere off—where the hell was that—?" His voice faded, then came back strong. "—Yeah, Wales. He's goin' north. There are two Tornados up his ass and a bunch of F-16s spread across the top of Scotland. What they're doin' is bottling him up, 'specially to the north and east. They *want* him to run low on fuel—then he doesn't make it over to the Russkies, see?"

"Oh, Jesus," Pentland said. "Look, do this for Christ's sake, will you? Make them understand over there that Joe'll loiter anyway, if he's *allowed* to. He'll know it's the only thing he *can* do. If I know Joe, he'll stay at max altitude over Russia until his fuel's almost out, and only then will he admit defeat and land. Once they know he's in their airspace they'll go along with that. They'll have no choice, right?"

"Right. Yeah, I guess that's what Joe'd do. It's what I'd do. But what's the point?"

"The point is, we *have* to have time to find Suzie. If we can somehow find her and tell Joe she's okay, he'll come home."

"Yeah, but how the fuck you gonna—?"

"Chuck, get them to leave him alone. There's no time to discuss it. Get the MI6 DO and Anderson on the line, will you?"

"Okay, Pentland, I'll do the best I can. Shi-it!" Lindley signed off, disgustedly.

The ambassador rose to his feet.

Ellington Landers was a big man: imposing, even clad, as he was, in a bathrobe over pajamas. He had a large, square face, iron-grey hair worn fashionably full, and piercing blue eyes. He was fluent in all major European languages, including Russian. Ambassador Landers was an ex-senior director of the CIA, which suited the Swiss position he held, since Switzerland was the major mixing pot for intelligence activity in Europe, and the country nations used to bank and distribute operational funds.

"You won't get the DIA to let that aircraft out of NATO airspace, Pentland," Landers said. "Not a chance."

The ambassador finished speaking as Pentland heard Simon's voice on the line. Pentland turned to Landers with red eyes.

"Well, *you* better get onto them, sir, in that case. Because if they don't pull those interceptors off, you'll lose your aircraft, and your diplomat, and the fucking Russians will slay Joe's wife."

"I don't think you quite understand, Mr. Pentland! The official position concerning this defection will be to prevent that aircraft from landing in, or being shot down over, the Soviet Union. The loss of Kenyon, and of his wife for that matter, are of less consequence, I regret to say—"

"Do you, Ambassador?" Pentland responded, his voice filled with bitterness. He drew his eyes from Landers's glare and addressed Simon.

Simon had rushed to the Defense Ministry's underground plotting room in the same complex as the War Room, deep in wooded countryside behind High Wycombe, surrounded by high, electrified security fences, and patrolled by Alsatian guard dogs and British Royal Marine Commandos. This was where the Royal Air Force and other NATO commanders assembled in the case of a national emergency. The loss of the SR80 was regarded as a national emergency.

On the way to the complex, Simon had phoned Farnborough and ordered that Chuck Lindley should be grabbed and hurried to the same complex. He had also telephoned the chief, Colonel Brynes, who was presently on his way. An open scrambler link had been established with the DIA in Arlington, Virginia, the operating agency of the SR80, Lindley's boss organization; and the United States Secretary of Defense had been alerted. Before he had left Whitehall, Simon also contacted the Head of Special Branch, who now linked with members of Scotland Yard in an all-out effort to trace the whereabouts of Suzie Kenyon.

Although no thread of evidence could so far be found to link Dimitri Olenko to Joe's defection, or the disappearance of his wife, a small force of experienced men were now at Farnborough. They were instructed to keep a very close eye on the Russian diplomat, with orders to do whatever was necessary to prevent Olenko from leaving the country.

"Simon," Pentland said into the speaker. "Is Anderson with you?"

"I'm right here," Anderson replied.

"Okay. Anderson, fill me in on every factor you can think of connected with Mrs. Kenyon's kidnapping from Brompton Square. How did whoever took her get past your man—the estimated time it happened—any clues as to how they took her away—any possible witnesses' descriptions—any theories anyone has as to where they might have taken her—*anything* which might give us a lead. You understand? *Anything* you can think of—"

Twenty seconds into the climb, Joe saw the blips of the two Tornados in pursuit of the cub out into the Atlantic suddenly change direction sharply. He had watched them close the range with the ghost, knowing that at any moment their IR screens would pick up the cub's image. He would have given a lot to have heard the flight commander's comments as the two Tornado pilots realized they had used up valuable fuel and time chasing an ECM missile.

While he had waited for the inevitable to occur, he had also kept flicking the contact readout screen to the F-16s. When he had programmed the second cub he had dispatched up the valley towards Loch Ness, he had purposely shrunk its counterdetection radar to its minimum of five miles. At mach two, the cub's exhaust gases would leave traceable heat behind the trailing ECM cover, so that even should the cub not be picked up on the six radar scopes in the F-16s above, one of the pilots would be bound to notice the fast-moving IR trace. For a few moments then they would assume the trace would be him, cutting across Scotland for the North Sea.

Joe felt a peculiar mixture of satisfaction and depression as he watched three of the F-16s lose altitude like falcons stooping as they plummeted down to intercept the cub close to Scotland's east coast. A part of him knew he must land in Russia, and therefore evade these RAF boys, but something in his gut, which he supposed resulted from the years of training and conditioning in the U.S. Air Force, willed the F-16s pilots to see through the bluff. He knew if they eventually shot him out of the sky that he would experience relief in those final moments. But at the same time he also knew that if he allowed that to happen, if he did not do all he could to evade these interceptors, then those final moments would be filled with an irrevocable remorse that he had caused the death of his wife.

The two Tornados were now closing fast from the left, streaking back in from the open reaches of the dark Atlantic, once more on an intercept course.

However, Joe knew that they had no hope of catching him now. The gap had widened too far; the intercept angle had become too acute, and the SR80's rate of climb and speed too great. The two pilots must have known this, but they came on flat-out anyway, pushing their aircraft to maximum performance at mach four.

I hope you guys have enough fuel, Joe thought.

Dracula howled over John o' Groats at three thousand miles an hour, climbing through one hundred and forty-five thousand feet, heading due north. The remaining three F-16s swung in behind from Joe's right as the whole flight realized they had been duped by the Loch Ness ghost. Joe watched their IR trails extend as the three higher aircraft went flat-out on afterburner in an effort to catch him. He could afford to ignore them, and sent the contact readout screens questing in a half-circle ahead, the only area from which he might expect any further trouble.

He watched the two Tornados drop down in a steep glide off the screens, merging with the ground fuzz of Scotland to the rear; he was relieved that they had made it back to land and hoped that they would touch down safely at some Scottish base.

Then, one by one, the F-16s fell back, reversed course, and dropped from the screen as they reached the critical point of their fuel flow.

By now, Dracula was slicing through the few thin remaining air molecules that existed at two hundred thousand feet, and Joe pulled back the throttles and programmed the computer to adjust for the most fuel-efficient cruise mode. Dracula settled down to a speed of mach one point six.

Joe noticed that back to his right, now practically out of radar range, a series of blips moved out across the North Sea. This told him that NATO now planned to build another fence, stretching up the Scandinavian Peninsula and beyond the North Cape of Norway into the Barents Sea. This time, when he eventually turned south, they would do their level best to shoot him down.

Meanwhile, Joe Kenyon sat back in the acceleration couch and glanced around him at the new dawn, and ahead to the blinding white of the Arctic reaching to both sides of the far horizon. There was no sensation of movement, just a steady, almost-imperceptible unrolling of the curved surface of the planet toward him. The deep blackness of space, clustered with brilliant stars, canopied above the cockpit. Immediately below, the north Atlantic was still hidden in darkness.

The computer told Joe that he had three and a half hours of fuel remaining at cruise. He called up the chart display and adjusted it to cover an area bounded by Iceland to the extreme left and Novaya Zemlya to the extreme right, with a baseline that stretched between Glasgow and the Urals. He studied the details. Then he reached forward and selected a course that would run from his present position just north of the Faroes to Jan Mayen Island in the Greenland Basin; from there east to Bear Island at the western limit of the Barents Sea, then southeast to the Urals with a short final leg due south to Berezniky. The computer read out a distance of three thousand eight hundred and thirty-three nautical miles. He could cut that a bit shorter, he thought, by turning south five hundred miles northeast of the North Cape and then running direct for the destination, leaving out Novaya Zemlya. That would save five hundred miles. So, at the best, he thought, the distance to run was thirty-three hundred miles. Two hours.

He checked the chronometer.

It was five minutes to three in the morning, British Summer Time. He had been in the air for fifty minutes.

It felt like fifty hours.

CHAPTER FIFTEEN

At the moment Joe Kenyon launched the second "cub" toward the entrance to Loch Linne, David Pentland was once again speaking to Chuck Lindley from the embassy in Switzerland. Pentland felt light-headed with fatigue and more depressed at Lindley's words.

"They think they've got him, David," Lindley was saying. "There must be something wrong with the ECM gear. He's using it, but every so often they see him clearly. He's fooled the sumbitches once with a cub—sent a couple of Tornados tearing out into the Atlantic. They don't know it yet, but I do, because it's what I would have done!" Lindley laughed. "Now they've picked up some IR trace pissing up the valley toward Loch Ness. I don't think that's him either. There ain't no flies on Joe Kenyon!"

"Is he answering, Chuck, anything at all?" Pentland knew what the answer would be.

"Nope. Not a goddamn bleep. They'd track him in seconds if he transmitted. He won't risk that. The only chance might be if he gets clear. We're trying him on every frequency, meantime."

"Isn't there some emergency frequency? Something

he can't ignore? What about the superbrain you people stuffed into that plane? Isn't there any way we could talk to him—?"

"Jesus!" Lindley exclaimed. "I think he might be *through*! That *was* a cub he sent up that Loch. Three sixteens dropped down after it. Now they've reported a brief contact just south of Cape Wrath. It's gotta be Joe! Shit, the boys here're madder 'n hell! It *is* him! This is like watchin' the fuckin' Battle of Britain all over again. Goddamn! I think he's gonna *make* it—' and then, "Hell! I guess I shouldn't be pleased—'"

"Chuck! We've *got* to get through to him. Concentrate. *Is* there any other way than by radio? There's got to be *something*—"

"There's only one way, and that's by using a SAMOS satellite. Washington could send a coded transmission to his computer via a SAMOS. They could do that—"

"Then why the hell *don't* they?" Pentland's spirits lifted at the thought.

"What—just to tell him to come back? *Everyone's* telling the poor sumbitch to do that!"

"Okay, Chuck. But who has the authority to use that method of communication?"

"My boss."

"Well, who *is* your boss?"

"The director of the DIA."

"Then get hold of him and ask him. Maybe someone, somewhere, will get a break on where Suzie is. We'll need it then. Imagine if we couldn't contact the poor bastard then!"

"Yeah, that's a good point. I'll get on it."

"Meantime, put Anderson on, will you?"

Pentland drank some cold coffee from a styrene cup and lit a fresh cigarette from the end of the one he'd just finished. Stenning coughed. The radio man yawned.

Then Anderson announced himself.

"As far as we can track it," Andrews said, "Allan Briggs tried to get in touch with the guy he posted to keep an eye on the Kenyons' house. When he couldn't raise him, Briggs went to Brompton Square himself. There was no sign of our man. Briggs was killed later in Stanton Street—"

"Stanton Street! What was Briggs doing in Stanton Street?" That was close to where Gail lived. "Whereabouts in Stanton Street?"

"On the corner of Heathstead Mews."

That was right *by* Gail's place! "What was he *doing* there?"

"Visiting some woman who was a friend of Mrs. Kenyon. He said he was going there to check someth—"

"Gail!" Pentland exclaimed.

"What?" Anderson said.

"Gail Seldon? Was that the woman?"

"Yeah! How did *you* know?"

"Get her. Get her on the line. Patch her in." He gave Anderson Gail's number. Why had Briggs gone to see Gail? Had Briggs been killed *because* he had gone to see Gail? Did that mean that whoever killed Briggs overheard whatever Briggs and Gail talked about? Oh my God, he thought. Where did that leave Gail?

Then Pentland heard the sleepy voice of the woman he loved. He felt like shouting with relief.

"David!" she said. "Where on earth *are* you?"

"Switzerland. Look, darling, just listen. We're in the middle of an emergency. It involves Joe and Suzie Kenyon. Allan Briggs visited you tonight—last night. Why?"

"He thought that someone might have been impersonating Suzie. He asked me questions about her. He got on to me because I called her while he was at the house. From what he said it didn't sound like Suzie—the woman there, I mean—"

"Everybody's looking for her, Gail. She's been kidnapped—"

"Oh my God, so it *is* true!"

"Think, Gail, did Briggs say anything more? Did he have any theories? Did you and he discuss anything else?"

"Only about the ambulance. Some kids—"

"Ambulance?"

"My God, you sound *terrible*! Are you all right, David?" she asked anxiously.

"Yes. Yes, I'm sorry." Pentland made an effort to calm himself.

"Tell me what you were saying about an ambulance," he urged her.

"Allan Briggs said some children in Brompton Square saw his man there talking to some people from an ambulance. Then the man disappeared. Briggs went to the Kenyons' house and Susie was there. Or, at least, someone who *looked* to him like Susie. But there was something—well—wrong about her, which is why he came to see me. He said she was smoking and drinking Scotch, you see, and, well of course, she doesn't do either, does she?"

Pentland closed his eyes and drew deeply on the cigarette.

"Are you there, David?"

Coming away from the cabin—running back down the mountain road towards Monthey. Before Maurice and the chopper had arrived. The vehicle that had passed him . . .

"David?" Gail's voice anxious from the speaker.

"Pentland—are you all right?" asked the ambassalor.

The vehicle that had passed him on its way up that
small mountain road had been an ambulance, hadn't
it? And the woman—Olga—the woman who had
expertly dressed his hand. She said she'd been trained
as a nurse. That was why he had known she would
never use the shotgun on him. And there'd been
something else, hadn't there? He'd advised them to
leave, the woman and Ernst. He remembered his own
words, "—*foolish to trust the Soviets, Olga. You have
done what they asked. Leave now*—"

And the expression on her face immediately afterward. A mixture of fear and resignation, and weary
acceptance.

Perhaps they *hadn't* finished up there in the cabin.

Two hundred thousand feet below the aircraft,
Bjorn Oya, Bear Island, protruded from the icy grip
of the Barents Sea. Beyond Bear Island, due north,
Vest Spitsbergen stretched in a long white hump
toward the curve of the brilliant white horizon, the
only relief in the flat, dazzling-white Arctic waste
which capped the latitudes north of seventy degrees.
The sun was now a bright-red orb over Russia to the
east, brilliantly lighting the upper surfaces of cloud
layers scattered a hundred and twenty thousand feet
below the aircraft.

The SR80 dipped its right wing and tilted into a
steep banking turn onto the heading to run directly
for the Soviet Union. Joe had flight-planned his
landfall on the Pol Kanin Peninsula at the entrance of
the White Sea. From there, the aircraft would quickly
transit Cheshskaya Guba, the deep bay below the
hook of Kanin, and then run down the Timanskiy
Kryash mountain range on a course slightly east of

south to where the range joined the massive Urals two hundred miles north of Berezniky.

A chain of contact blips had folded with him up the west coast of Scandinavia, five hundred miles to the east, as NATO interceptors sought to keep the spyplane out into the wastes of the Barents Sea. They now curved toward him from the North Cape in a last threatening gesture, folding north into the Barents Sea in a string extending three hundred miles, replacing each other in a predictable routine as the front runners grew short of fuel and turned back. Now, rising up from Murmansk to the southeast, another series of radar contacts flickered onto the screen as Soviet interceptors spread across his course between Murmansk and Novaya Zemlya, high to the east. The lines of NATO and Soviet aircraft maintained a distance of three hundred miles apart, and Joe sped across the no man's land between, forty thousand feet higher than the highest of the interceptor flights.

Joe knew that neither air force could see him. Both would have an approximate idea of his position from the limits of the electromagnetic disturbances of the ECM counterdetection radar emittance from Dracula, which normally he would have varied, increasing and decreasing the range to confuse the radar operators and prevent them from comparing their signals to define his ECM limits so that they could establish the emittance source.

Now he saw no need to bother. The Soviets knew he was coming—NATO knew he was leaving. Neither had aircraft or missiles that could reach him unless he descended, and he had no intention of descending until the last possible moment.

If he maintained this speed, mach two, he had an hour and a half remaining to run. An hour and a half of pilot-in-command of the most advanced reconnaissance aircraft the world had ever known, and an hour and a half of being Colonel Joseph Kenyon, USAF, fighter pilot, test pilot, and diplomat. Ninety minutes before he became Joseph Kenyon, defector, and prisoner of the Union of Soviet Socialist Republics—and Dimitri Olenko.

"David—can you hear me? David—"

Gail's voice pleaded from the speaker on the formica-topped table in the embassy communications room.

The others were peering at Pentland with expressions varying from concern, to irritation, to puzzlement, as the MI6 agent stood close to the table, unconsciously cradling his left arm with its bulbous, white, plastic-covered bandage clubbing his fist. Pentland stood with his eyes staring at the speaker, unseeing for a moment, not hearing Gail's voice.

"Yes," he whispered at last. He cleared his throat. "Gail, thanks. Thanks!" His voice grew louder. "Chuck!" he shouted, folding forward, thrusting his face toward the speaker. "Lindley!"

Simon's voice replaced Gail's.

"He's—at—over with the command-plot. Shall I get him?"

"Yes, Simon. Get him over. Get him fast."

Pentland turned to the ambassador.

"There's no time to explain, sir," he said. He found himself breathing hard. "But I know where they're holding Kenyon's wife. And it's here. Here in Switzerland—"

"Yeah, David. Lindley here—" from the speaker, before the ambassador could reply.

"Chuck, where is he? How long before he—?"

"He's turned south, north of Norway. He's running

289

for the Soviet coast. He's gonna cross the coast somewhere between Lapland and Novaya Zemlya. We don't know where because the ECM's still cranked out to max range. But if it's, say, midway between—over Indiga—then he'll have a straight run south to the Urals. He's movin' at mach two, so that'll take him about an hour and fifteen minutes from now. He's real high—maybe two hundred thousand—and our boys got no way to get at him—"

"An hour and fifteen! Jesus. Chuck, I think I know where they're holding Suzie—"

"What! Where, for Christ's sake—"

"Here—in Switzerland. Did you clear with the DIA—to use the SAMOS?"

"Yeah, but only for an approved transmission—"

"Okay. Never mind the approved bit. They'll approve! How long would it take for us to tell them what to say, and then for them to relay it to the aircraft by satellite?"

"Well, they should be able to transmit instantly. A minute to code up, maybe, but—"

"Then stand by this phone link, whatever you do. Don't leave for a moment, you understand? I've got to leave. There's no time to explain. Just stay there and be ready. We might have a chance of stopping him. And Chuck?"

"Yeah!"

"Get a tanker to stand by—"

"What! From where? When?"

"I don't *know* for Christ's sake! It's your aircraft. Talk to someone. What about Thule? That's closest, isn't it? If he makes it back out of the Soviet Union, one thing he's going to need is fuel. It looks like you'll have two hours, not much more. Get me?"

Pentland whirled away from the speaker.

"Maurice, she's at that cabin. Close to where you

picked me up. We've got one hour. One fucking *hour*, at the most. We'll need men and weapons. Our only chance is to use choppers. There's no time to drive—"

"We should inform the Swiss Police," Ambassador Landers announced.

Pentland sunk onto one of the grey steel chairs in the room.

The quiet CIA man, Stenning, spoke:

"No time, sir. They'd want explanations. Too late by then." He looked down quickly at his watch. Pentland looked at his own. It was four-fifty. Outside, the sky would soon be lightening into dawn.

"There is one I know," Maurice put in. " 'E is 'igh up in the police. It is possible 'e will 'elp us." Maurice smiled briefly. "I 'ave 'elped 'im before." Maurice turned to the ambassador.

"*Monsieur l'Ambassadeur*, your permission to use this telephone, *hein*?"

"Anything, Fennel. Anything you want!" Landers waved his hand.

Landers could see some light now, Pentland thought. He would have contributed to an interesting piece of history if somehow they could get Joe Kenyon to turn back. Landers would help all he could, now.

Fennel was using the phone privately, his head bent over the receiver with his back to the rest of them, talking French fast. Pentland translated in his head snatches of what Fennel said.

"—sorry to disturb your undoubted sexual exercise—" Fennel was saying.

"—emergency—woman of a USAF pilot kidnapped, being held here, near Monthey—no time to talk to the commissioner, *hein*—one hour before *un cris extraordinaire*—"

The seconds clicked by.

"Yes, my friend, of course I know I have one of

291

your pilots and one of your machines! But the machine, it is at Cointrin at this moment, you understand? How shall we get there to obtain it, and have sufficient time to travel to this place beyond Monthey? How would it be possible to eject these KGB people and transport the wife of the diplomat to safety, *hein*?''

Pentland groaned to himself in frustration. Why were the French-speaking people so verbose? Why couldn't the silly bastard on the other end of the telephone leave the goddamn woman in his arms, and snap to it?

"—financial implications," Maurice was finishing, staring up at the ceiling.

"*Oui*, you have heard that which I have said." A pause. Maurice smiled and held the receiver a little way from his ear for the moment, before pressing it back. Maurice was very adroit among the banking fraternity, Pentland remembered. It sounded like he had something on the person at the other end of the line.

"I regret, my friend, that in the circumstances, I would be unable to consider any alternative course of action!" Then Maurice nodded his head. Pentland and the others in the room held their breath.

"*Oui, d'accord!*" Maurice said, and let out an explosive sigh, with his hand over the mouthpiece for a second. He winked at Pentland. Pentland's shoulders slumped in relief.

Dix minutes—oui! Nous t'attendons, mon cher ami!"

Maurice replaced the receiver and turned to face the occupants of the room.

"My friend, 'oo is with the special branch of the Swiss Police which concerns itself with the action against drug enthusiasts, will arrive 'ere in ten min-

utes. 'E will bring one man. Both will 'ave weapons—
les carbines. 'E will land the machine on the road,"
Maurice waved a hand to indicate the front of the
embassy building.

"Then it's you and me, Maurice—"

"Not you, Pentland," the ambassador said.
"You're in a bad way. Stenning can go with Fennel."

Pentland got to his feet.

"I know the place. I know Suzie Kenyon. And I
know the two people who will be holding her. Of
course, there'll be others there, but I do have that
advantage." Pentland glanced at Stenning. "I think it
would be better, don't you, Mr. Stenning?"

"I guess so," the CIA man said doubtfully, uncom-
fortable not to be able to agree with his boss.

"Do you have any weapons here?" Pentland asked.

"We have a few—er—emergency pieces," Stenning
said, with a grin.

"Two machine pistols, spare ammunition, three or
four clips each," Pentland said. "Can do?"

Stenning nodded and walked quickly toward the
door. "Couple minutes," he said and went out.

"I hope you're right, Pentland," the ambassador
said. "The Swiss will take an extremely dim view of
this if you're not."

Pentland smiled tiredly back at Landers.

"I hope I'm right too, Ambassador."

They left the stale, smoke-filled communications
room and went down to the lobby of the embassy. The
ambassador drew back curtains from a high window,
which looked out into the forecourt behind the high
iron gates. The cul-de-sac was beyond, and through a
gap between the tall trees that lined the road, the sky
was losing its blackness as the first of the morning
light glanced down from the atmosphere above. The
trees were becoming something just slightly more than

bulky silhouettes. Then a pinpoint of light appeared beyond the end of the road and quickly grew, and a few seconds later a sound grew with it, rapidly developing into a regular beat with a background drone. Then, the light, now as strong as a single automobile headlight, dropped steeply downward. With a loud clatter, a helicopter's dark shape emerged from the darkness and lightly touched down onto the road.

Now the contact readout had become confusing. It was full of blips. Aircraft streamed up in series from Murmansk, Archangel, from Krestovaya Guba in Novya Zemlya and Pechora at the northern limit of the Urals. Short of all-out nuclear war, it was a sight unlikely to be viewed by any other U.S. pilot, as the strength of the Soviet air force grouped across the Russian shores of the Barents Sea to form an impenetrable barrier, on the possibility that NATO would order some wild Kamikaze effort to shoot Joe down as he descended toward Berezniky.

The computer was going wild in an effort to identify and print out the statistics of the numerous types of aircraft cross-pinning the skies below the SR80. Joe cancelled the ID program and instructed the computer to signal only those idents that appeared on an intercept course with him. None were. They knew he was there, but not where he was. On impulse, Joe changed the range briefly to pick up the remaining NATO fighters, now back to his right, beyond the border of Finland and Sweden, with some converging down to the North Cape of Norway, dropping lower as he watched. Men like him at the controls of the F-20s and F-16s and Tornados, Mirages, and Swedish Viggens. Men who spoke his language, some his dialect, from his own country. All allies . . .

Joe, for the last time, switched the screen to delete friendly contacts, and left the computer to monitor any Soviet intercepts as before.

He wanted to smoke a cigarette. He felt like a condemned man, and like a condemned man he wanted a last cigarette. There was a pack in his trouser pocket, the same pack he'd taken from the room in Farnborough. Farnborough, in another world: far from the featureless wastes which were now unrolling below him, too far down for him to see any detail—just white and grey shapes, with a broad dark area to the right, the Russian Taiga, last of the great natural forests of the Soviet, where men still lived by hunting and trapping, and sold their goods at a profit; wild people, uncaring of communism. At the moment, Joe Kenyon envied every free man on the planet. Unconsciously, he found he had lit a cigarette.

At the flare of the lighter, Dracula sprang into action, sensing the tiny fire in the cockpit. The audio alarm sounded, and Joe stiffened as the PCMS pumped him up to deal with the emergency. Then he realized what all the fuss was about, and cancelled the alarm, switching off the circuit breaker controlling the visual flashing red light that indicated cockpit fire. No one had ever smoked a cigarette in Dracula before, he thought. No one ever would again. He drew the smoke deep into his lungs and sat back in the couch. Something about sitting up at two hundred thousand feet with half the world's air forces beating contrails below him, East and West both sweating on his next move, suddenly appeared to him as hysterically funny and he began to laugh quietly, a low chuckle in the cockpit. The chuckle grew and he threw his head back and roared with laughter, until tears ran down his cheeks. The laughter surged until he was unable to breathe and he gasped through a dragged-down, open mouth, his eyes squeezed shut, his body shaking, and then no sound came from his lips, except the gasps of the laughter. Gradually, the laughter changed to sobs and he found himself saying her name over and over: "Suzie, Suzie—"

The PCMS dosed him with tranquilizers; he grew calm and the features of the cockpit swam back into his vision. Joe gave one long shuddering sigh, spat on the end of the cigarette, which he made sure had stopped burning, and leaned forward to consult the ground readout.

He had crossed the coast, and was now flying over Russia. Down to the right the Mezen River wound its way back up to Cheshskaya Guba, a barely perceived strip of frozen, winding smoothness at the foot of the Tamanskiy. A hundred and fifty miles beyond the river to the west lay Archangel, with its naval base on the White Sea and its air defense system, now so agitated about his survival as streams of blips ascended and descended from its bases.

Joe punched the keys to give him distance readout and time-to-go.

Fifty-two minutes overhead Berezniky.

He reached forward with his left hand and eased the two throttle levers aft. Dracula began to sink at undiminished speed toward the soil of the Soviet Union.

Once he had established Dracula in the descent, Joe switched the radios back on.

Last chance, he thought. Last chance. He tuned the HF wavebands and instructed the computer to search for transmits on the frequencies used by NATO and Britain and the United States. They were still calling him on practically every existing frequency, but no one said they'd found Suzie. They pleaded with him to return, ordered him to return, but none had the key that would allow him to return. Depressed, he switched off and returned to the silence of the cockpit, with the barely heard mutter of the Pratt and Whitney exhausts far back to the rear, and the subdued whine of hydraulics and the hum of electrical systems—sounds he knew and was comfortable with; the sound of the computer clacking quietly in the panel, and, when he eased his helmet off his sweating head, the high hiss of the slipstream past the thickened plexiglass and the glowing hot skin of the airframe.

Gradually, the slopes of the Timanskiy beneath and the Urals way off ahead and slightly to the left, became discernible from the featureless humps they had appeared at the higher altitude. Now he could see their peaks and valleys and, far to his left, beyond the Urals, the flat featureless swamps of the Zapadno Sibirskaya threaded by the massive River Ob.

Dracula cut a thousand mile an hour invisible line at a shallow downward angle through one hundred thousand feet, plunging like a black dart toward the earth below.

CHAPTER SIXTEEN

The eastern-oriented faces of the highest alpine peaks were turning pink as the dawn crept down. So were the edges of small white puffy clouds high above them. The raw reds of dawn reminded David Pentland of blood. I've got blood on the mind, he thought. It had been the bloodiest night he could remember, and it wasn't over yet. With a sinking feeling in his stomach he thought of what had to be done in the next forty minutes as the helicopter, with two uniformed narcotics men in the front, sped from Geneva toward the Alps.

Pentland unfolded a Swiss ordnance chart on his knees, obtained from Stenning, and asked Maurice, who sat beside him in the rear of the helicopter, to tell the pilot to switch on an overhead light. The pilot's name was Claude and the other man was introduced as Jean-Jacques. There had been no time for further detail as he and Maurice bundled themselves and the weapons into the helicopter. Claude reached forward and switched on the light.

Pentland traced the small road up from Monthey with a finger. Maurice leaned over to look. The cabin was marked with a small square at the end of a dotted line which signified a track from the main road. It sat in a bowl below the high peaks at the head of the valley up which the road climbed. The bowl was in fact a large corrie, once the starting point of the glacier that had undoubtedly carved the valley down to Monthey. The nearest building to the cabin was an alpine farm four miles away across the base of the corrie to the north, which was where the mountain road terminated. From there a dotted line ran up into a high valley in the peaks to the west, probably an access track up to summer grazing for cattle and sheep, which in this part of the world spent practically all their lives munching on forty-five-degree slopes. The alpine farmers were hardy people, like their animals. The Soviets couldn't have found anywhere more remote to hide Suzie, if in fact this was where they had hidden her, and it didn't turn out that he was following a hunch like a rotten apple.

There had been no time to get Simon to find out from the police back in England whether they had been able to trace an ambulance to an airport, and from there to determine if someone had been loaded onto a flight for Switzerland. It could have been a commercial flight or a private one—more likely the latter, Pentland thought. He wondered if the plane the Soviets had used might have been sitting quietly close to where they had landed earlier in the helicopter, back at Cointrin; it was very likely. He concentrated on the map again, and tried to avoid thinking about what the results would be if he was proved wrong.

"Maurice. See to the south of the place—here." He placed his finger on the map. "Behind the cabin—the other side from the road, see?"

"Yes. The flat area, *hein*?"

"That's right. It seems to me I remember half-noticing when I first got there that there was an open area back behind the place. The front is thick with trees, all pines. The track winds up between the trees. I can't remember any place I saw around the front— the north side—where you could put a chopper down. That area on the map that looks flat may in fact be the only place Claude could land this thing. And I'm pretty sure that the Soviets would pick somewhere they could get a chopper to, so for the moment we'll assume we can get down on that spot. The hills rise pretty steeply from what I can see from this, but I reckon there's enough room for Claude to get in."

Maurice nodded. "They will, of course, 'ear us coming kilometers away."

"Yeah, I know."

The helicopter's racket would echo from the surrounding peaks in the predawn silence. Any kind of a stealthy approach was going to be impossible, unless they landed well back, somewhere on the road, and went in on foot; but there was no time for that.

"Anyway, this is what I remember of the place. There are only two ground-floor rooms, I'm certain. There may be two more above, but since the roof is one of those very steeply pitched affairs, there could be only one. The front entrance is in the center of the building, between the two rooms. The room to the left of the entrance is the living room. Part of it is a small kitchen to the left, at the south end. There are windows from the kitchen, and these will be the only windows in that room that might overlook the landing sight. With me?"

"*Oui—d'accord*," Maurice murmured. "So the kitchen, it regards to the south. The entrance, it is on the east side, *hein*?"

"Right. And the track from the road comes up from the north. Now, the other ground-floor room will be on the north side, the opposite end of the building

300

from where Claude lands."

"*Oui?*"

"Olga, the nurse came out of that room when I got there. She went back into the same room to get her bag with the medical equipment, to fix my hand. I think it's a good bet that if Suzie Kenyon is in the cabin, she'll be in that room. She'll either be there or upstairs, but I'm going to bet she'll be downstairs where they can keep an eye on her more easily."

Pentland glanced up into Maurice's eyes. The Swiss nodded, frowning with concentration. They were in the mountains now and Claude was easing the chopper into a steady climb, maintaining as much speed as possible. The peaks were growing steadily lighter, but the ground below was still in darkness.

"So this is what I suggest we do, and if you agree, the main factor will be surprise and speed. I have no idea how many will be there. Probably four, possibly five, because there were two in the front of that ambulance, and Olga and Ernst at the cabin. There could have been another in the rear of the ambulance, but I don't see why there would have been more. How many bloody KGB people do you need to guard a pregnant woman in a cabin in the Swiss Alps?— especially if you can safely assume that no one knows you're there?"

Pentland then told Maurice his plan. When he had finished he asked Maurice to tell the two narcotics men the details and to be sure they thoroughly understood. The timing, he stressed, was vital.

While Maurice was leaning forward with his head and shoulders thrust between the two men in front, rattling away in French, Pentland sat back and thought of Joe.

The transmission from the SAMOS would be a code-one message which the computer would auto-

301

matically decode and print out on the screen, Lindley
had told him. The only way Joe could clear it would
be to acknowledge receipt of the signal. If he didn't do
that, Dracula would keep flashing it at him. So Joe
would get the message, if by then he hadn't already
landed. And if that was the case, the Russians could
dine out on the story.

But supposing Joe refused to believe the information?

It was a very real possibility. He would expect the
DIA to try that—lie to him about Suzie, to get him to
turn round and streak back home. In the same
circumstances, Pentland thought, I would expect a
last-ditch message like that from the DIA and assume
it would be a lie. So even a code-one signal would fail
to stop him.

There would have to be something special in that
signal, he thought. Something that would make Joe
believe it to be true. But what? As far as he knew, he
was the only one who knew Suzie was pregnant, so if
the signal the DIA sent was signed by him, and
included wording such as "pregnant wife safe" would
that be enough? Would Joe understand that?

No, Pentland decided. He would be more likely to
assume that Pentland had sided with the authorities
in order to get the aircraft back. Joe would think that
his friend would respond to the dreadful loss of the
SR80—and what it would mean in terms of losing the
edge the Americans held over the Soviets in the area of
electronics and engine technology and countermeasure systems. Years of design and technology in the
aerospace world wrapped up in the SR80; years of
NASA research and billions of capitalist dollars. And
whatever the motivation, however strong that motivation was, Joe was indisputably a defector. He was no
different from Soviet Lieutenant Belenko who had

flown the MIG-25 to Japan. Except that American pilots didn't defect, and what Joe was taking to Russia was a far greater prize than the MIG-25, which had turned out to be built largely of stainless steel, with archaic electronics by Western standards: a dated barrel of an aircraft incapable of matching the best of the West. Not much of a prize at all, in fact.

Joe was in deep shit, Pentland thought tiredly. The shit would be less if he brought Dracula back; there was no doubt of that. But it could only be a question of degree. However, at least he would have Suzie, and he would be free—and he might have his son.

Son!—Or daughter! Joe and Suzie Kenyon would have discussed a name for their child, wouldn't they? The prospect of a child so late—so longed for—would have become the major topic of their private moments, and they would have discussed a name— probably argued about it, sharing the prospect of their delight.

And if that name, or those names, were included in the signal, that would make Kenyon sit up! They would have told no one what they planned to call the baby—no one! He would make Suzie tell him.

If Suzie wasn't there, or couldn't tell him for some unthinkable reason, then the whole thing would be academic anyway, and Joe and the SR80 would be gone for good.

With a grunt, Maurice Fennel sat back into the seat beside Pentland.

Claude glanced around, caught Pentland's eye, and winked, and Jean-Jacques stuck a thumb up between them.

Thank God for Maurice, Pentland thought.

"What did they think, Maurice?"

"They think you are a crazy dog, but they also think the plan 'as a chance." Maurice turned his head toward Pentland and grinned in the darkness. Claude had switched the light off, and handed something to Maurice—a small flask, Pentland now saw. The big Swiss passed it to him.

"Drink some of this. It is cognac. Compliments of Claude. 'E says you could not be crazier if you were drunk, so you might as well be drunk. I agreed with 'im."

Unanimous, Pentland thought, and tipped his head back. He coughed as the brandy coursed down his throat and then he felt the psychological warmth spread through his system. Bullshit to the experts who said alcohol was useless in an emergency, he decided. It did three things: it gave you a kick in the ass when you most needed it—it gave you a false sense of security, which was a damned sight better than no sense of security at all—and it made you feel warm.

"Ah!" Pentland said, handing the flask back to Maurice. "Tell Claude he is an intelligent man."

"The strength of Claude," Maurice replied, "is not 'is intelligence; it is 'is prick! *Hein*, Claude?" Maurice let out one of his stentorian bellows of laughter. Claude lifted a fist briefly from the cyclic controls and shook it over his shoulder.

The chopper swept over the small town of Monthey, still sleeping in the darkness, and they could now dimly see the small mountain road as it wound up into the peaks below them. Five minutes, Pentland thought. It was five-thirty. If Lindley's estimates were correct, Joe would be on the ground in the Soviet Union in twenty minutes. And in twenty minutes the sun would be up. Five minutes to get there, and fifteen minutes to get Suzie and signal Joe.

Oh shit, he thought. He reached for the flask of cognac and took another swig.

"Maurice," he said, wiping his lips. "Tell Claude to

stay by the radio in the chopper at all costs. And leave the radio on—tuned to the embassy frequency. He must *not* leave the chopper, understand?"

"Of course."

"Any one of us could be, well, put out of action, right? So the message we send to be relayed to Joe is this: 'Suzie and blank safe. Come home. David.' Just that. 'Blank' is the name of their future son or daughter. Only Suzie knows this. Tell her that you *must* know this name to save Joe's life. Now tell Claude and Jean-Jacques. Make them understand. Okay?"

My God, Pentland thought, as once again Maurice heaved himself forward to talk to the two men in front, suppose Joe and Suzie *haven't* thought of a name! After the previous miscarriages they might even have decided it would be bad luck. What the hell to do then?

Stop worrying, he told himself. What was the use of worrying? What else could he do?

Maurice's shouted French over the noise of the engine and rotors ceased, and he settled back.

"I 'ave told them, David. Claude says, 'what if she 'as not decided on a name for this future child?' You 'ave thought of this?"

Pentland smiled grimly back at his friend.

"Ask him if he has any better ideas, Maurice," he said tiredly.

Claude raised his right hand and pointed his thumb downward. He relaxed on the collective and eased the cyclic forward, and the helicopter began to descend.

Maurice smacked Pentland's left knee and leaned toward him.

"If she is there," he said, "and we get 'er away, and 'er 'usband returns, David; Maurice Fennel and," he jerked his head toward the two men in the front,

"Claude and Jean-Jacques, will be your guests for the biggest piss-up which Geneva ever 'as seen!"

"You bet your sweet ass, Maurice," Pentland shouted back in a reasonable American accent.

They were low over the road now, banking and pitching, following the winding tarmac along the cliff to the left and the precipice to the right; close, David recognized, to where Renko had shot his tires away hours ago—years, now, it seemed.

"Gail can be with us, of course," Maurice added.

"I wouldn't like to try to keep her away."

Maurice laughed.

Claude set the machine down lightly on the road, a quarter of a mile down from where the track led up to the cabin. Jean-Jacques leapt out, followed quickly by Pentland, and then the bulk of Maurice. Jean-Jacques climbed back into his seat and shouted "*Bonchance!*" as he slammed the door, and then Claude lifted the machine up, tilted the nose down, and thrashed away up the valley.

To any listeners in the cabin, there would have been no discontinuity of sound, nothing to indicate the helicopter had landed.

Maurice Fennel and David Pentland began to run up the road toward the track that led to the cabin.

As the aircraft dropped down to forty thousand feet, Joe tiredly reached forward and switched off the autopilot, pulled back Dracula's throttles to reduce to subsonic flight, then adjusted power to maintain the descent rate.

"What the hell!" he muttered to himself, and again reached forward, this time to switch off the counterdetection system. There was now no point in remaining a blank hole in the Soviet sky. Berezniky was a busy base, and the area unknown to him, and he'd need their control assistance to make the approach. There were no charts in the aircraft to illustrate approach procedures to a Soviet military base, and if for some stupid reason he cracked the aircraft up just because he hadn't a clue where he was, that would be the end of Suzie.

The transponders immediately began winking frantically as the questing beams of airborne and ground-based radar transmitters found him and bounced their signals back to their dish antennas.

Joe slowed Dracula to two hundred and fifty knots. The course plot indicated he was seventy nautical miles north of Berezniky.

Marshall Gorlov, if not the highest ranking officer among those clustered in the control tower at Berezniky, was perhaps the most respected—as were all top-ranking KGB officers. It was, therefore, familiar to his austere figure that he should stand within his own space, where no others might accidentally brush shoulders with him. He was used to it. The nearest officer to him was a colonel of the Soviet air force, one Svetlin, commander of the base. Svetlin was alert and ready to jump in any direction Gorlov should suggest by gesture or direct command. The tension, as they awaited the appearance of the American spy-plane, was an almost-tangible presence.

The sun had risen from behind the Urals at their backs and now bathed the acres of grey concrete beyond the tinted control-tower windows. Dew still glistened on parked military aircraft in rows below the tower, stretching from left to right. Beyond the parked aircraft the taxiway, and then the rubber-streaked north-south runway, provided flattened gashes in the summer grass, and to the west, beyond the airport boundary, heat was already shimmering above the brown fields that stretched to the lake. At the moment it was quiet. Thirty minutes previously, the air had been filled with the roar of intercepters taking off to cover the American's approach to the base. The dozen or so officers clustered within the tower strained their ears for the voices of the approach controllers who would likely be the first to actually speak to Kenyon.

Colonel Svetlin moved closer to the back of the Soviet captain who sat before his banks of VHF equipment built into a long desklike unit below the high outward-sloping tower windows. Two radar screens showed the deployment of covering Soviet aircraft at ranges of fifty and two hundred and fifty miles.

"Well?" Svetlin demanded in a voice of authority.

The captain turned his head fractionally in deference to his CO, then shook it slowly. "Nothing as yet, Comrade Colonel."

Others in the room leaned slightly forward, all eyes on the backs of the two officers.

Svetlin looked at his watch briefly, automatically. "I do not," he said, "understand why we cannot yet see him on the screen. He must by now be within range, you agree? Switch back to the transmissions from the Centers," he ordered.

Gorlov moved close up behind them. For a minute they listened to a series of radar-intercept bearings issuing from the Center controllers. To the Captain, these lines of position translated into a mental image of a circle of airspace radiating two hundred and fifty miles from the centerpoint of Berezniky. The radar bearings altered swiftly, and as the picture changed in the tower controller's mind he became aware that a blankness was moving south toward Berezniky. The

Centers were tracking the circumference of this blankness, at the center of which they knew the American aircraft to be.

"Sir, the electronic radar interference capability of this machine can be varied, we now know, to a diameter of sixteen hundred kilometers. The controllers are tracking the center of this. From what I can make out, the American will be within Berezniky airspace within perhaps twelve minutes. The speed is constant at mach one point five. He is coming, Comrade Colonel."

Gorlov moved closer to peer through the windows to the north.

My God, he thought with his heart accelerating. My God, we have him. Twelve minutes. And I have done this. Still wearing his coat, he thrust his hands deep into the side pockets to conceal their trembling fingers.

The controller flicked back to the approach radar. "*There* he is!" he cried. "There he is—he has switched off the interference—"

There was a stampede of feet across the linoleum floor behind him as top-ranking military and scientific personnel rushed to peer first at the radar image centered in the screen, and then to focus on the blue sky north of the airfield.

Then they heard the American's voice.

Sixteen minutes to go.

Get out! he thought. Get out now! There was still time. What the hell was he doing? A traitor—a defector, the very word evoking a feeling of disgust—like defecator. A shitter, a filthy treacherous shitter—wasn't he that? All he had to do was ram the throttles forward, and punch the afterburners—maybe even use the emergency liquid-oxygen system to shove her up to near-orbital speeds. They'd never catch him then! He wouldn't make it to the coast—not on one hour's fuel if he used the rocket mode, but so fucking what, Joe thought, sweat pouring down his face. So fucking what? He could set the self-destruct timer for the aircraft and blow Dracula and himself into so many pieces, so many fiercely burning pieces, there would be nothing left—nothing for the bastards to find. And at least he could die with the satisfaction of not having betrayed his country—not having become a treacherous shitter.

But what of Suzie then? What of the child?

They *had* to live. Whatever the dreadful consequences of this, they had to *live*. It was beyond his capabilities to sentence them to death, a sacrifice for military secrets. He would just never go back—never shame them—even if one day, one gray day in the future, the Soviets released him, or traded him for some other poor, broken wretch from whom his own country would have milked all they could. No, if that happened, he thought, he would find some remote place, somewhere no one would ever know his real name, never associate him with the traitor in the news a few years back—the miserable bastard who'd flown that secret plane over to the goddamn Russkies.

Joe settled back in the acceleration couch and stared vacantly through the perspex at the Ural Mountains rising up to meet him on the left side of the aircraft. They looked like the Sierra Nevadas: white-clad peaks shining in the morning sun, wisps of cloud blowing from the highest of the summits, white vapor curling against a deep-blue sky. As Dracula slid on down, the mountains swelled into their true perspective, and valleys opened up to Joe's view. High, green valleys below the snow peaks, among forests of fir, and, lower down the slopes, birch and aspens above the green of foothill pastures, where, no doubt, as on the western slopes of the Sierras or the Rockies, fields were grazed by cattle and sheep, tended by farmers who were uninterested in politics and the machines of destruction and surveillance.

To the right of the aircraft, a wide river twisted through country varying between verdant cultivated patches and the burnt-umber of higher grazing, browning in the fall. Ahead, hazy still in the distance, the river widened into a long lake, and Joe could see from the map readout that this was the lake at the head of which Berezniky sat—Dimitri Olenko's home.

The land over which he now flew so much resembled his own country. Why, he wondered, had it not worked out that nations could exist in peace, so that down there not only would there be Russians, but also Americans—and British and French, Germans, Chinese, and all the rest? Why was it that the peoples of this largely beautiful planet found it necessary to build walls from each other, and complicated machines to wreak havoc on each other—when there were mountains like these, with green alpine meadows and running streams with fish to be caught, and soaring birds and running deer—beauty as far as the eye could see?

In spite of the balance the PCMS system exerted on his mind and body, Joe experienced an overwhelming sadness, and shook his head. Too late now, he thought. Too late for him. He took several deep breaths, then reached forward with his left hand to tune to the international emergency frequency on one of the VHF radios. He was unfamiliar with Soviet approach-control frequencies, but guessed they would be listening out on 121.5.

He cleared his throat, noticing before he spoke that his right arm was running with blood. It surprised him. There had been no time to notice before. He realized that the vein he had rammed onto Dracula's needle was pumping his blood slowly over the armrest behind the stick. Perhaps that was why he felt so strange now, he thought. He wondered idly how much blood he had lost during this dreadful flight. But it was of no matter now. The inquisitors would take good care of him in little more than twelve minutes.

"This is United States aircraft, Sierra Romeo Eight-Zero," he transmitted. "For landing at Berezniky. Advise your approach frequency for further transmission—Over."

A light burned in the sitting room of the cabin. It spilled from the window to the left of the door and lit up the thick pines that grew twenty feet back from the doorway. A tiny breeze rustled the needles, the sound whispering through the dense trees. High above the roof of the building the alpine peaks were bright with the rising sun, and as he watched, Pentland could see the black crags and planes below the peaks lighting up brilliantly as the earth rotated to the east and brought the sun down onto them. Over to the west, the black sky was shading to a deep violet, and in a few minutes the dawn would creep down into the corrie, and then it might be too late.

Maurice Fennel breathed heavily beside him. Their combined breathing from the exertion of the fast run up the road and then the track—to their present position five feet into the pines, as close as they could get to the window of the room facing north—was noisy in the stillness. That window, which they both watched, was dark. Empty panes of glass reflected the

312

lightened sky, and it was impossible to see inside.

There was only one distant noise to disturb the peace of the corrie. Far to the west, close to the rim of the mountains, the helicopter clattered. Unless someone inside the cabin was especially alert it would be unlikely that they would hear it—yet. As Maurice and Pentland listened, the sound of the machine grew a little.

" 'E is coming, I think," Maurice murmured close to Pentland's ear.

Pentland nodded. He peered down at his watch every few seconds now. The digits seemed a blur of speed, seconds clicking off like tenths of seconds. The time was flying. There were now only eleven minutes until the deadline. It was twenty-one minutes to six.

The sound of the machine grew. It seemed very high above them as it approached. You must arrive on time, Claude, Pentland urged silently to himself. You have one minute. Have you misjudged, Claude? If you have, and you are late, there will be insufficient time . . .

Pentland eased the position of the machine pistol resting across his left arm, his bundled fist glimmering palely in the darkness of the trees. A bird, alerted by the dawn, started to sing liquidly somewhere close-by in the tops of the branches. Both men kept their eyes glued to the door in the front of the cabin. When they had first crept up to the building through the cover of the pines, Pentland had gone round to the back of the building, the west side, and found no rear door. The only entrance was the one they now watched. It had been a relief, knowing that. It meant that he and Maurice could together cover the one entrance—until Pentland went to the north window.

Was she there? She had to be there . . .

Claude and Jean-Jacques were now high to the

313

south and the noise was becoming very loud as they approached. Someone inside would hear soon. Perhaps they wouldn't, though. Perhaps they were asleep. No shadow had passed across the light in the window as they watched. Whoever was inside would be thinking they were home and dry. They nearly *were* home and dry.

The digits of Pentland's watch sped through the ten minute deadline. It was twenty to six. Pentland felt panic rise as they kept on going—five, six, ten, fifteen . . .

Claude! He peered up into the sky.

Beyond the roof of the cabin, against the mountains, a bright light appeared. It dropped out of the sky like a falling meteor, accompanied by a whistling clatter of blades as Claude cut the power and autorotated downward in a simulation of an emergency—a powerless landing. Pentland could now see the machine behind the single light, dropping like a stone for the flat spot south of the cabin. It swooped out of the sky like a falcon, plunging toward the ground, and now the noise was very loud, and someone was bound to hear.

Pentland started for the window in the north room. The noise was tremendous—a loud whistling and clatter of blades, a rushing of wind in the pine trees, and a blast of shattering noise as Claude applied full power to arrest the descent of the helicopter. The door of the building was flung open and a figure emerged, a dark silhouette in the flood of interior light from behind. The figure stood transfixed for a second, his back to Maurice and where Pentland had been, staring at the single powerful light searing from the area beyond the end of the building, paralyzed by the massive onslaught of sudden, unexpected noise. Then Maurice's machine pistol roared,

314

heard only as a staccato stitching noise nearly submerged by the beating racket of the helicopter, and the silhouetted figure was picked from its feet and bundled forward, jerking down into the dead pine needles like a mad puppet.

Pentland sprang out of the darkness toward the blank window. Beyond the panes of glass, an oblong of light grew rapidly as someone from the lighted room beyond opened a door. The light slanted across the floor of the room, but still Pentland could still see nothing that indicated that Suzie was in there. He raised the weapon. Against the light of the now-open door a figure was silhouetted, hurrying into the room, carrying something; something long, held at the hip. Pentland fired through the glass of the window. The roar of the chattering weapon and the simultaneous crash of breaking, flying glass assaulted his ears; the sound causing him to stagger back a step. The figure inside, in the doorway, was blown back through it, back into the light of the room beyond. Then a woman screamed. A dreadful, panicky, animal scream, as Pentland used the barrel of the machine pistol to clear the jagged ends of broken glass with a scythelike sweep.

He heard the roar of Maurice's weapon again from the front of the house and the woman still screamed as Pentland clambered through into the room.

He saw the woman through the lighted doorway, then. It was the nurse, Olga. Her hands were up to her mouth and she had reeled back against the table where she had treated his hand, her eyes staring wide, focused down to the floor of the cabin before her, where the person Pentland had shot lay like a bleeding bundle of rags. The man, Ernst, turned dazedly around close to her, his eyes wide, shifting

315

between the window—through which the light of
the helicopter still glared like some demonic thing
as it clattered and whistled and roared—and the
doorway, where someone had disappeared with a
jerking scream. Ernst clutched the shotgun.

And then close to him in the darkness Pentland
heard someone sob—a terrified, stifled sob, and he
sprang round to face back toward the window, his
eyes searching the darkness to the window's left,
picking out the shape of a bed, and a figure on the
bed, indistinguishable in the darkness. As he moved
he was conscious of a change in the quality of the
light from the open doorway and he whirled his
body to the left, raising the weapon. The room was
filled with the crashing, deep-throated boom of the
shotgun and the staccato chatter of Pentland's
weapon. Simultaneously, Pentland was thrown
heavily against the wooden wall of the room, close
to the smashed window, and a figure shot back from
the doorway with a short cut-off cry. Pentland's left
thigh felt as if a thousand white-hot pins had been
thrust deep into his skin. He slithered down the wall
to the carpeted floor.

He crawled toward the bed, unable to use the leg,
feeling blood flowing from it in a thousand places
and pain like fire from the fusillade of shotgun
pellets.

"Suzie!" he gasped. "Suzie?"

Christ, it had to be her. Who else could it be?
Answer me, answer me.

He felt the bed and pulled himself up so that his
head and shoulders were over the edge, his eyes wide
and straining to recognize Suzie Kenyon.

"No!" a female voice sobbed. "Go away—leave
me—"

She was turned away from him, a bunch of hair

316

slightly reflecting the light from the open door, the rest of her covered by a blanket. But the light in the hair was golden.

"Suzie!" Pentland whispered. "Suzie, it's me— David." He reached forward and felt her flinch as his hands touched her covered shoulder. He gently pulled the shoulder, turning her to face him, seeing the paleness of her face roll into view.

"It's me!" he murmured. "You're all right now. You're all right. You're going home soon. The Russians—they've gone. You're all right, now—"

She opened her eyes. They opened wide and stared at him uncomprehendingly for a moment. Then they focused.

"David?" she whispered.

"Yes." Pentland drew her to him, and she began to sob.

"Suzie. Joe's in the SR80, on his way to Russia. We have to send a message to him. He'll ignore it unless we tell him something he'll believe." She was shaking in his arms, sobbing. "Do you understand, Suzie?" He squeezed her shoulders and rolled her away from him a little so that he could see her face, and she his.

"The only way he'll believe anything I say on the radio is if you tell me the name you and he plan to give to your child."

Suzie Kenyon stared up at him, her eyes puzzled, hurt, anxious.

"But, I don't *understand*. Joe—where is he? I—"

"Suzie, Suzie," Pentland urged, shaking her softly, desperately trying to contain his impatience. Christ, what was the *time*—?

"Tell me the name, sweetheart," he whispered. She was like a frightened little animal.

317

"Victor," she whispered back huskily. "Or Rachel, if it was a—"

Pentland eased away from her and turned toward the door. The big bulk of Maurice Fennel stood in the doorway. Pentland hadn't noticed before.

"Use them both, Maurice. Use them both," Pentland said, feeling infinitely weary. "Victor and Rachel—did you get that?"

The MIG-25s had closed in as he ran down to the base at Berezniky. There was one on either side of him now, each keeping station a hundred yards to right and left. The contact screen showed others behind and above him. He was in a box of Russian interceptors—the best they had.

The approach controller had ordered him to overfly the base from north to south and then to make a procedural, teardrop turn, beyond the outer marker, to bring him back on a reciprocal course from south to north to the runway. The base spread out below him—acres of gray concrete with rows of flat-topped buildings on the mountainside. The town of Berezniky clustered beyond the buildings, no more than five miles or so from the airfield. Mostly civilian employees, he thought, and aircrew.

Lines of aircraft stood close to the hangars, their shadows long and black, looking like plastic models in the sunlight. He recognized most of their shapes—various models of operational MIGs and some transports which looked like Ilyushins—and then the flat, base expanse slid back below him as he continued to the south at five thousand feet and one hundred and ninety knots. At the low speed, Dracula's nose was high to produce the required angle of attack. The ramjets were rumbling at eighty-percent power, and the aircraft pitched and yawed lazily in the turbulence as the morning sun heated air and sent it soaring upward in invisible bubbles. Two minutes later, Joe crossed the outer marker and began his three hundred and sixty-degree procedural turn to bring him back to the runway.

"Eight-Zero, contact now the Berezniky control tower on one one six decimal three for your final approach, and confirm." The Russian voice pronounced it "Preshniki", but the voice was neutral and the English accented, but clear.

"One one six decimal three," Joe confirmed.

As he switched frequency he could imagine them down there. They would be practically drooling to get their hands on Dracula. There would probably be crowds of technicians and scientists, and air force experts, eagerly watching him as he became a speck to the south before expanding in their eager vision again as he slid down the glide slope and flared for landing. Joe wondered whether Olenko would have returned directly to Russia after he had left Farnborough. How long ago had that been? It seemed so long—somehow another dimension of time, but he supposed it was no more than three hours or so. The chronometer told him that it was eleven minutes to six, British Summer Time—two hours later here in the Soviet Union.

Joe completed the procedural turn and leveled Dracula for the final approach. The two MIGs closed back in to either side.

Here we go, he thought. In four minutes the American tires would smoke on Russian concrete, and a few minutes after that he would take a giant step back for American military superiority.

319

Gorlov thrust Svetlin aside. "Where?" he demanded hoarsely. "Where?"

They had listened to the approach controller's transmissions to the American aircraft, and their own tower controller's instructions to Joe to overfly the airfield and make a procedural turn to reappear from the south.

"There—look!" the controller had half-risen from his seat, arm outstretched, pointing toward the northern boundary of the airfield.

Then Gorlov saw what he had yearned to see for so many months. At the center of a box of MIGs trailing long plumes of black unburned fuel, as if appearing for a ceremonial fly-past, Dracula, with her immense, long fuselage angled upward and the huge engines shimmering the air to her rear, flew past the control tower, the length of the field, paralleling the north-south runway.

Yob tvaiyou mat!" Gorlov breathed. "This aircraft, for one pilot—is—*immense.*" His eyes followed the flight, neck slowly swiveling. From the other personnel clustered around him, slightly to the rear, came a combined gasp of amazement. In contrast to the gleaming aluminum of the stubby MIGs, Dracula appeared as a delta-plan black swan, shrinking the MIGs to toys. As she flew past, the secret paint-coating of her surfaces absorbed the light. There was no gleam, no reflection. Gorlov narrowed his eyes to concentrate on keeping the peculiar aircraft in his vision. One moment he could see her clearly—at others she appeared like a shimmering ghost. And then the flight receded to the south, preparatory to turning back to the field to land.

Then the backslapping began. Soviet officers and Soviet scientists, forgetting protocol for the moment in the extremes of their triumphant excitement, became like enthusiastic children. Gradually they calmed and concentrated on Gorlov again, the central figure—the figure from Moscow and the KGB, who had conceived, planned, and engineered this perfect scheme, which the rest of the world could only, whatever they might suspect, regard as an unprecedented, disastrous defection by a United States Air Force colonel.

"Congratulations, Comrade Marshall!" someone shouted. Others joined in.

Gorlov turned to quickly survey the faces with the briefest of smiles, then jerked his hand for silence.

"Where does he turn?" he asked the controller.

"Five kilometers, sir. He will be at the threshold in—no more than three minutes." Sensing that Gorlov's anxiety resulted from watching this triumph of the KGB director's career pass out of sight again, he quickly added, "It is a standard approach procedure, Comrade Marshall."

Gorlov grunted, watching through the south-facing screens. Then he saw the larger speck surrounded by blocks of smaller aircraft appear and grow steadily larger.

Already, military vehicles were dispersing from somewhere at the base of the tower, fanning out across the field to line the runway. Fire-control vehicles were stationed at strategic points, their strobe lights flashing brightly against the sun. Heavily armed troops lined the fences of the airfield boundaries, and others thickly patrolled the buildings. Roads within ten miles of the base were sealed with armored vehicles and road blocks. All routine air traffic had been diverted from the area for a two-hundred-mile radius. The town of Berezniky was stiff with men of the KGB. In his preparations, Gorlov had taken no chances. No chances that some

CIA penetration attempt mounted at the last minute could have a semblance of a chance of success—no chance that dissident elements could stage a sabotage effort.

In the air, half the Soviet air force patrolled at flight levels to fifty thousand feet, and every conceivable electronic surveillance apparatus focused its attention on the skies above this base below the Urals.

Discreetly, the Soviet Union had gone to a Forward Alert stage, ready for any potential retaliation from the West. Overtly, Soviet ships and aircraft faced those of NATO forces in a line stretching east from Finland across the Barents Sea. Gorlov had done everything he could conceive to earn himself the status of Hero of the Soviet Union.

He felt an advanced sense of the immensity of his stature, even now, in this control tower full of men and the smell of working electronics. His breath came deeply as he instinctively held it for long moments while he watched Dracula grow in size as she slipped down toward the airfield from the south.

The controller was reading out the radar-computed height and distance to go. "—and one kilometer. Five hundred meters, and half a kilometer. Two hundred meters and one third of a kilometer—"

Dracula was now lower than the MIGs which had previously hugged her. The flight above her had remained at the same speed as the American, but one thousand meters above, ready for any maneuver which the American might try during the last seconds. As Dracula slowed further for the touchdown, the MIGs alongside her crept forward of her, maintaining their own low maneuvering speed and an altitude of one thousand meters above ground level.

Gorlov watched as the great, long nose raised even

higher as the aircraft slowed—watched the long legs drop down from beneath the fuselage.

He smiled tightly. "It is—*evil*—this thing," he said to himself as he became aware of Dracula's flattened, snakelike fuselage. "It is like a dragon!" he breathed. He shook his head slowly, his neck turning as his eyes trained unblinkingly on the *Americanski spion* reaching its long talons down toward the concrete runway of Berezniky.

Joe could see the airfield again now, hazy-gray, ten miles ahead. He adjusted the throttles to drop the aircraft's speed to one hundred and forty knots, then wound out flap and made pitch-trim adjustments to set the SR80 into a steady descent down the ILS to the distant runway.

Dracula's computer clacked, the peculiar rustling noise loud in the cockpit.

Joe's eyes flickered down to the screen from his concentration ahead. One of the audio-alert signals started a persistent beeping—a tone he had never previously heard. He brought his eyes down to the screen again. Words were printing fast, jerkily from left to right. Dracula pitched up a little in a small windshear and he quickly, automatically, raised his eyes to the horizon. He had to concentrate now. The runway was sliding up to meet him. Were they still trying to get him to return? Had they now resorted to using a direct order from the Pentagon—perhaps the president himself? It was too late—too late. They could never understand about Suzie. It was too late.

Joe's eyes flicked to the altimeter. Eight hundred feet, rate of descent nine hundred feet per minute. The screen flashed in his peripheral vision and the audio screamed increasingly loud. He knew the flashing—and audio—would continue until he reached forward to flick the contact, which would signify his receipt of the priority message. Then the message would be automatically stored in the computer's memory. After that, the screen would quit flashing and the audio would switch off. He needed to concentrate for the landing, goddamn it—but he reached forward for the contact.

—And read the flashing words:

**SUZIE VICTOR RACHEL SAFE
COME HOME DAVID**

CHAPTER SEVENTEEN

The transmission to Joe flashed onto the Ops screen in front of Chuck Lindley and Colonel Byrnes and the clustered military personnel. Tired, lined faces with shadowed stubbles of late-night beard regarded it soundlessly for long moments, as each man imagined what would be going through Kenyon's mind, thousands of miles east beneath the Urals. Would he have received it before his tires hit Russian soil? Would he believe it?"

Who in hell were Victor and Rachel, Lindley wondered? And *how* in hell was the poor sonofabitch going to make it back?

"Now he's in *real* trouble," Lindley muttered to the British MI6 chief.

"What precisely do you have in mind?" Byrnes said.

"Well, shit," Lindley shook his head. "Think about it. Jesus, if he ain't on the deck, he's close, right? He'll be up to his eyeballs in an escort of MIG-25s, and I'd guess he'd have an hour's fuel left in the tanks. Where in fuck *can* he go?" Lindley clapped his mouth shut and lit another cigarette, then began to walk around in small circles. Everyone watched.

Byrnes looked haggard and worried, as they all did. "Is there perhaps some way we can divert their attention from him?" he said to the American.

Lindley laughed shortly. "Just supposing, Colonel, there was a Foxbat on final to Farnborough, escorted by a bunch of F-16s—and the whole RAF out there watching. You'd need a goddamn nuclear explosion to shift the attention, right?"

"Yes, of course," Byrnes shook his head, "however, there must be *something* we can do—"

Pentland came on the line then, and they turned to the transceivers.

"Chuck?" Pentland's voice said. The MI6 man sounded strained and tired.

"Yeah, right here, Dave—you did a great job back there."

"Did Joe get the transmission?" Pentland interrupted. "Is he on his way back?"

"We don't know as yet, son," Lindley told him. "Any minute we'll know. I'd guess it's one of two things—he's down, or he's up to his ass in Soviet fighters making a break for it. Whichever it is, he's in big trouble."

"Look, we're on our way to Cointrin," Pentland put in. "I'm arranging transport direct to Farnborough. I'll be on the end of a phone or radio the whole time. Chuck, we must think of a way to help him."

"I know that, goddammit!"

"Well, what've you come up with?"

"Shit, Dave, what is there—?"

"Think—for Christ's sake. What about staging some alert to draw them off?"

"This is bad enough, ain't it. NATO and the Soviets are right on each other's asses over there. It wouldn't take much more to start World War Three—"

326

"Wait, wait," Pentland's voice was suddenly urgent. "Is there another overflight in process over there? A U2, or whatever—"

"Jesus—a '71?" Lindley whispered, standing very still. "Maybe there's a '71 up there somewhere—"

"What? What did you say? I can't hear you! Chuck?"

"Yeah, yeah—look Dave, maybe we *can* do something. Stand by, will ya? Just stand by." He whirled to face Byrnes. "Get my boss back on the line."

"The director of the DIA—?"

"Shit, *yes*, man. Hurry, for Christ's sake!"

Major Slim O'Leary and his copilot Major Cleeve Hanson were contemplating the new morning as it lit the brown land eighty thousand feet below. As they watched, the sun gained sufficient altitude to pour over the Yablonovyy Khrebet range to the east of Lake Baykal and cause the surface of the lake to gleam like burnished silver in a long ribbon roughly paralleling their course line, which at this moment was very nearly due north.

Fifteen hours ago their Blackbird had left Beale Air Force Base in California for a routine surveillance mission, starting at T'aiyuan in northern China, where it appeared from infrared information received by satellites that the Chinese might be up to something new in the mountains just south of the Great Wall. Then they had proceeded due north into the Gobi Desert, overflying Ulaaan Baatar in the Mongolian Republic, to sniff at the Russo-Chinese guerilla war at the border on the way; and now they were still heading due north across the southern Soviet, with the intention of swinging eastward across the Sea of Okhotsk, from where they would run down the Aleutians to refuel off Alaska.

O'Leary yawned. "Shit—this gets old, don' it? What's the next contact, Cleeve?"

"Place called Chagda—fifteen minutes—on the Aldan River, boss, then we turn east. One pass over a new missile site which the Nips're unhappy about—"

At that moment their headphones were filled with a repetitive beep that brought their adrenalin count up sharply.

"What the hell?" O'Leary murmured. "That's a code three!" He reached forward in the front cockpit to change frequencies, and switched on the decoder.

PROCEED AREA BEREZNIKY URGENT
COORDS FOLLOW
ADVISE FUEL REMAINING

O'Leary's voice was crisp now. "What's the fuel, Cleeve?"

Hansen took a couple of seconds to key his computer. "Five hours mach one point five at sixty thousand."

"Okay—new course three two zero. Give me an ETA for Berezniky at mach three."

The SR71 Blackbird's nose eased down a couple of degrees as her engines accelerated her to mach three, and the earth's curve tilted in the forward screen as the autopilot swung to the new course. Both officers took a keen interest in things from that moment, and all feelings of boredom and tiredness bled away.

"ETA Berezniky one eight minutes, boss," Hansen said from the rear cockpit.

While the SR71 pilots had been receiving their new mission instructions, Byrnes had remained on the line with his counterpart, the director of the DIA, General McMullen. McMullen was Lindley's boss, in addition to being the ultimate authority over in Washington, next to the President, for reconnaissance missions, and the general was perched on the edge of his bed in his pajamas with three phones going at once.

"A'right!" the general snapped. "They're on their way, ETA eighteen minutes."

"General," Byrnes's voice said. "Colonel Lindley has requested that he be patched in for voice transmissions to the SR71 and Kenyon—would this be possible?"

"What the fuck for?" said the general irritably.

Byrnes coughed. "He is the only one here, or there, who is familiar with the flight characteristics of both the SR71 and the—er—new aircraft, General. We believe that communication with the two aircraft over the Soviet in the next few minutes will be vital, if we're to have any chance at all of sneaking Kenyon out. It will be an exceedingly slim chance at best, as I know you appreciate. Colonel Lindley would like this arranged via the SAMOS on the ELF, if this is possible, to minimize the chances of the Soviets picking up transmissions—"

"All right, all right, all right," the general interrupted. "I'll arrange it. Stand by. Get him out, Byrnes, okay?"

"Yes, of course, General."

"God*damn* this!" McMullen said.

Byrnes looked over to Lindley, who was grinning.

"Tell Pentland," Lindley said to Byrnes, "while I get in contact with Joe."

SUZIE VICTOR RACHEL
SAFE COME HOME DAVID

329

The significance of the words flooded Joe's tired brain, flushing it with an explosive feeling, a feeling like ice cascading through his mind; a feeling that was a mixture of relief and fear, nostalgic emotion, and abject terror. It sent his pulse rate soaring and adrenalin pouring into his bloodstream. The hair on his scalp prickled and the PCMS sensed the absolute, urgent, immediate, highest-priority requirement for massive action, and flooded him with a tide of drugs that sent his left hand for the throttles at laser-speed.

At the same time Joe's eyes took in the scene around him with crystal clarity. No longer was he hazed by an overwhelming sense of defeat. The runway stretched ahead of him, grey and shining in the morning light. To the right, the buildings of the base with the lines of parked Soviet aircraft clustered before them. Beyond the buildings, the Urals clouded aloft in shimmering blues and violets, with the snow-capped peaks white against the sky. To left and right, the pairs of MIG-25s were accelerating to stay in the air as Dracula sank below them for the touchdown. A glance above revealed a flight of three others drawing ahead of him.

The immediate, instinctive thing to do was to ram the throttles to the stops—through the gates into emergency power, to bring liquid oxygen sluicing into the engine combustion chambers, and use suborbital power to jump the aircraft as high as he could. But they would be waiting for an escape maneuver like that. He would be, if he was them. He would be climbing through a haze of missiles. It would have to be something else.

There was no time to be aware of the speed at which his brain now functioned under the influence of Dracula's dispensary. Joe was only conscious of a strange, icy calm, during which split seconds played out like minutes. It seemed to him that he had all the time in the world.

In fact, only three-tenths of a second passed before he implemented his decision.

He eased Dracula into a lazy, skidding turn to the right, diverging from the runway at an increasing angle toward the base buildings and parked aircraft. He was, by now, no more than fifty feet above the flat ground.

"Eight-Zero," came the voice from the Soviet tower. "Eight-Zero, what is your intention?" the voice rose with alarm. It would look to them as though he was out of control.

Dracula lurched over the parked aircraft directly toward the tower, the highest building in the cluster.

"Eight-Zero, return to your heading and land immediately!"

By now the MIGs were well beyond the end of the runway, flying to as-yet-unchanged orders.

Beyond the base buildings there were a short stretch of flat countryside before the town of Berezniky, which stretched in a low huddle across the land below the mountains.

Keeping his eyes on the MIGs, with the angle between he and them diverging constantly, and Dracula wobbling and lurching still at little more than fifty feet, Joe cleared the buildings. The farm country stretched before him, the town approaching at little more than one hundred and thirty knots. The Soviets would be, he hoped, completely confused.

"Eight-Zero," the controller commanded, report *immediately* your problem, over." A pause and another mile. Then the controller lost his cool and began to shriek in Russian. Joe watched the MIGs, distant specks now, circling in a left turn, conforming to the pattern, drawing away from him. All hell will be erupting down there, he thought. All hell will be erupting up here soon. Then the MIGs suddenly banked to reverse their direction back toward him, plumes of black smoke paying out to their rear. Joe's left hand rammed the throttles to the stops.

Dracula surged ahead with a shattering, vibrating, tympanic roar. Joe's hand switched the emergency-power lever to flood the engines with liquid oxygen and turn the great engines into rockets nearly powerful enough to hurl the aircraft into orbit.

Dracula's insidious horizontal movement across the airfield toward the Soviets in the control tower was not immediately apparent. What was apparent, however, was that the American was no longer descending, but appeared to be flying at an altitude of no more than twenty meters above the runway. Then the controller, with eyes experienced in judging the relative position of an aircraft to the horizon and other features of the landscape beyond the airfield, uttered a gasp and reached for his mike.

"Eight-Zero, Eight-Zero," he rapped out in English, "what are your intentions, over?"

There was no reply.

Gorlov whipped his head round and shot a glance at the side of the controller's face as the man was transmitting. "What does he do?" he bellowed.

The captain transmitted again. Dracula now plainly was veering toward them, growing larger by the microsecond.

"Eight-Zero, Eight-Zero, what is your problem?" the controller's voice rose up the scale.

"Eight-Zero, *Eight-Zero*—"Then his voice betrayed his panic. Dracula had turned toward them, beginning to fill the morning sky to the west. They looked up through the windows at her as she flew toward them at an altitude only marginally higher than their own. They shrank back a little in the room as her menacing shape grew at them.

"Comrade Marshall!" the controller screamed into the open mike in his native Russian. "He is mad. He is out of *control*. I—"

Gorlov snatched the microphone, and spat out orders to Joe in English. "You will *return* to your course and *land*. Return and land *immediately*—"

Then for a moment the light was blanked out as Dracula passed over the tower in a shrieking, trembling whistle of sound.

Gorlov grabbed the controller's shoulder. "He is making a break—don't you see, you fool! Alert the interceptors. *Alert them!*—"

Someone hit the emergency alarm at the console of the controller, and the wailing of sirens filled the air.

For a moment, no one moved. All were frozen, paralyzed, their minds stretched as they tried to adjust to this totally unexpected event. No fisherman who had fought long and hard for, then watched, a thirty-pound king salmon flop back over the side of his boat to disappear into the invisible, unattainable depths, had ever expressed the sense of loss so clearly visible on the faces of the twelve men in the Berezniky control tower.

Then came the most hideous vibration and cacophony of sound any of them had ever experienced. The building shuddered. Equipment jumped and rattled, and one by one the toughened glass panes of the huge windows cracked and split into jagged plates, crashing into the room and disintegrating onto the concrete below.

The tympanic roar was replaced by the amplified

wail of sirens and racing engines, and the sound of fighters reacting on full afterburners.

The mountains were Joe's only hope. To put the wall of high rock between him and them was his only salvation. Short salvation, but time perhaps to plan—time to think. Time—the greatest commodity of life . . .

The wall of the Urals grew in the forward screen as an onrushing express train might appear to a fly with its feet stuck to the rails.

Dracula vibrated with the enormous power—two hundred thousand pounds of flaming plasma thrusting from the massive white-hot gaping afterburner nozzles. The sprawl of Berezniky snapped past in a momentary blur of speed-elongated buildings as Dracula tore for the foothills of the Urals.

In the relentless, vicious force of acceleration, the blood drained from Joe's face and head. His unsuited body was forced back into the oil-yielding couch with the oil compressed now to the consistency of clay. His mouth wide open, the lips pressed back to expose whitened gums, a thin scream of agony forced itself from his throat. The PCMS lit into a total array of warning lights as it monitored the pilot's failing systems while it spurted accelerated jabs of chemicals into his body and brain.

The land below became featureless with speed. Reaching out of sight above the limits of the screen, the mountains, which had been bands of ochres and greens and blues in the morning sun, capped by the line of snow-whitened peaks, fuzzed into a featureless grey wall before him. The gentle foehn wind, spilling down from the cooler peaks to replace the warmer air over the foothills, presented itself to the hurtling density of the aircraft as a compression of multidirectional molecules that hammered the titanium like pile drivers, slamming the body of the pilot within the harness, the helmet vibrating viciously in the padded cradle.

Young, like the Sierra Nevadas of California, the Ural mountains of Russia thrust themselves in places to fourteen thousand feet above sea level; jagged pinnacles of, as yet-unrounded peaks of granite and fissures. The valleys were steep-sided: V-shaped and deep-lined with scrub at the lower altitudes, phasing to birch and aspens that gave way before the snowline to the bright green of perennial fir. Above the treeline, the rugged slopes were fissured granite, the clefts full of greying, aged snow.

Into the first of these narrow, steep-sided valleys, Joe pressed the aircraft, his eyes perceiving only the blurred topography. With his guts plastered against his spine, he kicked her through vertical, climbing turns, while the grey granite walls of rock reached for the thin titanium of her underbelly.

Behind them, sound and shock waves loosened clinging rock, which avalanched in cascades to the valley floor, uprooting trees. Undergrowth was blasted to cinders in the violent torch heat.

Hauling narrowly over the lip of a vertically faced corrie, the aircraft burst into the still, cool air of a higher valley, its sides lined with pine, aspens glinting gold among the banks of emerald. From knife-edge to opposite knife-edge, using the elevators to suck her into turns that caused him to scream with agony, and the PCMS, as if sympathetically, to scream with visual and audio alarms, Joe flew Dracula as he had never flown any aircraft before in his career.

As if rising to the occasion with him through the physiological link of her computers, Dracula responded with an agility which, without doubt, the engineers who had designed and built her could never have credited her with even in their most optimistic moments; and an envelope of maneuverability which certainly neither Joe nor Lindley had approached as they had progressively tested her to her designers' ultimate load factors.

Totally unaware, as his nerve endings responded to the flashing inputs of the speed-drawn topography, and, in turn, as Dracula's superb systems reacted with synchronized speed in this surrealistic roller-coaster ride through the peaks, the G-forces worked on Joe's abdomen like a mechanical bellows in a steel furnace, evacuating his bowels and squeezing his bladder to the consistency of a sun-dried lemon. The miles of his unprotected intestines flattened to empty tubes and threw through his mouth a geyser of yellow bile which, like lava, spread across his chest and knees.

Time and again, with the organism choking for the breath from which its drug-laced blood and coursing adrenalin could extract the oxygen fuel to maintain needed muscular movements, Joe kept the aircraft swooping close to the racing crags to both sides—and sometimes above—until he had worked them over the divide and down into the far, sloping valleys, pitching the needle-nose lower until the eastern flats of the deserts were glimpsed, and the peaks rose higher and higher to their rear.

They came out into the lower foothills before the desert in a great, decelerating, sweeping vertical turn, made by Joe instinctively to the south, and from there he urged the slowing aircraft back close into the lines of cliffs that marked the plunge of the Urals to the lower ground of the desert.

With his eyes in a haze of blurred red he reached

forward and keyed on the terrain-following radar. He programmed it to maintain three hundred feet AGL, then interfaced the autopilot, punched up a speed of three hundred knots, and sank, totally exhausted, back into the couch.

"Ah, Christ," he heard his own cracked voice. "What the hell now?"

He remembered the antidetection system, which he cranked out to maximum range. Once again this new effort exhausted him. He leaned back and wiped the bile unconsciously from his lips with a sweep of his left hand while Dracula lifted, and lowered, and banked, in an electronic invisibility above the undulating, unclad rock.

From a grey kaleidoscope of confused vision and erratic, exhausted thought pattern, the never-absent ministrations of the PCMS pushed and shifted Joe's thinking processes and visibility patterns back into a semblance of order, as Dracula continued to take them south at three hundred knots. In no more than thirty seconds Joe's mind was starting to make enquiries about the advisability of this direction. The original reason had been the result of an instinctive reaction to the thought that the Soviets would assume, once clear of the mountains, that he would turn north and go for altitude like a bat out of hell. In the rush of the moment he had therefore turned south, slowed down, and stayed on the deck. But he knew there was no future in that. There would be a short-term gain in time, but no prospect of a future at all, because the fuel would throttle Dracula very shortly, and that, of course, would be that.

This line of thought brought his focus back to the contact-readout. Spitting drying bile from his desert mouth, Joe reached forward to flick on the screen. To the north, the sky was strewn with echoes, moving into patrol patterns, busy at this moment stepping into layers up to maximum altitudes. As he watched, echoes resolved into north-south pockets above the long line of the Urals. At the moment, none of them appeared to be on an intercept course with him. With a surge of relief, Joe realized that the dash through the Urals had confused them, and he had broken clear for the moment.

He would have given anything for a drink of something—anything. His tongue was swollen and he felt himself going brittle with dehydration. He worked his tongue around his sour mouth, in an effort to squeeze some relief from the salivary glands, with no effect. For a moment he closed his eyes and contemplated the vision of the destruct contact with longing. But then he thought of the words which had acted on him—how long ago? His eyes opened and focused on the chronometer. Three minutes? God, what was happening to time in this foul-smelling module? How could it have only been three minutes? That meant he had been aloft in the SR80 for only three hours thirty-six minutes? He shook his head and went back to concentrating on how to extend his existence a minute at a time—seconds, if it came down to that. Suzie and Victor-Rachel—he smiled—and David, were safe! He *must* somehow see them again. Compulsively, he switched the autopilot out and swung Dracula back to the north, squeezing tight against the mountainsides. To reduce his IR trace, he throttled back and stabilized the speed at one hundred and fifty knots, and the height again at three hundred feet above the ground.

The desert shimmered in growing heat and brown humps to his right, and the mountains grew aloft to peaks to his left. Invisible, except perhaps to wide-eyed Soviet shepherds or lonely prospectors and

338

hunters, he slowly began to move toward the north; it was all he was capable of doing at the moment.

Comforted by the awareness that a growing intercept would provoke Dracula to kick his guts into action, Joe closed his eyes. Someone was talking in his head, the sound tiny—rising and falling, the words coming through in gaps and tumbles. Sometimes the voice was there, sometimes not. It irritated him. All he wanted was to be left alone—like a small animal harried by predators until its whole life-drive was focused on seeking a dark hole, and peace. But the voice was speaking English.

Joe forced his eyes open and focused on the radio frequencies. One had switched to an ELF band—rarely used—the same band that had brought the news—the words—to the computer screen earlier. Alerted now, he made himself listen, and the words became clearer—became not English, but *American*.

Who?

Lindley? *Lindley's* voice?

"Dracula, Dracula, Dracula—do you read—?" Over and over again.

Joe nodded, his eyes glazed, a stupid smile of pleasure forming on his dried, cracked lips.

"Yeah—" he responded finally. "Yeah—I read. Come in, Chuck."

Oh, this was great, he thought. Speaking to his friend Chuck Lindley? Just *great*. He was so happy now that he began to smile widely and then to laugh.

"Joe, Joe, do you read my transmission? Over."

Fantastic, Joe thought. Superdocious! Fantasticlasmic! "Ha, ha, ha!" he laughed delightedly. "Aaah, ha, ha, haaah—"

"Joe, Joe, state your condition, come in please—"

Dracula sensed Joe's imbalance, analyzed it, dosed him. Joe felt a tingling sensation in his brain as if he were standing below a shower of ice-needled water. Lindley—Jesus!

"Dracula to base," he transmitted. "Come in now, over."

"Joe! What's your condition, self and aircraft? Over."

"At the moment clear and undamaged." He read Lindley the latitude and longitude.

There was a combined gasp of relief in the NATO Ops room near High Wycombe as Joe's weak, distant voice interrupted the subdued conversations and the humming of the computers.

"We got him, we *got* him!" Lindley yelled. Lindley turned quickly back to the bank of radios he stood by and spoke urgently into the microphone he held. Everyone else froze, some with their heads cocked, tense to hear the voice of Joe Kenyon again as it drifted through the ionosphere from somewhere in the depths of the Soviet Union.

"Joe, give me your position, present course and altitude, airspeed, and fuel. Over," Lindley transmitted.

For a moment the speaker's were full of the dead sounds of empty carrier waves, the dry winter rustle of an empty universe. Then, faintly, Kenyon's voice was heard in the room.

"Heading north—three five five, east side of Urals—stand by—I got twenty—twenty-two minutes fuel at cruise. They're stringing out along the mountains north and south at various altitudes like a swarm of starlings. I've about had it, Chuck. I'm setting up for self-destruct—plan to bail out somewhere over water—make it difficult for the sumbitches, right? Over."

An agonized look clouded Lindley's features as he violently shook his head.

"No, no, *no*, Joe. Listen! We got a seventy-one on intercept with you from the south. We just worked out he'll be over you in less than seven minutes. Now, you-all hold in there. We need you *back*, goddamn it!"

"You're—you're an—optimist, Lindley. I'm about beat—got no fuel. What's he got—a tow-rope?"

"Now you listen to me, Joe. You're under my orders from this moment. Head north at your present speed and hold in close to the mountains. We got a plot here that is following you. We can see your terrain on a sat-relay, right? Now execute that and standby, over."

"That is roger, Colonel," they heard faintly, cynically. "Will stand by your further transmission."

Lindley shook his head with the trace of a wry smile. He keyed the mike switch again. "You follow that, O'Leary?"

"Affirmative, Colonel," came from the SR71.

"OK, O'Leary, here are your orders. Begin a descent at max speed with full ECM on a course of three five two degrees. I'll vector you to a position close behind our man. At that point, we'll have him clear to max altitude, and hopefully you will become the target. Immediately Kenyon has cleared the lower altitudes, you'll operate your ECM gear as if it is malfunctioning intermittently, to draw them onto you. Do you copy? Over."

There was a short, stunned silence. They could all appreciate O'Leary's thoughts.

"We got that, Colonel," came leadenly over the air.

"You copy that, Joe?"

"Yeah—I copy. I'm at one five zero knots to minimize IR, but it'll only be a matter of moments before they pick up the trace. Right now I'm close to a

341

line of cliffs giving me good cover, but the ground's dropping ahead. Over."

"OK, hold in there, stand by."

Lindley turned to the NATO commander. "General, we'll need an ECM-equipped tanker off Kirkenes ASAP, no escort. We keep the other tanker and escort orbiting south of Spitzbergen—give 'em all somethin' to watch. We can hide the Kirkenes tanker among your boys standing off from the North Cape, right?"

The general turned to a senior RAF officer close to his shoulder. They conferred in low tones. Lindley scratched his balding scalp and rubbed at the stubble on his chin, impatient for their information. Both NATO officers consulted the plot, filled with the hieroglyphics of aircraft and naval deployment. A dense bank of Russian activity swarmed over the White Sea, stretching eastward to Novaya Zemlya. The Soviets were bolting the northern door with unprecedented thoroughness, perfectly aware that Dracula had insufficient fuel to make it out in any other direction.

Dracula's cockpit module stank disgustingly with a mixture of bile, feces, and the metallic sweat of intense exertion and fear.

The PCMS had, by its own measurement, manipulated Joe to maintain a relatively relaxed state of awareness. But by Joe's, his body felt as if it had been squeezed between the rollers of an old-fashioned mangle. His heart pumped in a heavy rhythm in an effort to push the drug-dosed blood through his veins. His breath was short—harsh and shallow, and sometimes deteriorating to shuddering spasms of shock. Whenever this occurred, the PCMS caught him with an appropriate mixture, similar to the method a motorist uses to catch a cold engine with his throttle foot.

An increased source of strain to Joe was now the knowledge that Lindley was about to risk the lives of two SR71 pilots somewhere behind him. He made an effort to rationalize that it wasn't his own ass with which the brass were concerned. The ass of Colonel Joseph Kenyon, USAF, diplomat—recently defector—defecator—was less than worthless. It was probably very unfortunate, from everyone's point of view—except possibly that of his closest friends and Suzie—that his ass was currently attached immovably to this conglomeration of precious metals and electronics labeled, for the sake of identification, as Strategic Reconnaisance Eight-Zero. He knew that would be all they cared about receiving undamaged back there.

The problem was that this would not be the way O'Leary and Hansen would see things. Those poor bastards would know that they were about to put their own asses in the ring so that *he* might have the chance to run.

He kept making his mind up to destruct—and two concerns kept delaying the action. The first was his vision of Suzie—purely, unredeemably, selfish. And the second was the urge he felt to return government property he had stolen. He had never committed even a minor criminal act in his life. With Suzie apparently safe, whatever would be his own personal destiny, his newly reestablished sense of duty made it mandatory that he use his best efforts to get Dracula back. He also knew that his country would be perfectly prepared to sacrifice the lives of a thousand O'Learys and Hansens to retain the secrets of this infernal, goddamn machine plugged to his wrist.

In his detached frame of mind, a result of the drug

343

doses, his expanded sense of the passing of time allowing him the luxury in this lull in the action, Joe regarded Dracula's panel, alive with its lights and signals and the flickering digits and animated screens that were her nerve endings.

"We are man and machine," Joe murmured to her. "Or are we? We need each other like—like lovers. If we go, we're gonna go together. So for now together we stay." He remembered the climactic escape from Berezniky. And remembered also a sense of being one with this machine—as if the machine had responded to the stimulation of fear almost as a human would—to put out an effort beyond its designed capabilities. During those moments, above the force-induced pain in his body, he recalled that he had felt a sense of oneness, as though Dracula had fused with him, their brains and muscles locked in a macabre orgasm of action. Joe found the recollection unsettling. A pilot was a pilot, an aircraft an aircraft—but Dracula seemed to have become something more than an aircraft. Because of her ministrations to his bodily fluids, had he become less of a man? Disturbingly, he visualized the fetus connection within the womb. He shook his head tiredly.

"Somehow, Sierra Romeo Eight-fuckin'-Zero," he said, "whoever you are, *we* gotta find a way back."

Joe rested his head back into the cradle.

There comes a moment when, regardless of chemical or any other form of stimulation, nervous and physical exhaustion finally cause the brain to shut down all functions not concerned with immediate survival. Then the organism will subside into a coma state for as long as it takes itself to reconstitute the ability to perform.

Sensing this droop to oblivion, Dracula went into an emergency mode via the PCMS—but to no avail.

It was like cranking an engine when there was no spark.

Joe Kenyon was a dead weight in the acceleration couch, while the tireless aircraft loped along the foothills of the Urals, undulating to conform to the terrain below, the necessary instruments to maintain this mode programmed into the autopilot. Thus, she would continue until her arteries dried from lack of fuel, and shortly after that happened she would die, reduced to minute fragments on the rocks one hundred yards below.

CHAPTER EIGHTEEN

In spite of the fact that at their current altitude and distance from their target there was no earthly possibility of picking out the SR80, O'Leary once again peered forward and downward through the triangular-shaped windshield of the SR71.

"Give me time to intercept, Cleeve," he said.

In the rear cockpit, Hansen narrowed his eyes in slight irritation. He'd given the skipper an update three times in the last three minutes. He sighed. "Seven an' a bit, boss," he said.

O'Leary's voice burst into his eardrums, harsh, and tense. "A bit! A *bit*! God-*damn*, Major—"

"Seven minutes and nineteen seconds by the mark," Hansen said quickly. "Mark!"

There was a silence, only the sound of the '71 engines, muted, and the hiss of their own breath in the headsets.

Then O'Leary said, "OK, Cleeve." The pilot gave a short laugh. "I—" he began, and paused. "Okay," he breathed. "Okay."

Hansen smiled at O'Leary's helmet in the front cockpit.

"As I see it, Cleeve," O'Leary said, "we gotta sort

of jump in the pond an' splash around so Kenyon c'n move out without the sharks noticing, huh?"

"That's about the fit, boss," Hansen said.

"Yeah. Well—this mother's sure fast enough, I guess, but jus' look at that screen, will ya?"

This time it was Hansen's turn to laugh. "I can't take my eyes off it, boss," he said.

For a moment they both regarded the array of echoes, into the thick of which they shortly planned to plunge.

"I never saw anythin' like this in 'Nam—did you, Cleeve?"

"Nope. Looks real shitty."

O'Leary sighed. "Well—we got speed, no doubt about that. An' we got surprise—"

"And four IR needles," Cleeve put in. They carried four only, and no cannon, no other armament, due to weight and range considerations.

"If needs be," O'Leary said, philosophically, "we could take four of 'em with us, then, right?"

"Jesus, boss," Hansen said, "you have a mind like a laser!"

"Fuck you, Hansen."

In the back, Cleeve Hansen laughed again and in the front O'Leary joined in. Then suddenly O'Leary said, "Well, now—jus' look at that!"

Both pilots studied their contact-readout screens. There had been a flight of two Soviet intercepters— identified as MIGs on the key readout—which for the last few minutes had been headed in the same general direction as Joe, although they of course were unable to read his echo. Now these two intercepters were turning, swinging out into the desert, and accelerating.

"What do you think they're up to, huh?"

Hansen didn't answer.

347

The two Soviet aircraft continued the turn, still accelerating.

"I'll tell you what I think, boss—I think they're on his IR trace!"

"Ah, Jesus—I think you're right. Shit! '71 to base," he called. " '71 to base, come in."

"Go ahead, O'Leary," said Lindley's voice.

Already the two MIGs seemed to have established station exactly at Joe's position—same speed, even, and altitude. O'Leary relayed this information to Lindley.

Lindley's voice came back harsh and businesslike. "Is there any sign they're attacking?"

"Negative."

"Stand by while I raise Joe. Joe, do you copy? Come in."

No answer.

"Goddamn, is he asleep or something?" they heard Lindley say. Then they listened to him calling Kenyon nonstop for the next two minutes, after which he came back to O'Leary.

"Okay, hear this," Lindley's voice spat urgently, "you will range on to those two MIGs and loose one heat-seeker at each—blow them off him. In the meantime, if we can raise Joe, we'll have him execute a double unstart so it'll only be their IR trace—got it? When he restarts, his instructions will be to take his ass as high and as fast as he can, by which time you guys will have inserted yourselves into his slot. Got that?"

O'Leary's calm voice belied the rising beat of his heart. "Roger," he said. "I got that. Over."

"Do it," Lindley commanded. Then, "Good luck. Meanwhile rattle Kenyon's eardrums—get the sumbitch to answer. Over."

"Roger, base," O'Leary said.

Joe's eyes opened and took in the instrument panel in front of him. Slowly, the realization of where he was soaked into his mind. At the same time, someone was transmitting to him, the voice desperate.

"Dracula, Dracula, come in you sonofabitch! *Respond* to this transmission. Dracula, Dracula, do you read, do you read—"

"Loud and clear," Joe replied. "Over."

There seemed to be an astonished silence, then, "Jesus, Joe, this is O'Leary, have you looked sideways recently? From our position it appears that—"

"Oh, my Christ," Joe breathed. What the hell had happened? How could he not have seen them—seen the contact readout? What about the audios, and the PCMS? He stared from left to right. One hundred feet away only, to each side, flew the Soviet star against the matte-green aluminum of two MIG-25s. They were close enough for Joe to see the unit insignias on each pilot's helmet. Joe's eyes went to the screen. Aircraft were closing with him from most directions, the closest a matter of two minutes from contact.

"Listen, Joe," O'Leary's voice burst into his thoughts. "This is what Lindley has asked us to do." He relayed the plan to Joe.

"What's your ETA in range," Joe asked.

"Forty-five seconds."

"Holy mother," Joe breathed. No time to think of anything else. "Okay—we'll try it. Over."

"Roger—on my count of seven, repeat seven."

"Roger that," Joe said.

A double unstart at one hundred and fifty knots three hundred feet off the deck? Not a hope. However, what other hope was there now anyway? He looked quickly back at the two fighters on his wing tips. It was plain that these guys were going to stay with him if they could, until others arrived to box him in, then they would swing him back to base. They were doing their level best to get him undamaged—gently persuasive. Joe smiled.

He realized he felt sharper now. Nodding off like that must have done it, he thought. His brain had had a chance to relax, and the PCMS no doubt had worked with it. But the whole thing couldn't have lasted more than a few minutes.

"Mark!" he heard. Missiles away. Then O'Leary's voice again, counting. "Ten—nine—eight—" Joe's left hand was on the contacts. "Seve—"

Dracula sank and slowed as though caught in a net. The drag of the maws of the massive Pratt and Whitneys was equivalent to the side of a house. The two MIGs appeared to accelerate and climb, rising above him. As quickly as he had caused the unstart, he had flicked back the contacts for restart and rammed the throttles to full advance. Dracula wobbled with her nose reaching up into the stall. As he fought to control her, Joe was conscious of two simultaneous explosions of black and red half a mile ahead, and at the same moment he was thrust back into the couch as the engines ignited and spooled up to full throttle. The rocks thrust up toward him as Dracula sank while thrust fought to overcome drag, and lift to triumph over weight. As the power increased, he pulled her nose back, his eyes flicking to the airspeed and the angle-of-attack readout on the director. For a moment, Dracula appeared to have settled tail-down into the rocks.

"Come *on*, goddamn you," Joe bellowed, using full-rudder deflection and aileron to hold her level as she veered and lunged, dipping in and out of a stall. Then she began to accelerate, and when this happened, it

350

happened so fast it was almost impossible to keep up with her. Joe lowered the nose, which improved the whole thing, and then he was blasting through the debris of the Russian fighters, plowing through the shock waves that beat at her like shotgun blasts.

Joe pulled the nose increasingly upward until she accelerated vertically. He felt the shudder as she went through mach one, sensed the cones in her inlets catch and trap the spreading supersonic shock wave to feed it to the afterburners, and then she howled up through the reducing pressure of molecules with her nose pointed to the stars. Mach two, two point five, three—still accelerating.

As Joe trimmed and retrimmed, O'Leary's voice screamed in his ears. "Go for broke, Joe. Go for *broke*—"

Forty thousand feet below Joe and ten miles now to his rear, O'Leary brought the SR71 bursting through the debris of flaming, boiling black smoke that was all that remained of the two escorting Soviet interceptors. He leveled out at three hundred feet, went to full afterburner, and the Blackbird tore northward along the side of the Urals, down on the deck in Joe Kenyon's place.

"Make a report," O'Leary gasped as he concentrated on hand-flying the rocketing reconnaissance jet.

Behind him he was aware of Hansen transmitting, his own voice strained and high. "Come in, base, come in—" As he spoke the words, Hansen was thinking that this could well be the start of World War Three. Could it be true that they had just blatantly destroyed two Soviet aircraft deep within Soviet airspace? Holy *Mother*.

"Go ahead," he heard Lindley. "Go ahead."

"I think we did it," Hansen transmitted.

"Give me the plot," Lindley snapped.

"They're on us now. Oh, Holy Mother, they're *all* on us now."

"Hear this, now," Lindley transmitted, his voice at speed. "Head due west, climb like fuck, and use everything you've got to get clear. Don't worry about fuel—we'll meet you, understand? Go, *Go!*"

"Roger on that," Hansen said as his guts were crushed in a great left-hand climbing turn into the Urals.

A babble of conversation broke out in the Ops room at High Wycombe. Excited voices questioned each other amid expressions of amazement at the sheer all-or-nothing maneuver that Lindley had imposed on Kenyon and the two SR71 pilots.

Chuck Lindley wiped sweat from his face and lit another cigarette with trembling fingers. He grinned briefly at the MI6 chief standing beside him. "This ain't good for the guts," he said. He wiped his lips. "The Russkies gonna be *real* mad now," he said. "They ain't gonna pussyfoot now, no sir! They are gonna be ree-eel mad. Shi-it."

"What next, Lindley?" Brynes asked tiredly. He had barely understood the maneuver, so fast had Lindley conceived it, and so quickly had the pilots executed it.

"What happens now, my good man," Lindley grinned, "is we got to get Kenyon's ass over to Kirkenes an' that theah tanker, without them pickin' up on him, that's what." He turned back to the mike linking them with Dracula through the SAMOS on the ELF.

"Dracula, Dracula, Dracula," he transmitted. "Position. Over."

352

They heard Joe again on the speakers.

"Flight level eight zero zero and climbing, mach three two, two eight zero degrees. What is O'Leary's status? Over."

"O'Leary's runnin' west, balls to the wall, son. You will RV with a tanker at these following coords—ready?"

"Roger for the coords," Kenyon's voice said.

"Correction—give me a fuel status, Joe."

There was a short pause. "I—calculate seventeen minutes plus one minute liquid oxygen—no reserve. Over."

Lindley turned to the RAF officer standing by with the charts and computer. "Can he make it?" he asked.

The officer shook his head doubtfully. "He'll need five minutes for positioning and a minimum squirt to keep him going. That leaves him twelve to get there." He shook his head again. "I doubt it," he went on.

"Any better ideas?" Lindley snapped.

The officer shook his head, recoiling from Lindley's thrust-forward face.

"OK, then, goddammit," the test pilot said. "Let's make it happen."

Gorlov stood with Svetlin and the young captain who was the controller in the shattered control tower. In the previous few seconds, he had ordered all other personnel out of the place. Now, he and Svetlin stood behind the controller. Both officers' faces ran with sweat—Gorlov's from an almost uncontrollable anger and Svetlin's from an almost-uncontainable fear of the livid KGB chief beside him.

From the bank of radios that the controller had tuned to all the frequencies in use for the massive search for the American aircraft, issued orders of flight commanders to squadrons, electronic search centers to flight commanders, and flight leaders to other pilots.

Gorlov now knew that Kenyon, once he had burst through to the east side of the mountain range, had feinted to the south. The Soviet air chief—currently a disembodied voice from the radio—had been heard to correctly assess the situation as perceived by Gorlov, and had immediately concentrated the radar and infrared searches in a line on the same latitude as Berezniky running due north along the east side of the mountains. For the moment there was nothing the KGB chief could do except wait. And waiting was like having someone slowly poke a red-hot needle into his chest, such was the agony of it.

"Fuel," he once again muttered to Svetlin. "He *cannot* have sufficient fuel to clear our airspace."

Svetlin nodded vehemently, his eyes darting to the KGB man's thin face. "Absolutely, Comrade Marshall. It will be impossible for him to get clear—however advanced his antidetection systems might prove to be. Absolutely impossible. It can only be a matter of ti—"

"Shut up," Gorlov rapped.

The colonel clicked his heels, his knees trembling within his uniform trousers. "I apologize, Comrade Marshall. I was only trying—"

"Shut up, man. Control your blabber," Gorlov hissed.

The intensity of transmissions from the radios stepped up. Voices became more urgent; lengths of transmissions decreased, became staccato, excited. Gorlov leaned forward, straining to catch the drift, his hand held up to restrain any possible interruption from the shaking colonel beside him.

"They're onto him, sir," the controller breathed excitedly. "They've picked up his IR trace." They listened. The controller's fingers leapt at the topographical chart laid out on the desktop, his finger reacting spasmodically to the coordinates coming from the radio. The finger jabbed down. "Here—moving slowly, very low." Then, "My God!—they have him visually!"

Gorlov reached for the mike. "Connect me to the flight commander controlling those aircraft who see him," he snapped. "Then advise Marshall Surnov that I will issue their immediate orders—quickly!"

The voice of the MIG flight-leader filled the speakers.

"Give me the situation!" Gorlov snapped.

"We have the American in sight, sir," the pilot transmitted. "We are circling to close with him from the rear. We are within firing range, sir. Over."

"Listen to me. On no account will you fire on that aircraft. The American is short of fuel. He is praying for a miracle. You will close with him. I want him boxed in—sides, top, and from below, you understand? Box him so closely that he will be unable to alter course without a collision. Then get him back here. Over."

"Affirmative, sir, will do," the MIG pilot transmitted. "We are close to each side of him. The pilot appears exhausted. He—he's asleep—possibly sick! He is making no effort to avoid us. Over."

"You have other aircraft close at hand for support, yes? Over."

"Affirmative."

"Good. You will remain in open communication with me, you understand, and advise me of the position constantly. Now, box him in tight—"

Static hissed.

"Did you receive my last transmission? Over."
Nothing.

"Do you read? Do you *read*? Come in, come *in*—"
Nothing.

"Fuck your mother!" Gorlov bellowed as he smashed his fist down onto the console. *"Come in, come in."*

They overheard another of the interceptor flight-leaders reporting to base and listened in horror. "—destroyed. The American must have weapons of which we are unaware. From the relative positions, it was impossible—"

As they listened, Gorlov made his own connection to the Soviet air chief.

"Surnov, what in the *name* of Lenin is happening—?"

"With respect, Comrade, may I suggest that too many cooks will spoil the broth."

"*Yob tvaiyou mat*, Surnov! Where *is* he?"

"We have picked up two IR traces. One has—"

"Two?" Gorlov snapped his head back to stare at the speaker above him.

"Two," the air marshall repeated calmly. "Both have climbed at an unprecedented rate. One heads north—the other due west."

"How can there be *two*?" Gorlov rasped.

"A good question, Comrade Marshall. I can only assume that the Americans had another of these aircraft within our airspace—and used it."

"Well, which of these are you pursuing?"

There was a sharp barked laugh from the chief of the Soviet air force. "Both, of course. Now, I will keep you advised. Meanwhile I would appreciate—"

"Da, da, da," Gorlov spat out. "You do understand, Surnov, that one of them has little fuel, and the other could be recently refueled?"

356

"*You* run the KGB, Gorlov—and now let *me* run the Air Force."

"Surnov, you will *pay*—"

"Listen to me, Comrade Marshall Gorlov of the KGB; as I see it, the only one who will *pay*, if we should be unsuccessful in capturing this American aircraft, will be you, correct? Think about that while I do my utmost to secure your position as a Hero of the USSR."

Gorlov's mouth snapped shut into a thin, white line as the air force chief broke the connection.

CHAPTER NINETEEN

Thursday morning in England was a beautiful one.

The storms which had raged across the country from the southwest had now raged off into the wastes of the North Sea and left the sky bright and washed clean. Only a few small rounded puffs of clouds floated in the remaining breeze from the west, and the sky above them was a deep blue. The air was clear, and trees and buildings on the Hampshire horizons were etched against the browns and greens of low distant hills.

From all points around the Farnborough airfield, streams of traffic filled the small roads as Airshow visitors tried for an early arrival to position themselves in the best spots from which to view the world's most important aircraft.

Within the airfield the public enclosures were already filling with people, and the stands were dotted with color as the crowd quickly filled the open spots. In the car-parks, booths were open and groups sprawled on the grass eating picnic breakfasts. Some people clambered onto car roofs at every new sound of engines as aircrafts taxied to a display position, or engines were checked in preparation for the day's flying. There was a mood of expectation and a sense of carnival atmosphere, helped by the brilliant Indian-summer weather.

The Soviet air attaché to Britain breakfasted alone in his room. The *mokre dela* man had driven back to London in the early hours.

The window of the room looked out across the Farnborough airfield. Close-packed terraced houses and industrial buildings lined the airfield perimeters. Olenko noticed that, for a change, it was a sunlit morning. The roads were already packed with incoming traffic, and heat already shivered the air above the town and the long stretches of concrete runways and taxiways.

Olenko picked at some cold croissants and sipped at a large cup of disgusting coffee. His stomach felt rotten, in a turmoil from the emotional strain of the night and the waiting. Every so often he looked at his wrist watch, wondering whether Joe had landed, trying to visualize his position, picturing the revolutionary aircraft he had never seen, as it stood silent on the apron at his home base. He wondered if Natalia might notice the strange craft on final approach. The house was near the approach path. She might see it, he thought, and the girls. Ah, God—how he yearned to see the three of them again.

Gorlov would send no signal. Nothing would be done to risk compromising Olenko's position as a Soviet diplomat in a Western city. As far as the world was concerned, Joe Kenyon would become known as a defector. As far as the kidnapping of his wife was concerned, this could have been the action of any number of unconnected terrorist groups. Sometime today the U.S. embassy would receive a ransom demand for her, and when it was paid she would turn up in Switzerland.

And the only way, he thought, he would learn his own fate would be from the newspapers, or the newscasters—or, God forbid, when the KGB came to hustle him home.

So far the radio had made no mention of anything that might be connected with Joe's departure, and the morning newspapers were clean. He had had them sent up with the breakfast. The British and American authorities would keep an unprecedentedly tight rein on any possible leakage of something like this.

Olenko rose from the small round table at the window, and began to pace restlessly around the hotel room. His mind kept returning to Joe. He prayed that Joe was safely down. In a few days he would see Joe—meet him at Berezniky, and do his level best to ease the American's lot.

He longed to tell Joe that no harm had come to Suzie—tell him how adamant he had been as to how Suzie was to be treated in Switzerland. While the operation was running she was to be looked after by a qualified nurse, and treated as gently as humanly possible. He wanted to tell Joe that the scream Kenyon had heard over the telephone was rigged—from recorded laughter and exclamations at various parties, and tennis matches down in Wiltshire. My God, what you couldn't do with electronics these days, he thought. Of course, Suzie had been genuinely depressed and upset when she had spoken to Joe for those few moments. What woman wouldn't be—snatched away by strangers. But there had been no physical duress—he was sure of that. And the nurse had been instructed to administer the gentlest doses of calming drugs.

He wanted Joe to meet Natalia. It was possible, he thought, that Natalia, soft and gentle like Suzie, would be able in some way to ease Joe's predicament.

And one day Joe would go home, anyway. One day he would be united with Suzie—and by then she would have a son, or a daughter. He would mend, then, at home with them—wouldn't he? He shook his head tiredly. Of course the American would mend. Time was the thing. Time healed everything in the end. Time, perhaps, might heal his own conscience in the long run. Olenko stopped pacing and stared for a few moments through the window, out across the airfield.

There was a flash of white beyond the far end of the runway. An aircraft was on final approach. He watched it idly, as all pilots do, automatically waiting to see what kind of landing the pilot would manage. Two small white puffs of smoke appeared as the tires hit. He saw the aircraft was a white business jet; but didn't recognize the make. He knew little of the West's enormous fleets of biz-jets. On its tail he saw, as it turned from the runway, that it wore a large red cross. Ah, Switzerland, he thought as he gathered his coat. He paused for a moment to look back through the window, but the aircraft had taxied into obscurity. A civilian Swiss jet arriving at Farnborough an hour before the show started? Odd. He decided that some VIPs were late. Then he left the room.

Olenko stepped into the elevator, unaware of the figure that seemed to emerge from the wall of the corridor two doors down.

In the elevator he faced a dour-faced individual, quite unnoticeable in his ordinariness. The man seemed intent on watching the little lights flash their downward progress. As the elevator descended, it occurred to Dimitri Olenko that in a few hours it might be announced that he had become a Hero of the Soviet.

But he wished he knew for sure. He sighed as the doors opened at the ground floor.

He failed, in his preoccupation, to notice that two unnoticeable types followed him through the doors of the front entrance according to their instructions.

The chartered Cessna Citation halted close to one of the maintenance hangars, its white paintwork and red Swiss colors gleaming in the morning sun. An ambulance was drawn close to the boarding door, which was unfolding with its own small whine as the whine of the engines died to nothing behind. Uniformed police had cordoned the area off fifty yards back. By the side of the ambulance waited a black Mercedes with the U.S. flag atop its radiator. Beside it, watching the now-open door of the aircraft, stood the United States ambassador and three security men.

A man in a wheelchair, with a bandaged leg thrust out before him supported on cushions and his left arm in a sling, bandaged thickly to his elbow, was gently eased down the steps to the ground. Shortly afterwards a big man, rapping at the attendants in French while he looked around him carefully, escorted a pale, shaky woman with ash-blond hair. She was, in spite of the Indian-summer warmth, wrapped in a blanket. The man in the wheelchair was eased into the rear of the waiting ambulance, and the big Swiss helped the woman into the ambassador's car, then climbed in after her. The car immediately moved off.

In the background, jet engines whined and roared in preparation for the show, and loudspeakers atop steel poles crackled and said, "Testing, testing."

In the ambulance, David Pentland looked anxiously forward through the tinted windshield—anxious because for the first time since leaving the cabin up in the Swiss Alps he was out of touch with Chuck Lindley, in spite of the fact that it would only be a matter of moments before they unloaded him into a quickly prepared operations room in Dracula's maintenance facility at Farnborough. He was fully aware of the speed at which events were occurring in the skies above the Soviet Union, and he hated the feeling of being out of touch—even for two minutes.

"Come on, come *on*," he breathed at the back of the driver's head. The nurse sitting alongside the driver chose that moment to turn in her seat. She smiled at him. She of course had no idea of what was going on.

"Can't he go faster?" he asked her.

"Well, we don't want to jog you, do we?" she said comfortably.

They were following the ambassador's car. Back in the Citation, Pentland had insisted on occupying the copilot's seat and had instructed the pilot to patch him into a telephone number. He had talked to Lindley during the forty-seven minutes of the plane's priority routing to Farnborough. Used to the quirks of business clients the pilot had remained uninterested, while the copilot had read a magazine contentedly in the rear cabin, pleased, for once, to be able to leave it all to his skipper.

Two minutes later, Pentland was unloaded into the hangar and rolled to an office at the rear to join up with the ambassador, Maurice Fennel, and Suzie Kenyon.

Dimitri Olenko's car dropped him off in the VIP enclosure close to the Soviet pavilion.

He went inside and mixed with his own countrymen—other Soviet officials based in London, and aerospace engineers and industrial teams visiting from the Soviet Union. People greeted him deferentially and he acknowledged them while most of his mind continued to calculate what Joe's fuel endurance would have been. One thing he was sure of was that either Joe was down at Berezniky or he was down somewhere else. But he was certainly down. The subjects of conversation around him were confined to the upcoming show, and it was clear that whatever news there might now exist within the Soviet Union, none had leaked—even through channels in the Soviet embassy—to anyone here. Olenko had been prepared for perhaps a whispered comment, or at least a penetrating look, but there was nothing. He hadn't really expected there would be.

"Ladies and gentlemen," boomed a cultured British voice from the loudspeakers beyond the pavilion. "A very good morning to you all."

The announcer went on to provide details of the opening address and the day's activities. Olenko crooked a finger at a passing waiter and ordered coffee, then decided to pay a visit to the nearest toilet, his stomach churning with tension.

The waiter who had taken his order for coffee quickly checked on the positions of the two other Special Branch men, then disappeared into the kitchen.

Once again above Joe the sky was black and full of stars, and below him the earth's surface was bright, stretching away to the west in increasing darkness, until at the extent of his vision, night lingered on the hazy curve of the horizon.

After the initial burst to altitude from the base of the Urals, Joe had, with the help of the PCMS, concentrated his energy on the computer in an effort to make the graphs of remaining fuel and the coordinates that Lindley had given of the position of the tanker resolve into a positive result. But whichever way he had worked it—balancing remaining fuel with distance to go, juggling with altitudes and speeds—the lines of the graph had refused to cross.

A number of times he found himself falling back in the couch, unable to concentrate or even hold himself in a position to operate the computer, and his mind would begin to hallucinate. Each time, Dracula edged him back, almost as if expressing her own vital interest in his success, and he would attack the computer anew with a short-term spark of energy—like a flashlight battery awakened to a tiny glow by the warmth of a hand. The low-warning indicators had been lit red on all tanks for God-knew-how-long. And now they flashed in a permanent effort to assure him that at any second the great Pratt and Whitneys would die to silence behind him, and Dracula's nose would gently lower in a two hundred and fifty-knot glide down to a hornet's nest of interceptors and missiles.

A minute ago he had remembered the remaining cub and its own weight, and quickly sent this off to his rear, programmed for mach three and a shallow dive back to the Urals—which might make them think he'd decided to head for a safe landing after all. As it dropped below sixty thousand feet the cub had been quickly obliterated by at least six missiles, which reinforced Joe's opinion that the Soviets were now in a killing frame of mind.

He wondered what had become of O'Leary. Lindley had refused to advise him—told him to use his energy on making it to the RV. At first Joe had ranted at his friend, desperate to hear that the SR71 had made it to safety, but Lindley had shut him up with no indication of what was happening, except that O'Leary was heading due west for Finland.

Joe keyed the course-plot once more. Eight minutes to the RV—better than two hundred and sixty nautical miles at his present cruise speed of two thousand knots. But it wasn't the distance that mattered, of course. It was the time. It was always the time. He knew he might just make it to the tanker, but it would take maneuvering during the descent and hook-up, then a minimum period of three minutes to feed Dracula. It was the three minutes he was short of. He might possibly, he thought, have gained ten seconds with the dispatch of the cub and its weight. This was the result the computer had given after he had programmed it to dredge up the weight of the aircraft and the weight of the cub, and then apply the result to the fuel remaining. It still looked hopeless.

Desperately, he ran through his mind a routine to minimize the link-up maneuvers. To this end he had begun a slow descent from the one hundred and eighty thousand feet he had been maintaining, to bring him to the tanker's level of forty-five thousand at the RV point. This would deal with skin-cooling and descent in one go—but, of course, as he dropped lower it would also increase his exposure to the Soviets below.

The contact radar showed clearly the build-up of NATO aircraft ahead in which the tanker was buried. As far as Joe was now concerned, the Russians occupied a low position in his priorities—unless they would be lucky enough to lock onto him in the next few minutes and try a zooming maneuver. But the element of risk in that had reduced to a low percentage.

Time and fuel. Time and *fuel*.

His eyes were drawn by some change in the pattern of the contact-readout. Below him the Soviets probed in a net stretching clear across to Archangel. The northern extension of the Pol Janin Peninsula seemed to be the line drawn between the westward extent of their patrols and the advanced front of the NATO fighters.

In a little over seven minutes now he would be overhead Ostrov Kalguyev, the Soviet island in the south Barents Sea which guarded the mouth of the Cheshkaya Guba. From the disposition of both Soviet and NATO forces, it appeared from the long-range radar that the airspace above the island had become no-man's-land for the time being. The coordinates for the waiting tanker put it some one hundred and fifty nautical miles further west, in a position off Kirkenes. From the plot, Joe could understand now why it had not been possible to move the tanker further east.

Joe considered these factors while he examined the contact-readout. Now he saw three Soviet interceptors climbing up toward him from the southwest on an intercept course. He watched calmly, with one eye on the chronometer—his senses poised for the deceleration of the flame-out as Dracula ran out of fuel. As he watched the plot he was more concerned with the fuel than the climbing interceptors. He was sliding at a shallow angle down through one hundred and ten thousand feet. He had never heard of a Soviet machine that could climb beyond ninety thousand, let alone maintain controlled flight in the thin environment. But on they came.

And as they came on, he realized that they were tracking him, as he perceived their slight alterations in course to converge with him.

Five minutes now.

On they came. Sonofabitch, he thought. These guys

are special. Eighty thousand and still climbing at mach two? The computer advised him that the closing speed was in excess of mach five—time in seconds, twelve.

Any moment, you'll fall away, Joe thought.

Nine seconds!

Missiles away—six of them, fanning up toward him across his course. And now the MIGs *were* falling away, spinning and flashing as their loads reached up for him.

Dracula's computer was flashing the estimate of strike in red seconds and tenths . . .

Five one—*Four* nine eight seven six five four three two one *Three* . . .

Joe's left hand leapt for the oxygen levers. He hauled Dracula's nose upward as the engines kicked her forward, at the same time pulling her round in the thin air, shaking with the advent of a high-speed stall at three thousand miles an hour, as his body crushed into the couch.

The missiles came on, their momentum established—Dracula's still increasing. Dracula now streaked north, climbing at a shallow angle.

Joe's eyes were glued to the screen.

Two nine eight, seven, six . . .

One nine eight seven six . . . six, five, five, five, four, five, six, seven eight nine *Two* . . .

His eyes watched the screen unblinkingly as one by one the missiles flamed out and spun down into the space below. At that moment the oxygen gave out, and Dracula threw Joe forward in his straps. He swung her back on course, shaken that they should have made it so close. He knew what they had done. Three of them had volunteered to zoom for the center of the ECM blank, in the hope of locking onto him visually. They had achieved this and run themselves out of supporting air at the moment they had fired the missiles. They had spun back toward the earth, while others watched the screens for the telltale flowerlike bloom of a new radar image.

Three minutes to the tanker now, and by all accounts four minutes of fuel remaining.

The burst of emergency power had given him a bank of height, which he now intended to draw from as he throttled back to idle, conserving his precious fuel, gaining seconds—perhaps as much as an extra minute—holding the altitude as the speed bled off in the almost-nonexistent air. As the speed bled down through five hundred knots, Joe stabilized it and established Dracula into a steady sink down toward the waiting tanker.

"Ladies and gentlemen," the cultured English tones of the commentator started, booming forth from the hundreds of strategically placed speakers throughout the airfield. "As many of you know, this year at Farnborough we shall have the privilege of viewing perhaps the most advanced aircraft the world has yet witnessed—"

What was the man saying? Olenko stood stock-still in the shade of the tent. It was a second before he realized that, in an effort to cover up, the United States would have flown an SR71 over for the show. The SR71 would be a good substitute. Only very recently had the Americans been forced to be rather more cautious with the routing of the twenty-two-year-old spy plane's overflights as Soviet technology provided an ever-increasing threat to its previously untouchable speed and altitude performance.

"—was scheduled to arrive in this country during the early hours of this morning," the commentator continued. "However, due to weather conditions which affected arrangements for the inflight refueling of this incredible aircraft, its departure was delayed—perhaps to our advantage! Because now you will have an opportunity to see the SR80 actually make its approach and landing in a few minutes; actually see this great black dart of an aircraft in action—"

Were the Americans bringing another SR80? Did they *have* another? Surely there was, so far, only one?

"—and as you will see from your program of events, the SR80 was scheduled as a static display. Well, I am here in the control tower sitting close to Squadron Leader Michael Horton, who is the officer in charge of flight operations for this great Farnborough Airshow, and in a matter of moments now you will hear his voice and that of the American pilot who is flying America's newest and most advanced, perhaps miraculous, strategic reconnaissance aircraft. Good morning, Squadron Leader."

"Good morning, Raymond," a very RAF voice boomed over the airfield. "Yes, we should—ah—be able to see the aircraft coming in from the east, that is, roughly from the direction of London in just—a—er—few seconds now. We are already in contact with the aircraft, Raymond, as London Center has just switched him through to our frequency, so that we—ah—can bring him in, so to speak. So, if you'll forgive me for just a *few* moments, I will address myself to the incoming aircraft control procedures—"

"Of course, Squadron Leader. Well, ladies and gentlemen, here he comes, the sight many of you will have been keenly looking forward to for so long now, as we listen to the voices of Squadron Leader Horton and Colonel Joseph Kenyon of the—"

"Yob tvaiyou mat!" Olenko whispered. Kenyon? What did the fool mean, *Kenyon*!

Olenko felt the blood drain from his face.

Other Soviet officials were streaming past Olenko toward the entrance of the marquee, some clutching cups of coffee, all keen to see this new American aircraft. For a moment, Olenko stood alone inside as the marquee walls flapped gently in a light, summer breeze. Then he forced himself to move, to follow the crowd outside, to listen to the voice of the controller with a growing sense of horror.

And then he heard Joe Kenyon's voice, distorted slightly, or perhaps the voice just reflected fatigue, but it was most undoubtedly the voice of Joe Kenyon.

"—Good morning Farnborough, this is Sierra Romeo Eight-Zero, Three Three DME East for landing—Over."

And then the brief hiss of static before Horton's voice replied.

"Farnborough—ah—Tower, to Sierra Romeo Eight-Zero, good morning, sir. You are cleared number one for a straight-in to runway Two-Five, QFE One Zero One Two millibars, wind variable, no reported traffic."

And then Joe replying:

"Eight-Zero, Roger for straight-in to Two-Five, One Zero One Two on the altimeter—"

Olenko stood behind his comrades, who all now stared toward the east. He felt numb and cold, hardly aware of the scene around him, seeing and hearing as if in some disconnected nightmare, unable to think, immovable as a statue.

From the east there came a whine and a distant thunder.

And then Horton's voice came over the speakers:

"Ladies and *gentlemen*," the controller said excitedly, "Colonel Kenyon has agreed to execute a flypast for us—keep your eyes on the end of the runway now, as the aircraft will approach extremely fast—"

And then something came into view, something black, moving toward the assembly at a colossal, silent speed, low over the distant hedgerows on the boundary of the airfield.

"He knows," Olenko whispered. "He knows I'll be here. He knows I'll be watching. He knows my life is ruined. He knows I've lost Natalia—and the girls—he *knows*—"

A long, black streak hurtled along the runway toward them. Heads snapped from left to right in an effort to follow, to keep eyes focused on the black blur.

"Oh my *God!*" someone said in a voice of utter awe, just before there came a sound like Thor himself, a previously unimaginable, shattering, thunderous, vibrating cacophony of noise, which sent the soles of shoes bouncing on the concrete; and then upturned heads with open mouths saw the dartlike silhouette of Dracula as Joe pulled up from the far end of the long runway into a series of vertical rolls, flicking razor-thin, dart-flat, razor-thin, growing smaller, smaller, until finally disappearing into the limitless blue of the sky, while the thunder rolled and grumbled into silence.

In the new silence there was a peculiar sigh as thousands of people breathed "Ahhh," to themselves in a murmur that expressed awe, and wonder, and incomprehension.

"Ladies and gentlemen," the commentator's voice from the speakers broke the spell. "I don't think any of you will disagree when I say that what we have just seen was one of the most remarkable sights of current aviation. In a few minutes Colonel Kenyon will once again bring the aircraft in from the east and this time you will have an opportunity to rest your eyes on it as he approaches at—what, a hundred and forty knots or so, Squadron Leader?"

"Yes, Raymond. One hundred and thirty-five, actually. He'll touch the wheels onto the concrete at no more than one hundred and ten, which itself is one illustration of the amazing flexibility of this remarkable aircraft—"

The voices droned on.

Olenko remained standing, staring across the airfield at nothing. After a minute he walked slowly back into the tent to wait.

As he waited he heard the aircraft approach, heard the quieter, but still substantial, roar of the enormous engines, could imagine the plane as it slowed practically opposite the tent, heard the hubbub of conversation break out as people beyond the canvas walls discussed the SR80 excitedly, and then a brief roar of engines as Kenyon turned at the far end of the runway, and the steady whine as he taxied to the maintenance area.

One or two people seeing Olenko sitting there in the tent made comments to him, but passed on when they were ignored.

Slowly Olenko took a cigarette from his pocket and lit it with trembling fingers.

This time, Chuck Lindley stood alone on the small platform at the top of the boarding steps.

Dracula's canopy rose up before Lindley with its customary whine. Lindley's nose wrinkled in distaste. If he had been on the ground he would have taken a large step to the rear. Quickly remembering, he managed to restrain himself. "Holy shit!" he muttered as the stench from the cockpit enveloped him. He peered down onto the filthy figure of Joe Kenyon lying in the couch. Kenyon's helmet raised up and Lindley looked down into the pilot's face. The front of Joe's sweater was rimmed with vomit, as were parts of his face where he had made an effort to clear the mess. The eyes which stared up at Lindley's from the sunken, white features were big and staring, the pupils expanded. The bloodless lips were open in a grimace, which at first Lindley took for pain, before realizing that the expression could also perhaps be an attempt on Joe's part to smile. For once Chuck Lindley was speechless.

Joe's left hand moved slowly across toward the right wrist. The fingers trembled violently. Then the left hand flopped and Joe's head went back.

"Get her—off—me," Joe croaked.

"Jesus!" Lindley muttered and bent down into the cockpit, no longer conscious of the stink of excrement and vomit. "Don' she wanna let ya go, Joe?" he said gently. He caught Joe's right wrist and eased it from the PCMS needle, then noticed the blood and the spreading stain on the armrest and the instrumented bulkhead below it.

"She'll—never—touch my flesh—again, Chuck," Lindley heard the attaché croak. "Never again." Joe slowly shook his head still encased in the helmet. "Get this off."

Lindley gently removed the helmet to reveal Joe's sweat-matted head and looked down into his friend's eyes. He forced a smile.

"You sumbitch, Joe! You kep' a whole bunch of us up the whole goddamn night."

Joe nodded slowly. "Where's Suzie?" he said.

"Down there waitin' for ya—where the hell do ya

think she is?" Lindley said. Joe began to heave himself up to exit the cockpit.

"Now, wait a while, Joe. I think we need help—"

"I don't need—help. I got in—I'll goddamn well get myself out," Kenyon said. "Stand aside."

A sea of faces looked up at them as Joe rose upright, wobbling. Some were talking. Some knew, Joe realized. But others didn't. The ones who didn't know were the ones who were talking. One of the silent ones was the U.S. ambassador, Joe's immediate boss, waiting close to the bottom of the steps.

Lindley waved at the ambassador to come up. In the silence now, the ambassador's leather shoes rang loudly on the aluminum steps.

"He ain't in no shape for people to see, right now, sir," Lindley said quietly.

"All right," the ambassador said. "Hold him there for a moment, and I'll get them moved." He left to go down.

"I've really blown it, Chuck," Joe said.

Lindley took a deep breath. "Yep, old buddy," he said. "Yep—I guess you did. But you got your wife, right? An' your kid," he smiled. "What more does a guy need?"

Joe shook his head.

Security people were moving people away below them, stating loudly that there was a fuel leak and potential danger. Joe noticed that Harris was dealing with this. Harris. He'd never thought he would see that man's face again.

Once it was clear below, Lindley helped Joe Kenyon climb unsteadily down the steep steps.

With Lindley supporting him on one side and the ambassador on the other, they walked him to the door of the hangar.

Suddenly Joe stopped. "O'Leary?" he said.

"Where's O'Leary?"

Lindley glanced quickly at the ambassador.

"Lakenheath, Joe. He made it to Lakenheath."

"Oh, thank Christ for that," Kenyon said.

They went inside, into the gloom of the hangar.

When the door was shut, the ambassador said to Joe, "A few moments with you, if you can manage it, Kenyon? Then you can go and get cleaned up before you see your wife, okay?" He nodded to Lindley, who left them. The ambassador led Joe to an empty office. They went inside and the ambassador shut the door behind them.

Joe's ears were ringing in the unaccustomed silence, and from the blood still driving through his veins, urged on by Dracula's chemicals. He leaned weakly against the side of a table and lit one of Lindley's cigarettes.

"I'm—er—glad you made it back, Joe," the ambassador said.

"So am I, sir," Joe breathed. He drew on the cigarette.

"Olenko is on the field," the ambassador said quietly.

Joe nodded. "I figured he might be," he said.

"We're having him brought in. The British are handling it. I thought you might like to—er—talk to him. It might not be possible for you to see him—well—for quite a while."

Joe tried a smile. He knew what that meant. Who was worse-off now? he thought. Olenko or himself? "That will make my day, sir," he said to the ambassador.

"There's some coffee in that flask behind you. Help yourself. I'll arrange things." The ambassador left the room.

As Dimitri Olenko walked slowly and woodenly from the Soviet pavilion out into the fresh air, a man stepped forward. Olenko remembered seeing the same face in the elevator on his way out of the hotel. How *long* had they known? Olenko stopped and smiled slightly, making a small bow at the man, as was the custom of a well-mannered Soviet citizen.

"Good morning, sir," the man said. "My name is Inspector Jensen, I am with the Special Branch, sir. I will willingly show you any required identification, but I do not wish to do anything which might embarrass you."

"Yes, inspector. I, of course, understand," Olenko said quietly. "You wish me to accompany you, yes?"

Inspector Jensen coughed. "I do, sir."

"Very well, inspector."

As they walked off together, another man fell in loosely on the other side of Olenko. To a casual observer, the three of them were one of the crowd, strolling to a common destination. Within a few paces they approached a car. Sitting in the rear of the car was a man swathed in bandages. Jensen opened the rear door, and Olenko got in.

"How do you do?" the man with the bandages said briskly. "My name is Pentland. I'm with British Military Intelligence. I had a couple of accidents in Switzerland, by way of explanation of all this!" Pentland waved his right hand.

Olenko leaned back in the seat and stared at his knees as the car moved off.

"Your man Renko didn't come off quite as well, I am afraid," Pentland said. "I was forced to break his neck."

Olenko smiled then. He turned to the MI6 man.

"Do you know, Mr. Pentland?" he said. "You have given me my first good news of this day."

Pentland smiled in turn, then faced forward to address the driver. "Okay, Maurice," he said.

Joe Kenyon turned as the door opened. A big man he didn't know pushed a wheelchair into the room. From the wheelchair, Pentland raised a hand before Joe could say anything.

"Here's an old friend of yours," Pentland said in an even tone.

Then Joe saw Dimitri Olenko enter the dingy office followed by the ambassador. The ambassador closed the door. Olenko took a few steps toward Joe, then halted. He stood in the characteristic pose of a prisoner, hands clasped loosely in front of him, shoulders slightly stooped. Behind him, Pentland sat in the wheelchair between the big man and the ambassador.

In spite of Joe's state of exhaustion, he felt intense anger flush his blood through his veins. He had sworn that he would kill this man. He felt his hands ball into fists at his side and renewed sweat break out on his face.

Joe broke the deep silence. "While I was up to my ass doing my best to prevent my own people from shooting me down," he started, "I told myself that if I was going to accomplish anything when I got to Berezniky—if it was the last goddamn thing I ever did—I was going to find some way to kill you, Dimitri."

Once again the silence fell heavily in the small room.

Olenko looked down at the dirty linoleum, then a few seconds later back up to the American's face.

He took in the staring, drug-enlarged eyes, appallingly huge in the white, stretched skin of his exhausted face. He saw and smelled the man-in-the-street clothes, matted with excrement and vomit—noticed the violent trembling of Kenyon's fingers as the attaché lifted his cigarette shakily to his bloodless lips. He was aware of what he had done to this man—perhaps because of his own experience, so similar to Joe's, he was more aware than the others behind him—and was sick to his stomach. He thought of Susie, and the unborn child—and then, with a pain like a hot knife in his chest, he thought of Natalia and his children—knew he might never see them again. Twice, his lips moved as if he would speak. But in the end there was nothing he could think of saying. Both he and Joe were now men without careers, men who had, in their different ways, disgraced their respective nations.

Unable to remain on his feet any longer, Joe slumped down onto a chair close to the table. His breath came heavily and unevenly as his eyes continued to look at Olenko's. The Russian stood silent and motionless a few paces away.

Joe's cracked lips formed into the semblance of a smile.

"If you were in a MIG, my friend, I'd shoot you down—soon as step on a roach," he said. He nodded heavily, then held his hands out before him. For a moment he watched them tremble, then looked back up at the Russian's eyes. "I guess though, maybe, if it came right down to it—I couldn't do it with these." He shook his head. "Not when you come right down to it," he repeated, almost below his breath.

Olenko nodded slowly.

Joe's chin suddenly slumped to his chest. His hands came up to cover his face.

Olenko moved forward and placed a hand on the American's shoulder.

"I am told, Joe," Olenko looked down at Kenyon's head and smiled. "I am told—Zuzie is here." He paused. "You will see her soon, yes?"

Joe nodded. He removed his hands and revealed his gaunt features as he looked up at the Russian.

"Natalia?" he said bleakly. "Your two girls?"

Olenko released Joe's shoulder gently and turned a little toward the men by the door.

"Perhaps is possible," he said hesitatingly, "for me to see them again—sometime in the future?" He nodded to himself as the thought took hold. "*Da*, but first—America." He smiled suddenly and nodded again. "You and Zuzie have told me so much about your country. I would like to go to America." He trailed into silence.

The United States ambassador spoke up quietly.

"I imagine something like that will be arranged," he observed. He glanced down at Pentland by his side.

From his wheelchair, the British intelligence officer fixed his eyes on the Russian for a long moment, then he looked up at the ambassador with a small smile.

"After a—suitable—sojourn in England, do you think, sir?" He turned to face the Russian. "We English should have a better opportunity of making Mr. Olenko's acquaintance first." Then Pentland looked at Maurice Fennel. "Now, Maurice—if you wouldn't mind escorting our—guest—to the car, please?"

Olenko quickly squeezed Joe's shoulder and walked toward the door. Maurice Fennel held it

open and followed the Russian into the gloom of the
hangar. Joe rose from his chair and went over to the
door.

Dracula had been wheeled into the hangar.
Olenko, with Fennel on one side and Inspector
Holmes on the other, walked the length of the
fuselage without once looking up at the great black
aircraft. The three of them disappeared into the
gloom beyond the shadows of her port wing.

Joe stood by the door staring up at Dracula. Her
fuselage slanted away from him in the gloom of the
hangar. The strong lights in the hangar roof swelled
like small suns above his over-sensitized eyes. The
lights failed to outline Dracula. She sucked the
darkness around her. The flattened, snakelike fuselage wavered before him, and the slant of her
windshield seemed to regard him, as he regarded
her. Jets screamed beyond the grey barrier of the
closed hangar doors as the Show continued outside
in the sun. Her needle-nose pointed at the doors.
Joe trembled. She seemed to him like a great
confined beast—caged now—smothered.

Joe's mouth moved. His eyes flickered, and his
body shook as the drugs in his veins began to lose
their control of him. He felt the need for her. Inside
her, she would fondle his mind, and ease his body—
shut out the confusions of the world in the silence of
her womblike module.

She would comfort him. Wobbling, he moved
toward her.

An arm wrapped around his shoulders and
stopped him, but his eyes remained fixed on her.

Lindley's voice then came from close-by.

"You wanna know somethin', Joe?" his friend
asked. Joe leaned on Lindley's arm.

"What?" Joe managed.

They stood together, their eyes fixed on Dracula, both sensing that she in turn regarded them.

"I think," Lindley whispered"—I think that bitch—*likes* you." He gave a short laugh and tightened his grip on Joe's shoulders. "Come on, fellah—you got your wife waitin'."

Joe shuddered and looked back over his shoulder at the SR80 as Chuck Lindley led him away.